Solving crime isn't only for the living.

In turn-of-the-century New York City, the police have an off-the-books spiritual go-to when it comes to solving puzzling corporal crimes . . .

Her name is Eve Whitby, gifted medium and spearhead of the Ghost Precinct. When most women are traveling in a gilded society that promises only well-appointed marriage, the confident nineteen-year-old Eve navigates a social circle that carries a different kind of chill. Working with the diligent but skeptical Lieutenant Horowitz, as well as a group of fellow psychics and wayward ghosts, Eve holds her own against a host of dangers, detractors, and threats to solve New York's strangest crime as only her precinct can.

But as accustomed as Eve is to ghastly crimes and all matters of the uncanny, even she is unsettled by her department's latest mystery. Her ghostly conduits are starting to disappear one by one as though snatched away by some evil force determined to upset the balance between two realms, and most important—destroy the Ghost Precinct forever. Now Eve must brave the darkness to find the vanished souls. She has no choice. It's her job to make sure no one is ever left for dead.

Visit us at www.kensingtonbooks.com

Books by Leanna Renee Hieber

The Spectral City

Published by Kensington Publishing Corporation

The Spectral City

Leanna Renee Hieber

REBEL BASE
Kensington Book Corp.
www.kensingtonbooks.com

Rebel Base Books are published by
Kensington Publishing Corp. 119 West 40th Street New York, NY 10018

All Kensington titles, imprints, and distributed lines are available at special quantity discounts for bulk purchases for sales promotion, premiums, fundraising, and educational or institutional use.

To the extent that the image or images on the cover of this book depict a person or persons, such person or persons are merely models, and are not intended to portray any character or characters featured in the book.

Special book excerpts or customized printings can also be created to fit specific needs. For details, write or phone the office of the Kensington Special Sales Manager:
Kensington Publishing Corp.
119 West 40th Street
New York, NY 10018
Attn. Special Sales Department. Phone: 1-800-221-2647.

REBEL BASE Reg. U.S. Pat. & TM Off.
The RB logo is a trademark of Kensington Publishing Corp.

First Electronic Edition: November 2018
eISBN-13: 978-1-63573-058-6
eISBN-10: 1-63573-058-9

First Print Edition: November 2018
ISBN-13: 978-1-63573-061-6
ISBN-10: 1-63573-061-9

Printed in the United States of America

Prologue

Manhattan dinner parties in the gilded 1890s had become a studied spectacle in opulence for the ruling class of the country's wealthiest city. The bustling, ever striving, never sleeping metropolis's class of most fashionable, up-to-date, technologically accessorized, bejeweled and beholden to no one but themselves were the kinds of company that the Prenze family kept, curating people and their statuses like one might think of assembling a stock portfolio.

That's how it appeared to Margaret Hathorn as she floated into the parlor for light aperitifs and a bit of music and chatter before dinner. She knew the types, their predilections, and their concerns. Margaret had been born into wealth, and during her young life she'd been quite enamored of high society's trappings, dalliances and luxuries, their petty dramas and the consequential ways their decisions affected the city. From her vantage point, she could see the full scope.

She had seen and learned much since those days of carefree and impetuous youth. Not only had she come to understand the tired adage of money not buying happiness, but she realized that Poe had been on to something with *The Masque of the Red Death*. There were dangers in being too shielded, too gilded, too able to make up one's own rules for life, too easily sheltered away from the horrors and cares of the world. She could feel a sense of dread here, as if the Red Death were lurking in the hallway just beyond. Maybe it was, clad in some beautiful House of Worth gown or some finely tailored frock coat with satin lapels.

It should be noted that Margaret Hathorn, herself, was dead. Her perspective was one of two worlds, and for nearly two decades, she had floated between the living and the dead. Once, on the heels of her untimely and harrowing murder, she had nearly decided to seek out the light and go unto that great, sweet Summerland that the legitimate Spiritualists spoke of. Heaven. Peace. Almost . . . The corridor of light had opened before her and she had almost sought out forgiveness in the oblivion of some great and unknowable thing.

But the spectral city kept drawing her back. New York was a body she felt destined to orbit; an otherworldly magnet. There was so much to *do*. There was so much to learn. There was so much to fix, to reveal, to *fight* for that she now knew had deep meaning; meaning that had been lost to her in a life looking into gilded frames and too many mirrors in which she'd primped lustrous curls.

Looking into the mirror here, gazing into the center of its wide gold frame and etched glass detailing, as she floated in this gaudy and ostentatious mansion she'd been drawn into, she saw a wisp of herself. Nearly entirely transparent, there was just a slight contouring of the air where her figure floated. She was nothing but a slight shade of glowing lines delineating features frozen in youth.

She had agreed to stay a consistent New York City haunt because of the living. Her ongoing work with family and friends gave her a purpose and mission she'd never had as an admittedly vapid socialite whose ill-advised curiosity had killed her like the most inelegant of cats.

But to say she had full command over her immortal coil would be a lie. Take this evening, for example. She'd been drawn into a stranger's mansion and found herself floating about a fine parlor bedecked in marble, velvet, and seemingly unending gold trim, with no idea why.

Spiritualists, as the uniquely American version of the sect had been born of Quakers, would often utter that they spoke "as the spirits moved." Sometimes the spirits too, were moved. By unseen forces and unfathomable hands. She had been moved here for reasons she hoped would reveal themselves. Surveying the room, floating along behind the present company at a sufficient distance so as not to strike up complaints of drafts or chills, offered Maggie the clues of family name and fortune. A few framed images on the parlor walls featured images of beautiful women in frothy day-dresses holding decorative bottles trimmed with golden filigree, boasting the great calming and healing powers of Prenze Tonics.

This is where she was. The Prenze mansion. This family had been on her mind. Something wasn't right about this place. About this family. And the spirit world knew it.

Maggie had followed a series of incidences and instincts to this mansion, all in a rush. There were secrets to be exposed. She now floated by a mantelpiece littered with objects d'art from around the world, and watched the festivities unfold.

There was a medium present, or at least she was costumed as such, with an embroidered set of robes, a turban, and too much eye makeup. The most theatrical ones who appropriated religious aspects of other cultures and muddied the meaning right out of them with fetishistic Orientalism tended to be the most fraudulent ones, so Maggie was certain it wasn't the medium who had summoned her directly into this space.

No. Fellow ghosts had drawn her in. Two of them, children, one dressed in traditional garb of a skirt and vest, and the other in shorts with shoulder straps, straight out of a Bavarian folk tale. Fellow ghosts appeared to Maggie's eyes as fully greyscale figures, their features more solid and clear than any reflections she could see in mirrors.

The Grimm storybook children pointed to the mantel, towards a specific object. There, between a set of candelabras, sat a simple box with a latch; an etching in the wood proclaimed it to be something of smoking supplies.

"Open it," the little girl begged.

"You're a potent spirit," the boy, likely her brother, added hopefully.

"We've been weakened here and nothing responds to our touch. Open it. Show everyone. *Throw* it. This family can't keep hurting all of us."

Maggie knew from working with ghost colleagues and mediums on a spate of recent mysteries that living subjects under possible investigation react in vastly different ways to poltergeist activity. She had no idea what she was about to set in motion, but she also didn't have anything to lose.

Dear Eve, the young lady to whom Maggie had pledged the work and gifts of her spirit, would be cross with her for acting on a hunch without informing her. "There are protocols, paperwork, one can't just *barge* in and begin levitating family belongings," she'd chide gently as if she were a bemused mother and not a nineteen-year-old taskmaster; a brisk old soul in a youthful body.

But every time Maggie had an instinct about this mansion and the people in it, results eluded her. It's why she'd never brought the Prenze name to Eve's attention. She wasn't going to send Eve's new Precinct on a wild goose chase when she was trying to prove herself. Here was the opportunity to engage with an actual object that might be hard evidence and not conjecture. No detective could work with conjecture—she'd learned it was their least favorite word and a liability they couldn't afford.

It was clear that none of the living people in the room saw the three spirits, as there were no indications, no shudders, no looking around as if suddenly unsettled, no brushing down the hackle of small hairs up the backs of their bejeweled or satin-swathed necks. A poltergeist would prove the most surprising, unsettling, and least expected event of the night. The fact that the 'medium' didn't look around or sense any presences when Maggie or the children appeared revealed the woman as a fraud.

The trick would be mustering the energy, the momentum, to move an object. She'd long since forgotten what being corporeal felt like, and that had always been the easiest way, to simply interact with an object just like you would have done in life, feeling a phantom limb in reverse.

Overthinking it was also a curse, so she just allowed herself to rifle through a memory box of every time she'd been humiliated or patronized at an event like this during her corporeal life. Just because she'd been in high society didn't mean it had ever been kind to her. It treated young, eligible women as pretty cattle sold to the highest bidder in the marketplace of social climbing. This surge of frustration was enough. She swatted a weightless hand at the metal box. It went flying and landed in the center of a floral Persian rug, opening and spilling its contents—a stack of photographic images.

Cries went up, everyone, all eight adults in the room, reacted with a jump or a vocal start at the crash of the box. Bodies leaned in, but no one approached the box or its contents—they simply stared.

The photographs were recent, by their finish and the lack of yellowing around the edges.

Maggie took a moment to stare at the pictures she'd revealed to the company. Something bothered her deeply about their nature. They were all posed, with props and scenery, costumes and crowns or halos. There was something too stilted about the figures, something eerie about their features.

Postmortem photography. When it was so common, one learned to tell the difference between images of the living and the photographs of the dead. Often a photograph of a dead loved one was the only picture a family had of them. But these were more elaborately staged than Maggie had ever seen. Far more than was any sort of custom.

Maggie stared at the ghosts of the two young children—six, perhaps seven years old—who had fierce, defiant looks on their faces as they took in the horrified expressions of the living. She saw a photograph lying there of the two of them, in their Bavarian garb, posed with a shepherd's crook and a prop sheep. Their eyes were closed but their eyelids had been painted with eyes as if they were open.

A tall, thin, dour-looking man in a fine umber brown suitcoat strode forward, his long face elongated in a frown, his auburn hair greying at the temples. The man scooped up the strewn images with an irritated sigh, glaring in the direction of Maggie, but not directly at her. This man, she determined, must be a Prenze patriarch.

"What . . . what were those . . .?" a young woman sitting on a velvet settee asked, leaning forward curiously, her blue silk gown pooling around her.

Everyone stared at their host, who offered a thin-lipped smile. "Confiscated property from a recent wayward friend. I have been known to minister to those among my station who are lost. This is a friend's collection. What an unfortunate fetish; to covet deceased who are not his kin. I took them away, lest he be haunted. Perhaps I have brought a haunt upon us instead. What an ungodly thing. Isn't that right, Madame Nightstar?"

Maggie nearly snorted at the unoriginal stage name.

The man turned to the medium, who was white as a sheet. "Oh . . . of course . . . Mr. Prenze. Of course."

Maggie wanted to interject that there was nothing inherently 'ungodly' about a spirit in the least, but the man ushered everyone out of the room to go on to dinner, saying he would be right with them all. They did so, looking warily at the upturned box, at their host, and at the 'medium' before obeying and filing out to a feast.

Once the parlor door had closed behind the last guest, the towering man closed the distance between himself and Maggie in two easy strides.

"Ah, naughty girl," the man clucked his tongue, staring at Maggie directly, eye to eye. That answered whether or not she could be seen by him. He hadn't given her any clue before. Wily. "How did you get in?" he pressed.

Maggie turned toward the children. They were gone.

"Just passing by," Maggie replied, unsure if he could hear her.

"Well, now that you're here, stay indefinitely—" the man said with a leering grin. He moved to the door, to a switch along the wall that surely controlled the lighting. She had assumed from the opulence of the home that the lighting was electric; it was too bright and had a harsher quality, and the man made it only more so as he turned a knob and the lights grew even brighter. Impossibly so. The room grew blinding. Maggie squinted, raising an incorporeal arm over her eyes as if she could shield herself.

Along with the bright light came a hum, a rising, whining, whirring, grating noise like a mechanical roar. The sound hurt. The light burned. She felt as though she were being torn apart . . . she opened her mouth to scream . . .

And then . . . utter darkness.

Chapter One

Only the ghosts surrounding Eve Whitby could cool her blushing cheeks as the inimitable Theodore Roosevelt, Governor of New York, stood to toast her before a host of lieutenants, detectives and patrolmen, all of whom found her highly dubious.

Many of these same New York Police Department officers found Roosevelt just as problematic. He wasn't Police Commissioner anymore—he'd used the notoriety from having cleaned up corruption within police departments and ridden it straight to the governorship, but as some detractors noted, the man couldn't leave well enough alone. So here he was meddling again with the police, and Eve was at the center of it.

While Eve tried to appear confident in most situations, being at the center of a crowd made her nerve-wracked and flushed. She was surer of her mission than she was of herself. When one followed a calling, passion was often a driving force greater than self-assuredness.

Whole departments turning to her and lifting glasses made her stomach lurch and waver like the transparent, hovering ghosts glowing about the room who made her work possible. She looked down at the hem of her black dress—simple light wool attire of clean lines and polished buttons she'd designed to look like a police matron's uniform, but in the colors of mourning. When she took on this department, she donned mourning. Not out of sorrow, but in celebration of her co-workers, the dead.

I am a woman of particular purpose . . . she thought, an internal rallying cry. Any moment Roosevelt was going to make an announcement about

The Ghost Precinct, the project she'd put everything in her young life on hold to spearhead.

Taking a breath, she steadied her feet, shifting the heel of her black boots on the smooth wooden floor. She glanced in a mirror and tucked an errant thick black lock of hair back into her bun, trying to shift her pallid, nearly sickly-looking expression to something that appeared more commanding lest her wide green eyes give away her concerns.

The manner in which the three ghosts at the edges of the room were bobbing insistently in the air meant something. They had something to say and were her most vocal operatives. Vera, Olga, and little Zofia, who was actually wringing her hands. Eve had asked that her operative spirits not come tonight, for fear of distraction, but they had come regardless. She ignored them, though their behavior made her nervous. Something was wrong. But she couldn't ask what. Not now. Not in the spotlight in front of a crowd who didn't trust her.

Roosevelt, dressed in a white suit with a striped waistcoat, his iconic moustache moving with his expressive face as if it were punctuating his dialogue, adjusted his wire-rimmed glasses, lifted a glass, and bid his fellows do the same.

"I give you Miss Evelyn H. Whitby, daughter of Lord and Lady Denbury, and I bid you toast the inception of her Ghost Precinct. Now, because we live in an age of skeptics and charlatans in equal measure, we're not going public about this Precinct beyond our department heads here. We don't need undue fuss, we don't need hysterics. What we know conclusively is that this young woman's talents aided in solving two brutal murders to date. As we near a new century, no one knows what new crimes will come with it, but one thing we can count on is that there will always be the dead, with a perspective none of us have. It's foolish to leave such a resource untapped, especially as this city grows by the thousands every month.

"We await many more resolutions and have directed her to cases that have gone cold. Perhaps, dare I say, she and her colleagues may even garner a few premonitions to stop a crime before it's even begun! To the young lady and her ghosts! Whether you're a believer or not, she has assured me there's nothing to be afraid of!"

There was a polite if less than enthusiastic clap of hands.

Nothing to be afraid of . . . she repeated to herself. *That's exactly your purpose on this earth, to make ghosts a less frightful reality for those who do believe. For those who can see, for those who want to know. You are the voice of the departed, you are their champion. Be proud. Show these people how proud you are to be the advocate for the dead.*

Eve nodded to the politician, squared her shoulders, lifted her flute, and allowed herself to enjoy the distinct, sweet bite of a good champagne, feeling the chill of the dead on the air. If her spirits could not calm her nerves with their presence, at least their drastic temperature wafting towards her warm cheeks made her appear more poised and stoic than nervous in the spotlight.

While she was fairly certain she was the only one present who could fully see and interact with her spirit department, she didn't rule out that some members of the force might be aware that they were being watched from beyond the veil. While the ghosts had disobeyed Eve's orders to stay entirely away tonight, at least they were keeping their distance from the attendees, as some of her friends and family were too affected when more than one was in the room. When she had agreed to be noted in tonight's reception, she'd done everything in her power to avoid a scene.

The intense, inimitable Mister Roosevelt had never tried to convince the New York Metropolitan Police Force that creating a 'Ghost Precinct' was a good idea; he had simply done it. He made it Eve's purview and ensured, thanks to powerful allies, that she had access to departmental services, support, and resources. He had also kept the press out of it lest the Precinct become, as he'd said, "an unnecessary rodeo. I don't want to field calls for you to contact departed loved ones unless they can solve crimes." Roosevelt wasn't a man who much cared what other people thought when he was committed to a cause, and that quality was maybe the only thing she had in common with the bombastic legislator.

When Roosevelt had told her family he wanted to honor Eve and the Precinct, her grandmother Evelyn, whom she was named for, had taken control of the arrangements to ensure the reception was held in the grand downstairs foyer of The Players Club, Edwin Booth's beautiful brownstone complex in Gramercy Park, established in hopes of making the theatre more respectable—a much harder sell after his brother had killed President Lincoln.

While most of the city's grandest clubs were for men only, as was the Players Club's regular membership, Eve fought additional stigma regarding Spiritualists, mediums, psychics and the lot—a hierarchy of respectability that kept a celebration like this relegated only to theatrical spaces. Whether they were believed or exposed as frauds, people passionately loved or hated a woman who spoke with the dead. There was hardly a middle ground. She could not be entirely lauded, and would always be considered suspect. Eve had heard one detractor say that people like her were for 'parlor tricks, not politics'. The man had been a New York congressional representative and had stood in the way of her department when it was first being finalized with the police commissioner. Roosevelt had ignored him and had bid Eve do the same. She was hardly as positioned or as powerful as the Governor, but she tried to follow his lead.

Her parents, Lord and Lady Denbury, were sitting off to the side of the richly-appointed foyer. Poised on cushioned benches against the wood-paneled wall, they watched uncomfortably, in elegant but subdued evening dress, matching the tone of mourning dress Eve had taken on out of the kind of respect and engagement she hoped would ensure spirits' ongoing help. The mourning, she felt, was not only a uniform for this work, it was a mission.

To either side were her grandparents, Evelyn looking on in beaming pride in a stunning black gown direct from France, taking the mourning cue from her granddaughter. Her grandfather Gareth looked pleasantly baffled in a plain black suit, choosing to cope with a strange world by way of detached bemusement. This attitude had served him well thus far and kept relations with his clairvoyant wife at their most pleasant.

Eve's parents had come to know the paranormal by violent force. By murder and horror. Her father was a titled English Lord who had been targeted by a demonic society, her mother was a middle class New Yorker. She and Gran had been the only ones who had helped him and it was incredible they had survived at all, having both been targeted by abject evil. They'd survived thanks to cleverness, good friends and Gran's help. They'd fallen in love, married and remained in New York, hoping to have a normal life with their newborn Eve, praying none of what they went through would be passed on to her. They would never fully accept a life lived with ghosts at the fore and Eve could not expect them to.

The gifts Eve manifested placed a distinct strain on the family. Not wishing to bring such loving parents any inconvenience, let alone pain, she had tried to block out her gifts, once.

That effort had nearly killed her at age nine. When she'd tried to stop hearing the dead, migraines had seared her head for weeks, and she couldn't eat or sleep. Only when she opened back up to hear the murmurs of the spirit world could she breathe again, her fever breaking and life returning to her paranormal normal.

The reality of this precinct meant she could never go back on her talents. The dead would never let her. Her parents knew it, as she could tell by their haunted gazes. A new chapter had begun.

Roosevelt was staring at her. So were her ghosts, expectantly. So were all the men.

"Would you like to say a few words, Miss Whitby?" Roosevelt prompted.

"Ah." She wouldn't have liked to, really, as nerves always got the better of her if she was put on the spot in such a manner, but it was necessary. Taking a deep breath, she thought about what was best to say. The absence of trust in the room felt like an impossible gulf to cross. She wanted to thank her mediums but that seemed odd after not having invited them. She didn't want the patrolmen, detectives and lieutenants to look at a group of four young women of vastly different backgrounds and judge them all as a threat. She wanted that pressure to land solely upon herself, and keep her Sensitives sensitive, not defensive.

Taking a deep breath, she reminded herself that this department was her mission, it was not about her. It was about respect for the great work of mediums and all the good the dead could do for the living. Just like Edwin Booth had sought to lift up the profession of theatre by this grand space. This freed her to speak with a calm, crisp tone.

"In this day and age of charlatans and magicians in the guise of Spiritualism," she said. "I blame no one for their skepticism. In fact, I encourage it. Skepticism offers investigative integrity. A questioning mind solves a case. My specific and unprecedented Precinct hopes to earn continued trust by the thing we can all always agree on: solving crime and easing suffering."

She could see the unsure faces before her, some bemused, some seeming openly hostile. Every woman entering a predominantly male field had encountered these same faces, even without her subject matter being additional fodder for derision. Her nerves crested but she kept talking. She believed, above all, in her mission, and no critic would change that.

"However unorthodox the means," she continued, raising her voice and commanding more of the room, "however unprecedented the methods, our aims are mutual and always will be. Ghosts are far too often misunderstood, and I hope that by working with them in proven, positive ways, our work can begin to change the perception of hauntings. Spirits can walk where we cannot, hear what fails our mortal senses, and keep the most vigilant of watches when we must take our rest. I hope you will see them as a help, not a horror." She finished not with a request but a demand: "Thank you for your support."

"Hear, hear!" said Ambassador Bishop, a tall, striking, silver-haired man across the room. Impeccably dressed in a black silk tailcoat and charcoal brocade waistcoat, the diplomat to England and lifelong friend of the family lifted his champagne glass for a second toast. It was Bishop who had gotten Roosevelt involved in the first place, since his present ambassadorship did not carry the same legislative control as when he had been a New York senator. In those days he'd have seen to such a department himself.

Bishop's wife, Clara, a sharp-featured woman many years his junior, with dark golden hair that matched the gold core of her piercing eyes, stood at his elbow in a graceful plum gown. Clara stared at Eve with a fierce pride that held none of her family's hesitance. Eve owed more to Clara than either of them would admit to anyone but each other. Clara nodded at Eve as if she knew she was passing off work she could no longer do herself.

"Hear *indeed*, Ambassador!" Roosevelt exclaimed, grinning at the Bishops. "Now enjoy refreshments and the fine company! I'll be here if any of you men need me and Miss Whitby has been gracious enough to agree to answer some questions from the department present, provided they are posited with all due respect. Respect, and transparency. I didn't clean this filthy force up for nothing. Well, I reckon the Ghost Precinct will be our most *transparent* department yet! Ha!" Roosevelt slapped a hand on a serving table and enjoyed his pun amidst a few groans.

When asked Eve's opinion on Mister Roosevelt, she had once replied that he was a man who wanted to preserve wilderness so he could shoot things within it. That summed him up, she concluded. She found many of his ideas sensible but was often baffled by his road getting there. But no one could deny he was a compelling, larger-than-life character who never failed to surprise.

Gratitude was her most abundant sentiment, if she were asked how she felt in this moment. Thanks to Bishop and Roosevelt's machinations, she'd been given steady employment, without which, like all the many strong working women around her, she'd go mad. The moment she'd signed paperwork on the precinct, the constant, dull ache that rested at the base of her neck even if she wasn't having a migraine had eased. It was as if the whole of the spirit world that clutched at her from behind had released their talons ever so slightly. It was a world that wanted to be seen and acknowledged, and that's why it sought to communicate in such a wide array of methods. Now it was seen in a whole new light and given responsibilities.

At nineteen years old, when most young women of any kind of title and society were very busy with their 'seasons' and hoping for a well-placed marriage, Eve found she had no interest in following the path of her supposed peers in the city. Of course there was the occasional ball she attended due to the pressures of her father's Lordship, her gran's high-society dealings, her grandfather's Metropolitan Museum soirees, the Bishops' esteemed gatherings. But theirs were generally philanthropic functions that had great purpose, not dances meant to pair up eligible bachelors with debutantes. The former suited her, the latter bored her.

Her circle attracted a constant parade of ghosts whose chill presence ruined the warmth of a good party. Here at the Players, the fireplaces were roaring as the new electric fixtures were buzzing in a juxtaposition of ancient and modern light and heat, making the room so warm that the ghostly retinue on the margins caused a much-needed draft. But she couldn't keep ignoring them. If she did, they might start throwing things, and now was hardly the best time for a poltergeist.

Roosevelt held up his hand, hailing Eve as if he wished to speak with her, but men in tail-coats blocked his path as he took a step forward. As legislators were forever called upon for favors, the veritable inferno of energy that was Roosevelt was immediately beset by an entourage. Eve took this as a chance to slip away, into another room where the ghosts and she could speak freely.

Glancing around, she moved towards an opening in the crowd, preparing to make her way to whatever empty, dark space she could find in the grand place. But a young detective stepped into her path and she paused with a smile she hoped did not appear strained.

She recognized the dark-haired, clean-shaven, sharp-featured man with rich brown eyes ringed in blue; a distinct gaze that pierced her right to the core. During a recent case, Eve's ghosts had bid her examine a crime scene herself, as they were having trouble describing it. While she had not been welcome at the site, and it was assumed she would both be in the way and taint the evidence, this man had quelled the protesting officers on duty. He had found a place for her to stand within view of the exsanguinated body and take notes. It had been grim but her composure was a test that she'd passed.

"Detective Horowitz, it is good to see you again and I hope you're well. This is a more pleasant scene than when I last saw you."

"Ah, yes." He grimaced. "That ugly bloodletting."

"Have you figured that one out?"

"How a body could be that drained?" he asked. He shook his head with a humorless laugh. "There were suction marks near the puncture wounds—something drew it out of him."

"How odd. I believe in ghosts, but not vampires, detective."

"Well that's reassuring at least." His face transformed from angular to warm for a moment before cooling again.

"Thank you for honoring me this evening," Eve said, bobbing her head.

"I do have a question for you, if you don't mind."

"Go on," she said, glancing at Zofia, a ten-year-old in a simple pinafore, bobbing in the air impatiently, gesturing for her to hurry up with this chat. "I try, whenever I can, to work in new technologies. Fingerprinting, psychological profiles from alienists, taking exquisite stock of a scene so that not even a hair of evidence is tampered with. In regards to your department . . . Say one were to believe in poltergeists. To be clear, I don't believe, but if I did, wouldn't a host of spirits be liable to disrupt and thus corrupt a crime scene by moving objects? Couldn't any of the various ways the spirit world has been said to commune with mortals potentially foul a scene?" She stared at him. It was a valid point.

"My spirits aren't ones for moving things," she began. "They aren't the poltergeist sort, at least not that I've been aware, but it is a cogent point to bring up to them; to be aware of the ways their presences might affect a given environment. To be fair, my ghosts wouldn't leave any additional fingerprints," she offered. The young man twisted his lips as if he wanted to smile but was too focused to allow the indulgence.

"What I have tried, with my contacts, is to cultivate details *beyond* a crime scene," Eve explained. "My ghosts and mediums pick up on expansive aspects, specifics of place, people, setting, weather, clothes, and they're drawn to things the living might find mundane. And they do so in a non-linear manner, so I have to constantly sift for relevance. That's what was so maddening to me at first, why ghosts kept coming and telling me far too many details about seemingly meaningless things. Until I finally saw a pattern in the noise. These patterns led to the arrests and cases solved that Mister Roosevelt so kindly referenced."

"While I am glad of the eventual outcome, how can you be sure all the facts presented to you were real and not just luck?" Horowitz pressed.

Suddenly Roosevelt was behind him like some bold, pouncing apparition. "Because she has spies!" the man cried, waggling his great moustache. "Her ladies, both living and dead, are everywhere and in *everything*," he added delightedly. "And if any man here underestimates a woman's craftiness, or her ability to pick up a litany of detail so intense as to leave you breathlessly disarmed from argument, well then you've never had a single one of them cross with you!"

This broke a distinct layer of ice. The entourage of fine suits swarmed the Governor again and Eve edged away, Horowitz following a pace behind.

"When he's right, he's right," Eve said, turning to the detective with a smile. Just as Eve felt that the man was beginning to warm to her, the temperature around her went ice cold. A plummeting of twenty-some degrees wasn't just a draft; it meant only one thing. A ghost wasn't just nearby, but directly behind her, toying with a lock of her hair, threatening to lift it up into thin air. She was familiar with the trick to get her attention. Eve smoothed the lock back down again and gave a sideways glare to the spirit.

"I look forward to your further questions, Detective. But if you'll excuse me for the moment . . ." she turned away, crossed around the corner of the next threshold and stared into the eyes of the chill directly.

Her best scout, young Zofia, floated before her in full greyscale, dark hair back in a haphazard bun, in a plain work dress blackened just slightly at the hem; the only reminder of her premature death in a garment district fire. Because the ghosts who communed with Eve were full-consciousness spirits, her burned body wasn't what became a shade; this was her silvery soul. The agony of death was long shed—souls were a glowing whole while the body's raw materials returned to dust. Spiritualism's greatest and most comforting gift was this reassurance.

"I'm sorry to disturb you, Eve, I really am, but you have to know . . ." she said in a thick Polish accent, her ghostly voice never heard above a whisper, no matter how emphatic. "I know you told us to hang back, to not to talk to you, but . . ."

Eve turned her head away from the crowd, moving into the shadows of the hall beyond so that she couldn't be seen talking to thin air.

"But?" she murmured through clenched teeth.

"Margaret is gone," the spirit replied.

Eve blinked at the spirit. The spirit wavered in the air, blinking back.

"Gone?" Eve prompted, not entirely sure what Zofia meant. The spirit world was full of comings and goings.

"*Gone*, gone," Zofia insisted. "None of us ghosts have any sense of her. Her candle is out. We've tried everything. There is no waking her. There is no summoning her. This world, or the next, we cannot find her. Our Maggie. She's gone."

Eve reeled. What could be worse timing? Just as she was on the cusp of being taken seriously, her best asset was dead. Again.

Chapter Two

Eve began taking her leave from the club, begging forgiveness; saying that she'd received an important lead on a brand new missing person case. She didn't say it was one of her own. She managed a few words of appreciation to Roosevelt and to those who had facilitated her offices; the men who had been particularly unobtrusive and taken the information she gave without snide commentary. They deserved particular thanks. She pressed the Bishops' hands in hers, quietly thanking them for being gifted Sensitives who had paved the way for her. They quietly smiled, and Eve could sense how much more Clara wished to say, but didn't. Those who kept rolling their eyes in her direction she pointedly ignored.

A glance back at Horowitz proved to Eve that he'd been staring at her as she gathered her things; a drawstring bag and a light wool evening cloak. Catching his eye, she could see him attempting to discern the cause of her departure. His look seemed to ask if she was all right. With a shrug, she turned away, a wresting sensation in her stomach telling her the obvious: that he was one of the rare young men who had the ability to affect her. Most, she didn't even notice.

Eve enjoyed the art of flirting, she enjoyed the challenge of charming and captivating people, all people, who might be helpful to her. What to *do* with that once the game was afoot was hardly her strong suit. She frankly didn't have time for callers. The detective would, of course, remain a colleague, but the game could remain, silently, in play, ensuring an ally in him and a source of secret pleasure if she could keep him on a bit of a hook.

Grandmother Evelyn, having watched Eve's face from the moment Zofia burst to her side, rose quietly from her perch at the side of the room as if on cue. When Eve glanced at her gran—her mentor, her inspiration, and her very best friend—she knew she'd been heard; that the ripple of the spirit world Zofia sent across Spiritualist waters had been felt there too. Her grandmother turned to Lord and Lady Denbury and smiled that gracious, warm smile that eased the sting of whatever she might say next.

"Something has happened," Evelyn said gently. "Information has just arrived with some urgency and demands Eve's attention. Let me go, I'll see after her."

Eve's mother, sitting bolt upright and yet distant-eyed, as if trying to somehow be both alert and far away at the same time, nodded to her elder, knowing better than to fight the inevitable and acquiescing that she couldn't come between two such kindred spirits who remained so driven by their gifts, talents that precluded all else.

"Mother, Father," Eve swept over to them and kissed their cheeks in turn, feeling the draft the spirits left in her wake wash over them in a subtle breeze. Her mother physically recoiled from the chill while keeping a strained smile on her face.

She gazed between the two of them, speaking with a mournful earnestness. "I know you hardly know what to say to me anymore. I am so sorry all of this pains you. I love you very much."

Her raven-haired and unearthly blue-eyed father, Jonathon, described by ladies of the city as breathtakingly handsome, managed a reply. "Congratulations, my dear, on this accolade from the Governor. Whatever you do that solves the unsolved, eases pain, and makes this city safer, we love and support you."

Her mother fought for words, the white lace collar that swept up from the taffeta of her fine purple gown quavering a moment. The cameo at her throat and the small auburn pin curls that framed her lovely face shook before she finally murmured, "Grandmother Helen's loving ghost would be very proud."

At this, Eve's grandfather, Gareth, squeezed his daughter's hand and reached out to pat Eve on the head as she bent over them, shifting the careful braid she'd put her dark hair into to manage her thick locks. "Yes. Be good. Be safe, child," he said, maintaining his nearly fixed, pleasant smile.

They meant their words, but all of this was a kind of torture and Eve didn't want to subject them to it any further, and she urged the whole family to go home and rest.

Her parents and grandfather went on ahead, Evelyn insisting she and Eve would hail a hansom cab and all would be well after a breath of fresh air.

'A breath of fresh air' was their code for a full leave to talk with spirits.

Eve needed that air, and she needed her girls, without constraint. She could gain no reliable intelligence if she herself was surrounded by the uninitiated, the uncomfortable or anyone who might worry about appearances. Her communication with the dead was unorthodox even by the varying standards of mediums and clairvoyants. Roughly interrogating thin air would only lose her ground in front of skeptics.

Bursting down the Player's Club stairs and onto the path around Gramercy Park, it was only a moment before Zofia reappeared at her side in a freezing gust. While Evelyn hailed the hansom cab, she alerted the driver as to what might ensue.

"I warn you, sir, my granddaughter here is an actress in grave need of learning lines. If you hear her shouting from the compartment, let it be. Take us around Washington Square Park a few rounds if you please."

The man shrugged. "So long as you pay me, scream to the heavens if you like."

"Thank you, Gran, as always," Eve murmured, hopping into the cab.

"Of course, now get on with it. I've hardly the connection with your girls you have, but I could tell in that room something was wrong. And not just the officers' general opinions, though I could have given a whole battalion of them a piece of my mind," the elder woman scoffed. "There have been police matrons in the force now for nearly two *decades*, for heavens' sake, what *century* are they in?"

With a chilly blast, the compartment was illuminated in an eerie grey light as Zofia floated across from Eve. "Go on, Zofia," Eve prompted, "now we all can speak freely. Tell me more. Everything."

The ghost, her dark eyes mesmerizing and entirely unsettling if Eve looked into them for long, shifted as if uncomfortable, staring at Evelyn, biting her lip before whispering to her medium.

"Will your grandmother want to hear about this, Eve?" the girl began, shifting closer, so that Eve saw her own breath cloud before her. "Considering . . ."

"Considering what?" Eve pressed.

"*Margaret*. Maggie was her niece and you are family. You met her long after she died. You taught me to be sensitive to how the living still grieve, Eve," Zofia insisted.

Eve sighed. "Yes, so I did. Of course." She turned to her grandmother. "Can you hear Zofia, Gran?" Eve asked carefully.

"A few words." She swallowed hard. "I heard *Margaret*. I know what . . . *who* . . . you're being careful about." There was a flash of distinct pain across Gran's lovely face—her stoic, distinct face lined by a fully-lived life, the picture of elegance who held the weight of a room with spirited grace, all the more vibrant a presence for her sixty-eight years. She shifted her shoulders, a rustle of luminous satin, as if she were readjusting some great weight to a more manageable position.

"Don't worry for me," she continued quietly and patted Eve's knee absently with a long-fingered hand creased with veins and accented by a large garnet ring and one of polished lapis lazuli; both powerful stones with distinct powers of lending clarity to divination. "My poor Maggie has visited me and our souls are at peace; we are more loving now than we were in life. Go on, dear, you must get to the bottom of this if she's missing from her usual haunts."

Eve squeezed that hand that had wrought so much out of this world and the next, a hand that had guided and saved her mind when so much was screaming around and within it. Maggie too, had helped, inordinately. It was Eve's job now to help her in whatever void she'd been lost to.

"When did you know Margaret was gone, Zofia?" Eve began.

"Today. She wasn't at our appointed rounds," Zofia insisted. "She never misses our Friday Frights."

"Friday Frights?" Eve narrowed her eyes.

"You know she and I like to terrorize any old codger giving a working girl a hard time in the business district. Every Friday. Eyes seem to wander more, lips are looser and hands lose their way the day before a weekend. We like to appear before the face of any man who won't leave a girl well enough alone, in hopes he'll wet himself or scream like a baby . . ." Zofia's luminous grey face lit with a smile ". . . or both."

Eve couldn't hold back a laugh. Her darling girls. When they weren't helping solve crimes or alerting her to possible threats they were making their own kind of righteous trouble.

"Something is wrong indeed," Eve replied, "if Margaret Hathorn missed her chance to knock a bowler off a lecher's head."

"Exactly!" Zofia exclaimed. "She's the ringleader. When she didn't appear downtown—on Fridays we meet at the Bowling Green—I wafted about to any of her known haunts. Nothing. I told the rest of the girls when I could find them. We came back to the Precinct office, but you weren't there. That's when we remembered about the ceremony tonight."

The carriage came to a halt along the street. "Here," the driver called down.

"No," Eve shook her head emphatically. "Gran, I can't leave now— whenever I go home, I always lose their focus. They become fixated on the property and forget their details."

Evelyn opened her door and called back to the driver. "A few more turns around the Square, if you please, sir, we'll account for them all."

"Suit yourself. Anything for art, I suppose," the driver retorted as Evelyn shut the door, gesturing for Eve to continue.

As the clop of the horses sounded again and the jolt of the carriage rocked them, Zofia wavered.

"Go on, Zofia dear," Eve stated. "Please. What words do you remember as the last you heard from Maggie before this disappearance?"

They circled Washington Square Park, the old parade ground renamed in honor of the first president's inauguration downtown. There along the northern side, facing Fifth Avenue, the newly erected Washington Arch glowed eerie in the moonlight, a grand homage to the Arc de Triomphe that appeared like a ghost in its own right, a mystical beacon rising from the dark shadows of the gas-lit park. The spirit was instantly distracted.

"Did you know," Zofia began mournfully, "that there are ten-thousand-some human remains underground there, in the park? Just below the earth. Taken by yellow fever, choleras, one disease or another, the city didn't have the room . . . A pit of ten thousand bones . . . Disregarded. Tromped and *paraded* over . . ."

"Yes, Zofia, of course we know that," Eve said, gritting her teeth. "But their deaths were long ago. We need to talk about what's happening *now*."

This was the point when patience never won her. Extracting useful, prescient details was the most difficult part. A ghost who came right to the point was a spirit Eve longed to cultivate.

"When you realized she was gone, you said you went to find the other girls. Did you come to the office together?"

"Yes," Zofia nodded, wisps of hair floating in the air as if she were in water. "Just like you taught us, we floated around the table and called out for her, we held our own séance to get her to come out, but nothing. We tried lighting her candle, but we couldn't. We looked into the scrying glass. We even tried moving that silly spirit board. We tried everything we could think of."

The ghost was getting agitated, as the temperature was dropping further and further, and her form was wavering as if she were an image interrupted from a projected screen. "The more we did, the more worried all of us got. We made a promise we'd let each other know if we were going to cross over for good, go onto the sweet Summerland. She promised she wouldn't go without telling us . . ." Zofia's voice hitched.

"There now, Zofia love, don't you cry," Eve said softly. She felt as though she were an elder sister to some of the ghosts. "We'll find her. Can you remember the last thing she said to you?"

The ghost thought a moment before answering. "You know how you and Gran have said that there are times when we might hear a knocking sound?"

Eve nodded. "From the Corridors of life and death itself," she replied. "Fate, destiny, eternal rest, all may come knocking at any time from that space between the living and the dead."

"She said she was hearing lots of sounds," the ghost continued, cocking her head as if she too were straining to listen, "and she couldn't tell where they were coming from. She said they were loudest outside some of the largest mansions in the city. Knocking, singing. Calling. Murmuring. Bidding her come in . . ."

"Was this the last that she spoke to you?" Eve pressed. "About these sounds?"

"Yes. It was Sunday, two days past. What if . . ." Zofia whispered, the mesmeric irises of her grey, luminous eyes widening. "What if something came from the corridor of death and Maggie answered the door . . .?"

Eve's blood went from cold to a distinct ice; the chill of the spirit and the fog of her breath was nothing compared to the shiver that went from the top of her head to the tip of her toes, and along that shuddering course was a ghostly whisper that seemed to be echoed by the whole of the spirit world itself:

Don't invite anything in . . .

Chapter Three

This thought of the finality of death, a concept a ghost was always at odds with, was enough to frighten Zofia's spectral form into disappearing, snuffing her from the cab, leaving only a misty, luminous wisp, then nothing. The carriage came around the north side of the park and halted.

"Well then . . ." Eve muttered.

"How many more times round, ladies?" the driver asked, calling down to them in a wary tone.

"Let's go home," Gran said, opening the door and calling up. "We'll alight at the corner of the park and Waverly, if you please, sir, thank you."

"As you wish," he replied as they jostled forward again.

She turned to Eve. "You know there's only so much you can get out of them at once. This will take time. Maggie has all the time in the world; surely this is but a pause on her eternal journey," she continued, though Eve could tell she was trying to rally herself as much as anything. It was Maggie's interest in dark things, in the paranormal, that had led to her death, a fact Gran would never fully accept or forgive herself for not intercepting.

Upon arriving, Evelyn finally relieved the driver of his rounds and went in to check on the rest of her family while Eve approached the adjacent townhouse she shared. While Evelyn and her grandfather Gareth had their own home further uptown, along the part of Fifth Avenue that constituted old New York money, they spent a great deal of time here; these two addresses were far more the center of their world since Eve had taken up residence with her team.

The privilege of a fairly comfortable life that Eve was wise enough not to take for granted only came by fortuitous marriage at a ghostly cost.

The families entwined out of deep love, respect, and the particular, inimitable bonds created by spiritual battle at the precipice of life and death. Evelyn was a natural stepmother to Natalie, and Gareth was an understanding husband. Regardless of class, neither Eve's father, a British Lord, nor Gran, who had inherited more money than any of them, ever made the family feel that they were anything lesser. While Evelyn Northe-Stewart was not Eve's grandmother by blood, she most certainly was by soul and spirit.

Gran and Grandpa weren't going back uptown tonight, Eve was certain. They had their own floor, below her parents, in 'Fort Denbury' as Eve was fond of calling the attached townhouses her father had procured on Waverly Place, west of the park, before she was born; fine brick and brownstone buildings with the sort of exquisite detail one would expect of an era that called itself gilded.

Eve walked up the grand stoop, let herself in the glass-paneled door covered in wrought-iron tracery, and with a turn of an ornate key, the gas lamps that glowed in round orb sconces all about the property flamed to life. Gliding past the open pocket doors of the first-floor parlor, she turned a few more gas lamps bright, banishing the night's shadows but keeping shutters closed from prying eyes. There in her parlor, filled neither with finery nor useless knick-knacks but a wide circular table and many places to sit, she would conduct the necessary séance to continue the search for Maggie.

At sixteen years old, the ghosts had been at their zenith, pressing upon Eve all the time, in constant agitation. It had nearly torn the whole family apart, not to mention wrecked a good number of fine furnishings and objects. It wasn't because the ghosts plaguing Eve were poltergeists, but often ghosts would startle any number of family members, and teacups in the hand, fine bone china, and any nearby objects easily unsettled were none the safer for a cavalcade of spiritual interruption.

It was Grandmother Evelyn who'd suggested that since the Denburys had bought the adjoining townhouse as an investment on Jonathon's instinct, the instinct had actually been preservation of family rather than a real-estate venture. Eve moved into the empty home next door, and the ghosts followed. Within the month, both buildings were more peaceful for the separation and Eve grew accustomed to living alone while never being left alone.

Ghosts *loved* Eve. There was something about her soul, her energy, her presence, that drew them to her. While she could always talk to Gran about it, thankfully being a Sensitive and a part-time medium herself, even Gran was baffled by how many spirits kept Eve company. It was Gran's questions about the spirits that had set the course of her life and made something meaningful out of what could have felt like a curse.

"What on earth do they all want to talk about?" Gran asked once, just after her sixteenth birthday, when a horde of spirits had swooped in and blown out the candles on her cake.

Eve shrugged. "Gossip! I told them to go find some high-society medium instead."

"Well, your father *is* a titled Lord—"

"I mean a high-society girl who *cares*. I couldn't care less about the petty goings on of others. What point is there? Heaven forbid I haunt the earth to *gossip*. They go on and on. About particulars. Details. Clothing, comings and goings. Shouldn't they be trying to sort out their greatest mortal failure and make peace? If I were a detective, I'd write down all these details, as someone might find them useful at some point."

Gran just stared at her, thunderstruck. "Maybe you should."

Eve had blinked at her. "What?"

"Become a . . . sort of detective." Gran's compelling gaze twinkled—a sure sign she was in possession of a particularly good idea. "If the restless dead won't leave you alone, then why not give the busybodies something to do?"

At this, Eve had snorted. But the idea stuck.

Within the next years she was asking relevant people in the Spiritualist movement important questions, questions that, thanks to Ambassador Bishop, even caught the ear of the newly elected Governor Roosevelt, and her precinct was born. With stipulations, of course, as her operatives were 'just young women' and her department a collection of spirits. For some people in the world, Eve had learned with frustration, there were always qualifiers. Sometimes one could rise above them, but her and her 'girls' would have to work twice as hard for the same amount of respect.

The Precinct mediums and ghosts, every living or dead soul who had sought her out, enjoyed their work. They did seem to know they were a part of something important, working for a greater good. The spirits that bound themselves to the Precinct, serving the city from beyond the veil, clearly shared in a passion for justice that helped ease any injustices during their often too-short lives. Living and dead, Eve's girls were full of purpose and dogged determination. They knew they were unique and whatever progress they made would break barriers, leaving room for who might come next. Eve hoped future generations of young women would have it a bit easier and would be taken more seriously in roles of leadership.

Now Eve lived in-house with her three mediums. They had been working together on various cases and clues for nearly a year now, though the Precinct itself was only officially a few months old. The ghosts who had chosen to support the mediums called Eve's side of "Fort Denbury" their best haunt. The whole lot of them were generally unflappable souls. But in the past year of work, Eve had never seen a ghost as upset as Zofia was while reporting on Margaret's disappearance. It went beyond a ghost's inherent interior melancholy. Zofia was despondent. Sad ghosts carried a melancholy with them like a weight in the air. This was like a millstone.

Just as Eve was about to send out a psychic siren, a call for her mediums to come back home for a meeting, cutting what had been their night off short, there was a knock at the door. Eve knew who it was immediately. Gran didn't like the doorbell, stating that it was 'far too jarring' and why couldn't she have a door knocker like the rest of civilized society for the past centuries?

Letting her Grandmother in, still in the same fine gown from the evening's festivities, Eve left her in the parlor and went to stoke coals under the back stove to brew a pot of tea.

When Eve returned, Gran asked, "I assume you'll call back your operatives?"

Eve nodded. "Because of the event tonight, I had told them to go out and have a nice dinner somewhere. I couldn't have predicted we'd have a crisis on our hands."

Zofia burst through the parlor wall, her phantom hands wringing the edges of her pinafore apron. "I want Maggie back *now*."

"Indeed, Zofia, indeed. We'll do everything we can," Eve assured the ghost.

"I'd like to go freshen up before I sit down to a séance," Gran said. "Did you get the plumbing fixed in the upstairs water closet?"

"I did, thankfully."

"Good." Gran turned and held onto the rail tightly as she climbed the stairs to Eve's floor, moving with deliberate steps. Gran was getting older, and it took a maturing Eve to see that, noticing the barely perceptible change in pace, every movement taking a hair's breadth more time as the years went on.

A sense of guilt washed over Eve in a cool inundation. She should be letting this woman rest.

Turning at the landing, Gran looked down at her. "Well? While you're waiting for your girls, we could be brainstorming. While I wash my face and put some peppermint oils behind my ears to perk myself up, come and talk to me."

Gran was so very wise but didn't know the first thing about the fine art of rest. Eve had learned every habit from this indomitable woman, who immediately picked up on her granddaughter's hesitation. "What is it, my dear? You have a look about you."

"I worry I'm taxing you too much," Eve replied sheepishly as she ascended after her to the second floor. Gran entered Eve's boudoir and sat down at her rosewood vanity inlaid with pearl and floral marquetry, the fanciest item of furniture she'd allowed Gran to procure for her. Eve followed behind, sitting on a nearby settee whose burgundy brocade matched the vanity stool. "Mother and Father are one thing, but you . . . You've earned rest and then some. I think the spirits sense that too, perhaps wanting to spare you—"

Gran swiveled the chair to stare Eve down, a dainty bottle of scented oil that she herself had gifted Eve clutched in her hand. She withdrew the delicate blown glass stopper to dab a drop of lavender mint oil onto her finger. "I've nearly died many times," Gran began, rubbing a finger behind one ear, then the next, breathing in deeply and squaring her shoulders. "I've been haunted by the dead as long as you, them coming to me in childhood and never leaving me alone. If I were to truly stop, the silence would be maddening. I wouldn't be able to think, I wouldn't know what to do with myself."

Gran continued with the routine of the oil, pressing a dab of it on pressure points about her face, continuing in an ardent tone. "I've made mistakes in life. I've been selfish, short-sighted. If the spirits stop murmuring I'm left only with guilt." She stared at herself in the mirror, and Eve sensed Gran feeling her age even if she didn't look it.

"We all make mistakes," Eve said to Gran's reflection, seeing herself in part profile in the mirror. "You can't keep taking on Maggie's as your own. It won't help her peace or yours."

"As a clairvoyant who should know better, I've never been able to content myself with that adage of everyone making mistakes. Why have the gift if it won't keep us from making them?"

"The rhetorical question of the ages."

"Your turn. If I've taught you anything it's how to take care of yourself with simple, restorative comforts," Gran said, handing her the bottle that had been procured for these precise holistic purposes, when the night was young and full of trying work ahead. Eve placed a dab of oil on her finger, touched each temple and pressed hard upon them, trying to open the channel of her third eye, internally blinking between those two temple points, as wide as she could.

Just then, the doorbell buzzed, a loud, jarring noise letting them know to expect an entrance. Evelyn jumped and grumbled at the raucous interruption, hating the noise.

"I know you hate the bell, Gran, but my colleagues and I have made it a sensible practice to ring it even if we have keys, so that if someone was mid-trance, they wouldn't be surprised by a quiet entrance."

"That's sensible and all, I just hate how jarring it is. I'll be down in a moment."

As Eve descended the stair, Cora opened the door with her key and waved at Eve as she hung her coat in the wardrobe. Cora's hazel-brown skin was dotted with moisture, her black, tightly spiraled curls up in a lace bonnet. She adjusted the eyelet cuffs of her high-necked blouse and unclasped the pin at her collar sculpted in the shape of an eagle, keeping it pressed in her hand as she gave herself more air, as if the evening had strained her breath.

"Heavens, they won't leave me be," Cora stated. Gesturing behind her, she added. "You feel them? Have they *all* come out on parade tonight?"

The icy wake that had been trailing behind the young medium two years Eve's junior caught up and two ghosts burst across the threshold, bobbing frenetically. Winnie and Cyril, who must have been the ones to collect Cora. The two greyscale spirits were transparent and floating, both holding slight clues as to how they died in their appearance. Winnie, a little girl in a choir robe with dark circles under her silver eyes, having died of consumption; Cyril, a young, broad-shouldered man in shirtsleeves and suspenders, a piano player who had been lost to the same fate, years later. The two spirits of different hue and opacity were drawn to wherever music was most prevalent, tied to this, the city of their birth. They were infrequent haunts of Eve's association, but it was clear they cared deeply for the precinct's well-being.

"Margaret's gone," the spirits and Cora all stated at once. The effect was quite an ethereal echo of sorrow.

"She knows, I told her," replied Zofia from down the hall, a glowing form at the base of the stairs who wafted to the group, refreshing the chill. Cora and Eve shuddered in tandem.

"Hello, Cora, my dear," Evelyn called from the upper landing. "I'll be down with you in a moment."

"Oh, hello, Gran," Cora replied. Evelyn was everyone's relative. Eve had never met another woman people admired or took on as their own so much. Leading Cora into the parlor, Eve bid her take a seat on the settee.

"I can hear crying. Not just from our usual haunts, but everywhere," Cora stated, shaking her head. At the mention of their names, the ghosts entered the parlor from the hall. Cora continued. "I hear the *air* crying. At least, that's what it sounds like. Do you hear it like that?"

"I can't say I heard crying. What I did hear was a warning. A warning not to 'let anything in'. Wish I knew what that meant," Eve said rising as her kettle whistled from the back stove. Preparing the pot and wheeling a tea service in, she set a warm cup before the shivering Cora, who took it gratefully. Eve prepared herself for another late night.

When the dead couldn't sleep, the living who could hear them wouldn't either.

Either Eve would hold a séance or the séance would hold them. If she wasn't mistaken, a life hung in the balance in a way they'd never experienced and had never thought to protect against. What would cause an incorporeal being to vanish? How did one kill the already dead?

Chapter Four

Antonia Morelli was the next to return, taking her seat silently, young Jenny behind her; the last of their medium quartet.

Eve didn't need to say a word or send a wire in times of an emergency. All she had to do was open herself in a certain, clear and unmistakable way—a psychic alarm, a siren's wail let the souls connected to hers feel her concern and they would, almost always, take their natural places around the circle as soon as was possible.

Eve and the girls didn't know much about Antonia's past. All they knew and cared about was the striking night they had all met, which was telling in and of itself.

Antonia had knocked on the door mid-séance, in the middle of a hunt for information about an abusive doctor. When Eve snapped out of her trance to answer the bell, there was tall Antonia, brown-black hair swept up into a bun atop her head, dressed in a lace-collared shirtwaist and a plain black skirt, sporting a bruised cheek and a half-smile. She'd worn a hint of rouge and lip color, and her hazel eyes framed by long black lashes were sharply focused.

"Hello . . ." Eve had begun, but before she could ask if she could be of service, the young woman—perhaps Eve's age, but it was hard to tell, as it was clear the soul inside was an elder one—had explained herself in a soft, tremulous voice.

"When I . . . wasn't what was *expected*, the spirits said to come here. And . . . I wasn't in a position to argue. Sorry to interrupt you. I'm Antonia. I wasn't born so by name, but I *am* Antonia. I've no family, as the sex they assigned to me upon my entrance into this world is not who I am and I had to part ways with them for my safety.

"The spirits told me Eve wouldn't mind and, if I spoke forthrightly, would take me as I am, without question. You're Eve?"

Antonia had stared at Eve, boldly willing her understanding, and Eve's senses had warmed to this clearly feminine soul who was so very much like herself—elegant and fierce, brave enough to presume, in fact, *demand* her safe passage as the woman she had become.

"I am," Eve replied. "And who am I to argue with Providence? I'm looking for a new hire, and the universe provides. Welcome," Eve said, gesturing her in. "We're in the midst of a séance."

"I know," Antonia replied with a smile that won Eve over entirely. "May I please join and prove myself?"

* * * *

That was how they'd begun. Antonia dove in and got right to work. During the séance her first night, Antonia identified and communicated with the spirits of two missing persons, one having fled home only to die of illness and one murdered. This closed two of Eve's open cases before the precinct had even been officially codified.

Due to her nearly preternatural understanding of others and their needs, Antonia got along with everyone. The Precinct gave her purpose, belonging, and a safe haven. Now she was here at another critical juncture, and her whole being was alertness.

The same had been true of eight-year-old Jenny Friel. She had simply arrived, a bright-eyed, bronze-haired little girl in a calico dress, escorted by the ghost of her mother who had drowned in a boating accident with her Catholic parish. Jenny hadn't been on the boat, but the trauma of losing her mother after having already lost her father when she was a baby back in Ireland cut her voice to the quick and she barely spoke.

When she had arrived on the stoop and Eve opened the door, Jenny looked up at her, wide green eyes sad but determined, her light brown hair bedraggled. Her Ma floated to her side and explained to Eve the situation, asking if she could help, as the only family she'd had here went down on that boat.

"Fellow spirits told me my girl would be understood here," her mother said in a gentle Irish lilt. "Not just because she's got the gift of Sight, but because she's gone right quiet . . ."

Eve had told the spirit that her own mother stopped speaking after the death of her maternal grandmother and they were well equipped to understand and even to teach sign language if need be. Eve opened the door to little Jenny and that was that.

Lady Denbury, Eve's mother, suffered from selective mutism when she was a child. She had been sent off to the Connecticut Asylum to learn American Sign Language. Her voice had recovered, but she instilled the value of Sign in her daughter, saying that she had a feeling she'd need it. It had proven quite true. Gran also spoke Sign, maintaining that after having learned five vocal languages she had felt it high time to learn a different kind. That had been the initial connection between Natalie and Gran; their ability to converse. Being understood created families out of orphans and the disenfranchised, communication being a shelter for a heart and mind battling the elements.

There was no taking away little Jenny's immense grief, but at least she was championed. Natalie had agreed to teach Jenny American Sign and Jenny was eager to learn and to take her mind off the pain of loss.

Much like Eve, Jenny had grown up hearing spirits and didn't know any different. Antonia and Cora had both opened to the gifts at thirteen. Altogether, the quartet was equally haunted and equally understood. Jenny's face on this night, facing another loss as she strode in behind Antonia into the front foyer, was stoic.

"So our Maggie is mysteriously gone?" Antonia asked.

Eve nodded confirmation. "I don't even need to be upset, Zofia is beside herself enough for all of us," Eve said, trying to force a smile.

Jenny signed to Eve that she could hear Zofia's sob from what felt like a mile away. Eve nodded.

"Don't worry," Antonia said to Jenny. While Antonia hadn't fully learned Sign, she had taken to Jenny like an older sister and the two were intuitively connected. "I know you and Maggie are close." Antonia gestured towards the direction where Zofia had wafted. "I know she's like your sister too. We'll find her. She'd never go on to the undiscovered country without telling you. Without telling all of us."

Eve nodded. "She wouldn't go without warning. That's why we're all worried." Eve tried to hold back a torrent of emotion but she had no artifice around these women and she allowed a few tears to fall as she sat a moment with a cup of tea. Jenny slid next to Eve, her small body only taking up a part of the cushion next to her and grabbed her hand and held it as memories of Maggie overtook Eve.

Eve was young when the ghost of Margaret Hathorn had first come to say hello. The ice had been broken in the house about her seeing ghosts for three years by this point, her first interaction with the dead having

been her grandmother Helen, who'd died pushing Eve's mother Natalie out of the way of an oncoming carriage when Natalie was only a toddler. From the first black-eyed-Susan flower that her grandmother's ghost had mysteriously placed on the Whitby mantle, to Eve's present employment, Eve's gifts had been a source of tension with no resolution—only a battle-tested knowledge of what would and wouldn't upset her parents at the dinner table.

"Don't tell your mother that I've come to you," Maggie had said to Eve that first day. She had appeared in full greyscale, her image very potent, her hair up in a coiffure and dressed in a beautiful, trailing ball-gown of early eighties French style, with a prominent bustle and layers of frills everywhere.

"Oh, so you know she doesn't like my talking to ghosts?" Eve asked with a wary eye.

"I don't want to make it any harder for her. It was . . . hard for her when I died. She blames herself. Gran too." Maggie batted a hand and laughed. "They're so *stupid* about it."

There was a long pause. "Care to elaborate?" Eve pressed. This ghost clearly knew her family but she didn't know her.

"I was Evelyn's niece," the ghost explained, wafting over to hover at Eve's vanity, taking a look at herself in the tall oval mirror and frowning, reaching up a translucent hand to tuck a floating lock of hair back into her coiffure. "I wasn't very nice to Natalie in life. It was complicated and I was a complete *snot*, but remember the 'horror' that brought your parents together?"

"One of the many things they won't talk about?" Eve asked.

"Yes." The ghost swiveled around to face Eve, bobbing gently as she perched on the velvet vanity stool. "I got caught up in all that too. I made it worse for us all. It became the death of me."

"I'm sorry," Eve said. "So why haunt me? Is our family unfinished business?"

"I came to your mother after I died and we forgave each other. I thought I'd move on for good. But truth be told, I was drawn back to you. I had been in a pleasant 'between' for some time when I saw a light and I followed. Right before I stepped through, from the Corridors and into this world again, your grandmother Helen was there. She grabbed my hand, helped me step across and told me she was confident you'd welcome me."

Eve had done exactly so, just as she had with each medium and spirit who had been drawn to her. This magnitude of purpose had driven Eve right to a legislator to ask for that purpose to be given a job. The feeling of water on her hand, her own tear, roused Eve back to the moment.

"It's so odd . . ." Eve murmured. "You understand, friends, why this is so strange. When one works with the dead and becomes so very fond of them, as we all have of Maggie, there is a comfort in the idea that they would never be gone. Grief here is so changed, specific and hollow. I've never felt anything like it."

"What do we do, beyond the usual?" Cora asked.

Eve gestured for her fellows to follow her to the single round table perfect for a small séance.

"I don't know," Eve replied. "But we can begin with our usual rite whenever searching for information on a missing person. We treat Maggie just like we would any living soul gone without a trace."

Her mediums nodded, taking a seat and placing their palms flush upon the black tablecloth and allowing their gaze to move to a soft focus before them. At the center of the table sat a box of matches and a white taper on a silver candlestick, at the base of which sat a wreath of juniper berries. To the right of this was a small silver bell.

Eve took in a deep breath and released it slowly. As she did, she struck the match and lit the taper. "Heavens, grace us," she murmured.

In response, Antonia murmured something private, Jenny made the sign of the cross, and Cora bowed her head. Picking up the small bell, Eve rang it once, a glitteringly sharp, pure little sound that echoed around the room.

She sat, placing her hands flush upon the table too, taking another deep breath. Leaning into the table, she extended her hands, one to each of her compatriots, who did the same, creating a circle of held hands.

There were no other tricks of their trade, no other divinatory devices. Eve surmised that the more contraptions one relied on, the easier it was for a medium, whether legitimately gifted or toying with the craft, to begin relying on theatrical effects to make sure an audience received what they wanted. The spirit world was unpredictable. A career in divination either meant one weathered the fits and starts, or fashioned fail-safes for consistent results and became a fraud.

Eve knew she would never attain respect for her mission or her ghosts if their Precinct was revealed as leaning on trick tables, spirit cabinets or other easily manipulated objects. They relied only on a candle, a bell, a few symbols of respective faiths and of the natural world, and their own gifted souls. She hoped in time their simple truths would prove themselves and she'd write it all down to show to the world, when ready.

"Heavens, we ask that you grant us," Eve continued quietly, "by way of the spirits we have come to know and trust, information regarding the soul of Margaret Hathorn, our friend and colleague, absent from us this day. We wish to be connected with her or any spirit who knows something of her."

Eve watched the candle flicker a moment. She closed her eyes and spoke more directly. "Maggie, are you there?" Eve continued. "Why have you worried us so?"

The candle went out entirely in a burst of chill breeze and the room lit with the additional eerie light of a new attendant spirit, like the glow of a bright moon against Eve's closed eyelids.

"She's gone, Eve," came a worried, thickly accented voice, wafting into the room. Eve didn't open her eyes but knew it was Olga, a young Ukrainian woman who had died in the same industrial fire as Zofia. Their spirits had found one another in the corridor between life and death that the spirits so often talked about. They agreed to stay on and haunt the earth on behalf of those who died in industrial accidents and try whatever they could think of to prevent them. While Zofia wanted to stay on as a constant Precinct haunt, Olga only manifested during a séance.

"Maggie has never missed telling us goodnight unless she's told me and Zofia that she's gone on a case hunt," Olga insisted. "Something *must* be wrong."

"Any idea where she might have gone that might have caused trouble for her?" Eve asked calmly, even though her own nerves were fraying.

"Yesterday she said she wanted to see something mid-town, that something didn't feel right, and now she's gone," Olga exclaimed, her voice breaking.

The varied ghosts that agreed to work with the Precinct knew one another, were often called forth in a séance, and occasionally went off on their own adventures together.

Many of the Precinct spirits, whether they haunted Eve regularly or only came when called, had become close, filling in for family lost, drawn to their common causes and untimely ends. Any encounter with the spirit world offered a chance for family found and a bit of life restored.

"We'll find her," Eve promised, opening her eyes to comfort both Olga and Zofia as they floated before her in their plain, drab, greyscale dresses. Turning towards the small form of the eight-year-old floating at Eve's right, where the air was cooler, Eve placed her hand supportively at the side of the draft, where Zofia placed incorporeal hands atop her open palm. "She's the mascot and the heart of the whole Precinct. Something must be so important that it drew her away from us, but she'll tell us all about it as soon as we find her," Eve stated, wishing she felt as confident as she was trying to be for these young spirits who bravely went into fires and all manner of industrial accidents hoping they could do any small thing to save a life or alert help, even if every time it meant reliving the trauma of their own deaths. These spirits were so inspiring.

Cora Dupris spoke in French, reaching out to her closest and best haunt. Uncle Louis spent most of his time haunting New Orleans but was always ready to help his talented niece. After a benediction, he appeared before them, a handsome-featured man whose grey skin would once have been the same light brown as Cora's, with close-shorn black hair, expressive eyes, and a plain dark suit.

"*Bonne nuit, ma chérie,*" the spirit murmured. "*Ça va?*"

Cora shifted to English for the sake of her colleagues. "Uncle Louis, *mon cher*, have you seen Maggie? She's gone and hasn't shown up at any of her haunts. It's unlike her . . ."

Louis Dupris, the twin of Cora's father, had died in a mysterious research accident. He had a complicated past relationship with assisting Gran and other acquaintances of the family, and Eve had been instructed never to bring that up; his presence might cause pain if mentioned beyond their circle.

"I've no additional insights," Louis replied, "but I pledge to keep a spiritual ear tuned for her. I cannot claim closeness with Maggie, beyond awareness of her as a Precinct asset. Usually we try to allow the spirits to let go. This runs counterintuitive to the momentum that urges us onward."

"I know, Uncle," Cora replied gently. "But our Precinct has its own protocols. Maggie's disappearance is antithetical to her pledge to us."

"Anyone who is important to this divinely wrought group is important to me, tied together in soul bonds. I shall remain aware and come to you with any clues."

"Thank you, Mister Dupris," Eve murmured, "you are always so gracious and helpful."

"Anything for my family," he said, smiling at Cora. He wafted down to kiss the crown of her head with ghostly lips and vanished. Cora stared after him, turned towards the wake of his departing chill until the next ghost joined their ensemble.

Vera was the next to arrive, an old woman who had been brought to New York as a child from Mexico City. She'd found her passion and calling late in life studying at the Metropolitan Museum of Art, where many women found fulfilling instruction at an elite level in the school. She'd died at a ripe old age on the far Upper East Side and loved the raucous metropolis so much she simply didn't want to leave. Manifest in the room, white-haired and floating behind Antonia, her favorite of the Precinct mediums, she drew her large, greyscale, once-colorful floral shawl over her bony shoulders. Antonia didn't know Spanish, but she was fluent when Vera was around.

"*Amigas*," she began gently, speaking through Antonia, her youthful voice transformed to something gravelly, old, and warm. Vera had an accent but had learned English well during life and spoke it today for the benefit of the group. "You know the ways of the spirit world do not concur with the timelines of your own," she said. "A friend missing for only a day, and there's this much fuss?" She scoffed and laughed.

"It's her patterns being off that concern us, Vera dear," Eve replied. "I know ghosts to be creatures of habit."

"She never misses saying a goodnight," Zofia insisted, floating from her place beside Eve over towards Vera, tugging on the old woman's spectral shawl. "I can always *feel* her. Or I could. Until today. She's gone," the child murmured, trying not to burst into tears again.

"I'll walk the Corridors and look," Vera said.

"Thank you," Eve stated. "Be careful they don't draw you too close."

Vera laughed. "The Walks cannot have me. I am not done with New York yet and it is not done with me any more than it is with Maggie."

Gran had always called the space between life and death "the two walks", a corridor where souls came and went from between worlds, "for better or for worse." She had described seeing her life flash before her eyes in a near death experience as a sequence of still moments, like pictures at an exhibition, hanging on the walls of that corridor. In one brief moment of candor her mother expressed having seen the same thing.

This place had been further verified by the spirits that worked for her, something akin to a long hallway, although everyone's experience was slightly different. It was best not to spend too much time in the Corridors. Nightmares lurked there, forces and energies that the living and the dead could not quite explain. The darkest of negativities that had coalesced all the way into demonic form could come and go from them too . . .

"What else can we do?" Antonia asked the spirits.

"Hold on to her," Vera replied. "Find things of hers—relics, special places—think of her, and magnetize her to you."

"There's such a sadness," Zofia said. "Not just mine. It's . . . it's like I can't breathe . . ." Olga, who had been quiet so that other spirits could speak, wafted closer to the child.

The candle guttered and there was a sob from the spirit world, a soft, aching cry from many spirit voices, echoing in the room in an uncanny reverberation, and then silence. Silence in the dark. An otherworldly echo of a bell ringing meant the spirit world was closing its door, as if the ringing of the bell had a parentheses, a closure of thought.

"Goodnight, Eve," Zofia said, grabbing Olga's hand and fading. "See you tomorrow."

Vera waved to the group and faded. Antonia blew Vera a kiss.

That was the end of the session.

"Thank you, spirits, for your services," Eve murmured. "Good night."

Everyone was silent for a long time. The room warmed. Eve got up, moving slowly in the dim gaslight to the sconce where she turned the key and brightened the flames.

"Tomorrow we'll haunt her haunts," Eve instructed, trying to sound more hopeful than she felt. "For now, get some rest."

Her colleagues filed upstairs while Eve wandered to her library. There, she kept a small box of Maggie's things that had been given to her via Gran's intervention, things Maggie had wanted Eve to have of the few things left of her, before her family moved out of New York.

Sitting at her writing desk she pulled out an engraved fountain pen that had been, in life, Maggie's favorite writing instrument for letters, diary entries and the occasional ill-advised love note. Eve sat with it in her hand, weighing its heaviness, picturing Maggie writing with it, dreaming with it, exorcising her old demons with it.

Plucking a fresh sheet of paper, Eve closed her eyes and let the pen take her hand. Maggie had imbued part of herself into the implement. She called upon the echo of her friend that had conversed so much in paper and ink with this vital object.

True mediums might engage in any number of methods to transcribe messages from the spirit world. Eve employed any of them that struck her and in the moment, automatic writing seemed the only salve for the sharp, distinct pain that was growing just behind her forehead, as if her third eye were weeping and the tears were swelling up beneath her skin . . .

If a migraine resulted from overwork or undue pressure, so be it.

"Where are you, Margaret Hathorn?" Eve murmured to the air. "Give me a sign."

As Eve wrote the first phrase, her hand moving before she even had a grasp of the words, she heard a thousand murmurs echo a repetition of the earlier chilling warning that came softly from dead lips:

Don't let anything in . . .

Then there was no sensation at all.

Chapter Five

When Eve awoke, it was with a wave of pain that crashed over her body as she gained consciousness. She was no stranger to pain—it was a state she often found herself in, one way or another, to varying levels, depending on her circumstances. She avoided too-bright light, she tried not to be overtired, she made sure to drink water and always travel with aspirin. Her clairvoyance and clairaudience came with pressures and pain associated with her eyes and head, and the only thing that eased the feeling like the tightening of a vise grip around her skull was letting the spirit world in, letting it pass through her field of vision and murmur in her ear as it pleased, in and out like an exhaled breath.

Eve had long ago learned to live with the spirit world as a second luminous, transparent layer of movement and form as well as an additional murmuring layer of sound superimposed upon the living layer of reality. Having made a certain peace with aches and pains, today felt sharper than most.

There was a time, three years prior, when she had applied and was accepted to Barnard Women's college. Gran's idea of putting the ghosts to work in a department was all well and good, she'd thought, but she wanted to be a fully educated woman. She'd excitedly begun her first semester studying history, having taken up residence in a small, simple dormitory just off Broadway, where she could see the edges of the Columbia green, its grand new concourses taking over the Morningside area.

Of course, Eve saw and heard the spirits all through the halls and floating across the lawns, but she had assumed they'd leave her well enough alone to study. Instead, the migraines got worse. Ghosts who had ignored her before became insistent that she listen.

"*We* are your course of study," Vera had said, when Eve looked up from a book to find her dormitory room had become overrun with ghosts. She asked why they couldn't leave her be to study for a night, and they all told her that they were her sole discipline, her sole purpose.

In what became a workable truce, Eve left school and with the help of her mentors in the many months that followed, took steps to open the Ghost Precinct, provided the spirits let her alone enough to read books and study what interested her at her own pace. The migraines dimmed to the dullest of roars before fading entirely most days.

But after last night's session of automatic writing, she was sore in an entirely different way, as if she'd run miles and fallen on her face rather than just collapsing from strain on the writing desk. Her arm was numb and before her lay Maggie's fountain pen with a drop of ink splattered onto the paper below it as if it had been a thumb-prick of black blood. She almost didn't want to read what she had written.

Whispers and cold, whispers and cold.
All there is.
Drawn in, something was wrong, I was found, now am lost.
Am I between again?
Whispers and cold.
Don't let anything in. Don't open doors, I don't know what's around me.
If I go somewhere, will I ever return? Did I live or did I die? Again.
Did I die to live?
There are thoughts in the void.
Is everything overturned? Do I still exist?
Someone is very wrong. The children know. Inversed.
Don't let anything in, not the monstrous hum.

A phrase written there chilled Eve's blood in the instant. She remembered that recurring phrase about not letting anything in, but the rest was done in a subconscious state, where memory was far away. The last line struck her most.

Don't play God lest you play the Devil instead.

The automatic writing was personal, intimate. Was she actually able to access Maggie's state of mind in some strange, transient place? It was baffling, but it seemed like she had listened in on a frightened internal monologue.

From the earliest inclination of self, Eve wanted to help. She wanted to heal, soothe, and make things better for all around her. It was why the ghosts were so drawn to her. They wanted the same peace she wanted for them, and they came to her desperate, unwitting vampires draining her energy and life force. In order to survive, Eve had to toughen herself a bit, put up psychic shields, harden her heart and soul only so much as to not die of a broken heart like old romantic poets, exhausted and drained of all capability before she ever had the chance to fall in love herself. She couldn't care about every little thing; she had to constantly prioritize.

But Maggie. She cared about Maggie. Eve closed her eyes and pressed back tears of worry.

"Beloved friend," she murmured into the places of her mind and bidding the spirit that traveled back and forth across the veil with such impunity to hear her, "do not be afraid. You were the first of the spirits to ever bind your soul to mine, and I will never desert you even if you've lost your way in the labyrinth of eternity's corridors. I love you . . ."

She folded up the paper of this entranced writing session and carefully tucked the results into a small envelope. In a hissing gust and a suddenly plummeting temperature, the air around her taking on a preternatural glow, Eve turned to see that Vera had burst in on her and floated about two feet away, about a foot in the air, her arms folded in her floral shawl, glowering.

"There's something you're going to need to write up," the ghost said, agitated. "In Preventative Protocol."

"Well let's get going to the offices then, you can tell me when I'm at my typewriter," Eve said, stretching and sliding open the pocket doors. Vera nodded and vanished again as abruptly as she'd entered.

"I pray Antonia did us all the extreme favor of making coffee . . ." Eve said to herself as she stepped into the entrance hall.

Antonia, who was just tidying up, whirled to Eve, looking her up and down and pursing her lips in disapproval. "Why, of course I did, but *heavens*, did you not go to bed last night? Last I saw you, you went to the study. I didn't think to check on you."

Eve chuckled. "I fell asleep face down on the writing desk."

"I'm sorry, you poor dear! I should have come down to see how you were faring."

"I'm not your responsibility," Eve said, following her into the dining room where a warm carafe was still sitting on the hutch.

"Of course you are—we all are each other's beautiful burden," Antonia countered with a cluck of her tongue, pouring a cup and handing it to her. "If I'd known you were going to sleep in there I'd have at least moved you to the settee."

Eve took a sip of coffee and groaned in palpable relief. "Well, thank you for the sentiment," Eve conceded. "No irreparable physical harm done, but no answers gained either in the writing. But I must be off. Vera needs a report made up."

* * * *

Eve walked the several blocks east to her Precinct office on Mercer Street, north of the 15th Ward Station House. The Ghost Precinct had been shoe-horned into an unmarked Metropolitan Police records building whose second floor was all theirs to make reports, hold meetings and do the work of séances and divination. This plain red brick building was where hundreds of unsolved cases sat languishing in file cabinets, most of them dating from a time of unparalleled corruption before Theodore Roosevelt had overturned every rock and cleaned up the force. Paperwork and records were irregular and varied ward to ward, with many in the offices incomplete. The idea was that if Eve and her mediums were ever at a loss for something to do, any number of cases gone cold were readily available to their psychic meddling.

As exciting as their work might seem to anyone interested in spectral phenomena and the occult, there really was a great deal of mundane paperwork, resulting from an effort towards raising inter-departmental standards of procedure. But it was the paperwork that made any of it legitimate. Without thorough, documented process, so much would be left up to ghostly whispers and the vague pull of instinct, those first clues that, when finally leading to evidence, created a full picture. It was Eve's plan that after several years at the Precinct, she'd collect her findings and publish a book about all of it.

It was Preventative Protocol that required the most care—a slippery moral slope that would prove the most dangerous and questionable aspect of the group's aims. There were two reports from last week Eve hadn't written up yet. They were seen by one of Roosevelt's most trusted lieutenants, Mr. Bonhoff, and Roosevelt himself.

When Eve's offerings to a now retired sergeant got her noticed by Mr. Bonhoff in the first place, he had engaged Roosevelt directly. It was a discussion the three of them, under Gran's supervision, had from the start.

"The rights of our citizens are sacred," Roosevelt had explained. "In the cases you worked, where you couldn't have known the circumstances, where you brought clues right to the department's door, those were at a stage where a murder would have gone unsolved. One already committed and where we were entirely at a loss."

"*Preventative* crime is a trickier wicket," Roosevelt had continued. "Innocent until *proven* guilty."

"I've given this a great deal of thought, sir," Eve replied. "I agree with you entirely. I would never want a clairvoyant, a ghost, or any activity in the spectral realm, to supersede human free will and independence. Where I believe the ghosts loyal to me can be of most direct use is to perhaps expose the elements of a possible crime and leave it to the living to sort it out amongst themselves. With the dynamics of power in consideration."

Roosevelt raised a bushy brow. "In some cases, the helpless just need help," Eve explained. "I can't police what ghosts try to affect; they have minds—and missions—of their own. What they will ask me to help with are things they cannot influence all on their own. Sometimes we may need to give things a little push."

"Can you give us an example?" Mr. Bonhoff said. He was a quiet, level-headed, steady-handed man interested only in the city's greater good.

"I have often held a séance not to draw out information from the dead but to magnify their abilities. Many of them aren't just here on earth for their own unfinished business, but that of our own mortal failures."

"Go on . . ." Bonhoff urged.

"Why, just last week I was contacted by a ghost begging for intervention on behalf of a child apprenticed to a brute, a child who would not survive another beating. Henry Bergh's creation of the ASPCA passed animal cruelty laws decades prior. This is, of course, a huge boon, where cases of animal cruelty and domestic abuse can be linked and animals and children might be removed from deadly situations if their plight is *known*.

"As my Gran and her circle of philanthropists and clergy have many associates, a contact from the ASPCA was able to go see for himself, and they found both horse and child with open, bleeding sores. The horse was collected and turned over to care, and thanks to an Episcopalian organization the child was able to choose a different apprenticeship. The child chose to work with the church itself, saying that God had saved him so he wished to work to help others in turn. But it was the ghosts that saved him. God didn't swoop down, the ghosts did, reaching out for a listening ear. I was glad I was there to hear the spirit of the boy's elder sibling, who came asking if someone could look in on his battered brother. Whatever entity serves as God, I can't be sure of, but I believe the dead are used to great purpose. Angels among us, even. It would only be fair to stop fearing ghosts and start appreciating what they can do if we but only listen, and act before it's too late."

The gentlemen were very moved by this account, and thusly the protocols for preventative services were quietly instated.

If an alarm was sounded, a network of various charitable contacts curated by Gran and her dear friend Reverend Blessing, a dynamic man and sometimes exorcist, might be deployed in an instant to check in on a precarious situation where an innocent creature might be in danger.

The origin of this protocol was particularly on Eve's mind today as just a few days before Maggie disappeared nearly an identical case to the one she'd used as an example crossed Cora's spiritual threshold. The same strategy had been deployed to resituate the powerless into a safer environment of their own choosing, rather than merely being a victim of fate.

The Preventative Protocol was new and the cases thus far were few, as the grounds for stepping in had to be an iron-clad case. Eve required more than one spirit to relate their insights on the person and place. She'd had no second thoughts about what had been done so far, but she wanted to be sure there was continued oversight.

The latest issue with a farrier and his hired hand needed to be written up, and it had to be documented which ghosts would be checking in on the subject after his transfer to a better condition. Zofia had volunteered, saying that if she could never grow up to have a life of her own, at least she could watch over these young squires mired in pain and try to bring them a life of hope instead.

Eve wanted to capture the most human and moving details her department oversaw. This was what she wanted the world to know about the dead; just how beautiful they were. She'd convince the world, report by report.

* * * *

Only Jenny was in ahead of Eve, paid an hour extra per day to tidy the place up and prepare coffee and tea. It was something Jenny had asked to do, indicating that her parents never wanted their daughter to go without, encouraging her to take as much as she could from a job willing to pay her well.

The matron who had been assigned to sit watch by the exterior door, Mrs. McDonnell, wasn't due in for another fifteen minutes or so. She was generally unpleasant to the girls, so Eve liked to avoid her.

Whenever Jenny was in the office alone, the spirits of her parents often joined her, singing Irish ballads of a faraway home. Mary and Connor Friel's spirits looked after orphans as an ongoing mission, and Jenny willingly shared them, provided they returned to her when they could. Eve paused outside the door for a long while. The Friels' ethereal voices hit a keening note and rendered Eve breathless. The music of spirits could stop time. It was perhaps the most civilizing thing, music, the way to bring the whole world together, living and dead, offering some comfort and peace, no matter where or when.

Eve didn't want to interrupt—she knew that these moments of privacy were very important for Jenny, the only way she could still feel like she had her own family. Living communally with co-workers, time alone was vital and she tried to be a respectful manager in that regard.

But the telephone rang from within and that forced Eve into entering, placing her warm hand on the cool glass doorknob, the frosted glass panel of the wooden door reading "Ghost Precinct: E. Whitby, managing official" in gilt letters. Every time Eve looked at her name on that door, her heart raced, daunted and thrilled in equal measure by the weight of responsibility.

What a jarring, unnatural sound the telephone was, a vibrating, clattering noise that was far louder than the size of its two small brass bells would have indicated. Eve wondered if she was already becoming her Grandmother, hating modern, clanging sounds that jarred a contemplative mind. The alarming notification had shattered the timeless spell of the Friel family song.

The first NYPD telephone had gone into the Center Street station in 1880. Nineteen years later stations often communicated by wire or courier instead. The force hadn't wanted to pay for what was still a relative luxury when the women working there weren't switchboard operators or secretaries, so Gran paid for the installation on the wall as a matter of convenience, expediency and safety for Eve's precinct, even though she herself hated using one.

Eve was designated as the Precinct contact, so it had to be her that answered the phone. This also made sure that if there was a problem or a disciplinary action it would fall on Eve and not her colleagues. When she created the Precinct, she insisted this be so. She wouldn't subject a fellow Sensitive to reprimand or censure, if she could help it.

As Eve entered, the startled sadness on Jenny's face had Eve blushing with an apology, knowing she was interrupting something beyond precious. The Friels wafted to the back of the room as if concerned they might be too intrusive otherwise. Eve gestured to the ghosts that they were welcome to stay, and then gestured at the phone that she'd have to answer, bowing her head in respect and care before changing her focus.

Their office was dim. Jenny hadn't turned on the one large electric lamp that hung too low and buzzed too loud. Their group often relied on what meager sunlight came through the thin, tall lancet windows that peppered the back of the records building.

Eve went to the wall where the telephone box was mounted, picked up the handle of the receiver and leaned in, speaking close and loud into the voice box. "Whitby here. How can I help you?" she said, in a loud, strong tone. She didn't announce herself as a woman, even if her voice might belie it, as she wanted to be spoken to on merit, not on impressions of her sex and their aptitude in such a work environment as this.

There was only a hiss on the other line.

Breathing—shallow, soft, and far away.

"Hello?" Eve repeated. There was an intake of breath, as if whoever was on the other side of the line wanted very much to say something but couldn't.

The hissing of the line continued for a moment, a static buzzing overtaking any sound of breathing. As if it were coming out from the telephone itself, a chill emanated, and the tiny hairs across Eve's face froze. She shuddered. The static hiss grew loud, unbearable.

But no one was on the line.

Eve shook herself free from the chill and hung up, placing the black cylinder with a fluted end on its designated hook.

Turning around, she noticed Jenny was gesturing to her parents, who were reaching out to her, placing incorporeal hands upon her small shoulders. Eve turned back away, not wanting to interrupt the family.

The most interesting feature of the room was its narrow, glowing windows; it sported nothing but file cabinets, a rickety shelf, and a few small tables with drawers that were more suited for school children's desks than for professionals facing the wall, each set with a wooden sorting tray full of various papers and guides. At the back of the room, dressed with a black tablecloth and set with notebooks, a small bell and a candle, was a small circular séance table with five seats, one for each medium and one for Gran whenever she felt like joining them, their mascot and patron saint.

"Where is my coffee?" Eve muttered to herself.

Vera lifted her transparent hands in the air. "Incorporeal. Don't look to me."

At her elbow, Eve's favorite cup appeared, presented by Jenny, who looked up at her with narrow, angry eyes. Eve took a step back at the small and inexplicably furious girl. Jenny gestured between the cup and a spirit board planchette, signing that setting the cup down upon it was quite disrespectful. She folded her arms, fuming.

Eve frowned a moment before offering a counter argument.

"But you don't *use* a spirit board or a planchette, Jenny."

The girl turned away, her thin braid swinging out from her small head. In the next moment she whirled back, the braid again airborne before it thumped down on her shoulder as she emphatically began signing that even if Eve didn't use a board with letters and numbers and a small disc spirits guided to point to them, perhaps some of their company might want to use one.

"If you'd like to use a board, Jenny, then say so. And then I won't think of it as décor."

Jenny slammed a drawer closed on her desk that had been open. She looked into the air and shook her fist at Vera, gesturing between her desk and the ghost that things had been moved. She signed, emphatically, not to move her things.

Eve came close and put both hands on the girl's shaking shoulders. "What's really going on, my dear?"

The girl burst into tears.

Mrs. Friel wafted over to Eve. A ghost's voice came as a distant but clear whisper, carrying with it an intense atmospheric quality as well as words, almost as if a spirit's words were underscored with a sorrowful note of music, evoking a Sensitive's empathy. "I'm sorry, Miss Whitby. It is the anniversary of my death in the waters of the East River. It has only been a year."

"Oh, my goodness!" Eve exclaimed, putting a hand to her mouth. "I had no idea!"

The ghost continued. "She lost everyone that day. Nearly our whole parish, the last of any family. She's been overwhelmed with emotion of late."

"Of course," Eve murmured. Mr. Friel just stared at his daughter, having hardly gotten to know her in life, illness striking him down back in Dublin when she'd been a baby. Eve caught the glimmer of tears in his vaguely transparent form, sparkling in small luminous silvery stars, there in his welling eyes.

Eve knelt, holding her arms out for Jenny. The girl didn't wish to be held; she shook her head.

"I'm here for you as you need," Eve murmured. "Please let me know."

Jenny nodded, wiped her eyes and went to one set of the lancet windows at the back of the room that let in light in distinct shafts at this hour of the day, if the sun was bright. She climbed a step-stool and began cleaning the thick panes studiously, a creature of constant movement.

Much like the house chores, Eve wanted everything to be fair, but Jenny had asked for extra hours. It seemed like working was a drive, a constant urge for Jenny, a way to stay afloat from her grief. She was such a restless spirit and Eve, wishing she could take the girl's grief away, empathized with the complications of missing a body when there still was a spirit there to see. Her parents weren't gone. They just couldn't hold her anymore. The loss of touch was the most unbearable of all changes between the parallel worlds of life and death.

Eve took to her desk and examined what had been left upon it. There was an envelope that read *Miss W* in small script.

That was slid under the door, Jenny signed to Eve after she'd placed her washcloth in a tin bucket, strode over, and stopped across Eve's supervisor desk. The young girl's expression indicated the missive was both important and likely unwelcome. Eve shared a worried look with her colleague and opened the envelope. Her heart immediately sank.

The memorandum was on a slip of paper with red ink.

Complaint, 11am.

She glanced at Jenny who pursed her lips and rolled her eyes, signing somewhat of a rhetorical question, wondering if anyone would ever be satisfied by what they do.

"Satisfaction doesn't seem to be in human nature, but still, we strive," Eve replied with a sigh.

The rallying sentiment of striving seemed to brighten Jenny's sadness and she nodded, squaring her shoulders, moving to her own desk: a small, simple surface with one drawer like one might have had in a one room school-house. What 'budget' they had went to giving them a salary; the furnishings had been done thanks to Evelyn and her friends cleaning out closets and storage spaces. Jenny didn't mind her small corner of the world. She sat there and closed her eyes, perhaps in listening to what the spirits had to say to her today, perhaps in prayer—Eve didn't know. She didn't dare presume to understand the vast internal mysteries of another psychic. It was very important they each respect separate processes and moments of quietude.

It wasn't long before a tall grandfather clock in the corner of the room—a gift from the Bishops—began to chime a morning sequence in deep tones. The last reverberating bell faded into silence just as Cora and Antonia walked in, bobbing their heads to Eve and Jenny and the spirits that wafted in from the walls, all keeping their appointed hour.

When her team was assembled, they turned to Eve expectantly for the day's orders. Before offering any instruction or command, she took in their faces. Everyone was tired from the séance, but more than that, worried.

"There has been a departmental complaint, my dears," Eve declared, setting her jaw, allowing for the group to groan in response. "We'll be getting a visit."

"What kind of complaint?" Cora asked.

"A complaint of *meddling*."

Antonia sighed irritably. "What are we to do if we can't be left to do what we're meant to do?"

Eve didn't even look at Vera but the spirit was immediately forthcoming with her own indictment, splaying incorporeal hands.

"A man in a townhouse had a photograph," Vera began, wafting to and fro in the ghostly version of pacing. "A single, post mortem photograph of a child. There was something very wrong about it. A mistress's child. I wouldn't stand for it and I was sure neither would his wife. So I winged the photograph out into the hallway for her to find. Managed a good shove from his study."

"Is this what you were trying to tell me would need written up?"

Vera nodded.

"And how were you drawn to the house?" Eve said, picking up a notebook and writing down particulars. "You know we can't mess in the living's dirty business, affairs or no, only abuse and crime, so I hope you've got something better than that or we *are* guilty of meddling."

"A crying child in a rumpled frock who looked very much alive to me when the poor creature approached me on the street pointed inside a house, saying "I'm lost . . . And there are more . . . Please help . . ." When I turned to look at the house, then back at the child, there was no one; a ghost after all. You know it's hard for us to tell. We don't always appear between ourselves as transparent phantasms. We even forget we are incorporeal. I look down and see myself as I always was, find myself reaching for things my hand passes through."

"That's because you're indomitable and this city can't bear to let go of you," Eve said fondly, thinking of Vera's painting from a year before she died that Eve had seen in the Metropolitan Museum of Art's schoolrooms, where she had continued her lifelong studies. The painting had been so pulsing with life, it was no wonder she was so often more solid than most spirits Eve had met, and didn't need the power of a séance to manifest her.

"So I went into the house," Vera continued, "to have a look around. Instinct said go to the study. I did. Something—a spirit I couldn't even see—winged the image out at me from I don't know even where, in a leather Memento Mori frame, a lock of hair affixed and all. I looked around for the child that had vanished, but I saw the same plaintive face there on that photo, uncomfortable even in death . . ."

"What did you do next?" Antonia asked.

"Once I managed to fling the image into the hall, the lady of the house stepped on it before exclaiming. It was not well met. Evidently that child was not hers, nor any relation, and what the photo was doing there was a mystery, but must have aroused or confirmed the wife's suspicion. I hung back and listened to the excuse of a mousy, evasive man saying he had no idea where it came from. Didn't believe a word. Felt my essence had been drained in the force of throwing the image so I faded out from the house, finding myself again near my old apartment."

"And you're sure *this* is the complaint we've gotten?" Eve asked. Vera thought a moment.

"Oh." She wafted back on spirit heels. "Well, I suppose it could be something else. I just . . . I felt very strongly so I volunteered the information as pre-emptive, in case the man takes any action against the wife or the mistress if that was his child. Since Maggie's disappearance, I'm just a bit off . . . I feel like she'd have done the same thing I did, would have responded to the same sort of call; it would have been like us, to attend to this matter ourselves. She'd have wanted me to . . ." The spirit's voice broke.

"Yes, this does sound like your mission," Eve agreed, "exposing truths to women to help them look out for themselves. But this young ghost was . . . lost? Not concerned for that lady of the house, it would seem?"

"Yes," Vera replied. "In this, I'm not sure if I did more harm than good by exposing the fact. I'm sorry. I should have tried to gather more context before acting. It was unwise, I see now."

"It is always so hard to know," Eve said, her empathy clear. "That's why we have to take these kinds of acts and cases with such care. The child wants to be acknowledged, that is often the case. What about the child saying there were more?"

"Oh, yes—that, I've no idea," Vera scratched her head, thinking, bobbing a bit in the air as she did. "More children? That he fathered? More pictures? I don't know. I'm sorry. I'll try to find my way back . . ." Vera trailed off, her charcoal eyes staring at her blankly. Eve sighed.

"How many detectives even *know* about us to be able to lodge such a complaint?" Cora asked.

"That's a fair question . . ." Eve murmured, and thought about the gala, the attendees. There were maybe ten people from the department total that were there. Despite the initial call for discretion, perhaps Mr. Roosevelt had boasted of the department beyond the usual channels.

"I can't be sure," Eve replied finally. "Not many, but enough to make any friend to the lieutenant a possible snitch. What they don't necessarily know about, and shouldn't, is about our Preventative Protocol measures. I'll not have our every move subjected to an ethics board."

"We have complete, plausible deniability and a solid alibi," Antonia said. "Cora, Jenny and I were at the theatre while you were at the gala—"

"Antonia, just let me do the talking," Eve explained. "Let me be the front of this."

Her dark eyes flashed defensively and she opened her mouth as if to retort but closed it again, a pain crossing over her olive complexion. Eve, trying not to tread upon anxiety regarding presentation, clarified gently. "Please don't misunderstand me. I want no one to feel hidden behind me for any reason. But *I* must bear the brunt of scrutiny—that's what being the director means."

Antonia's brow remained furrowed. "You are all my charges and my responsibility," she added. "I *asked* for this; to make sense of my life and to retain my sanity. Let me be what I am made for and support me as is needed. I have armor that won't be pierced; it was forged in childhood when I had to decide if the gifts would kill me or make me their soldier. Let me fight for all of us."

Her colleagues each nodded.

A rough knock on the door. Eve answered it and a barrel-chested man in uniform entered, his actions suiting his frame as he strode into the room. Vera wafted towards the wall, hovering in the same dimensions as a file cabinet and watched.

"I don't give any part of a rat's anatomy what you ladies think you're doing in this fanciful department," the short-haired, burly man stated, "but if you send your spooky minions into good people's fine homes, you're going to find the full weight of the NYPD against you—certainly not behind you as our former chief would like to have you believe."

"And you are?" Eve prompted.

The man pointed to his badge.

"Sergeant Mahoney. Yes, I can read," Eve replied. "I just assumed you'd do us the courtesy, as your colleagues, of introducing yourself like a gentleman."

"You want manners?" the gruff man frowned. "Why'd you join a bunch of officers? Go have a séance in a lady's parlor and be done with wasting our time."

"Who complained to you to warrant this?" Cora asked, her nostrils flaring. Her light brown face was flushed with frustration. Eve held out a hand.

"We don't know anything about the *nature* of your complaint," Eve clarified, trying to keep an edge from her tone.

"That's not germane to the discussion."

"Of course it is," Eve countered, stepping forward. "How can we avoid something if we know nothing about it?"

"Of course you know about it, you sent a ghost in to go snooping."

Eve cocked her head to the side. "To be fair, Sergeant, only a fraction of the city's ghostly goings on have anything to do with us. It is a very big city. A very *haunted* big city. We work with some seven to at most ten of the thousands that float about the boroughs."

"The Prenze family is off-limits," Mahoney declared. "They are boons to the Police and we owe them our thanks. Consider this a warning with no second chances."

"Barging in, demanding, accusing and threatening, all with no proof nor details, and all in one breath," Eve said, in awe of the confidence it took to be so rude.

"Like I said, you don't like it—"

"Leave the force, yes, I heard you the first time. I'll have you know I've not authorized anything related to the name Prenze. We'll be sure not to trouble such a *helpful* family with any of our direct actions should they come to our attention. However, if their house is just simply haunted, don't rush to accuse us. Take that up with an Exorcist. I know two, I can make a referral if you like—"

He harrumphed and exited.

"Good day, Mister Mahoney," she called after him.

All the girls' fists were clenched. Vera cursed after him in Spanish with a wide, emphatic gesture, wafting forward to Eve's side and making the papers on her desk float away with the breeze of her gesticulation. It was clear Vera hadn't been noticed by Mahoney, but per Eve's orders, as none of them knew how much the spirit world affected everyday folk, when their office had company the ghosts were to keep their profiles low.

"So how do we surreptitiously spy on this Prenze family? No one is that threatening who's doing the right thing," Antonia stated.

Eve held up her hands. "I agree, such an unwarranted attack dog is suspicious in and of itself, but we must proceed carefully, if at all. We've hardly any friends; we can't afford enemies and I'm sure Mahoney's banking on it. Vera, was this the family in question? Were you in the Prenze mansion regarding that post mortem photograph?"

The ghost, still fuming over the man, whirled towards Eve, sending a chill on the air as she moved and Eve saw her own breath come out in a cloud. "Oh, I've no idea," the ghost responded. "I'm sorry, I was so caught up, I didn't look at any of the papers. It was a townhouse, no mansion, but I didn't get names . . ."

The girls groaned. "You *know* protocol, Vera," Eve muttered. "How else can we follow up without a name or address? And how else can we be careful after this complaint?"

"I got carried away . . ." the ghost said, wafting to and fro in a nervous, spectral pace.

There was another knock, more timid. Eve went to the door and opened it just a crack. Detective Horowitz was outside, standing with his arms behind his back and a pleasant, hopeful not to be troublesome look on his sharp-featured face. Seeing Eve, he bobbed his head but kept her gaze, and the bright light of the day streaming in from outside the windows highlighted the flecks of blue in his light chestnut eyes, a dynamic touch to his visage.

"Hello, Detective, do come in," Eve stated. His manner was the opposite of the man before him and Eve found herself relieved at the contrast, though surprised he'd sought her out.

"How can we help you?" she asked. She thought to offer him tea or coffee, but she didn't want to give anyone the impression her department were glorified maids or secretaries. "Do you know the rest of my associates?" He shook his head and Eve introduced her colleagues, who all turned back to their desks after bobbing their heads, a subtle reminder that they were all professionals at work.

Eve gestured Horowitz towards her desk where a plain wooden chair sat opposite.

"Mr. Bonhoff is leaving New York," the detective said, taking his seat and surveying her desk carefully.

Eve, thunderstruck by this news, sunk into her chair across the desk. Out of the corner of her eye, Eve noticed that little Zofia had wafted in and come to float by Jenny, her usual haunt, who ignored her at her small desk, both ghost and living child keeping their eyes focused on the detective. Vera frowned, folding herself back to the file cabinets again.

Eve tried to keep her face neutral. Her dearest champion, Bonhoff, was liaison to Roosevelt and to the chief of police, and he knew every step of the delicate dance of advocating for working women in men's fields. Perhaps that's why the 'complaint'—more like the threat—had been so easily and flippantly leveled the moment he was gone, whether there were grounds on the family's behalf or not.

"Roosevelt spoke to those of us detectives and officers who know about you, that ten or twelve or so at your reception, to choose a liaison to replace him. I volunteered immediately."

"Ah." Eve tried to keep her face expressionless. Needing something with which to busy herself, she moved to a tea tray and poured herself some, gesturing to a row of cups hanging from hooks upon a wall. The detective shook his head.

"I anticipated your disappointment," he stated after a moment.

Eve forced a small, conciliatory smile as she returned to her chair with tea. "No, it isn't that . . . I am, well, fond of Mr. Bonhoff, you see."

"I am aware Mr. Bonhoff was a great advocate for you and I have no intention of proving otherwise. But I will say that I'm not as enamored of the secrecy in which you work as you are. I believe a liaison should be more involved."

Eve bristled, sitting up straight, practically floating at the edge of her chair, trying not to notice the whispers of disapproval from the present ghosts whom Horowitz appeared oblivious to. "Secrecy is for everyone's safety," Eve replied. "For *myriad* reasons."

"Reasons I'm sure I'll appreciate, but I would like initial transparency, here."

"We're entirely transparent, detective," Vera stated, wafting a bit closer, unable to help herself.

The detective cocked his head. "What's that?"

Eve flashed a look at Vera and bit back a chuckle. "Vera here, one of our ghostly operatives, made a joke about transparency." Eve waited a moment for the detective to laugh. He did not.

"You mean . . . one is present right now?" He asked, his bright eyes widening. He raked a hand through warm brown curls.

"Oh, yes. She's right behind you," Eve replied. "For a moment, it seemed as though you heard her speak. It's best if you don't second guess it." The detective whipped his head behind him, frowned, then turned around and shuddered.

"I feel something, a chill, but it's likely just a breeze," he declared. He crossed his arms, as if punctuating his denial.

"No, that's Vera. Ghosts bring a delicate frost with them wherever they go. I maintain that everyone has the capability to hear and see spirits," Eve countered, "and most certainly to feel them, it's just trained out of most people. Like any sense," she gestured to her colleagues, "ours is more highly calibrated. So you'll have to remind me what you can and can't ascertain, detective, as I take for granted that my department is all of the same skill set." She looked at him pointedly, the intruder. He just nodded, taking no offense. "Can you see them in any way?"

He looked behind him tentatively again. Vera waved. A more unruly curl on the top of his head bounced. "If I were to presume I saw a spectral entity or movement, it would likely be the extremely potent power of suggestion at work. We must be careful not to let fanciful notions run away with themselves," he replied carefully.

"Is that what you think of this department?" Eve said with an arch of her brow and a squaring of her shoulders. "Fanciful notions?"

"No," Horowitz replied honestly. Eve set her jaw. "Is something wrong?" Horowitz asked, looking at the women. "You all seem to be out of sorts and I don't think it's just me who has ruffled communal feathers."

Eve sighed. "Among several concerns, we dealt with a complaint this morning, and a positive boor of a sergeant yelled at us for something we know nothing about, blaming us for some sort of spectral meddling we didn't order."

"I'm sorry," Horowitz said earnestly. "I dealt with a complaint from the same boor just yesterday myself. I'd bet money it was Mahoney, wasn't it? He's on a rampage trying to get promoted."

"What was he on about? Maybe I won't feel so targeted if you commiserate with me."

"I was pointedly told by a family member of a deceased victim that they 'did not want a . . .'" Horowitz's mouth thinned as he took a moment to deliberately choose more delicate words, the truth biting behind the flash of his eyes. He gestured. "Let's just say they proceeded to hurl every Jewish slur and absurd misapprehension they could think of, horns and all, '—in their house, let alone working the case of their dearly departed."

Eve's hand went to her sternum. "That's horrific."

All Eve's precinct nodded and offered empathetic noises. As Horowitz had spoken, they had all stood, almost as if ready to fight for this man's dignity. Vera muttered in Spanish. Eve didn't know the language but she didn't have to, the spirit regularly cursed cruelty and intolerance. It took a lot to raise Vera's hackles; that was the second time today, and it wasn't even noon.

"Let me be honest with you all," Horowitz stated. "I volunteered to be the liaison because I heard an epithet being used towards you, collectively, yesterday, likely from the same part of the department that lodged your complaint. I promise I will stand in the way of such hateful ignorance if it's the last thing I do. For your sake, for my own, for all of us working in this city made from a thousand cities. I may be skeptical of your methods and practices, but not of your right to respect."

"Thank you," Eve stated. "We need to stand together, not divided."

"Agreed . . ." Horowitz said, rising. "And now, I'm sure we've all work to do."

"I'll respond that we have registered the complaint and will take steps to avoid a recurrence in yet another report," Eve said, rolling her eyes. "Did you think that working for a department such as the police that your life would be filled up with just so much paperwork?"

"No." He leaned forward with a half-smile. "My father wanted me to be an academic but I said I didn't want all the paperwork. How naïve of me. I'll leave you to it. Good luck and don't be strangers. Give me concrete things that can continue to cast you in a positive light. I don't want to be anyone's enemy save the criminal mind."

"Noted."

Horowitz bowed his head and went for the door.

"Thank you again, Detective," Eve said. "Any disappointment at losing Mr. Bonhoff has been alleviated by your promise to champion us."

"I'm not sure about champion, just standing against hateful rhetoric. I still expect results, I just won't undermine you or expect less of you because you're women."

"Noted," Eve said again, pursing her lips in a prim smile that generally meant *touché*.

The detective left and Eve took charge of the room immediately.

"No gossip about the man, not one word," Eve barked and went to her desk. "Paperwork, all of you, note anything at any stage of a case. The spirit world seems unsettled and we need to know why, talk to your contacts, I'll handle the complaint report and then we're off to search for Maggie."

Everyone eyed her a moment but said nothing and went to their respective desks.

She didn't want to hear any of her colleagues comment on the dark-haired detective being uniquely handsome or compelling, not to mention noting any kind of spark between the two, because she thought all of those things and was not going to entertain a single one of the notions.

Once paperwork carefully, courteously, but thoroughly countering the complaint was all in envelopes to be sent to the right higher-ups, and when the nearby church chimed the hour of five, Eve glanced up to find her colleagues looking at her diligently. Sometimes they stayed after hours, for no extra pay. Their department was not afforded any extra wages past their time, and while labor unions were fighting for over-time payments in other industries, she doubted that progress would flow their direction. Regardless, none of her staff, there because of passion and mission, were the sort to abandon any work left at a precarious stage. Today, as Eve clapped her hands she didn't even need to say the words to follow; they all simply did, rising and going to the door in unison. Half the time Eve didn't have to give orders, her staff intuited them. The benefits of working with Sensitives.

"Let us waft Maggie's wafts," Vera stated, wafting to and fro as if setting an example of a pattern.

Just then, the phone rang. The clanging trill that made everyone jump. They hadn't received many calls in the months that they'd been official, but this was the second today.

It took a second clattering sound for Eve to pick up the receiver from the wall. Did anyone other than her family even know the number? Would someone speak this time or just hiss on the line like the last call?

"Hello?" Eve said. After a moment, straining to listen for a voice, she thought to sound professional and announce herself. Theirs wasn't a public number, it was only for inter-departmental use and the occasional coordination with Gran. "Whitby here."

"I have a message for you, Eve," said a faraway, soft alto voice.

"Yes? Who am I speaking to?"

"Lily. I am calling in regards to a missing girl. Her name is Ingrid. Ingrid Schwerin."

"Yes?" Eve gestured for someone to bring her a piece of paper to take notes. Vera was closest so the ghost gestured on the air and wafted a piece from her desk that floated to her feet. She bent and picked it up, using the pen that had been attached to the original wall fixture.

"There is something wrong," Lily said worriedly, her faint voice catching. There was a sequence of ragged breaths as if the woman had been running. Eve felt sure this was who had called earlier, only now having screwed up the courage to complete the warning.

"How do you mean?" Eve asked calmly.

"Go to Grace. My poor children, and the poor girls who had them. Protect them all, I beg you. Poor Ingrid is gone and unwell. Look after her."

Eve was trying to take dictation, capture her every word. "Grace who?"

A shaking breath on the line. A whisper. "Grace."

"Do you mean Grace Church? The Memorial House?" She pressed. "What is your full name?"

"I'm Lily Strand and I've got to go now."

There was a hiss on the line. "Hello? Miss Strand?" Nothing. Eve hung up the black cone of a receiver.

"It sounds like *you* have a clue to track down," Cora said, moving towards the door, gesturing to her colleagues. "Let us look for Maggie." Cora pointed to the telephone box. "You go and find out whatever that was all about."

Eve stared at the phone, puzzled. So much for being thankful they had a clean slate of cases. "Thank you, that's probably best. I think we just received a new case."

"I know," Cora replied with a smile and Eve reached out to squeeze her hand. Cora always knew, due to an innate read on Eve and the situation, when it was her turn to take charge, and she did so seamlessly.

They all exited, their stern matron eyeing them as they left. Eve thought to tell Mrs. McDonnell where they were going but she stopped herself, as it wasn't any of the matron's business and she needn't continue trying to justify their existence and every move. Really, when even the police matrons found them suspect, how could they ever gain respect amongst male colleagues? At least the detective's support was heartening, and Eve was determined to approach this new clue with hope, zeal, and immediate, discernible progress.

Chapter Six

Eve couldn't be sure it was Grace Memorial House that the woman meant. The Grace parish was a font of resources for struggling mothers and children and there weren't many other buildings in the city with the name, so she had to start with the most likely. Missing person cases were mostly either solved or not in the first few days—according to long-time officers that Eve listened to whenever she could, looking to soak up any advice from any reputable service members who would talk to her.

The building was a gothic edifice just south of Union Square. Larger and bulkier than the small, elegant, beautiful chapel that lent its name to the parish, the Memorial House interior was as sober and straightforward as its mission.

Eve knocked and was granted admittance by a young woman in what may have been a novice's garb, a simple white dress and white scarf over her head. She showed the superior on duty the small card signed by Roosevelt that noted Eve was a part of a special city police task force. Eve had never been given an actual badge and doubted she ever would. The novice introduced Deaconess Brower, bowed her head and exited.

The deaconess was a tall, willowy woman in a blue habit. It was a simple clerical uniform that often got mistaken for that of a nun, but considering Gran's involvement in the Episcopal Church, Eve knew better. Deaconesses were given special offices by the church to care for the sick, afflicted, and poor, and there was a conclave of them in New York. Perhaps in her thirties, the deaconess was thin as a rail but carried great gravitas.

"I'm here because I have been told that a girl has gone missing," Eve explained. "Ingrid Schwerin. Was she one of your charges?"

The Deaconess looked aggrieved.

"She was. And I thought we could do her some good here. But her mother . . ." The woman looked away.

Eve pressed further. "Lily Strand called my office and told me to come to Grace."

At this name the woman was even further affected and she bowed her head, her hand fluttering in front of her for a moment. "Oh, our poor Sister. She was just about to become a deaconess herself. You must have spoken with her some time ago."

"No, she called my Precinct office today."

The woman looked at her blankly. "Today. No. Why . . . she *couldn't* have. Lily Strand has been dead over a month."

"Oh." Eve tried to appear as suitably reactive as propriety would dictate. Her being unsurprised wouldn't play well. "I'm so sorry to hear that. Perhaps I misheard." She knew she didn't mishear.

Why had the late Lily Strand gone to the spectral trouble of calling when she could have just floated into the office herself to offer a message and clue? The ways of communication across the veil were varied and new technologies certainly expanded the possibilities. Perhaps, much like specters liked to disrupt electrical currents, some discovered they could more easily access telephone wires, using their flickering spark to send whispers murmuring down the line? Even as inured to it as Eve was, a shudder still went down her spine.

It was healthy to always be a bit afraid of the dead.

"Do you have records of Ingrid and who brought her here?" Eve asked.

"Not available to the public."

"But I am a public servant working on behalf of the law," Eve pressed gently, showing the piece of paper again to reinforce her position.

"Yes, of course. I'm sorry. I do want to help you." The woman was shaking. "This is just . . . very nerve-wracking, Our Lily calling you . . ."

"I'm sure I misheard," Eve said gently.

"No, maybe you didn't," the Deaconess replied, a nervous laugh escaping from her grimace. "One of our girls who tells us she always sees ghosts says she sees Miss Strand all the time. I should be relieved, shouldn't I? Proof of life after death just like our Savior?"

Before Eve could answer, the woman rose, disappeared a moment to a nearby room and returned with a ledger in what clearly were shaking hands. "Here's a ledger noting that Ingrid wasn't feeling well. She had a telling cough, but she didn't die here. Her mother brought her here abruptly and left with her just as abruptly."

Eve looked for Ingrid's name. There she was, with a question mark after her name.

"Ingrid was a special case. Her . . . mother was going through a difficult time. From what I remember, her husband, Ingrid's father, abandoned them and she asked if Ingrid could be kept here while she found employment. That is what we do, supply hope to the hopeless, with a special eye towards mothers and children. I try my best to remember their circumstances." The woman paused.

"You're doing very well at that; this is all very helpful, thank you," Eve said. She found that people needed encouragement when discussing unpleasant things, especially if the police were involved.

"Mrs. Schwerin never returned until the day after Ingrid began showing signs of consumption and was then beside herself. She insisted she had to take her before the father found and 'stole' her. I've not seen either of them again."

"What do you think?"

"I've no idea," the Deaconess said, wide-eyed. "I try never to judge. We're here for the children. I don't care where they come from or what forces a mother to give a child over to us, even if for a short time, but I always believe in the good we can do for them, and we can't step in to separate a mother and child. When she took her I had hoped that was for the best, warning her about her cough and the possibility of tuberculosis. Beyond that, it's in God's hands."

"Do you think anyone was ever violent towards Ingrid?"

Brower clenched her jaw, making her too-thin face fiercely sharp. "The day she arrived I thought I saw a bruise on her arm during an initial physical examination. We have to examine everyone before they are housed in our dormitories. Years ago someone dropped off a child with cholera and a third of the girls' wing died."

At this, Eve made a sound of empathy. Her sensitivities could literally feel the lifting of the weight of souls ascending all at once when such a heavy toll was left on earth. Eve didn't just empathize with the moment, she felt it too, more than anyone without those gifts could know, so she tried not to show the physical pain across her face.

"So . . . seeing that bruise," Eve prompted the Deaconess to continue.

"Perhaps there was violence before, with the father. The mother was distracted, but I couldn't imagine her being violent. Of course, never here. Beyond general punishment, the slap of a ruler on knuckles during lessons, nothing is severe here."

"Of course. I understand."

"From what Mrs. Schwerin indicated in my first interview with her, her husband seemed to very much need the Lord, let me put it that way. But it is our duty never to judge."

"I never do until given just cause."

"They're letting women do actual detective work now?" the woman asked, leaning forward as if sharing a secret.

"Haven't we always done the work?" Eve countered. At this, the Deaconess smiled. "Within the Police Department, some of us are allowed certain duties, in certain capacities," Eve added. "It is still limited but I have been granted a certain amount of freedom and jurisdiction many haven't, and my small department of women take our duties very seriously."

"Good," she replied, pleased. "I'm not sure how to tell you to follow up on Ingrid's family; she left no forwarding address even though we asked for one, saying she was going to take refuge with her sister." The woman looked at the book again, flipping to a page full of notes. She found a line and showed it to Eve.

Ingrid Schwerin removed from premises by mother on account of fear of father, said going to sister, within city. Thought to have croup or bronchitis. Worst case tuberculosis.

"Thank you," Eve said. "I can look for family but I don't suppose you have a maiden name?" The woman shook her head. "Any belongings left behind?"

"We try not to keep things—we reuse them—but this is recent enough there might be a few things in a bin . . ."

The woman disappeared again. Eve loosed a prayer that even one item from this mother or child might have been left behind. Cora's powers of psychometry—touching an item and gaining information from it—were burgeoning, and she might be the only one who could give them a solid lead on any whereabouts.

She returned with a simple pinafore and a small wooden cross with a golden lacquer hanging from a braided cord. "We took these off when treating her for her cough. I remember she was wearing these when she first came in."

"How long ago was that?"

Deaconess Brower turned to a different book, an intake ledger. She scanned alphabetically. "Last month to the day."

Eve took out a notebook from her vest pocket and put down notes lest she forget them, it was easy to get caught up in the emotions and think all the details that were searing at the time would remain emblazoned but memory was a difficult beast.

"May I take the items? They will be very helpful in a further investigation. I promise they won't be discarded. We'll bring them back here if we can't find the family."

The deaconess seemed hesitant at first but then folded them, wrapping the chain of the cross around a button, then taking twine from a desk drawer and making a little bundle. There was such diligent care, even in this small act of respect, that Eve was very moved by her deliberation.

"Thank you," she said, and was surprised as she had to hold back tears. She didn't know Ingrid, but she felt like she did just a little bit now, a sweet, quiet girl who just needed to be given the peace and breadth to live well and safely.

In a small fold in the notebook cover Eve had a few business cards she'd typed out herself.

"You have been so very, very helpful, Deaconess Brower. This is my card if you think of or find out anything more." Eve handed over her card and the woman took it with a bow of her head. "And if there are any other issues with missing children, or any delicate matter best left to women, please don't hesitate to contact me."

It was the Deaconess' turn to have a certain empathetic reaction, as if there were many more things she wished she could share, or wished Eve had been there for in the past. It was a vault of pain, this place, as much as it was a place of refuge, healing, second chances, bare survival—a place of study, worship or starting over. Eve could feel it all.

The ghostly Lily who had called about one girl could have chosen many stories, Eve felt, but she could glean no further specifics from within the walls or from the mouths of any spirits; none were close enough to hear.

Eve's stomach growling brought her back to corporeal realities as she removed her ungloved hand from the carved stone doorway and stepped back out onto Fourth Avenue.

Dinner. Tonight was Antonia's turn. Good, Eve thought, as she wasn't sure she had the energy to make anything but a bland soup and Antonia was the best cook of them all. To go home to a wonderful meal and leave all this behind . . . Sometimes easier said than done when living with co-workers.

When Eve first began the Ghost Precinct, she hadn't intended to live with her co-workers, but it had just simply unfolded that way. When Cora had come to join Eve in New York, per her own visions and prophecy, it was obvious she should stay in Eve's large, empty house. Then Jenny, then Antonia, both needing a refuge of safety and understanding. The household then became the sort of family that Eve had always envisioned. Eve's heart was full but her mind was always wary. Together they were very powerful. Uncomfortable things always sniffed out the powerful who, if separated, were vulnerable.

Divesting work from home life was critical. In the first months, it had been impossible; every discussion was trying to solve a case. But Cora, in her infinite wisdom and uncanny gauge of her own limits and those of others, called a stop to the practice of discussing work after a certain hour. For the past few weeks they'd done a better job of creating and maintaining boundaries.

By the time Eve got home, dinner was simmering in pots, the house smelling gloriously of stewed tomatoes and Italian spices.

"If I just could have stayed in Grandmother's kitchen with all the women, making art out of food and telling endless stories, I'd never have left," Antonia said quietly when Eve complimented her on how delicious it all seemed.

Even though Eve could tell it was on the tips of their tongues, no one asked about the results of the phone call, or what she had gleaned from Grace. Eve made one exception. Drawing Cora aside, she explained that there was an item for her to 'read' when she was ready, set in the foyer table, in one of the side drawers.

"What is it?" Cora asked.

"A bundle of a dress with a cross inside," Eve murmured a reply.

"Ah, something worn near the heart always gives off the best light," Cora murmured.

"Secrets, secrets?" Antonia admonished from the dining room.

"We're coming," Cora called.

Sitting down together, the colleagues ate dinner and talked about what they each were reading.

"What is your latest?" Eve asked Cora.

"The whole canon of Alexandre Dumas," she replied. "I'd like to think he was an ancestor. She opened the book to show his daguerreotype. "Doesn't he look like he could be a relative?"

"He does, in fact."

"Not many people know he was a man of color," Cora added. "I like that this edition wants to remind people of the fact."

"W. E. B. Du Bois's *The Souls of Black Folk* is truly important," Antonia offered. "I want to understand struggles beyond my own. I want to understand the pains that have plagued those I love." Antonia spoke so forthrightly that Cora almost blushed at this.

"I'm also working my way through as many Brontë books as I can," Antonia added. "It is very clear I prefer Rochester to Heathcliff, wife in the attic notwithstanding," she stated. "But it is a low bar to reach for romance concerning either, so I think if I had to pick a companion, I'd just choose Jane herself."

"Can't blame you," Eve replied with a laugh. Turning to Jenny, the girl signed she was reading Irish folktales and dreaming of green fields.

"That's lovely, Jenny," Eve replied. "For my part, I'm overdue to pick up something new," she confessed. "I just finished *Persuasion* a few days ago. I don't know why it took me so long to get to this when I've read all of Austen's others."

Your thoughts? Jenny signed, her face very serious, as if she were a teacher prompting a report.

"I confess my guilt," Eve responded with a laugh. "I had to skip to the end of the novel to make sure the two of them fell in love and were able to be together. You never quite know with Austen, and those two were simply unbearable. It hurt."

"I know," Antonia gasped. "*Agony.* I did the same and I feel better hearing you say so."

"I'm usually strict on chronology," Eve added. "I never skip ahead, I think that's childish but I was *unprepared* for *that* level of pining . . ."

"That book should come with a *warning* attached," Antonia added.

The women laughed and shared a few trivialities and discussions of the news of the day, such as Roosevelt's latest doings as governor— there was always a story with that bold man. There were consistent odes complimenting the cook, at which Antonia beamed. Cora mixed engagement with moments where she looked far away. Eve could nearly hear her powerful mind whirring and chewing on things Eve knew she wouldn't discuss until ideas were fully formed or whatever voices she was hearing from beyond became clearer. Perhaps Ingrid was already speaking to her, or something related.

In addition to the rules about keeping work at bay after hours, the women had to make a strict boundary about when the ghosts could or could not keep company with them. That was a line that still had to be held in the sand, and it was constantly difficult, if not impossible, to enforce without jeopardizing their channels. Their boisterous conversation and camaraderie was a draw to the dead, who wafted toward bright signs of life like moths to flames.

The laughter had the youngest of their ghostly compatriots wafting through the walls, as if the sound were a siren call. Eve looked at Cora, who waved her hand to let Zofia be, even if it was past what was regarded as a sort of bedtime, a time when a spirit shouldn't continue to maintain their energy to be physically manifest. The ghost child didn't want to fade and their Mediums didn't make her. Tonight, no one shooed anyone away, and they let laughter and shared stories continue to warm them, even the dead—no spectral chill grew too much for the hearth of their souls.

* * * *

Once Antonia and Jenny were fast asleep, Eve's door opened a crack and she knew Cora was on the other side.

Without looking up or turning to the door, she murmured for her colleague to come in. Eve was at her desk writing, a discipline she tried to do daily, both in taking notes for her cases and also in the memoir that the trajectory of the Precinct would result in; her broader lifetime mission.

"I'm ready," Cora stated. "Would you like to take notes?"

Eve picked up the notebook she was immersed in and without another word, the women went downstairs. One of Eve's rules had been to keep séances out of their bedrooms in an effort to maintain boundaries. Of all the rules, she was strictest about this. They would do their business in the parlor.

Cora paused, standing before the foyer console table where the items rested.

Zofia floated in the hallway, right near the door, her small form transparent and floating at eye level to the taller women, the spirit clearly waiting for them.

"Zofia, you needn't wait up with us," Eve murmured. "Fade and rest a while, dear."

The little girl shrugged. Eve wanted the ghosts to feel, just as she wanted for her living team, that they could all take time away from their work, regardless of it being their calling and lifestyle. Eve didn't want it to be all-consuming every moment of the day; that was unhealthy.

"Ingrid is a child," the ghost replied, the name sounding lovely in her Polish accent. Eve opened her mouth, asking how she knew the name of the girl and Zofia bobbed forward, anticipating her. "I was with you for a time at Grace today. I didn't want to disturb you, but it all felt very important. I wanted to help watch over my sisters . . ."

Zofia called any girl around her age her 'sisters' and Eve never dissuaded her. It was that passion that made the ghost one of their best assets in missing children's cases. She had been the one to crack the clues for the last child they'd saved. A senile old woman had taken a child from a playground thinking it was her granddaughter, and the poor child—whom Cora had deemed a painfully gifted empath—was too polite and too emotionally stricken to tell the distracted woman otherwise for whole two days. Heartbreaking all around, but thankfully no one was hurt or dead. It was the happiest of results and Eve knew none of them should be spoiled by it. It was good Zofia wanted to know more about Ingrid. Perhaps it would help take the ghost's mind of her missing 'big sister' Maggie.

"Would you mind?" Cora asked, gesturing to the drawer before her. Eve moved to retrieve the items. As Cora's senses were sharpening for this particular gift, the more she touched around the object of focus, the more scattered the imagery.

Belongings in one hand, Eve slid open the parlor door and turned up the gas just at a low trim, a dim glow from the frosted glass sconces. Cora followed and sat down beside Eve at the séance table.

"Ready?" Eve asked. Cora nodded. Eve handed her the girl's dress and necklace.

Cora placed the small dress between her hands, Eve noticed its seams were hand-stitched, made of a floral print with eyelet cuffs with an uneven ribbon woven through, every bit of it speaking of tiny details made with love for a small being.

From what Eve had seen of the way Cora's psychometry worked, it didn't activate for just anything she touched, in the same way Eve didn't listen in on every spirit—that way lay madness. She had to be intentional. Focused. Open. But most of all, safe.

Cora took a deep breath and murmured a French phrase of benediction long cherished in the Dupris line and Eve bowed her head, magnifying her colleague's request for grace and insight. As she spoke, she entwined the cord of Ingrid's little wooden cross between her fingers.

Her breath quickened into a pant.

The cross slipped down from its careful, gentle press between thumb and forefinger and swung from the cord still wound around her finger, to and fro like a hypnotist's pendulum.

"Mama," Cora exclaimed. Her eyes snapped open. The pinafore fluttered to the floor while the cross kept swinging from Cora's shaking fingertips.

"I think I know where she is," Cora gasped.

Chapter Seven

At breakfast, an exhausted Cora shared the psychometry of the previous evening with the whole group. During the visions touching Ingrid's dress and necklace she saw a tenement house east of Greenwich Village, and had a strong vision of looking out a window onto Ninth Street.

"It was one of the clearer visions I've had," Cora confessed. "But it took from me more than most."

"If you needed any help, you could have woken us," Antonia said.

"Not all of us will work on every case, and not all the time," Eve clarified. "There are things Cora and I will undertake together that I don't want you to think you're not included in, but we have to use our resources," Eve gestured to her head and heart, "sparingly."

Her tone indicated that was that.

"Protocol is on the docket for me first thing," Eve stated. "I need to turn in *my* written response to Mahoney's 'complaint' to headquarters before I can return to the office. In my estimation, any response appears an admission of guilt but the politics of keeping one's doors open at new thresholds . . . means sometimes dancing to overarching departmental music."

"Perhaps Antonia and Jenny can escort me to the vision location and we can make inquiries while you're at Mulberry," Cora offered. Jenny looked between Cora and Eve and nodded enthusiastically.

Eve paused a moment, feeling a surge of protectiveness over the case and over her team, then realized that there was a selfish impulse in wanting to be at the center of every development. If she wanted a strong team, she had to let them take the helm sometimes.

"That would be wise, thank you. Please take detailed notes," Eve stated and tried not to let her associates see any hesitation in the delegation.

* * * *

At the police headquarters at 300 Mulberry Street, a plain, multi-storied stone building ironically located near one of the more vice-ridden parts of the city, Eve showed her card to an embittered clerk at reception who, for whatever reason or another, refused to acknowledge her as part of the department and went to drop off the response with some other clerk. She realized she didn't know the hierarchy of these complaints, where they went to after her response, and she needed to know that—who was responsible for making decisions positively or negatively about her department. Naïvely, she'd assumed all things would go through Mr. Bonhoff, but she needed to be more careful.

As she wondered which office she should even ask about this, wandering down a back hall, she overheard a voice she recognized as Horowitz's arguing with a beat officer. She hung back, not wanting to interrupt.

"What do you mean the body was moved?"

"It's in the morgue. Talk to the folks at the 19th Precinct. The Dakota was being very difficult."

"So you're saying I can't see the crime scene as it was discovered."

"Suicide, man, no crime scene. From what I was told he had a big bottle of laudanum or something in his pocket. I don't even know why you care."

"Because people like you just write things *off* as suicides is why I have to care."

The man snorted and made for the door, calling derisively over his shoulder back at the detective. "Bah, you and your kind, always wanting to think you're somehow better than us, eh? With your sly ways, trying to get your grubby, greedy upper hand over us all no matter what, to hell with ye."

The man barreled forward and charged right into Eve as she stood in the shadows of the corridor, mouth open in horror. Stumbling back from the collision, she managed to hold her ground and stay upright.

"I'm sorry, Miss—"

"You never mind me, you mind what you said to *our colleague*. This man is your peer, as am I, and we demand better."

"Or what, or you'll sic Roosevelt on me? He loves any excuse to come tearing back in as if he still owns the place," the man muttered. "Go on then, tattle. I didn't do nothing wrong."

"I don't need to say a word to the former Police Chief—now Governor— though I could. I'm not interested in enemies, but I won't hear prejudice without objection. You can say whatever you wish—it is a free country—but you're not free from being called to account by those who won't tolerate it." "Lord free me from prattling women," he grumbled, walking away. "I've more prattling where that comes from, and worse, so you'd best start respecting all your peers," Eve called after him. "We're not going anywhere." He disappeared around the corner of the hall.

Squaring her shoulders, Eve strode into Horowitz's small office to see him staring at her a bit slack-jawed, his face still flushed with humiliation, but dazed by her railing.

"Thank you . . ." he said after a moment, "You didn't have to—"

"Of course I did. If anyone can wield any amount of resistance when it comes to bullying, in any situation, it is their job to speak up. Did you not do so for me recently? Would you not think I'd do the same?"

"Of course, and thank you."

"It is our duty. What's the matter, then? You seem frustrated, beyond just the obvious rudeness."

Horowitz sighed, deflated. "I'm getting nowhere on a recent 'suicide' I think sounds suspicious and I can't get a look at any of it. That's part of the reason so much mess is going on around it. I didn't make immediate progress on an anonymous tip, so there's additional sabotage from the uptown precinct."

Eve thought a moment and weighed a few concerns before positing a careful query. "Would you like to hold a séance about it in my office?"

He stared at her for a moment at first thinking she might be joking, then realized that of course she wasn't. "Ah . . ." He too was being careful. He wasn't a believer, but he was trying, still, to respect her position.

Eve smiled. A gentle smile was one way to disarm a skeptic. "What do you have to lose?"

Another uncomfortable shift in his chair. She took a step forward, adjusting her tactics. It wasn't that she needed him to believe, but if she could help him, it would give her a stronger ally in the department. "We don't just *let* men *in*, you know," she explained, "so you should be grateful I'm even extending this invitation."

"It isn't that, I . . ."

Eve kept a patient tone but spoke matter-of-factly. "I don't care if you do or you don't believe in what I do. I'm asking if you want to pursue what you will deem a shot in the dark at your wits' end. I won't tell anyone if you're worried about your *reputation*."

"You heard what colleagues assume of me come out of that man's mouth as he left the room." He raked his hand through his thick brown curls and rose with a sigh. "Lead on. I can't promise I . . ."

"Just listen. It's all we can ever do. It's not a science and I'm not pretending it is. It's a labor of love, every time."

He strode to the door and gestured ahead. "Lead on, then, Miss Whitby." They stepped out of the precinct, ignoring a glare from the attendant matron. Eve was very unsure what she'd done to anger the matrons, but it seemed that they, as a group, disliked her. Sometimes other women weren't always the stalwart supports she hoped they would be. Perhaps it was more a matter of distrusting youth. Eve had not yet paid her proverbial dues.

Once out on the bustling street, heading north and west, Horowitz resumed their conversation with care. "How you speak about what you do is . . ."

"Blunt?"

"Refreshing. I assume you'd like to know about the case, then?"

"Not right now. Wait to tell the spirits, we'll all hear it fresh for first impressions when we've got several pens set to papers, to take down any pertinent details. I don't trust conversation alone; my memory can become very unreliable if I'm in a spiritual state. Writing everything down is key, as the mind fills in blanks as a routine problem-solving technique. Not helpful if it's just imagination."

"Don't you think we should extrapolate, though? Try to get into the mind of a suspect or a victim? Doesn't that require a certain amount of imagination?"

"You're speaking more like an alienist than a detective."

"I don't think the disciplines should be separate," Horowitz said with enthusiasm. "I think they should be complementary. How can we try to understand motive or patterns without considering whole people and whole pictures?"

Horowitz gestured towards a trolley car, but Eve waved and gestured to the sidewalk instead, and they continued uptown at a leisurely stroll.

"I agree. But empathy and understanding—are those not considered 'feminine' disciplines? I can't imagine you've gotten much support in that vein from the average officer," Eve said.

"I don't talk about my methods publicly, I just employ them privately. I figured you wouldn't judge—if anything, you've been employing the same."

"Indeed, instinctually. It's good if we start taking note of instinct and creating a methodology, for the benefit and employment of those who come after us."

"Is this a legacy, for you, this Precinct?"

"I most certainly hope so. One of the things about dealing with the dead is you think about time, the long stretch of time, very differently. You realize you are only one small part in such a timeless whole."

"When did it start for you? Hearing sprits? And how did that lead to all this, to a whole department?"

"If it had been solely up to me, I wouldn't have created a department necessarily—I'd just have taken on the spirits' information and, in concert with my Gran, relay it to officers and detectives as we saw fit. I've always planned to write a book about my experiences as a way of 'teaching' and 'helping' more broadly. I want people not to be afraid of ghosts any more but to welcome them when they are being helpful. The department began when my gifts became too much for either me or my dear Gran to handle on our own."

"How did you recruit? There are so many frauds."

"I didn't. I said a few prayers, Gran talked to a few colleagues of hers from her time in the thick of paranormal battles—long, incredible stories you should get her to tell you—and it unfolded from there. A shared dream brought Cora Dupris to my side. Her parents having worked with Gran meant her transition from New Orleans was smooth, and both Antonia and Jenny were sent by the spirits. As Fate saw fit."

"I see." Horowitz said.

"But, I confess, there are times when I miss the moments when it was just Gran and me, helping the world one piece of information at a time. Now I've so much responsibility, and while I wouldn't admit this to my colleagues—so don't you dare repeat it—it feels all so precarious. The recent complaint drove that point home sharply."

Horowitz nodded. "I understand. I'm the first in my family to be a detective, not an academic. My parents don't know a whit about my world. Not that they can't comprehend it, it's just that they feel safer with their heads in philosophical clouds. Can't say I blame them. The moment I saw my first murder victim's corpse, I wondered if I shouldn't have taken up Plato after all. It was my father's dream that I follow in his footsteps at New York University, and goodness if sometimes our parents don't try to live through us."

Eve laughed hollowly. "Not mine. Mine would rather distance themselves. They are aware of the paranormal—it targeted them—but they want nothing to do with it."

"And so the drama continues, family to family, each with our own burdens to bear."

Walking by a theatrical poster hailing a newly emerged king of card tricks by the title of Thurston who was doing a run at a little theatre on 14th Street, Horowitz asked:

"How do you gather your information for a séance? Do you operate like all the fantastical acts do?" He gestured to the billets.

Eve stared for a moment at the somewhat garish posters sporting an array of red devils supporting the man.

"Heavens no. And I'll never understand why so many seem to embrace the imagery of devilry. Doesn't help a Spiritualist's cause, that's for certain. We've no magic tricks up our sleeves. We use any number of methods, though," Eve replied, and went on an excited tear. "Automatic writing. Direct channeling. Clairvoyant visions, with one of us taking down dictations. Indications of aura changes. If there's an object available, psychometry. Yes or no questions involving an electric light. Slates for the dead to write with."

"I heard that's *definitely* a magician's trick."

"Usually. But I've found a word or two left by a spirit. Not enough to build a case on but a clue. Nothing is ruled out. Everything is allowed, we fine-tune from there. Wheat from chaff and all that. There's a lot of mundane noise from the spirit world you know. When I first began hearing and seeing I dismissed it outright as boring. I was drawn in once I started listening for patterns, afraid I would miss my chance at a Rosetta stone clue."

"I know that obsession. I do. I respect it. It gets cases solved."

The two walked another few blocks in quiet, but took in the cacophony of the city—a constant variation on a theme, a symphony of haphazard sounds blending one into the next.

She unlocked the Precinct door and he held it open for her. Stepping ahead of him and bobbing her head to McDonnell, she asked if he wouldn't mind waiting in the anteroom and didn't wait for his reply as she charged towards her office.

Sure enough her colleagues were back from their morning inquiries.

"Darlings, we've a gentleman caller," Eve announced to Cora and Jenny who sat at their séance table with papers and notebooks, likely writing up the goings-on of their morning, details of which Eve was eager to discuss later.

A few spirits who were floating about, running absent, incorporeal fingers about the lighting fixtures, turned to Eve and looked between her and the detective, curious. The detective's eyes didn't follow any of the spirits, but he did suddenly shiver from the change in temperature and a bit of his breath fogged before him.

"*Que pasa?*" Vera wafted closer. The quieter spirits, ones who Eve had seen before floating in the neighborhood but hadn't made themselves known hung back.

"Ooh, good thing I'm decent," Antonia said with a flirtatious intonation, poking her head around from a carved wooden screen at the back of the room opened when any of them had to make wardrobe adjustments or freshen up, grabbing the long, dark braid that she'd let down and pinning it back up with haphazard propriety.

"What does Horowitz want?" Cora, her senses already anticipating him, was furrowing her brow trying to make out why he was back so soon. Eve couldn't blame her protectiveness, but she wished she wouldn't be so sharp about it.

"The detective here has hit a wall," Eve began gamesomely, "and our ghosts will go through it for him. If he's going to be our liaison, he'd best know what we do and see it first-hand."

Jenny nodded at this, her frown shifting into defiance.

"I know we've matters that need our attention, but let's give the detective something useful and he'll be on his way," Eve said, turning to him. "Have a seat." She pulled her own desk chair over, placing it with its back to the door. None of the rest of them liked having their eyes closed facing away from an entrance, so it would be the guest's chair in the most vulnerable position.

The detective took the seat while the rest assembled. He looked around him, eyes narrowed, his lips pursed as if he were gathering evidence. Vera waved at him again. It was clear he was sensing something, but said nothing, probably just chalking whatever he felt up to the power of suggestion. Eve did not press, as this process was often uncomfortable for people coming to terms with a new aspect of their mortal reality.

Jenny returned to the table with a notebook and charcoal. Antonia brought over the box of matches. The candle was already placed at the center.

"What do I do?" He asked finally. "How can I be of help and not a hindrance?"

"Give us time, as mortal time and the clock of the spirits are profoundly different mechanisms," Cora instructed. "When we bid you ask questions, ask pertinent ones." Her eyes scrutinized him mercilessly, her hands perched on the back of her chair, squeezing the wood a moment before slowly taking a seat and steepling her fingers at her chin, her body going rigid as she began to take measured breaths. Glancing at Eve, the reluctance to do this essentially vulnerable thing before a stranger was clear, but she closed her eyes and began nonetheless.

To varying degrees each of them was a clairvoyant and clairaudient, but Cora didn't want her hands fussing with anything. Everything she shared was verbal and it was up to Eve to take down notes, Eve also being the one most prone to automatic writing.

Jenny was the next to sit, pulling her chair close, resting her book against the lip of the round table, charcoal poised, ready to transpose images that she saw or words her gifts heard onto the page.

Antonia was an increasing encyclopedia of knowledge of every divinatory form, from Tarot to tea leaves, so she could be conversant with any sign or practitioner. Today she withdrew from her pocket a small weighted pendulum, a carved quartz hanging from a plain silver chain. "To focus," she explained to Horowitz, who was looking at the implement with curiosity. "One's mind must be still to hear the echoes of others, the center of oneself must be level."

"This . . ." Horowitz murmured, gesturing to the implements and then to the table and its small array: its plain burgundy tablecloth, a silver candle holder sporting a tallow candle, a small, painted box of matches at its base, and a palm-sized brass bell with a slender handle cast in the shape of a holly leaf. "This is so simple."

"Anything much more complicated and you're looking at a performance, not a practitioner," Eve said quietly, taking her seat last. Cora took one more measured breath and opened her eyes, the mesmerizing hazel spheres piercing Eve, and nodded the indication that she was ready. Eve gestured to Cora, who picked up the matchbox placed before the candle.

The matchbox was exquisitely painted, featuring a bright red heart with a plume of fire leaping up from it like a blossom, the edges of it trimmed in golden paint—a religious icon. When Cora had departed New Orleans for New York, a relative had given her a wooden box filled with these painted treasures, and she brought it into the offices as a requisite for their work, explaining their importance. These matchboxes were a reminder of Haitian ancestors and certain beliefs of Vodoun that her Uncle Louis had died trying to champion. Cora did not follow exactly in those traditions but honored them as the core animating force of her gifts. These small boxes of faith and power were the perfect match to strike up their spiritual chorus.

Once the wick was lit, Cora carefully passed the lit match to Eve who then let the smoke unfurl once she'd shook it free of its flame, waiting almost until the flame had reached her fingernails, drawing out every moment of this lighting as a physical, elemental call to prayer.

Eve placed the charred nub of the match upon the base ridge of the candlestick. When a few of these bits had accrued, Eve would place them in a medicine bottle and deposit them amongst flowers as if she were spreading someone's ashes. Eve deemed any aspect of prayer or meditation augmented by something physical should be returned to the earth with as much ceremony as the prayers themselves.

She could feel Horowitz watching every single movement, any and every detail, as a detective should, his expression one of pure curiosity.

The call to the séance was completed by Eve picking up the holly-trimmed bell, ringing it with one sure flick of her wrist and holding it upright for a moment until the clear tone that reverberated in the room and its echoes blended with the general milieu of city noise, an aural tapestry of transit and movement—trolley car bells, horse hooves and carriage wheels clattering along cobbles, the occasional shout or laugh from passersby. Tucking her finger into the bell to silence it from further noise, she set it down on the tablecloth, pressed her palms together and brought them to rest before her.

"Spirits. Those known and dear to us and those who newly hear us. We ask for your calm presence. For answers to our questions. Come, friendly folk from beyond the veil, make yourselves known." Eve opened her hands in supplication.

Her colleagues did the same. Horowitz, watching, did the same, placing open hands on either side of him. Eve made the first move, reaching out and grasping Cora's upturned palm to her left and Horowitz's to her right. Antonia joined hands with Cora and Jenny. Jenny hesitated a moment, watching Eve's hand commandeer the detective's, and she placed hers atop his with a wary expression.

"We join hearts and hands together in hopes you will respond to our plea," Eve continued. "Who will join us as we seek justice?"

Eve could feel the small hairs over her neck and down her arms, which always rose in the frisson of a séance, stand straight. She didn't have to look around the room to know that Vera, Zofia, and Olga—those who were most connected to her and her team—had appeared in response. Louis Dupris too, though his presence to Eve's mind was almost as if he were standing behind a thin curtain, because so much of his essence was devoted to and focused on his niece.

There were two other presences in the room that Eve could feel but not see. Vera and Zofia were always the most apparent to her eye. The rest mixed into a bit of a spirit stew and questions would be needed to filter out each voice.

"Will you tell us the name of the deceased, detective?" Eve asked.

Horowitz looked around the room, shuddering. His nervous breath came out in a cloud. "Do . . . Do I speak to you," he whispered to Eve, "or to . . . the . . . room? I mean, are they listening?"

"Yes," the Mediums all chorused, a bit forcefully. The detective sat back in his chair.

"I am . . ." He began shakily, then stopped, steadied his voice, cleared his throat, and spoke louder, deciding to stare at the candle flame as he made his announcement. "I am looking for information regarding Doctor Claude Font, deceased, reported missing by his family in Washington Square, found two days ago in the Dakota building with no visible signs of trauma," Horowitz replied. His eyes flicked about the room a moment before returning to the lit wick.

"I see an empty room," Cora stated. "A long room. Nothing in it. Nothing but black curtains. Black carpet. Everything drawn and dark."

"That . . . sounds like the room where the body was found," Horowitz said with wonder.

Eve could hear a rustling sound. It was the voices of spirits, but not ones talking to her. Whenever she served more as a protectorate, the leader of the séance rather than the conduit, her operatives heard more and she could only skim the surface. Admittedly, she was having a harder time than usual concentrating.

Jenny had unclasped the hands on either side of her and was rapidly sketching, charcoal flying about her page.

"Check for a substance, all over him, all over his clothes and the carpet. *Drowned* spirits say. It's as if he drowned . . ." Cora stated, her brow furrowed, trying to make sense out of a tumult of words and scraps of thoughts. "Something toxic, leached and leaking over dark fabrics."

"Did you even get to see the body?" Antonia asked the detective.

"No," he replied with a frustrated sigh. "He's been moved."

"Get his clothes and take his last words seriously, that's what everyone is saying," Antonia stated. Jenny's eyes flitted between her colleagues before she nodded.

"Everyone who?" Horowitz asked quietly, looking around the room cautiously.

"All the ghosts. We've a stable of regular correspondents. They've all weighed in. You should be flattered. Not all come when they're called," Antonia explained patiently.

"Doctor Claude Font," Eve called clearly. "We reach out to the spirit of Mr. Font. Could you help us understand your fate, Mr. Font?"

There was a hollowness, a sound of air whistling across a great expanse, as if the question itself had created a void. Finally:

"Don't invite anyone in . . ."

Eve repeated this to the room. "Mr. Font? Is that you? Is that your warning? Is that what happened to you? You let someone in who hurt you? If there were no signs of trauma as the detective said, what happened?"

This phrase had come up before, and it shook Eve to hear it again. A chilling theme with no further clarity.

Jenny held up her notebook. First was a sketch, then there were hastily scrawled sentences. She passed the notebook to Eve to interpret and explain.

Eve and Horowitz both examined the face sketched on the paper—a sunken-eyed, menacing-looking person with wild, dark hair beneath a wide-brimmed hat, a white collar, and black clothes, a bit like a priest. The face may once have been attractive but drawn features and a rather infernal frown was off-putting. It wasn't a face you'd want to confess to or seek absolution from.

"Do you have any idea who this is, Jenny?" Eve asked gently.

Jenny shrugged and signed. Eve explained to Horowitz that the little girl saw the face in her mind's eye, without context.

"Do you have a sense of how this face relates to Mr. Font?" Eve continued. "And you're doing very well, Jenny, thank you for this," she reassured.

Jenny pointed to the most legible of the sentences she'd scrawled. "Back from the dead. Open graves." Below it was another phrase. "Scared to death."

"Who was scared to death, Mr. Font?" Eve asked, turning her face back to the room. She didn't see him; she only saw her spirit regulars. But she felt a different weight. He was there, his heaviness was there. "Were you?"

A sad murmur, glancing through the room in a nearly imperceptible "Yes . . ." Each Medium echoed the response in the same aching sigh.

And then there was nothing else. Eve heard the reverberate bell, a distant chime from across the veil. Her Mediums bowed their heads, squeezed the hands they held and withdrew hands back into their laps.

"Our channel is closed," Eve murmured quietly and blew out the candle.

A respectful silence was held for several moments.

"Goodness," Horowitz murmured. "'Scared to death'. That's what I'd been told by the only relative of Mr. Font I could find, a cousin. The rest of his family was back in England; he'd come to New York to study medicine and remained. He'd written the family a strange note saying he was 'scared to death,' and that 'graves had yawned open before him' and the relative was sure when his body was found that he had, in fact, been scared to death."

It was clear the driven young detective, who seemed just as devoted to and emotionally invested in his work as they were, was shaken that Jenny had picked up on this phrase she couldn't have known about. His eyes shifted between Eve and Jenny with wonder.

"Keep the warnings in mind, Detective," Eve declared. "Let them echo. See if they hold any resonance as you continue with the investigation. Often the spirit world speaks generally, waiting for us to apply their insight onto our nuanced reality and from there make deductions."

"I very much appreciate this image," Horowitz said. "I don't have the same sensitivities as you all but I do have instincts as to what may be important. This will hold resonance if there is ever a lineup of suspects. May I keep this?"

Jenny nodded. Eve was continually impressed by the youngest of them. She didn't seem to need praise or approbation for her efforts; she simply presented the information she was given almost impartially, under no illusions that the information presented would always make sense, but patient for it to be a part of the greater vision, a wise old person inhabiting a young body. In the first week Jenny had joined the team, when Eve had asked about how long Jenny had been aware of her own clairvoyance, she'd written Eve a note explaining that she had always been a vessel and a messenger, for longer than she even knew, verifying Eve's sense of a far elder soul than the small body would suggest.

"Now you know what we do, and how," Eve said quietly. "A few things change; sometimes we're more focused on writing than speaking, or more images than words. We can't solve your mystery directly. But we hope to at least supply a few missing pieces of your puzzle that you can then place into your frame."

"Indeed. I'll check for substances on clothes and carpet immediately, provided I can regain access to the scene of the crime. The management of the building is particularly protective. I understand their wanting their residents, many of whom are high in profile, to feel safe, but we've been hamstrung by restricted access and inability to speak with possible witnesses." Horowitz rose, bowing his head. "Allow me to take up no more of your valuable time, I'd like to go follow up on this right away."

"The Dakota is a grand building that does have its own specters, I hope you know," Eve said with a smile. "A mere decade old and already haunted."

The detective's mouth twisted into a half-smile. "Can't say that surprises me, given the look of the place, I'd say it was built to attract a good ghost story. Again, I thank you for your time and your efforts. I truly do. I don't think I'd have been a proper liaison for you had I not seen you in action. I hope you'll do me the honor of this ceremony again."

"Let's hope you'll have enough tactile evidence you won't have to rely on the spectral," Eve said with a smile. "But we're here and listening."

They watched him go. He was careful not to let the door slam behind him.

"That was almost pleasant," Antonia said with a slight, surprised smile once he was well out the door. "He didn't affect us poorly at all, and I don't always receive my gifts well with strangers in the room."

"If we *have* to have a liaison other than Bonhoff, I think we've dodged a spiritual bullet with this one," Eve stated. Cora seemed a bit unconvinced, but said nothing. Jenny shrugged, her expression and gesture indicating that she had no objections thus far.

Taking a deep breath, Eve said, "I need to try again to find Maggie. The phrase 'don't invite anyone in' repeating itself can't be a coincidence. . . ." I think I need to go deeply, to see if I can find her."

"Into the Corridors?" Antonia asked with trepidation. Eve nodded.

"I think the Two Walks may be our only hope for information on Maggie."

"You warned Vera not to let the Corridors take her, and now you volunteer to go in them?" Cora said with a frown. "What can a living soul glean there better than the dead? Let Vera try before you barrel in."

In Eve and her family's experience, there were "Corridors" between the living and the dead, and information and spirits traveled between, helping the living to make choices. In Gran's experience, negative forces could also enter the world from the Two Walks between life and death, positivity and negativity being the two base choices for any soul. It was not a wise place for the living to be.

Don't you want to hear what happened today? Jenny signed. *Why rush elsewhere when there's information here?*

The piercing wisdom of the child hit her strongly.

"Of course!" Eve exclaimed. She'd forgotten about the inquiries they had made about Ingrid that morning without her. "I'm so sorry. Jenny, you're very right, thank you. I'm a bit off," Eve said with a slight, nervous chuckle. Cora eyed her. "Please, tell me everything."

"We found Mrs. Greta Schwerin, Ingrid's mother," Cora stated. "Well, at least, we know where she is. She was unconscious due to a fever and what her sister described as a declining mental state. The tenement I envisioned was the home of Ingrid's sister Susan Keller, the first place Greta went with Ingrid in tow after the father started to become aggressive. From this house, Ingrid was then taken to Grace. When Mrs. Schwerin feared Ingrid would be found at Grace, she took Ingrid away. To where, Susan did not know.

"Mrs. Schwerin returned to her sister, nearly hysterical after Ingrid had gone missing after being in her care. Susan didn't bring this right to the police as she confessed she wasn't sure what to believe of her sister's failing mind and didn't want her to be implicated in a crime. Susan has been trying to get information out of Greta but hasn't been able to glean a consistent answer. She doesn't know if the father did in fact find and steal Ingrid as described or if it was something else entirely, an unrecoverable lapse. She was so grateful that someone was looking into it for Ingrid's sake but was understandably worried for Greta."

Eve took this all in and thought about it for a moment. "Have you been back to the spirit world to see if they've any thoughts on this matter?"

"No, we were about to try when you came in with the detective," Cora stated.

Eve could tell there was something Cora didn't quite trust about Horowitz but she didn't want to press. Cora would come to her with her concerns when she was ready. At least, Eve hoped she had the right read on her. She couldn't know everyone's mind, as much as she tried.

Eve nodded. "And thank you for being so amenable with him. You understand departmental politics are now such that we have no choice but to be." She turned to Jenny. "You're wise in that I should pace myself. I'll not engage the Corridors until we've all rested. Sometimes I don't know my own limits."

The girl simply looked at her with that unsettling old soul in such a young face and nodded, signing that if she didn't learn, it would cost her.

Engaging in another séance on behalf of Ingrid offered snippets. Places. Sights. A few sounds and words. All of them jumbled and somewhat nonsensical.

Coming out of the session, Eve chuckled mordantly.

"The spirits seem as though they've had too much spirit . . ."

"It did seem like the one voice was drunk, didn't it?" Antonia said.

"Altered, somehow."

"If we're picking up on Ingrid's state, existence might, in fact, be incoherent; perhaps we're picking up on her fever dreams."

"Or that of her mother, her possibly dangerous father, or any number of narrators who may be, unfortunately, unreliable."

"I think we should try Susan again. If she wasn't forthcoming about Greta's life before Ingrid's disappearance, we need to pressure her for more. We'll make sense of this but not without help from the living to piece the patchwork of the dead together."

Eve rose and went towards the door. "Ninth Street, you said, and what—Second Avenue?" No one rose or moved to follow.

Jenny wrote on her notebook and held it up. *Limits.* As if Eve might take it more seriously if the suggestion was written down.

She looked at her operatives. Multiple séances in a row, in addition to interrogations of the living, was more than they'd ever done in one day. Their faces were stoic but their eyes were watery and weary. And her own head hurt too.

The push, the drive, the constant zealous need for movement and engagement—it was an addiction that Eve had to admit to. But she needed to stop and breathe, and she had to respect that she and her fellow Sensitives had different hours to keep.

"Rest a moment. Eternity will still be here for you, Eve. Listen to that child or it will be the death of you," Vera said, breezing through the room and then wafting right back out of it again. The Precinct followed her home.

Chapter Eight

After a contemplative night taking notes and transcribing everything she knew so far, Eve was at the office bright and early the next day, two cups of coffee in and standing at a precarious precipice.

Proposing to take to the Corridors rather than just coaxing open the door of the spirit world was a bold step that skipped their usual practices. But Maggie's spirit hadn't been found by surface channels. That could only mean she was deeper in the labyrinth. Eve would have to face the Minotaur. A prospect that was as thrilling as it was nerve-wracking.

Gran had once stated that a psychic who could travel in and out of the Corridors regularly was a transcendent being. Eve realized a part of her desire to dive in had to do with proving herself that gifted, that powerful.

Therein too, lay a great danger. The old myths warned more of hubris than they did of anything else.

When everyone was assembled, Eve called their day to order. "Let me now take on the burden of a deeper dive into the Corridors between life and death. For Maggie, for Ingrid, for anything we need to know."

Just as this decision was made, there was a knock at their door, and Gran walked in without waiting to have it opened for her, dressed in a mauve silk dress with pearl buttons, feathered hat in hand.

All the Precinct smiled as she stated: "I just . . . want to help." She set her hat upon a peg by the door and turned to look at Eve pointedly. "And protect."

"Of course, Gran. You must have sensed I was about to take to The Walks."

"Heaven help you. I wish you didn't feel called to," Gran replied, clucking her tongue, her full skirts swishing as she moved to Eve's side. "But yes. I sensed a particular weight and, as usual, I feel responsible for you. I lost Maggie already. You going in after her . . ." Gran swallowed hard.

"Perhaps you'll be the one to take me under, then?" Eve said brightly. "Gran, there shouldn't be fear about the Corridors. They're just a plane of existence like any other, life, death, pain, paradise—"

Gran's warm, maternal gaze shifted and steeled. "One should always be afraid of the Corridors. Healthy fear keeps you alive, dear." She looked at the rest of the company. "Don't any of you forget it!"

Everyone sat back, suitably chastened.

Gran took a deep breath and managed a smile. "Now then, let's begin."

Eve and Gran had been reading many journals about parapsychology, hypnotism, and the findings of England's Metaphysical Society trying to bridge faith and science, and between the two of them they'd developed the trusted relationship of guiding one another through a meditative state. Generally, it was Gran doing the guiding, as she'd be the first to admit the spirit world gave Eve greater access than she had ever seen in a medium. This responsibility was heavy and daunting, but Eve tried to take it in stride at every turn.

Gran murmured regarding what had been described to them by a fellow medium as The Descent. Neither Gran nor Eve liked that. To them, it was 'The Parallel'. The idea of going *down* to a spiritual place felt like a medieval idea of purgatory. Or worse.

"As above, so beside" was how Eve preferred to think of it. The spirit world was just a breath away. For anyone. Death but a few heartbeats away from a transition to another state. Eve didn't fear death. She feared the places beyond the spirit world's reach that she didn't dare try to cross, the places that spirits wouldn't speak of.

Gran stood behind Eve as she sat at her séance table and placed her hands on either side of Eve's head. Guiding Eve back to sit fully relaxed in her chair, Gran began and in the softest and sweetest of chants, spoke a few quiet Latin phrases they'd been fond of. It was their own sacred text, fashioned when she was a child when the two of them had been trying to figure out how Eve could live with the spirit world without it causing so much chronic pain in her head and all down her spine.

It was old, familiar. Spiritual muscle memory. Eve felt like she sank into her trance state. Heavy and distant. The darkness was complete, thicker than any darkness she'd ever experienced, whether in normal life or in a state like this.

Usually, there was a sort of architecture to the corridors; they were precisely that—long halls to wander, searching, especially for those who were lost or trapped between worlds. It was a beautifully haunted place, and even though it was so cold one could see one's living breath, which always caught the attention and the clamor of the dead, there was an aching beauty to the tall arches and the way souls trailed wakes of translucent energy from them like glittering streamers, the corridors filled with such spectral phosphorescence as to give the idea of ectoplasm credibility. The sheer magnitude of infinite magical possibility emanating from this realm was palpable.

Usually.

But there was nothing here.

They had taken the usual route to get her here. But there was no *here* . . . The darkness was so oppressive, there were no corridors to be seen. No choice of two walks, no shadows, no fellow searching spirits. No spectral clamor. No beautiful floating forms like underwater angels lit by starlight.

In that terrible darkness, she felt as though something grabbed her by the shoulders, something of sharp iron.

In a voice that was not entirely her own but another voice utilizing her, speaking through her as Medium, Eve cried out two terrible words.

"Help me!"

Eve was launched from her trance, as if she'd been pushed out of it and yanked up from the bottom of a well at the same time; a dizzying, sickening push and pull.

"No . . ." she mumbled. "I need to know more." She jerked against the séance table, her eyes snapping open to see her colleagues, Gran included, staring down at her in horror, which only added to her own. She felt a scream welling up inside her, but she suppressed it as if she were swallowing bile.

She got up clumsily, feeling like everything was too hot, too close, as if the darkness had been the close finality of a coffin, not a corridor.

"That was it? Just a cry for help and nothing more?" Cora asked, looking up at Eve. "I heard a voice through you, but I couldn't tell if it was Maggie."

"It . . . it sounded like Maggie," Gran said. Her face, usually so elegant in its character lines and distinguished creases, looked old, haggard. Scared.

A hundred voices said it, Jenny signed. *Maybe Maggie, many more . . .* . The youngest of them was not easily frightened but her green eyes were wide and there was a sheen of moisture on her smooth skin.

As if the whole blank corridor were filled with souls begging for help, Eve thought, but didn't want to put her voice to it.

"I don't know . . ." Eve murmured, still breathing heavily. "Take a lunch. I need some air."

Rushing outside the office, still feeling her mind and body as somewhat disconnected, Eve nearly collided with the same officer who had lodged the complaint. Mahoney. His fisted hands were full of paper. Perhaps he was here to ruin some other officer's day.

"What have you been meddling with today?" the man asked gruffly.

Eve squared her shoulders and stared up at the man. He was a full foot and a half taller than her, but she'd have liked to think the ire in her eyes gained her at least a few inches.

"Trying to ascertain the whereabouts of a missing girl, is that too objectionable for you?" she asked. "Your patron family isn't implicated, at least not yet, so you should reconsider questioning me about every action my department undertakes, because that in and of itself raises suspicion. Are those papers for me or do you have someone else to harangue?"

"City fines," the man grumbled, and continued on his way. A paranoid part of Eve thought perhaps he was tracking her, knowing just when to throw her off guard before a day's work, but she thought better of it—this was likely just on his beat.

The charitable part of her took a moment to consider that he seemed a miserable man who wanted to be more important than he was, stuck in clerical jobs when he might like to be seeing more action or advancement. But examples of empathy didn't do her any good; a bully was a bully regardless of motive or inner deficiencies.

Eve continued outside, unconsciously drawn to the church around the corner and the small patch of green it maintained between its eaves and hers. An important part of balancing one's living life with the dead was making sure a living soul saw some patch of green at least once a day.

Gran followed her within moments, saying nothing at first.

"What good are all these fragments . . . ?" Eve began, scuffing her boot edge against a flagstone.

"If they don't point us to a whole?" Gran finished. "That sounded a bit terrifying in there. The Corridors can be . . . traumatic. I warned you—"

"Yes, and I'm young and reckless. I know. I'm sorry," Eve barked. A sharp pain stabbed behind her eyes. She hadn't brought her dark glasses to fight against the bright light, which only added to the growing, searing sensation. The pain, however, was no excuse to lash out at Gran. She reached out for her hand, keeping her eyes closed against the light. "I'm sorry. I don't mean to snap." Her voice sounded as small and worried as she felt. "I . . . want to be a leader and provide victories . . . I can't seem to, here . . ."

"You put all the pressure on yourself."

She put the heel of her hand to her right eye and pressed. "Who else should bear it but me? I don't have any choice, it's been clear for as long as I can remember."

"You're not alone, you never are. You can't think of your gift of purpose as a curse, not now, it will hold you back. Now go back inside before you get a full migraine, please," Gran reminded her, squeezing her shoulder. Walking off, she called back to Eve. "You're not alone in this. Share that burden."

"Thank you," Eve called after her mentor, her best friend, her light in any darkness, blowing a kiss as her elegant form turned the corner.

Returning to her office with a hand shielding her eyes, Eve found the interior door open, Mrs. McDonnell gesturing inside. "Detective Horowitz is here for you, *milady*," she said with an exaggerated tone. "He's awaiting you within."

"You just let him in?" Eve asked, blinking, wondering how she'd missed him. He'd likely seen her and Gran talking off to the side and didn't want to interrupt. "I believe the man is trustworthy, but I have to have some boundaries for my colleagues."

"Then ask the chief for a reception space," the woman replied flatly. "I'm not entertaining your special company out here."

Eve bit her tongue, nearly saying it was precisely the matron's job to deal with company who called upon their office, but instead she forced a smile. "Very well we'll make a *parlor*," Eve retorted through clenched teeth. "With all our extra funds because we're so *popular*."

Striding forward, she opened the door and Horowitz stood from the chair he'd been sitting in, having faced it away from the nearest desk.

He was there alone. The rest of her department had taken her incident as a hasty cue for lunch and had vanished, likely wanting to leave that lingering, begging echo for *help* far behind. A chill still lingered in the air, as if Eve had brought it back with her from the Corridors.

"I'm sorry to intrude," Horowitz murmured, nodding towards the door. "I know I wouldn't want anyone in my office either, I understand, I'm just . . ."

"I'm sorry you heard that," Eve said, rubbing her eyes, willing the pain in her skull to edge to the side. She fumbled in her desk for a small bottle of aspirin. "I don't want it to seem that I distrust you—"

"Truly, I understand. I will always respect your autonomy."

"Thank you. Very much." She went to the table where a bottle of water sat next to the tea accoutrements, poured a bit into a small glass, and took the pills. "Are you still puzzled over yesterday?"

"Well, yes, but there's more. There is a case that was handed to me . . . no one else wanted to take it up at first, but now there's growing interest and before the case gets taken from me, I'd like to make headway enough to keep it under my jurisdiction." He sighed and raked a hand through his brown curls, a rather endearing gesture despite it indicating his building frustration.

"Is it related to yesterday?" Eve asked. "Mr. Font, was it? I've got lots of strings. None of them tying up. I'm not sure how much farther spread I can be."

"I doubt it is related." He looked horrified at the prospect of any correlation. "I don't see how it could be. But Angels."

Eve blinked. "Beg your pardon?"

"Angels have gone missing. Other items from religious institutions too, I couldn't ascribe to a pattern, but now . . . And I know your department has dealt, so far, mostly in children's cases, so, I thought your insights could be very useful . . ."

"Go on," Eve encouraged, "you don't have to justify why you want my help, just tell me how I can provide it."

"I think the Sisters at the New York Foundling Hospital might take more kindly to your presence, might allow you more clearance and might more readily follow up with you, especially considering you work in spiritual matters."

"Is this a missing children issue or a theft issue?"

"As far as I know now, this is a theft issue, of a small angel. They're a Catholic institution. But in your work you might see . . . more than meets the eye."

"Very well, let me leave a note for my colleagues to continue paperwork and research in my absence once they return from a lunch."

Eve did so, and as she was writing, Horowitz asked more questions.

"What do they do when remaining in office? Will they take calls or consultations as you do, or is that exclusively your purview?" he asked.

"If called upon to a safe environment, one might go accompanied by another. Otherwise my colleagues and I can spend whole days taking down dictation from all our ghost operatives, the eyes and ears and sleepless souls that see more than we ever could. Somewhere in there, often, are clues we must sift through like prospectors looking for gold."

"Like the initial mess of a crime scene," Horowitz replied, trying to liken their work to something he understood. "Sorting chaos into a narrative."

"Indeed, by words and thoughts. Less concrete than a scene, but evidence is sometimes there nonetheless. Lead on to the Hospital and tell me more as we go," Eve stated, grabbing her dark glasses and sliding them on her nose. "The spirit world sometimes conspires to give me a migraine, so forgive me the look of some nocturnal creature. Well, I should clarify that if I'm not serving the spirit world well enough they give me a migraine." She sighed irritably. "And it would seem I'm not doing my job as well as they'd like."

"Everyone's a critic," Horowitz said mordantly.

"Isn't *that* the truth," Eve choked a laugh.

"Thank you for coming with me, especially if you're feeling poorly," the detective said as they set off in the direction he gestured. Uptown.

After a moment, Eve added. "We women are useful. And resilient."

"I never said otherwise. Really, Miss Whitby. Please understand, not every man is out to end your calling. While I know you've had to fight complaints and threats of being shut down, I'm not one of the voices advocating for it." He spoke not with a sharpness or defensiveness but with a complete honesty, and it occurred to Eve that he had done so from the first. Eve stopped. She looked at him. He kept her gaze, undaunted by the dark glass between them.

"You're right," Eve murmured. "I'm sorry. I'm defensive. In addition to not feeling well, we've just been a bit rattled by a cry for help we can't answer." She pounded a gloved fist into her palm. "It's maddening."

"I do understand your barbs, your defenses. I've had to fight to be respected and taken seriously too. Remember that last incident I was sorry you overheard?"

"Oh, how could I forget?"

"That led to a complaint filed against me for meddling, not an apology. I was blamed for being a factor in impeding my own investigation. It isn't just the people I try to help. Most of the officers would prefer if I was their banker, not their colleague."

"I think most of the departments would prefer we all were housewives or matrons. Secretaries. All stereotypes in their respective places, I suppose?"

"It often feels like that's what most of the world feels more comfortable with. Everyone in their lanes. Everyone tucked cozily into boxes that cannot cross-contaminate."

"We're in New York, and we must do absolutely that. Cross-pollinate, not contaminate, but cross-examine. Co-exist. It is the very nature of this place."

"May we continue to live into that truth," the detective agreed.

"If what we're interviewing about today is an escalation or continuation of a pattern, where and when did it start?"

"The first was a Lower East Side synagogue. An immigrant congregation. No one at first seemed to care that velvet curtains in their synagogue, leading to the sanctuary, had been stolen. The Rabbi was insistent it was not someone from his congregation. They rotate a guard, and no one seemed to have noticed anyone come or go. A patrolman in the area said he'd pass it along to someone who cared. At least he said something. It came to me. Much like today with the Catholic angel, the story was almost entirely the same the first time, just in Yiddish, with the same baffling sense of wondering why."

"Maybe that's the point? Someone is doing this just because they can, knowing that taking items from anyone's sacred space is a unique kind of violation? Do you know if other practicing faiths have reported anything similar?"

"After the synagogue curtain incident, the same officer who alerted me to it said he would be following up with another Catholic church near Union Square that reported a small angel statue and garlands of silk flowers taken from one of their altars. He stayed on that case before he transferred, I'm not sure the outcome. Again, nothing particularly *valuable*, just unsettling and odd. I'll ask my Mother if she has heard of anything else in her alliance group, an academic wives' circle that includes many different faiths, even though my parents have asked me never to bring work home."

"My family asks the same." The two shared a weary chuckle.

"Have you ever regretted choosing detective work over academia?"

He shook his head. "I admire the discipline, but I can't stand the politics."

"But precinct politics are the worst!"

"Politics involving desks, libraries, the mind, the esoteric world, entirely cerebral ventures—somehow that's more maddening to me than men trying to jockey for sergeant by solving the most cases or working the most hours."

"You're saying you're too pragmatic to be a theologian?"

"Absolutely."

Eve laughed. She was glad for the walk. The Corridors had made her so tense that her muscles were in knots that only a long walk could untangle, but there was a limit to how much time they could spend strolling up Manhattan's length.

Looking up at street markers and realizing they still had some forty blocks to go, they ascended to the elevated rail along Third Avenue and looked out over the city, full of church-spires and ever-climbing stories, each taller than the last, and from that elevation everything looked like decorative building blocks as their compartment screeched and rolled by along the tall rails.

The Foundling Hospital's building on East 68th Street was a stately and impressive complex of red-brown brick with white sandstone detail over many windows, a mix of Federal façade and a mansard roof with the upper story featuring wide dormer windows. They walked past a hedgerow and up a stoop, walking below a religious frieze to the front door.

The Sister who answered the bell was an old, round woman in a full black habit, with a black capelet over her shoulders and a kind, expressive face shining from under a black bonnet; a radiant soul. As Eve introduced herself and Detective Horowitz at the front door, it was clear she was rattled.

"We are here to discuss the matter of a missing angel?" Eve began quietly.

"Ah. That. Yes." The woman frowned as she gestured them in. "I'm Sister Rose. Thank you very much for coming."

"Please tell me about your institution," Eve stated as they were led into an entrance foyer that was plain but well-lit, with many tall, large windows, white walls, and ceiling with graceful arch supports. The hall was blank save for a wooden crucifix over a table with a ledger. Thanks to Gran, Eve was familiar with many charitable institutions but she couldn't keep up with all of them considering the city boasted hundreds, one for every identity and need. It was a roster her family and friends took great pride in—New York was a city of agency and aid, of refuge and resource. The Sister smiled and any reservation vanished when she was given leave to extol their mission.

The two women of faith Eve had encountered recently, first Deaconess Brower and now Sister Rose, were the exact opposite in stature and size, but their commitment was identical. Where Brower was severe, Rose was effusive, yet either demeanor could keep an institution well-run.

"The New York Foundling Hospital believes no child should be abandoned, that every child should have a chance. As the Sisters of Charity we've helped thousands of orphans—so many, we had to move into this larger space. Sister Mary Irene Fitzgibbon had begun with her Sisters in a far smaller residential building further downtown, over thirty years ago, with just a cradle in an interior hall for desperate mothers to leave their child. Since then we have rehomed thousands across the country, with a focus on adopting them into Catholic homes, of course."

"Understood." Before the Sister could ask if they too were Catholic, just in case their protestant and Jewish backgrounds might impede gaining information, Eve continued. "The Detective here was the one who initially received the report about a stolen angel, and he later asked for my assistance," Eve explained. "Could you show us where it was taken from, and tell us anything else you think is important?"

The Sister nodded and gestured them forward down the long hall.

Eve could tell, and feel, a lot just from her first few moments in the door. For a place full of children it was relatively quiet. In the distance there was the sound of a piano and singing, so perhaps they were at a mass in a chapel. This was a place of last resort, but a place where second chances were made. Where lives were saved and the Sisters put their lives on the line to be providers. A circle of desperation and hope. It was as if Eve could feel their sense of calling and purpose, one believer to the next, even if the focus of belief differed between herself and these nuns.

They were led ahead into an open, clean white room with benches, tables and chairs; a school room, play room, meeting room—perhaps all of these things, depending on the hours of the day.

"That angel . . ." Sister Rose looked at the white wall, towards the back of the room, and back to Eve. "It's so odd. It was a gift from an orphan who was raised here and went on to form her own benevolent society. It meant . . . a lot to us. I don't understand how anyone could find a particular value in it other than it being a lovely little angel. Miss Loretta would have known we wouldn't have wanted something here that was made from gold or marble; we'd rather have those funds going to those in need. But it was simple plaster, she painted it herself."

"Was it visible from any of these windows?" Eve gestured to the arched windows on either side of the open, whitewashed room.

"Well, yes, I suppose it would have been, sitting here," she gestured across the room, where a small scallop in the wall indicated a lamp, fixture, or setting had been there at one time. It would have been visible from any window looking in, if one were looking close.

Eve felt a voice nag at her. The phrase that kept repeating; a murmur coming from the edge of the corridor itself, a distinct chill near her ear. *Don't invite anyone in . . .*

"Could someone have been invited in?" Eve said, picking up on the spirits' cue. "Could one of the children, having learned graciousness and generosity from you, have perhaps unwittingly invited in a thief?"

"Perhaps." Her round, beautifully expressive face fell at the thought of it. "I'll have to ask the children old enough to respond. Those in need in this neighborhood know they can receive a hot meal provided by the parish in more than one locale. It could be that someone needs that angel more than we do. In that case, then may God bless them. But if it is a portent for anything else going missing, or someone's excuse to come inside a safe haven, I thought it best to make a report."

"Of course. We're glad you did," Eve replied.

Horowitz joined in for the first time, adding; "There are a few other small things that have gone missing from various faiths and denominations. We've not gotten a sense that anything is violent or of particular concern, other than the indignity of stealing objects from sacred spaces. A particular fetish, one might say. This may be a part of that pattern and we'd like to keep an eye on it."

"Oh, goodness. That's sad."

It wasn't that the woman was naïve, but it was clear that the city had not hardened her heart one whit. It made Eve feel for her in a different way, a protective instinct she'd had since she was too young to be a protector. "Thank you, Sister. If you do think of anything," Eve handed over her card, "call, write, wire, drop by my office, or I'll come here—whatever makes you comfortable."

"I will, God bless. Thank you for coming on what may seem such a small matter," the Sister said, peering at them closely as if she might be able to determine from mannerisms or details whether either one of them was Catholic or had any interest in becoming one.

"Angels are no small matter," Eve replied, her hand fluttering over her heart, near an angel pendant Gran had given her when the Spirits first had begun overwhelming her. She hadn't worn it in a while; it had been hanging from a peg on her vanity and this morning she had unconsciously slipped it on, perhaps at the urging of the spirits ahead of her on the theme of the day. Angels as a concept had always been helpful to Eve, as the hierarchy of heaven offered her a system to balance an assault of spectral voices, staggering spirits into groups rather than being assaulted by their needs all at once. The archangels held sway over the rest of the heavenly host, and she sorted out the voices of spirits as if she were parsing out those tiers.

At Eve's earnest words, the Sister simply bobbed her head, smiling radiantly.

Horowitz bowed slightly and Eve turned to walk away.

Once out the door and a good ways on down the street, boots clicking sharply on the uneven sidewalk with Horowitz keeping pace at Eve's side as she clipped along, he finally spoke.

"Thank you for coming. No one else would have cared a whit about an item of no great monetary value that no one saw disappear."

"Thank you for bringing it to my attention," Eve said.

"Save for the man who brought this to me, my friend Erik, all this would have been ignored. He was going to be my partner before he transferred up to this area; his rounds stretch from here nearly all the way up the East Side. Sister Rose's report crossed his desk and he handed it to me, saying "I know you love patterns and obscure crime, so have at it," and so, here we are."

"If we're the patron saints of lost causes then so be it; may the supplications continue rolling in."

At this, Horowitz loosed a mordant chuckle.

"It is upsetting to me," Eve continued passionately, "that an icon that means something, that has had so many thoughts and prayers, so much thankfulness wrapped up in it, like those curtains that were drawn over so many hopes and concerns from that synagogue, should just vanish."

"That's precisely what has me so frustrated about this," the detective replied. "Why steal from an institution that is doing a demonstrable good for the city's most vulnerable? That synagogue hardly has any money to rub together yet they run food and shelter programs for the whole community. No matter your beliefs, you can see the good in what's being done. It isn't as though wealthy congregations are reporting thefts, although perhaps the fetish might escalate."

"I don't want to be seeing correlations where there are none, but I've been inside two benevolent institutions that exist for desperate women and children in the past few days: here, and Grace Memorial south of Union Square. And there's something about an "invitation" that keeps cropping up."

"How so?"

"The spirits keep telling me. "Don't invite anything in . . .""

"But you're not holding a séance . . ." Horowitz began, looking at her warily. "Do spirits speak to you so often outside it?"

"Yes," Eve said. "All the time. I don't always see them, but I hear whispers constantly, nearly always innocuous, nonsensical non sequiturs. I don't really know the meaning of silence."

"That must be maddening."

"I'm used to it."

"The warning to not let anything in that you're . . . hearing," Horowitz spoke as if he was processing taking that fact seriously, even after all he'd seen and experienced with them thus far. This chafed Eve, but she said nothing. "Suggesting an outside threat to an interior safety?"

"Yes. Perhaps."

"Hmm . . ." The Detective scratched his chin in thought. They ascended the elevated rail and stood waiting on the platform. "The doorman at the Dakota said there was someone who had asked after Mr. Font the day before he died, when he wasn't in."

"And?"

"Perhaps he invited someone in he shouldn't have? The man's name, or at least what he gave the doorman, was Lazarus."

Eve stared at Horowitz. "Wasn't there something about open graves and returning from the dead?"

Horowitz looked uncomfortable. "Yes."

"Scared to death. By someone raised from the dead . . ."

"I've been told I'll be able to access his Dakota room again. I'll examine the carpet as your spirits advised and retrieve his clothes. If I'm able to get you clearance, I can't promise, but would you like to see it yourself?"

"If you can, and if I won't be in the way, then certainly," Eve agreed.

"You won't be in the way," Horowitz said, with an odd sort of warmth. An invitation. Eve stared at him a moment. He stared back. She kept her expression blank. As did he. But then, at the same time, there was a slight, guarded smile.

Once they returned to 14th Street they went their separate west and downtown ways.

The moment Eve turned away from waving a goodbye her cheeks bloomed a slight blush and she began to walk quickly, pushing the dark glasses further up her nose, better to hide behind. She was glad she could shake herself free from the odd magnetism that was brewing between her and this detective—she didn't have time for such distractions. Walking quickly afforded her mind the full-tilt whirring space she needed. Her cheeks cooled as spirits whispered once more . . .

Don't invite anything in. The phrase repeated itself in her mind, echoed by spirit murmurs. That was ongoing, significant, and had the capability to apply to each puzzle: Maggie, the missing Ingrid, the strange case of this stolen Angel for no good reason, the dead Dr. Font . . . It was good advice, at least.

One of the most important aspects of Spiritualism that a young medium had to master was not inviting in negative energies. One mustn't entertain toxic presences, so it was vital to be able to tell the helpful from the vengeful in a matter of seconds. There could be no tolerance for seeds planted in the mind, home, or soul that would grow a certain and unavoidable poison. Eve and her colleagues were all for redemption and growth, but that capacity had to be already present and active for them to even begin to entertain a spirit or form. If the essence was shut to betterment and light, so would be their spiritual door.

So of course they wouldn't invite anything in that could cause a problem. They weren't vapid hacks with a spirit board made by a games manufacturer—they were serious, devoted professionals.

"It's insulting, really, when I think about it," Eve said to the spirit world, "to give such a generic and obvious warning to those who grew up knowing better. So you can't mean that on a surface level. What do you really mean?" she demanded.

The bustling metropolis swarmed all around her as she walked towards home; delivery wagons and errand runners with parcels, distinguished-looking persons out for strolls in perfect finery under parasols and wide-brimmed top-hats, the spirit world diving in, around, and through them in a chaotic but beautiful dance, stopping to stare at Eve a moment before bobbing on their way, sufficiently seen, chattering about some sort of loss, sadness, victory, or nothing at all. Eve tried not to focus in on the words, as she didn't have time to hear every story; she had to focus on the aural tapestry, the symphony of the dead as an ongoing overture.

"The warning is not enough . . ." she murmured insistently, tilting her face upward, looking at the increasing stories of buildings, cast iron facades sporting magnificent pressed details that could be ordered out of a catalog as easily as one might order a dress. Cherub and Green Man faces looked back at her from cornice pieces and window ledges.

Glancing down, a sign in the window of a shop proclaimed:
When the Spirit Fails, There's Always Tonic. Cure Any Ill Save Sin Itself!
—Prenze Brothers Co.

The slogan made her nearly want to snort with its grand claims and piety. The name was a reminder to consider the Complaint lodged against them. Vera's incident with the photograph hadn't yet been written up in Preventative—Eve made a mental note to do so—and she needed Vera to confirm the family identity. She doubted it was the same. Eve would ask Gran about the Prenze family company. As Antonia had declared straightaway, anyone who would send a lackey to admonish them was all the more interesting and most certainly more suspect.

That night, she had dinner with her family as was the custom three times a week, her parents and her grandmother alternating as hosts. Eve had offered her townhouse many times, but considering she was loath to exorcise the ghosts out of it just for the sake of her family's comfort, none but Gran had ever taken her up on her offer of hospitality.

On this night they were bid to join Gran in her sumptuous Fifth Avenue townhouse. It was a setting that everyone else tended to prefer, but to Eve, it was a jarring reminder of the different classes in which she moved. Every time she dined uptown, she thought about her colleagues that were making more meager fare for themselves in her own townhouse, and she felt torn between two worlds.

It had long been decided that Eve was not to talk spectral business at the table, so she contented herself with the most interesting sort of small talk she could manage, usually asking Grandfather about the latest goings on at the Metropolitan Museum, where he was a curator and fundraiser. He could have long since retired, but he genuinely loved art and it kept him out of the house that had been haunted one too many times for his comfort. Not that the house was haunted, but Gran always was.

Eve knew her parents felt the same about her, having prayed so hard for the cycle of hauntings to end once she was born, only to have her end up a more powerfully haunted creature than anyone in their respective bloodlines.

Arriving before her parents, Eve sought out her Grandmother in her library, a room towering floor to ceiling with books kept lovingly in exquisite glass cases. Evelyn had anticipated her, having already brought in tea and a plate of dates, one of Eve's favorite delights.

These quiet moments together before a lively meal were usual custom, as Eve nearly always had something that needed particular advising and today was no different. The moment the doors were closed behind them and Eve felt she had the freedom to ask pointed questions, she launched into what had been on her mind.

"Gran, what do you know about the Prenze family?"

Evelyn thought a moment, cocking her elegant head to the side, her silver hair coiffed in an immaculate sweep up to a braided bun and confined there by a spray of seed pearl pins. "Not much. I'd have to look up what industry they're in, how they made their name and fortune."

"Pharmaceuticals, if the sign at the chemist's shop was correct—Prenze Brothers. They were selling a tonic with helpings of piety on the side. But tonic could be anything these days. Just water in a fancy bottle," Eve stated. The rise of suspect 'cure-alls' was as ubiquitous as charlatan Spiritualists putting on magic acts and calling it a séance.

"The persuaded mind can be its own medicine," Gran mused. "If I recall correctly, the patriarchs are twin brothers who keep an ostentatious, nouveau riche sort of style. I think they're a few blocks away, south and west. I don't like the styles that scream of having something to prove. I believe they built near the Vanderbilts, in either admiration or competition—I tend not to care. I've seen them make the rounds of hosting things but I've not been to what they've offered; they seem particularly enamored of revolutionary history and that's just not my penchant. Why do you ask?"

"Received a warning not to trouble myself with them. A brute of an officer came directly into my office to intimidate my precinct. Which of course means I want to trouble myself a great deal."

"No one gives out warnings who doesn't have something to hide," Gran stated.

"Our sentiments precisely. I'm sure the department thinks women can be easily threatened. We were accused of meddling when I hadn't sent anyone in to do anything of the sort. At least, I didn't give any direct orders."

"What happened, though?"

"Vera was drawn in by a child and overturned a questionable photograph of the child, dead. Curious for the man to have had it, as it wasn't *his* relation. It seemed to have caused a ruckus. I just want to know why. And also, why we were so quickly blamed. I don't even know if what Vera related to me even was done in a Prenze house. She said it was a townhouse, so it couldn't have been their mansion, but perhaps a relative? She didn't know—she was too preoccupied with the events to check for names as per our Preventative Protocol."

"Unfortunately, if there is a ghost on the scene and something uncomfortable happens, if you are known to someone involved, you and yours will be blamed."

"I'm beginning to gather that . . ."

Gran thought a moment. Her lips drew into a pursed little smile. "Perhaps I'll go to one of the Prenze functions. They've one on Saturday, even. And you'll be sure to come with me. Your parents will be delighted you want to go out in society and they don't have to know it's scouting for work."

Eve grinned at this development. "I love you, you know."

"As well you should," she exclaimed, and the two laughed. "It will be good for me to be seen again too, I've been lax in making hypocrites squirm, and we can't let them get away with it for too long unquestioned."

It was a known fact that Evelyn Northe-Stewart had either started, been involved in, or was responsible for the continuation of many philanthropic and benevolent institutions since she was Eve's age. She had a charming way of guilting robber barons into offsetting various sins by direct action and monetary pledges.

Marie, one of the maids who had been with Evelyn the longest, poked her head in the door and bid them join the rest of the family, who had already been seated.

"Oh, goodness, and here we were just jabbering away . . ." Gran stated, rising to her feet.

"I know better than to interrupt two women talking about work," Marie murmured.

"And that is why you are beloved and appreciated beyond measure," Gran replied.

"Hello, Mother, Father, Grandad!" Eve exclaimed, gliding around the table to kiss each of them on the head before taking her seat opposite her father as dinner began.

They were hardly into their first course when Father, with a 'now, child, see here' look on his face—one Eve dreaded—caught her entirely off guard with something she'd feared her parents had been whispering about for weeks.

"There is a man I insist you meet, Eve," her father said, his tone amenable while his face was all seriousness. "A successful young man, well-placed, and I think you two would have a great deal in common. Perhaps a wonderful connection . . ."

She knew what this was. The wood-paneled walls of the beautiful dining room felt like they were about to close in on her. Her parents had been making hints. About courtship. Match-making. Setting her up. Marrying her off. Sealing her fate.

Eve's heart pounded and she felt as though she were going to panic. An obstacle. She had to throw something in the way. This was the worst timing for the imprisoning demands of society to close in on her. Deeply regretting that she hadn't expressed the magnitude of worry surrounding Maggie's disappearance, she suddenly felt a wave of anger at all the things her family preferences shackled her from discussing. She didn't care about a successful young man. Her best operative had vanished, among a host of other unfortunate things that required her attention, but she couldn't tell ghost stories at the dinner table . . .

And here they thought they knew what was best for her when they refused to see her for who she was. She was a woman of ghosts. Anyone who couldn't countenance that most basic fact . . .

"I'll be bringing him by to meet you this weekend," her father added.

Eve's mind spun. Something. It couldn't be this weekend, there was the Prenze function, and so much work to be done; all her loose ends as a patron saint . . .

Come up with something, she demanded of herself. *Someone.* She was already courting. Surely that would do the trick; to pause and to placate. She couldn't be seen courting multiple men; that would be unseemly!

"You will, will you?" Eve arched an eyebrow. "Well perhaps you'd like to know that I am already entertaining a suitor. We're professionals, both of us, so we haven't had time to make plans, but I'm not interested in being beset by multiple suitors and I've given him my first free calling hour. I have a *job* to do, you know, for the good of the city, so a suitable match hasn't been on my list of priorities."

Who was she lying about? Could she come up with a man she could stand? Evelyn was eyeing her. She knew Gran didn't believe a word of her excuse. Eve was thinking extemporaneously and Gran was the only one who knew all her tells. Bless that the woman remained silent.

It was her parents turn to raise eyebrows simultaneously, as if they'd choreographed it.

"You are *entertaining* a suitor, are you?" her father responded, leaning forward, his ice-blue eyes sharp. "Did you plan to mention courtship at any point? Do we not factor into any of your impetuous decisions? Or are you just trying to put us off the scent?"

Her father had begun trying to use policing metaphors lately, perhaps as a tactic for trust or simply understanding. Glancing over at her mother, Eve noted she just set her jaw and took to carving up her piece of chicken somewhat viciously.

"I'm mentioning this now!" Eve exclaimed. "The discussion only happened today, but I owe the detective a chance."

Horowitz. She was thinking of Horowitz, and she only realized it when the word *detective* left her lips.

"A detective?" Her mother frowned. "Isn't inter-office fraternization—"

"I don't know, I'm sure it's . . . well, I'll find out. It isn't as if he's in *my* precinct building, he's stationed out of Headquarters. One thing at a time. But I've no interest in any suitor, no matter how well-landed they are, who isn't engaged in the good solid work of making this world a better place. Since when has the aristocracy done the same?"

"Since *I* opened a clinic for the poor when I was younger than *you,* in London," her father said, making a motion to rise from the table. Eve's hands flew out in front of her.

"Of course, Father, I'm sorry, that was wrong of me," she said, earnestly contrite.

"And this man happens to have taken over my clinic in London," her father continued icily, "so don't make assumptions."

"Noted. But you know the subject of marrying me off is one I'm not fond of. I know you'd like me out of your hair entirely and to be someone else's responsibility . . ."

When Lord Denbury opened his mouth as if to protest, Eve continued gently, "It's true, I understand, and I want the best for the whole of our family. But come now, I'm hardly a spinster nearing twenty! I'll meet with those you wish, but not this weekend, please. The detective will come calling and I wouldn't want to be seen overextended with gentleman callers.

There's a limit to how much I can flirt," she said, and at this Grandpa laughed. It helped.

She had managed to ease the company and delay her doom. Gran didn't say a word, which Eve knew meant she'd get an earful later. But she had to break the news to Horowitz that she'd used him as a ruse. The idea that she wouldn't mind if he did come calling was something she buried at the bottom of her consciousness as if it were a file tucked in the back of a cabinet she didn't have a key to open.

Chapter Nine

The next day at the office Eve was terribly distracted. Mail had been brought in, and per Eve's request, it was stocked with all the publications having to do anything at all with Spiritualism, what could be considered 'the occult'—although Eve found most in this vein to be far too salacious and overblown—and any publication from the various Spiritualist societies that had cropped up after the advent of the Fox Sisters and their table rapping in upstate New York some fifty years prior.

At the top of the stack was W. T. Stead's *Borderland* magazine which had begun in England some six years prior, focusing on Spiritualism and Psychical research. Most of it amused Eve, as Mr. Stead was a bit more eccentric than was often helpful or convincing, but he had some sound points. The Society for Psychical Research as well as the British National Association of Spiritualists, extant for some seventeen years and now operating out of London, had taken on Spiritualism as somewhat of an export from New York, and Eve was interested in doing something different with her work than what she saw in these articles. Her book would be a long-standing compilation, giving the world not just scraps but complete stories from inception to fruition.

Most of these magazines read to Eve as desperate to believe, to prove, to be certain, and she just didn't trust 'authorities' claiming to have all the answers. The spirit world could not be pinpointed; it was ever changing and expanding. The fact that Eve had been able to so easily rely on several steadfast spirits had been a surprise. One she'd taken for granted, she realized, now that Maggie was gone without so much as a trace.

Something had to garner results, she hoped. The morning rounds had seen them try Susan Keller, Ingrid's aunt, but no one was home, just one sad spirit wafting up and down the block with nothing to say but how much she missed her husband. So back to the office it had been, and Eve now rifled through what to do next.

The idea of being on hand to attend a crime scene was a tempting one, and in case Horowitz forgot he had invited her on their return from the Foundling Hospital, perhaps she could fashion an excuse to just happen to be at headquarters to remind him. Not to mention telling him how he was being used.

Staring at her cabinets, Eve snapped her fingers and jumped up. Her own feelings might be locked away but so were her own cabinets. When she'd been given this room, she'd been promised for months that they'd be sent, but no keys had come, so she now decided to go down and get them herself, if they even existed. Yes, it was also an excuse to confess to the detective what he'd become and hope to goodness he was amenable.

There was commotion there at 300 Mulberry Street as Eve arrived—a lot of fuss and to-do around a jail cell on the main floor, an area that showcased an aggrandized Police history.

A man who looked vaguely familiar to Eve was inside the cell, handcuffed. He was handsome with dark, wavy hair that was cut neatly above his ears. He was in shirtsleeves and it was clear he was of a strong, athletic build. Photographers were at their camera stands with flashing apparatus, reporters were madly scribbling in notebooks, and sergeants and ranked officers were looking on, arms folded.

It took her a moment, but she remembered the man from a stage act she'd seen in Coney Island on a trip with her family to enjoy the beach last summer and see the amazing sights like the Elephant Hotel, rides, delights and shows. He'd done card tricks and magical acts. A rising star calling himself Houdini.

There was a billet sitting on a nearby desk that shed some light; picking it up, Eve read the proclamation:

IMPORTANT ANNOUNCEMENT
HARRY HOUDINI THE ESCAPOLOGIST
WILL ACCEPT CHALLENGES FOR EVERY EVENING DURING THIS CURRENT WEEK, AND ALSO WEDNESDAY MATINEE.
   THESE CHALLENGES WILL COME FROM VARIOUS SOURCES, EACH ONE DIFFERING FROM THE OTHERS.
   SEE THE DAILY PAPERS WHICH WILL ANNOUNCE EACH DAY THE TEST ACCEPTED FOR THE FOLLOWING DAY, AND ANNOUNCEMENTS OF THE SAME WILL BE MADE FROM THE STAGE. ALSO ON THE BULLETIN IN FRONT OF THEATRE. THOSE WISHING

TO CHALLENGE HOUDINI MUST BEAR IN MIND THAT HE CAN ONLY ACCEPT ONE TEST AT EVERY PERFORMANCE.

And today's Challenge was just about to commence as a group of officers joked together at the fore of the assembled group.

Eve felt this must be a ploy to increase funding for the city prison system, as she felt confident he could easily escape this old cell and the cuffs they put him in. She'd seen the papers and these announcements before; the man always escaped.

The man was soon out of what he'd been constrained in, releasing himself from chains around his ankles. Before long, he had undone the padlock on the jail cell and swung open the door, stepping forward with a bow and flourish to applause and more photography.

The man had an intensity about him that was searing, captivating, and the spirit world was murmuring about him. No spirit directly manifested before Eve, but she could hear spectral whispers about how important he was and how famous he might become.

What he longs to escape most from is the certainty of death . . . came one spirit voice.

Another joined in. *He seeks out eternal truths, never satisfied with the vagaries . . . He wants to know us and yet is terrified to acknowledge us in turn.*

Another voice cooed. *Beautiful paradox.*

In Eve's experience the spirit world didn't always weigh in on a person directly without being asked. That they were so forthcoming was telling.

Houdini was chatting with the sergeant overseeing the stunt, and she overheard him ask if he might keep the manacles as a trophy that he'd put on display outside of his theatre. As he put on a simple suit-coat over his shirtsleeves, the compelling performer glanced over and caught Eve's eye. Something about the look of her must have given him pause, for she arrested him somehow, and before long he made his way towards her.

"And what did you think, Miss?" he asked, glancing at her dress uniform. "Are you with the department?"

"I am, and I thought this was quite impressive. This stunt will likely be put forward as a need for better equipment from the city coffers and I hope it is beneficial for all involved."

"Your expression is as though you can't quite believe what you saw, or perhaps don't believe it at all, or think that it is entirely staged. I assure you, I was locked in."

"Are you not a magician? Is suspension of disbelief not your specialty?"

He smiled. "Escaping can be a bit different from magic. Different sets of skills will mean that my audience isn't being deceived in the same way. Everyone is willing to be deceived a bit; how much—gauging that balance—is half the trick."

"Ah," Eve smiled. "Here I pause at deception. In my line of work there are many impostors who try to make audiences believe they are more talented than they are, their results more meaningful, and they are pretending at things that are in fact quite sacred. I don't like for the grieving or the desperate to be taken advantage of, turning the sacred to sacrilege."

"In your . . . line of work?" He leaned in, having hung on her words.

Looking around, no one seemed concerned that they were talking. Everyone was occupied for this small moment, and Eve decided she would dare speak truth to this burgeoning star. "Believe it or not, I am a medium who works with other mediums," Eve explained, "alongside a small group of faithful spirits who help us help those in need and try to lend aid in what remains unsolved."

Here the magician's eyes went wide, taking on an almost hungry tone. "Really?"

"Yes, and the wealth of faux mediums, of charlatans who are really just stage magicians, no offense, means none of us can really be taken seriously. I'm sure you can empathize."

"I . . . well . . . I am not sure I can believe you, but I want to." He took a step forward. "I want to believe."

"I am heartened to hear it. I plan to publish a future book on my experiences in the department, to not only offer concrete proof, but the myriad ways in which spirits can be of service, out into the world. Ghosts are a help, not a horror."

"That is honorable and an improvement on texts that do exist. I try to familiarize myself with all that are out there. Lots of esoterica and theorizing, very little practical application."

"I don't blame anyone for not being able to distinguish fact from fiction or legitimacy from spectacle."

Houdini put a hand to his chiseled jaw, furrowing his brow, and leaned towards her as if he were about to ask if she could keep a great secret.

"Do you think, Miss," he began carefully, "it would behoove the world to have these magicians exposed as exactly that? Magicians, not seers? To let the world know?"

"Would that not be breaking a certain code, an oath as a fellow magician?"

"But they're not advertising themselves as such!" Houdini exclaimed, jumping back so that he didn't yell in her face. Some officers turned to them with raised eyebrows and turned back away, muttering about theatre people.

Houdini continued in a quieter tone, unfolding a new idea. "Perhaps I could be a mitigating force, letting an audience understand what they're in for, not duped in a way they wouldn't want. There's a sort of motto, for magicians: *Mundus vult decipi, ergo decipiatur.* That Latin translated means: "The world wants to be deceived, so let it be deceived." But there are limits to that, a decency in our profession. I want to believe in something so unknowable and, dare I say, sacred as the beyond; I don't want to be deceived about that." His eyes flashed, the truth of his sentiment was undoubtedly sincere. "Not about that."

"I would support you in whatever venture you would undertake in that regard, provided it does no one any harm," Eve offered.

"We must speak further, after my next tour," the escapologist said excitedly. "I'll be soon going to England. After that—"

Just then a large man in a suit stepped nearly between them. "Mister Houdini, sir, we have to get you to your next engagement," the handler said, eying Eve with suspicion.

"Forgive me," Eve said, looking at both men apologetically. "I didn't mean to keep you."

Houdini stepped around the handler, who folded his arms. "It was I who wanted your opinion, and I am left intrigued, Miss . . ."

"Whitby. Eve Whitby. Greenwich Ghost Precinct if you need me or want to know more about what we do. Come by any time."

"I do, I will, thank you."

"Good luck on your tour, you're good at what you do," she stated. He bowed his head and walked away. The handler frowned at her and she simply smiled.

If Eve, during her work, could gain the trust or at least endorsement from someone in the magical community like Houdini, her book, once compiled, might have a greater impact. And her work here might be more respected, at least by those willing to differentiate her from charlatans. She hoped they could speak further on the true justice and consummate wonder of the spirit world at some point. She thought he could be a good advocate, in ways she might not even know. The manager trundled Houdini off despite other officers trying to catch him and ask for autographs, but he glanced back at her as if to affirm these hopes.

Eve was left for a moment in the bustle of the department before reminding herself why she'd come. Keys. Keys to unlock what had been closed to her. The day was becoming themed. She wondered what else she would need access to.

A suitor. Yes. That too. How had she nearly forgotten that? She felt a blush threaten to overtake her face again; a violently rosy usurper of her otherwise vaguely sickly complexion.

She hadn't forgotten it in the least. What she was, clearly, was nervous. She didn't know how to bring it up, what Horowitz would say, or if this would jeopardize having him as a liaison. Clearly there would be a bias and they'd have to be secretive, which was in its own way far more interesting . . . Her cheeks were now scarlet and she wasn't even near his office.

The spirit world was chattering at her ear, gossipy and banal.

Hopefully Horowitz was in his office and hopefully he'd be amenable to a ruse. Upon inquiry on the upper floor she was seen into his rear office, the both of them relegated to dim, background spaces.

"Detective, I've a proposition for you," Eve declared, knocking on his door and entering it without awaiting permission. Horowitz looked up from a white piece of silk at his desk.

"Oh, what's that?" she asked, coming around the side.

"This ascot reeks of camphor which is ostensibly masking a more distinct undercurrent beneath. It was recovered from Mr. Font's body, which had been undressed and in the morgue."

"Oh?"

"Your colleagues said 'drowned'. His jacket, everything, reeked of this, as if he'd been doused in it. I took this to one of my dear friends, Mr. Liang Lee, a doctor whose practice is just north of Chinatown—he's a bit of a genius with toxicology. He thinks whatever tonic was found empty in his breast-pocket was in fact poison. Either willingly ingested as an intoxicant, perhaps to the point of suicide, or forced. That I can't tell, and Lee still has that bottle in study. But what I can say is that your séance helped crack this open and lend credence to what the cousin said about his being scared for his life. It's a whole new direction."

He brushed a lock of brown hair from his forehead, looking up at her openly and eagerly. This expression, in this gentle light, affected Eve as quite enchanting, and she felt her face flush a bit.

"The spirit world merely amplifies what should be obvious or already found. Were you able to get into the room?"

"I was. And the faint scent here was indeed all over the carpet, I just had to lean close to be sure. But it was all around the center of the floor where his body lay. As if he'd drowned in it. I can now open a wider case. I will credit your precinct's assistance."

"As you wish. I don't need the credit, I just want to be left alone by those who would grind axes," Eve said. "Being a medium is what I was born for."

There was a silence as they stared at one another again.

"Miss Whitby," Horowitz prompted with a smile, "didn't you barge in here saying something about a proposition?"

"Ah. Yes. That. Well . . . may I sit?" Eve gestured to a stool near the wall. Horowitz jumped up as she was going for it. "Oh, of course, allow me, I'm sorry—"

As they both went for the seat, their hands brushed and Eve nearly whipped hers back, and they both apologized, then laughed nervously.

She sat across from his desk as he returned to his side, shifting his work lamp to cast more equitable light between them. Glancing around, Eve was thankful that no one else was in his workspace.

"Do you ever . . ." Eve began, her nerves mounting. "Have you experienced your parents, perhaps . . . pressuring you about anything? In regards to your . . . future. Your . . . prospects? Do they have expectations of you?"

"Yes . . ." Horowitz replied warily. "Why?"

Eve took a deep breath and her proclamation came out in an inelegant torrent.

"My parents harangued me with pressure of a suitor last night. So I told them we were courting. Or . . . courting the *idea* of courting . . . I needed something to distract and put them off guard—don't worry, I didn't mean anything by it."

Horowitz's brown eyes widened. "You . . . told your family . . . your *titled* family . . . that we were *courting*?"

"Yes, I had to think of something and as I'd like to think we're friends, this can perhaps buy us an indefinite amount of time, you see . . ." Eve was trying to make all of this sound perfectly normal, convenient—brilliant, even. It had been in her head. But the man's surprise and evident nerves had her questioning herself and wondering if she'd just made the most terrible mistake.

"You know," Eve began in a genial ramble, "I hadn't really thought about the titled thing being any sort of complication; I mean, I don't give a whit my father is a Lord, it isn't like he inherited Royal sums—he'd been cheated out of all of it anyway and nothing's left, we're a regular, merchant-class family—"

"Do they know I'm Jewish?" he asked in almost a gasp.

"My family is an open-minded clan who love people of *all* faiths!" Eve protested earnestly. "I understand you may be suspicious, but in my family's circle, and in Spiritualist company, there's a broad range of understanding and alliance. My mother's best friend growing up was Jewish, and a Horowitz even, Rachel Horowitz. A medium, no less."

"Ah, yes, the 'I have a Jewish friend' response," he said, eyeing her. Then something shifted on his face.

"Rachel Horowitz?" The detective raised his eyebrows. "She doesn't happen to be deaf, does she?"

"That would be her." Eve rocked back a bit. "Are you related?"

"Second cousin." Horowitz leaned forward, excited. "Is your family still in touch with her? We had no idea what happened to her!"

"We are! She is a practitioner of the spiritual arts in Chicago and writes us often! See what we've discovered together? Old family and friends brought back together by fate! You're all the more perfect for playing the role of suitor!" Eve exclaimed, choosing a jovial affectation to hide the clench and twist in her stomach at the word 'suitor' attached to the man she was finding more and more pleasing with every meeting.

Horowitz tried to chuckle but it sounded more like a groan. "Be that as it may, all delightful happenstance aside, shouldn't you have asked for my . . . *participation* in a ruse before wrapping me up in your family drama?"

"Yes." Eve felt suitably chastened, her nerves roiling. "Yes, I should have. I am very sorry." She looked down at her hands, clasping them together lest he see them shaking. "Detective, please. I can't possibly be courted now, not when I've just got my work up and running . . . I *can't* have my life decided for me, I have to be the mistress of my own fate . . ."

The detective began a chuckle, quiet then bubbling up into an uproarious laugh.

"What?" Eve asked sheepishly.

The detective grinned at her. "I don't know anyone like you, Miss Whitby."

"I am a bit odd," Eve confessed.

"And I think what you've done is brilliant."

"You . . . do?" She eyed him.

"Yes. Because I'd be lying if I said my family wasn't giving me the same sort of nonsense as yours."

"So . . . you will? Be mine? I mean—in a—"

He smiled as she stammered and relieved her with a reply; "I will be your willing ruse and you mine, Miss Whitby."

"Thank you!" Eve presented her hand for a handshake.

The two shook on it and Eve turned away to hide scarlet cheeks. Horowitz clearing his throat was evidence of the awkwardness. That there was an undeniable draw between them made this equal parts hazardous and utterly, unexpectedly delicious. Eve returned her chair to its place at the wall.

"Well then, now that that's settled, Detective, I am in your debt. And I'm sorry for any discomfort—"

"You'll feel plenty of discomfort all for yourself if I ever invite you over for dinner. We're of the Reform tradition, and that allows for broader interpretation of law and practice, but still. Mother has always been terrified I'd take up with someone like you."

Eve cocked her head. "There's a term for courting a woman who isn't Jewish, right? *Shiksa*, is it?"

Horowitz burst into an even heartier laugh. "You're an attentive New Yorker to have picked that up. I may have fun with this. Father won't care, he's essentially an atheist but Mother . . ." He chuckled. "I like keeping my parents on edge. They think they have my life all planned and ruled out for me."

Eve nodded. "My parents wish they could corral me, but how haunted I am gives them pause. At least now, I hope, they'll stop badgering me about my abandoning every aspect of an average woman." She rolled her eyes. "I hope."

"How much time does this buy us?" he asked, musing. "When will they push for an engagement, and when will they insist on meeting your suitor?"

"Cross those bridges when we come to them! Ah. I've an idea and an invitation. The Prenze soiree on Saturday."

"Isn't that the family involved in the recent complaint? The one you were *expressly* told to stay away from?"

"The very one. Lodged on their behalf. Not sure they were the ones to actually lodge it, might have just been Mahoney trying to stir up trouble. My Grandmother, Evelyn Northe-Stewart, has standing invitations to every city soiree. If you come, it may prove informative." Eve pointed to Dr. Font's odorous scarf. "Not to mention the Prenze fortune is made in tonics. That could have been one of them the poor man was drenched in. Gran will escort us, if you're game."

Eve thought a moment and added. "The event should begin just after sundown, so it wouldn't interfere with Shabbat." When the detective raised his eyebrows in surprise, she explained. "We would sit with Rachel when she came to visit, she let me light the candles sometimes too."

"I appreciate your consideration," he said. "I am indeed game for the soiree."

They shared a smile. Mischievous. Definitely dangerous.

Eve bobbed slightly, turning away before she felt or revealed anything. While in the past few years she had begun to refine and enjoy the fine art of flirting; anything that might come *after* that she was petrified about. All she could commit to were the dead. Whatever would the ghosts say about a romance, even a feigned one to get parents off their backs?

Soon, Eve thought, they'd have to dance at a ball. A shudder that had nothing to do with spirits coursed down her spine.

* * * *

That night, there was another séance in the house with her colleagues. They'd keep trying until something broke through. Vague tatters of phrases. While Eve wrote everything down, she still couldn't make sense out of the chaos, there was no pattern in the noise. Only another bid not to *let anything in.*

Eve wondered to herself if they meant her heart.

Chapter Ten

Eve was not particularly fond of dressing up, save for the times work demanded it. But in those cases, she loved it. It was like taking on a role, playing a part . . . She supposed she'd gained a penchant for dramatics from friends of the family, the Veils, who put on Gothic shows around the world. It was on their advice that she'd revamped her entire wardrobe into mourning on account of her calling. But Gran's connections allowed her to dabble in society as she wished, and there were a few sumptuous ball-gowns she needed a good excuse to wear.

What would Horowitz think of the evening ahead? Would he feel out of place, coming from a distinctly academic, highly educated family disinterested in the social spheres, or would he, as she hoped, find it a fascinating sociological opportunity to gather data? If they were going to make their new 'partnership' work, it would have to be enjoyable and productive.

Eve was alone in her half of the joined townhouses, her housemates having taken the evening to go see a theatrical performance. She liked having moments of quiet, despite spirits passing through with their constant murmurs. She readied herself in silence, choosing to focus on the faint sounds of New York itself, a soft symphony past closed doors.

Ever since she was a child she felt New York had spoken to her as a stream-of-consciousness character, a murmuring sort of nursemaid storyteller, telling her about life and all its joys and pains in textures and layered noises, some immediately discernable, some unfolding through time.

Today New York was telling the story of going places, the clip of horse-hooves on cobblestones and the distant metal pitch of rails, the above-ground lines and the engines along the riverfront. With this story it was good that she was going out into the world.

The spirit of the former lady of the house wafted through the room. She never spoke. Eve deemed her a visible memory, the house remembering its mistress for itself, a bond having been created between her living energy and its inanimate bricks. The apparition wasn't concerned with the goings-on of the living and she never interacted with Eve, just passed through in a black, jet-beaded mourning dress that faded into mist at the skirt. It wasn't just people who did the haunting—buildings and spaces had memories too, and sometimes projected them briefly into the world, as a part of an unending routine trapped in time.

Time. When placing oneself in finery, it always took more time than Eve usually gave the practice. She opened her tall armoire with a wince, as it squeaked on its hinges from lack of use and a bit of dust flew into the air.

Thanks to her family's interest in seeing her married off well, they'd invested in a set of evening gowns, each year altering them slightly to fashion's dictates. The choice was easy: a deep purple satin gown her mother had just recently complained that she'd never seen her in. It hung from a cloth-wrapped hanger whose interior lavender buds had long since lost their fragrant potency.

This gown was an easier one to manage; she slipped it over her head, then adjusted and clasped the satin shell, crepe and beads falling into graceful place. She stared in the mirror and smiled. It was nice, every now and then, to be fancy.

When so many in the city had nothing, she took time to appreciate her circumstances. She could never look at a fine dress and not think of the city's most ragged. From an early age, the storyteller New York had murmured of its deep and aching contrasts.

She rushed to her writing desk and made a note for her family's banker to deliver the deposit of her next paycheck to one of Gran's mutual aid societies helping keep families above water. It was the only thing that made her able to look at herself in the mirror again. The fact that so many who lived so well never gave their position a second thought made her heart heavy, and she prayed for their souls to understand generosity and appreciation for blessings they ought not take for granted.

Eve turned to look at the bustle of her dress, which was minimal—more of a gathered train—and she made a slow circle to make sure the fabric trailing from the shoulders had settled into the right falls. It had been made by some designer, Worth House or something like it—Gran would know, she'd had it done for her. An expensive evening gown could make

Eve feel like an object; ornamentation not meant for general usefulness. But she realized this was unfair to women like Gran, who had done so much from within her 'traditional' place, and all in fine gowns, no less. Gran was always mitigating her family's expectations for Eve, and Eve didn't know what she'd do without her. It wasn't that she minded the idea of companionship or a family, she just knew her duty at the moment was to the spirits. It was nice that Horowitz was perhaps of a similar nature to hers, and what an incredible group of partners she had assembled in trying to keep her life purposeful and her sanity maintained.

All this was to say, she was very nervous. Days when she would be thrust into "society" always made her mind race, making her think of her place in the world, what the Heavens expected of her. No amount of esoterica, however, was going to pin her hair up for her.

The thick, dark hair she'd inherited as a combination of her father's raven hair and her mother's auburn locks was easy to twist and pin into a bun atop her head and make look as if she'd spent time on it. The marcasite hair accent she placed at the base of her coiffure; the silver cut mineral faceted like a gemstone and set into a wide comb was specifically chosen because Eve didn't like the gaudy glitz of diamonds or other gemstones but loved the slate grey; 'the luster of the ghosts' as she had once described it.

Around her neck she clasped an amethyst pendant in a matching marcasite setting. 'Amethyst, for peace and healing' Gran had said when she placed it around her neck on her thirteenth birthday. Securing matching teardrop earrings, her own fingers brushed her cheek and she was equally horrified and fascinated to imagine Horowitz's fingertips doing the same absent-minded caress.

"A *ruse,* this is a ruse," she demanded of herself. "So don't you go falling for the actor," she admonished in a heated murmur. Perhaps her artifice was its own trap; her heart acting out the act because it was mere fancy. She'd have been a terrible actor, unable to leave the theatrics on the stage. The play, she had to admit, was titillating in and of itself.

She dashed a bit of violet perfume along her neck and wrists. Violet flower was one of her earliest scent memories; when a lovely young ghost had trailed through her nursery and spent time playing hide and seek with her one afternoon, the spirit had borne the scent on the breeze and Eve had never forgotten it. The violet ghost never returned with another olfactory haunting, but the smell had been her favorite ever after. It was an early lesson to Eve: enjoy the moments you have with the dead, for you may never see them again.

The memory of that lost childhood ghost had her heart aching for Maggie. She'd never not say goodbye, traumatizing her living loved ones . . . Eve shook her head, rushing back into action. A capelet, a drawstring bag for little toiletries, a few bills tucked into her bodice, and a notebook and small pen—as no operative worth their salt traveled without the means to write notes—and she was nearly ready.

Sweeping down her staircase, enjoying the drama of the train, Eve lifted the gargoyle-headed doorknocker and let it go, creating an echoing boom on the hefty wooden door that had been put in to connect her home to that of her parents. Her mother let her in, and closed the door behind her quickly, as if a ghost would slip through if she left it open. That was in fact a distinct probability, even though Sensitives had warded the door against them.

Eve now stood in the central hallway of the main Denbury townhouse, which led to a grand staircase on one side, the front door on the other, and a little rounded foyer with rooms edging off of it—parlor and dining room, everything furnished in warm rosewoods and pale satin colors, with an airy palette diametrically contrasting the richer, heavier tones on her side.

"See?" she said triumphantly, opening the silk capelet to reveal the dress.

"Look at you, out of black and into something livelier for a change. And purple, no less!" her mother exclaimed.

"When Gran insisted I choose a color, I wanted to choose your favorite."

"It is indeed my favorite," her mother said with a smile, her green eyes lighting up. "And you wear it beautifully. Is there a particular interest in the Prenze family that has you out on this crisp night?"

Eve knew they were asking because this was outside of any of her social norms. She leaned in. "Do you really want to know?"

Mother turned to Father, who had stepped into the room to greet her. "Do we really want to know?"

"If she asks us that, you know it's about the ghosts, so I defer to you, dear," her father said quietly. Eve held up her hands, absolving herself of any responsibility should they be made uncomfortable. "You do look lovely, though, Eve, dear," he added. "Belle of the ball I'm sure."

"Say it, then," her mother prompted with exasperation.

"Our department was told to stay away from the family, that there had been 'spectral intrusion' when I had ordered no such thing. I want to see why they're defensive." When her mother opened her mouth, Eve anticipated her. "I'll be careful. They are of a certain social status. So is Gran. Nothing will be strange. Paths will cross. I hope to navigate the department that much more safely. No good comes from hiding one's head in the sand, you know that."

Her mother's lips thinned, but the expression on her face showed that she couldn't contradict her own advice. It wasn't that Eve's parents had ever wanted her to lie about the fact that spirits ruled her stars; they just wished the paranormal had at least skipped a generation. To give them all a longer respite away from something they'd never asked for. In her early life, Eve had not appreciated the pain of it. Only Gran could fully navigate the tension, and thankfully her arrival had cured all. Having let herself into the house, she exclaimed at the sight of Eve.

"Ah," Gran cooed, "you wore the House of Worth!" She kissed Eve on the head and moved to embrace her step-daughter.

"That's it," Eve muttered. "I was trying to remember who I was wearing."

"I would have thought," Gran began in a chastising tone, "considering you now serve the city in the de facto capacity of a detective, that you'd have a better mind for such details, noting every class in which you might find yourself moving in. Besides, they are the very best designers and I confess to loving a gorgeous gown as much as anything. Call me trivial." At this, Eve laughed and Gran gestured to the door.

"Let me take her off your hands. I promise to keep an eye out for promising suitors, the one she already has notwithstanding," Gran assured, and when Eve noticed how her parents lit up at this, Gran simply patted Eve on the hand as if there was nothing in the world to worry about.

Eve kissed her parents each on the cheek and they followed her to the front door. Outside, she again allowed herself a moment of grandeur descending the stoop in her gown before the heel of her nicest pair of shoes—some impractical, satin-covered concoction—nearly caught in one of her modest trains. A near tumble down the steps humbled her from any grander notions.

A few familiar ghosts whose spectral forms remained forever in their finest regalia swept up to her, drawn by her finery, and chattered away about their favorite moments from balls long gone and suitors long dead; a sudden, sentimental cacophony. Eve turned to all of them and offered a smile and a little curtsey, which seemed to content them. The burst of spectral onslaught faded, the knot of spirits wafting down the lane to haunt the edges of Central Park, still murmuring about stolen kisses. Eve allowed herself to enjoy their explosive sentiment, letting it kindle a fondness within her.

That's what she wanted the world to understand about spirits; they told you more about life than death. They were a constant reminder to appreciate it, every moment you could.

Once seated in Gran's carriage it would be a quick drive to the event. When Eve had suggested they simply walk the avenue and several blocks, Gran had taken one look at her fancy shoes, and Eve relented.

"Detective Horowitz agreed to meet me at the event. As social foundation, assurance and chaperone, Gran, can we wait for him at the entrance? I suppose I should have asked if that was all right before inviting him," Eve said rather sheepishly.

Gran chuckled. "The moment you said you had a 'suitor' I was prepared for any contingency."

Eve smiled. "You're the best friend anyone could ever ask for."

"It's my calling," Gran said, returning the smile. She thought a moment and the smile turned slightly worried. "Do you two intend to go searching the house?"

"As tempting as that might be, I think it highly unwise. I think instinct, and the whisper of spirits, will give us plenty to work with for now, lest my department receive another complaint."

Pulling up, there was a carriage ahead of them and they stared out the window at the property. It was a large white granite block of a building with golden metal details, ornate cornice pieces, and another rectangular extension of large garden grounds on either side. Tightly trimmed hedges with topiaries poked up from the hedgerows, and the top of what looked like a huge golden gazebo, with open lattice-work more like the top of an enormous bird-cage, could be seen at the rear of the complex.

"Well, it's a . . . statement, this place," Eve said. The carriage path cleared and their cab rolled ahead as the next to alight.

"The whole property feels like an elaborate series of traps," Gran muttered. "The walled garden, that outside cage affair, this portico—look, the stones in the arch are like teeth, a mouth ready to swallow guests . . ."

Gran's driver, a lovely man named John, helped them both out and whistled at the property. "I know it's not quite your style, ma'am, but it's something else."

"It's something else all right," Gran said with a little chuckle.

"Be back 'round by eleven?"

"Ten," Eve stated. The idea of being in that gilded box for hours made her feel ill.

"I'll be ready by ten, take whatever time you need. It's good to see you out socializing and not just working, Miss Whitby," John said, bowing his head.

"Oh, I'm working," she countered quietly. "That's the only reason I'm here. But don't tell them that," Eve nodded towards the house. "I'm here *incognito.*"

John laughed. "At least you all keep life interesting," he said, climbing atop his perch and driving off.

From under the portico maw, a raised portcullis gate with golden spikes hovering over them like waiting fangs, they ascended the few steps to the front door landing.

Once inside, a few guests in the wide entrance foyer were fussing with cloaks and capelets, handing them over to a footman dressed to the nines in livery.

"There's a young man who will be here on my invitation," Gran stated to the footman. "Should we simply wait for him here? I don't want to be in anyone's way, but I don't want any lost lambs."

Just as she said this, there was a tentative but familiar voice calling out from the shadows beyond the threshold of the open door, part of a head peeking in.

"Hello there, sorry if you're waiting for me!"

Stepping into the bright electric light of the stone shelter was the detective, his mop of curly brown hair tamed a bit, but not entirely. He was in a very fine black suit with a royal blue waistcoat, a small white rosebud in his lapel. Dashing, Eve had to admit. There was something about dressing up that had the capability to create magic and possibility.

"*Well,*" Gran murmured approvingly.

"Ah, the man of the hour," Eve declared as his warm brown eyes edged in blue flicked from her to Gran and he smiled a wide, dazzling smile. It's as if he knew he needed to play his role as charming gentleman and had stepped into it with ease. "Gran, may I introduce you to Mr. Horowitz, who has become a truly valuable asset to me and mine."

"Jacob Horowitz, at your service, madam," he declared, bowing slightly before holding out his hand. Gran gave hers. "I've heard you're the cleverest and the most important woman on the planet. I look forward to saying the same from personal experience."

Gran laughed. "Flattery, even before anyone's had a glass of champagne— what a lovely night so far. Come, let's have our cloaks taken up," Gran gestured to the waiting footman.

"I'm sorry I'm late," the detective murmured to Eve, his cheeks coloring scarlet. "Mother made a bit of a scene over me."

Gran graciously involved herself with talking to another lady she recognized. By the way they spoke of dogs and a Reverend it was clear they knew one another from Reverend Blessing's ASPCA events. The Reverend, one of Gran's best friends was an ardent rescuer of animals. It was lovely that Gran knew everyone, it was lovelier still that Gran knew everyone from *doing* amazing things.

"Mother was so overjoyed at the idea of my going to meet someone," Horowitz explained, still in a whisper, "well, to be specific, a *girl*, that she insisted, last minute, on a new suit. I didn't have the heart to tell her you weren't Jewish, she might have made me return it."

Eve chuckled. "Well, it's a very nice suit," she offered.

"Thanks," he said, trying to adjust the stiff collar with a grimace, to no avail. "But I can't move."

"That makes two of us," Eve said, gesturing to her own trappings.

"Well, it's a very nice gown," the detective offered in turn.

"Here we are, in the nicest of things, longing for shirtsleeves."

"You're telling me," he exclaimed. "And the ability to breathe."

"You're telling *me*," Eve countered, patting the doubled layers of boning and stiff satin. "I'm in the corset."

Horowitz shook his head. "I don't know how you ladies do it."

"I don't, usually. Thank goodness for modern times and dress reform."

"Agreed." Horowitz gestured ahead of him. "For this set, dressing like this is a uniform, part of their job. I don't envy it."

"And they don't envy us; keeping the distinction of classes comfortably each at their own level, not at one another's throats. I suppose we're a fine example of capitalism at its most gracious."

At this, Horowitz laughed a little too loudly. Everyone in the entrance foyer turned. Horowitz turned too, as if looking at someone behind him. Eve bit her tongue to hold in a guffaw.

"Come on, you two, into the fray," Gran said gently and the trio stepped forward.

Another liveried gentleman was checking guest names and Eve let Gran do all the talking. What was and wasn't acceptable Eve didn't dare presume; she didn't have the social intricacies to fathom it. While Gran didn't know the Prenze family personally, one of their relatives had insisted that any function that crossed Gran's notice was open under her name, and to lean on her association with the Metropolitan Museum of Art. This seemed to do the trick and they were allowed to pass into another reception area, an empty room with a marble floor and a reproduction of part of the Sistine chapel painted along the walls, with extra gilding added onto the paint. In this square room a few people stood milling and chatting, glancing around for others they knew.

A stream of people were progressing down another hall beyond the painted anteroom, towards music in the distance. They followed. Wooden pocket doors with golden inlay led to rooms off the main corridor, but all were shut. Small decorative tables were inset along the corridor, each one sporting a grand urn-like vase in 18th century French style that was positively tumbling with fragrant lilies. "Smells like a funeral," Gran murmured in Eve's ear, and she again bit her tongue so as not to bark a laugh, her tongue now sore from decorum. The hallway felt as long as a city avenue.

Everyone's shoes clicked and echoed along white, polished marble. The walls of the hall were painted light blue; everything was airy and brightly colored. Yet the feeling of such a large, long space still seemed so tight, narrow and confined; antithetical.

Their trio entered the ballroom and drank it in.

It was the very epitome of the *nouveau riche* that the old aristocracy abhorred. Gaudy and overblown, trying to make a statement not by saying something but by shouting it.

Everything was gilded, there were fountains at each corner hewn from marble, and electric light blazed from seashell sconces, illuminating a dome above them littered with hanging chandeliers of innumerable crystals along the circumference and a ceiling painted to be a blue sky with a golden sun at the epicenter.

The ballroom floor itself was marble, a theme through the house, but not the best choice for dancing; it made everyone too careful and there was no bounce to it, no give, making movement hard and stiff, not to mention noisy, as if it was all for show with no thought about the enjoyment of it.

A cluster of men in tailcoats were near one of the recesses of the ballroom, an inset dais of golden-backed, velvet covered chairs from which one figure stood. Eve followed Horowitz's eyes as they widened.

The most arresting woman Eve had ever seen descended from the dais with a laugh, her gaggle of admirers following her. A stunning flame-haired redhead, with hair so bright as to be nearly copper, her eyes were wide and crystalline, and her mouth a pink bow of a smile. She was dressed in what appeared to be a white Regency gown, with a length of sky blue crepe hanging from lithe arms. She wasn't clothed remotely in the style of recent fashion, but appeared to have stepped out of some costumed drama and Eve wondered if everyone had missed an instruction to appear in clothing from long ago.

It was obvious that everyone was murmuring about her as a centerpiece of the event. Eve glanced at an enormous portrait hanging at the back of the ballroom, and she understood this woman must be part of the family with her uncanny resemblance to the couple who stood painted in Regency finery, to which her dress was an homage.

Eve found herself moving towards the center of the room, almost unconsciously, as if everyone who looked at this woman was immediately magnetized and drawn into her orbit, when she caught sight of an unfortunate figure by the wall and paused.

Horowitz, at her side, followed her eyes and groaned. "Mahoney."

"After the complaint about this family I can't imagine he'll like seeing me here, so let's try not to be seen," Eve stated.

He was standing in a fine suit, arms folded over his barrel chest, his thinning hair swept back from his bulldog-jowled face, a frown drooping down below his bushy mustache. His eyes were affixed, as nearly all were, to the beauteous lady of the house.

This gave her cover to find Gran, who had taken up a gilded chair not far from the punch table. Her sitting there, as if on a throne, was its own breathtaking moment for Eve, looking at this regal creature in her saffron gown, like a ray of elder sunlight descending from the painted sky, there to illuminate them all with wisdom and wit. Though Eve wondered a moment about her needing to sit. In earlier years she likely would have been one of the first on the dance floor, regardless of the surface, there to shine radiant beams and catch everyone up in her glow.

Gran's eyes flicked behind Eve and as the three of them were close enough, Gran murmured, "Quite the family."

Eve turned to see the beautiful woman talking to a lanky, lean man who shared that same orange-flame hair, save his was streaked with bands of white at each temple. An elder brother.

"Do you have any sort of read on them?" Eve asked, taking in the tall, thin, mustached man. He was speaking animatedly to a group of about six guests who stared at him rapturously, and the arrival of his sister only magnified the effect.

"He's got a bit of thrall," Gran murmured. Additional movement caught Eve's eye.

"Oh, no, here comes a bit of trouble," Eve muttered. "Gran, I'll need your help on this. Mahoney is one of our chief critics."

At this, Gran stood and Eve was reminded just how towering she was—not just tall, but statuesque in her power.

The man approached them, his drooping scowl seemingly affixed to his face at rest. Evelyn stepped forward as if to defend Eve, but armed with an effervescent smile, and the parties kept a comfortable distance of a few feet while the music changed to a different baroque tune, something old-fashioned and courtly, matching the gilded, dated decor.

"Miss Whitby, Mrs. Northe-Stewart," Sergeant Mahoney bobbed his head. He turned to Horowitz. "Detective? What are you doing here?"

"The Horowitz family has been a long-time friend of our family," Gran stated, and Eve was grateful for the connection to her mother's school friend Rachel. "I've been telling the detective he needs to appreciate the finer things in life, a pastime this family so clearly delights in."

"I do hope you're simply here in the service of high society," he grumbled, choosing to address only the elder Evelyn.

"Oh, of course, why else would anyone attend a ball? Are you a relative or the hired help here this evening?" Evelyn asked pointedly.

Eve kept her face neutral but was surprised by Gran's directness. Her position, age and wealth afforded her this ability. Eve would hardly be given such breadth. Mahoney's jaw clenched.

"I believe in this family's philanthropic work."

"And just what all does that work entail? Usually the people in my sphere are very public about it, carving their names into cornerstones and naming institutions after themselves."

"And this family just so happens to be private about it. More godly, don't you think, to be private about one's service?"

"So you know nothing about it?"

"I know that Mister Prenze is a reformer to those who have sin in their hearts and minds. Those who are restless and seeking. He's saved lives and souls. After a family loss, the only succor is prayer." He spoke with such certainty Eve felt clear he was speaking for himself and some tragedy he personally sustained.

"Well that sounds very fine of him," Gran offered. "And I'm terribly sorry to hear of a loss."

The sergeant's eyes widened. "I'd have thought everyone in high society knew about the death of the Prenze twin."

"Ah, that's right," Gran exclaimed, clucking her tongue. "I'm terribly sorry, how rude of me. I do remember reading about that, my memory isn't what it used to be!" She shook her head. Eve wasn't sure if that was true or not. There were games one played in conversations in places like this. "I don't believe we've ever been introduced to Mr. Prenze directly—my connection here is through a mutual associate. Is that something you'd like to arrange or would it be best if I manage that myself?"

The sergeant glanced first at Eve, almost as if to ask if she'd put her Grandmother up to this, and then glanced back. "He's obviously very busy, as is his sister."

"Well, I'll just have to introduce myself when I see him unoccupied," Gran said with a winning smile. "Good evening, Sergeant. My dears," she turned to them. "Let's have more punch."

Eve and Horowitz nodded their heads in respect and followed Gran's lead of sweeping over to the refreshment table just as fresh champagne was brought out to the guests.

Mahoney's scowl remained fixed after them. Eve could feel it as if it were a hand on the back of her skull, but Gran paid no mind, continuing on with her effervescent smile.

"I am all *kinds* of curious," Horowitz whispered.

"If he has a certain 'ministry' I imagine he has loyal followers, if this is any indication," Eve said, watching the admiring crowds at work.

"Industry. I want to know what industry made the family's wealth," Horowitz stated. "Usually one can tell."

"Medicine. Tonics. Placations and palliatives," Eve offered. "I've seen the name in adverts. It's often obvious in design or motif in homes built from robber baron profit. You'd think there would be at least a caduceus or something, illuminating the source of their fortunes under all the garish light."

"It is bright, isn't it?" Horowitz said, looking around. "Almost *too* bright."

"Do you want to know the oddest thing of all?" Eve asked. The detective gestured for her to proceed. Eve drew closer, taking one of Gran's proffered cups and handing one to the detective. She leaned in toward Gran, so that both could hear her murmur. "There are *no* spirits. Not a one. Ghosts love balls. But there are none here. None passing through, none lingering to watch or pine, or to frolic. This is a void."

"It's true," Gran assented. "*Nothing.* That's the strangest thing, next to a marble ballroom floor. Who on earth wants to dance on the hardest stone and injure their feet? Everyone knows the best ballroom floor is a wooden one," Gran scoffed.

"Perhaps the Prenze family just thinks everyone will glide about their floor," Horowitz offered with a slight smile. "It does seem to be trying for a celestial sort of look."

"I suppose you're right," Eve replied with a little laugh. "I'm not sure God would be so gaudy, but who am I to guess? Not for mortal minds to fathom."

"But no spirits in the *least*," Gran said, glancing about a shallow clerestory level above the ballroom. "It's troubling, truly. Because I have felt, since I came onto these grounds, like I'm being watched. Do you?"

"Well, yes, by the sergeant," Eve answered.

"Beyond that man; he was harmless," Gran countered. "Just a loyal dog trying to feel very important. But right now, I feel watched. Distinctly. But I cannot find from where, or by whom."

They looked around, at everyone, at every level, at every bright corner, as there were no shadows to be seen, hoping for an answer.

"Do you dance, Miss Whitby?" the detective asked after a while. She looked at him. His unique face, angled and distinct, was more handsome to her the more she stared at it. He'd asked a question . . .

"I have. At least, I have been taught to dance. And I've been known to, occasionally." Goodness, she thought with terror, could she sound more awkward? And why did she even care? The whole point of her pretense was so that she wouldn't have to.

"Would you like to?" he prompted.

"Dance?"

"Well, yes," he replied haltingly. "We're at a dance. In a ballroom. It's what it's meant for, ill-suited floor notwithstanding."

Eve paused.

"We don't have to, I mean, I know we're not—I understand fully. I feel the same—"

"Ah, a waltz, my favorite!" Eve exclaimed as the music shifted and she tried to absolve them both of awkwardness.

Perhaps it was good there were no ghosts, lest they chatter about her and the detective and make her self-conscious. It was one of the reasons she'd been so reluctant to consider a suitor. Many people often insinuated themselves and offered unsolicited opinions when it came to romance, but none so much as the dead.

She'd struck a deal with spirits when she was fourteen that if they didn't stop fussing over what she wore or looked like, or whether they thought she'd gotten enough rest or had the right attitude about something, she'd never respond to them ever again, on the surety that they'd all, young and old and every kind equally henpeck her to death. *Treat me as you'd wish to be treated,* she'd had to remind the spirits. Right now, she didn't want ghostly editorializing as she felt Horowitz's firm palm cup her waist and his outstretched hand receive hers.

Twirling about, Eve caught Sergeant Mahoney's scowling gaze. On another twirl she caught Gran's bemused expression, seemingly delighted that Eve was at least playing at enjoying her pretense of a suitor.

On another spin, twirled under the detective's deft arm—and why did he also have to be so effortless a dancer—she watched as the Prenze brother and sister danced together, their fair faces beaming, like oscillating candles with their orange-flame hair, lighting up the whole room as they spun. There was a great deal of love there; that was clear.

And yet, without spirits hanging about in rafters or against walls or swooping down over the company in glee and abandon, as Eve had always known, something felt terribly empty here. There was no life when there was no death . . . This world was entirely incomplete.

They enjoyed one waltz but at the end, breaking apart, their eyes meeting in a flash as bright as the electric bulbs, it seemed clear with a resurging swell of awkwardness that they'd best not indulge in a second.

"Thank you," they said at the same time, and smiled.

Eve suggested another sip of champagne.

Glancing over to check on Evelyn, Eve found her Grandmother freshly ensconced in what seemed like pleasant conversation with the Prenze brother, the sister looking on, engaged.

Eve was glad she had a ballroom full of people to watch, as she couldn't be sure of not giving a bit too much away if she were to look into Horowitz's eyes again. By the time they were done with another glass of champagne, Gran returned to their side.

"How was your chat?" Eve asked.

"Fine. We talked about The Met. I asked about their tonics. They built their empire from a modest start, the great American story and all that. I got the distinct sense that there is a whole other world. A whole other side to them, and I don't have the least idea how to safely turn over their shell to get underneath."

"How did the Prenze twin die?" Eve asked.

"Industrial accident in Europe, evidently," Gran said, her tone such that it was clear the family didn't want to talk about it.

It was soon the appointed hour they'd agreed to leave.

"Thank you for the pleasant evening," Horowitz offered as they walked to the portico, Gran keeping a few paces ahead. "I feel it gives us something to build on."

Eve wasn't sure if he meant Prenze family information or their own rapport and she wasn't sure she should ask him to qualify it.

The driver dropped the detective off first. He was again the picture of graciousness, polite and charming.

Once it was just Gran and her in the cab again, Gran offered, "You've done well, my dear. He's handsome and kind. Kind is the most important thing, though, handsome is just a bonus. I think your parents will like him."

"It's . . . it's just for show, to keep them off my back; same for his family. He's a co-worker, this is convenient."

"Yes, of course," Gran said, and smiled.

"What, you don't believe me?" Eve countered, far too defensively.

"I said nothing of the sort."

"But you've a look, you've that *I know something you're not admitting* look."

"I think you're proving a point with your own protestations, dear. Shakespeare said something about that, didn't he?" Gran chuckled as Eve blushed and folded her arms. "Don't worry about it, just let it be. Whatever it will be."

"Come in with me for a post-event cordial, Gran. Don't go home just yet," Eve pleaded, as if she couldn't be trusted to be alone with her own thoughts.

"I'm tired, dear. I leave being out all night to the young."

Eve pouted but Gran dropped her off anyway and continued up to Fifth Avenue, a world away from the more modest Denbury homes.

Turning her key in the lock, Eve entered quietly and placed her cape in the wardrobe, glancing in the mirror to see her own ghostly face staring back at her, another side effect of having taken on spirits at so young an age. She had taken on some of their unearthly pallor, her black hairline meeting almost ashen skin. Behind her wafted Vera.

"*Que bella*," she murmured. "I would have loved to have joined you tonight, but I couldn't get near you," the ghost murmured. "I tried following your carriage, but I couldn't get past the iron gate."

"The place was *curiously* absent of spirits," Eve said to the specter. "It must be somehow repugnant to the dead. Lord knows it was gaudy and bright."

Eve could tell by angled lamplight streaming from partially closed doors above that her colleagues were upstairs in their rooms, leaving the downstairs floor unlit.

Vera drifted with Eve into the darkened parlor and floated before her as she sat.

"I'm the only Denbury descendent, you know," Eve mused.

"I know. Your father wanting to marry you off has you spooked."

Eve chuckled. "I really can't blame father for wanting to marry me off well."

"He wants assurance and insurance for you," Vera supplied.

"For the remaining scraps of a once-grand line, perhaps hoping I'd continue, if not in fact grow it back to even a fraction of its former glory. It isn't that he wants a house like the Prenze mansion for me, he knows I'd hate that. He just wants me not to worry, as he had done, that I would ever be without home, resource, name, or earnings."

He'd lost so much to demonic thieves before she was born, and sometimes in his arresting sky-blue eyes, eyes that were the talk of anyone who caught a glimpse of him, she could see the staggering depth of his haunted spirit. Thinking of it now, she understood his motivations.

"Those who undergo trauma often cling all the more tightly to what they've cobbled together in recovery," Vera offered.

"You know, *mi amiga*," Eve began gently, "I never did write up that preventative report about the post-mortem picture of the secret child. You said it was a townhouse."

"It was not as grand as the Prenze mansion, for certain, so your complaint couldn't have come from my actions. I don't know where it was and I'm so sorry. Ever since Maggie disappeared, I just feel so *scattered*."

"As do I. I feel my talent faltering."

She had begun the Ghost Precinct on a confident note, having helped solve three missing person cases before her associates had come to her and she'd opened her doors as they'd solved more. The surety was gone, replaced by missing loved ones and disconnected loose ends.

A step on the landing had Eve turn. Cora walked into the darkened parlor. One of the things she appreciated about her right-hand woman was that she never turned on the lights if Eve was keeping a room dark.

"How were the festivities?" Cora asked.

Eve explained the night.

"You and the detective . . . are enjoying each other, it would seem," Cora said carefully.

Eve paused a moment. Vera wafted back, realizing she'd best not insinuate herself into the conversation. Instead she floated through the hall and her form floated upstairs, presumably to tuck Jenny in if the spirits of her parents hadn't already done so.

"My dear, why do you have an edge?" Eve asked Cora. "It seems you either do not like the detective or there's something you're not telling me. I think he's a very valuable asset to us."

"More so than the assets you already have? Are we really so trained and eager to accept any capable man as greater than the sum of many women?"

Eve's eyes widened. "Cora, goodness, no . . ."

"Just . . . remember he's not a part of the Precinct," Cora said gently but firmly. "An asset, an associate, whatever need be, but we've built something here, you and I, and now we have a group who are dependent on us."

"Of course. I know that—"

"I rearranged my whole life to come to New York and build this department with you. Please don't take that for granted."

"I don't . . ." Eve murmured. Cora nodded curtly before changing the subject.

"In the morning I'll tell you the results of tonight's séance in regards to the Schwerin girl. I'd like you to step up your involvement on that case. That dead woman from Grace can't have called you for nothing," Cora stated and turned back into the shadows, quietly returning upstairs before Eve could respond.

She sat there in the darkness, registering the reason for Cora's words, what it had taken to get her to this point of frustration.

The simple fact was Eve had let flirting get the better of her. She had shifted the priorities of time and energy to her own needs and excuses to fashion their ruse. Their department was treading water when it had just begun and she was doing nothing to propel them forward. She was being a silly schoolgirl, not a leader. Shame overtook her and she went to bed fighting back tears.

The next day was Sunday, the department's unquestioned Sabbath, and when Eve woke a bit later than she'd intended, she found herself alone in the house, the rest of the women attending their own sacred spaces or areas that rejuvenated them. She was already late to meet Gran, who had insisted Eve come see the work on the new St. John the Divine Cathedral, a project she had spent a great deal of time and energy making happen over the course of the past two decades.

In the parlor on the séance table she found Antonia's brief note from the previous night's session while she had been at the Prenze ball. Eve assumed Antonia had left it out for her to find.

When asked about Ingrid, all that could be heard: "Dead."

"Dead, dead, dead . . ."

"The Beautiful, Sanctified Dead . . ."

That was the extent of it, and this was terribly disheartening.

* * * *

It was good she was going to the Cathedral site, because any sacred spot, especially one in progress, was a place that tended to help her transcend from worry to inspiration, a location that lent itself to breakthroughs. While Gran had heralded St. John as a cathedral honoring alliance between faiths from the very beginning, its completed floor plan would make it one of the largest and most impressive cathedrals in the entire world. It was also true that after the Catholics had built the beautiful St. Patrick's on 50th Street, the Episcopalians felt they had to keep up. They'd been trying for a grand space forever but various financial panics and logistical troubles had kept the cornerstone from being laid until 1892.

The builders, in a plan created by Heins and La Farge as a Romanesque behemoth, were doing this in the manner of the great cathedrals of Europe—stone on stone. To support such a massive building, the foundations themselves needed ever-deeper anchors into the Morningside bedrock of Upper West Manhattan.

There was a patch of green next to the construction site where one of the Bishops had suggested the board of directors, lay leaders, and involved clergy meet for prayer, in a part of the expansive array they planned to become their peace garden.

In an introductory welcome, the dean of the church sweetly reminded the crowd:

"As we are all unfinished works of sacred possibility designed by God, so should we worship in a place that reminds us of that humbling fact."

Unfinished works. How right he was.

A group of well-trained singers sang a few hymns and Eve felt transported. Encouraged. Unfinished, but a bit more whole. She felt the spirits, many of whom were floating about in a sort of procession, seemingly moved by the goings-on in the grass beside the heaps of cloven stone, were affirming her, encouraging her to keep the faith and keep moving on.

"Your head has been in the clouds," Gran said after the service, pointing to the first part of the central cathedral arches that were reaching up towards the sky.

"It has, I'm sorry. It's so very good to be contemplating mystical things with you, though, it always is," Eve said.

"Oh, I know, I just hope you've made some progress on whatever you're spinning about. I can hear you whirring over there, a drone under the choir."

"I think that little girl Ingrid is dead. That's all that seems to come back from the queries put out to the spirit world. We failed her." Eve explained what they'd gleaned thus far.

Chapter Eleven

The first thing Monday morning, Eve was in before her company, just to have some time to think and be alone and try to center herself. She was torn in two, trying to find two souls at once.

The echo of *"Find me . . ."* wouldn't leave her mind. She had to do as that voice bid. In life and in death.

Eve did not, however, arrive before McDonnell.

"Gift for you, *Madame*," McDonnell said with her recurring jab of exaggeration as Eve entered, making it quite clear she thought that Eve and her colleagues took themselves too seriously, or thought themselves beyond their station. Perhaps someday Eve could reach a breakthrough with this bitter pill of a woman, but her energy was too precious for that to be any time soon.

Eve walked to the unadorned table where a sorting tray sat against the wood-paneled wall. Next to it was a box. A small, unmarked, black box.

"Do you know who sent it?"

"As you can *see*, there's no return address. The postman just dropped it off with the rest of the mail. It smells sharply though. As if it's been run through some sort of process like some of these new associates tinker around with at crime scenes. Might blow up a building with untested chemistry if they're not careful," the matron grumbled. Whether it was fingerprinting or some women daring to wear pants, it had been clear from day one that matron McDonnell didn't seem to like any controversial new idea, however practical or innovative.

"How ever will you survive the coming century," Eve murmured. "Noted about the smell, I'll open a window," she replied, taking the box and the letters to her desk.

As she put her fingers to the lid of the box, a strong instinct urged her to proceed with caution, to brace herself.

However, gifts and anticipation notwithstanding, she had to stifle a scream when she opened it.

A finger. A cleanly severed finger lay within the box. Bloodless, cold, preserved with certain embalming fluid—therein lay the chemical stench to mask decay.

An accusatory digit pointing at her. Small. Delicate. A child's finger? No, an adult. Maybe someone her age. It was roughly the size of her own.

She looked up to find that several of her ghostly operatives were hovering over her. Her stifled scream must have been audible to the spirits, panic drawing her closest associates to her side. Vera had her eyes closed. Zofia had a hand over her mouth.

"What do you make of this grim offering?" Eve asked the ghosts. "Do you think we know who this belongs to?"

Zofia vanished, unable to respond. Sometimes when she would get overwhelmed, she would fade. She never entirely went away, though after Maggie's disappearance the girl's fading made Eve more nervous than it had before. Often she'd come back with an insight or just return the next day fresh.

"Meant to scare you, surely," Vera said, drawing her shawl between her fingers nervously. "*Dios mio.*"

Eve set her jaw and closed the lid again, inspecting the box. It was fresh, clean, and hadn't been used for another purpose but this—a gift box.

A potent memory struck Eve and she was lost to it, the closed black box on her desk becoming a portal to the past as she thought about one of the only warnings her mother ever gave her. . . .

* * * *

There had been a conversation between her mother and her father about a portrait. Though it wasn't at all about art. It was about a soul, and their conversation got more heated than Eve had ever heard.

Ever since she could remember, her parents had never raised their voices to one another until that day, and it had to do with her, what she should know and what she should never hear. When Eve found them in the parlor, they fell silent.

"You know I sense and hear things from the beyond," Eve had stated. "How can I avoid or keep at bay the things you fear most? I never want to be a cause of you and father fighting."

This gained her a fond look, and the furrowed brow of her lovely mother eased. She cupped her cheek. Such gestures were increasingly rare as Eve aged and grew more world-wise, a process that seemed to make her mother withdraw from her more and more. But this was a rare warmth.

"Don't you take that worry on yourself," she had said. "The only thing we'd ever fight about is the safety of this family."

"What about a portrait? I didn't mean to overhear . . . but I couldn't help it. Some kind of witchcraft and devilry? I'm forbidden to ask questions about how you and Father met, but I know it had to do with a painting and a sequence of improbable events. Is there something else I should be wary of? Be warned about?"

Her mother sighed. Her father had come to stand beside her as she sat, his arm instinctively reaching out as she so comfortably slid against him, an expert move they'd spent their whole adult lives performing, a loving choreography Eve had always taken specific note of.

Father took a deep breath and spoke in a tone that was almost rote, something he'd had to say many times before. "There were three prongs by which a horrific cabal once sought to gain power and terrorize cities. Ripping souls from bodies, reanimation of body parts, and chemical alteration of the mind."

"And that's about all we can or should say, for our part." Her mother had looked away. "My nerves. I'd thought I'd grow more steeled as I grew older, not less. If you could talk to Gran about one of those things, I think I'd sleep better at night. She was my mentor then, and she's yours now."

* * * *

Eve returned to the present, to the black gift box bearing ugly tidings. Time to talk to Gran about 'one of those things'.

Eve let herself into her Grandmother's Fifth Avenue townhouse and hesitated in the hall. Not wanting one of the maids to mistake the box for a gift and set it down on the wardrobe and vanity by the door, Eve unpinned her felt hat and tossed it over the lid, not wanting to bring the thing in any further.

Evelyn, hearing the unlocked door from the nearby parlor whose pocket doors were open, met her granddaughter in the hall, took one look at her, and knew something was wrong. "Hello, Eve, good to see you, but not with that look on your face. What is it?"

"Gran, I don't want to bring you into this in particular."

"Eve, dear. Am I not one of your operatives?"

"We're your operatives, rather," Eve said deferentially. "And we'd rather take the brunt."

"There's no extricating me from your work. Stop feeling so guilty about it."

"This is . . . ugly. But I do need your advice. As usual."

She gestured her granddaughter into the parlor. Fresh tea in a silver service steamed from a tray near to Gran's favorite velvet divan where a book lay open. Evelyn reached out and squeezed her hand, drawing her to sit next to her on the velvet cushions.

"Something gruesome was delivered to my office this morning. A threat, surely, but I have no idea to whom it relates."

"What was it?"

"A box, a plain black box with . . . something inside."

"A body part?" Gran asked warily.

"Yes . . . How did you know?" Eve exclaimed. The memory with her mother flared again. "This is like your old terror, isn't it? Come back again?" Eve asked ruefully.

"I can't tell you that unless I see it."

Eve went to the hall, brought in the box and passed it over. Gran lifted it and made no sign of fright at the sight of the severed finger therein. What Eve would give for such composure at all times.

"This is odd," Gran stated.

"Well, yes . . ."

"Beyond the disgusting fact of it, there's something different about this. It isn't like the others. At least, not to my recollection. Have you gotten any sense of a spirit attached to this digit?" Gran asked.

Eve shook her head. "I've not heard anything or seen anything in direct relation."

"And you say it was brought to you, delivered, not left for you to find?"

"Morning post," Eve said. "I couldn't even bear to finish my coffee."

"There's someone we're going to have to go see."

They were in Gran's hack in a heartbeat and off to the depot, where a train would take them north of the city. To Sleepy Hollow, home to the headless horseman, fanciful old myths, and a scarred, reclusive clairvoyant who impressed and worried Eve in equal measure.

The Hudson River Line was gorgeous all year round, but never so much as the fall. Eve felt as though she were journeying through a picture book of folklore and fairytales as their train curved along the river-bend past every array of turning leaf, the sunlight dancing golden and magical along the river water, dramatic cliff-sides dotted with civilization and mansions as they traveled under stone arches and sweeping vistas. The river opened wide, showcasing the beauty of the terrain and the churn of travel towards the world's busiest harbor, an equal mix of industry and leisure.

This would have seemed the most pleasant and lovely of jaunts were it not for Eve glancing next to her, to the plain paper bag that the box had been placed in, to remind herself of what drove them to this lovely landscape.

"I know," Gran said, watching Eve look at the bag and then out the window as if to make sense of the jarring juxtaposition. "Beauty and horror. It is the way of it, with our kind."

A hired cab took them away from the quaint brick station with a gabled roof and they were whisked a mile north, to a wide green lawn and extensive hedgerows marking the property lines of a multi-acre rectangle.

Before them lay a grand red brick home with tall turrets and a wide, hunter-green deck that spanned two lengths of the house, a distinctly Victorian mansion in its liberal use of Gothic, Romanesque, Norman, and Dutch Revival architecture styles blended into one whole, its greatest beauty in its carved brownstone details featuring arabesques of birds and floral themes.

Stepping out onto the pebbled drive, Eve could feel life-force buzzing against her skin, invigorating her. As they walked to the front door, Eve took in every last detail.

Each window sill sported a window box and the front flower garden was teeming with rejuvenated autumn blooms, extra vibrant for the perfectly balanced clime this month, butterflies darting from cornflower stalk to black-eyed Susan. Eve thought of her late grandmother Helen, who had brought her tokens of those flowers direct from the spirit world, in a manifestation process that baffled even the most gifted psychic.

She chose to think the presence of the flowers was a good omen as Gran lifted the door-knocker, an open-winged dove with an olive branch in its beak which flew below the brass plate that read THE BISHOPS.

An elderly woman came to the door. "Hello, Harper," Gran said. The long-time housekeeper threw open the door and gave Gran a hug, ushering them both in and turning the gas-lamps, set in stained-glass sconces along the hall, up a bit brighter. While their mansion was one of countless well-to-do estates lining the Hudson River Valley, the Bishops were not the electrical sort, an aberration among their peers.

Eve thought the aversion to electric lighting might have something to do with Clara's sensitivities, the idea that she could hear electricity as if it were a voice, her body a conduit for energy. When Eve had first asked if there were others like her, or if she were a freak, Evelyn had made sure to note that several of her closest colleagues were repositories of varied, expansive, awe-inspiring force. Clara had been the one she mentioned first. Ambassador Bishop, a mesmerist, Spiritualist and Sensitive twelve years Clara's senior, as well as an accomplished lawmaker and public figure, she had mentioned second. Eve knew she was in the presence of greatness, and she had never before needed that so much.

"We're here for Clara, please, Harper, I do hope she's in," Gran said as a woman stepped into the hall. "Ah, there you are, darling."

Clara Templeton Bishop entered the entrance foyer in a simple white day-dress backlit by golden stained glass. A Tiffany Studios angel was the centerpiece of the mansion's wide and open foyer, two wooden staircases curving up on either side of it to the second floor. The heavenly art-glass seraph was set in a wooden Gothic arch above a window-seat strewn with pillows and an open book. From the distance and angle Clara stood, it looked as if she were the one sporting wings, and it suited. There was something magical about Clara Templeton for certain, inscrutable and somewhat terrifying. If those wings were real, she'd have been sent here as an avenging angel, beautiful and terrible to behold.

"Hello, Evelyn dear. Miss Whitby, pleasure to see you," Clara said quietly. Her brow furrowed as if she were trying to figure out why they were here by psychic exchange instead of words. If she was telepathic, this was news to Eve.

With a languid wave of her long-fingered hand, Clara bid them follow her as she floated into the parlor, a beautiful, arched room with richly carved wood paneling in floral arabesques and glistening, peacock mosaic wall panels.

"Tea is already prepared. I had a feeling someone was coming," she stated, gliding to a Turkish suite where an array was set out with several chairs around the perimeter.

Clara glanced at Eve, as if measuring her, then smiled at Gran. "All right, you, out with it."

Gran chuckled humorlessly. "I've a simple question I hoped I'd not have to ask. Is Lady C. still in her asylum?"

Clara blinked her eerie green-gold eyes at Evelyn a moment. "Yes. Why?"

Gran took a deep breath. "In Eve's precinct work, a small black box turned up with a body part in it. A finger." She smiled and waved her hand nonchalantly. "I wanted to be sure no one was up to their old antics. I know it's been seventeen years. I think this is someone trying to get a rise out of the family."

Clara gestured for Eve to turn the box over to her. Eve reached into the paper bag, lifted it out gingerly and handed it across the table.

"Please take care," Eve murmured, "We've no way of knowing who this may have belonged to, it's frightful—"

"I would expect nothing less to be brought to my attention," Clara replied.

Lifting the lid, she exhibited the same uncannily calm composure that Eve had marveled at in Gran. Peering at it closely, Clara spoke quietly, explaining.

"I don't think it's the Society. It doesn't have their particular calling-card perversions. No carving, no inverted symbols, no horrid adornments. It's likely a warning, unfortunately, and if someone knows about the Society, it could be a way of trying to throw you off course. This doesn't have the feel of Society befouling. Terrible as it is, please don't misunderstand me."

She considered the box for another long moment before continuing.

"My own ear was in one of these boxes once. Used as a piece of tethering magic for a terrible display over the Washington Mall. Since then I'm particularly attuned to magic tied to severed flesh." She glanced at Eve with a twisted smile. "I've an . . . ear for it you could say."

Gran exclaimed a laugh that was part chuckle, part admonishment for the horrible pun. Clara continued examining the item, and explaining to Eve the differences she saw.

"The thing of it is, it's a clean cut. The Master's Society, the horrific cabal that targeted your family and returned to drag an even wider net into their demonic grasp was a bit more ragged about offerings such as these. Sometimes the flesh was torn, almost serrated. Irreverently. Messily. Sometimes a bit of tendon . . ."

The true horror and disgust of it hit Eve all at once. Her stomach lurched.

"If you'll excuse me," Eve blurted. She nearly ran to the powder room, where she leaned over the basin and she tried to keep from retching, but a heave came anyway.

In her time, she had seen and heard much from the spirit world. She was conversant with death. The incorporeal was what she was accustomed to.

The corporeal reality of this tactile horror was beyond her capacity.

Coming back into the parlor, sure she looked a bit green, she tried to explain that point.

"Please don't think I'm too delicate," Eve said quietly. "I can't let any of the rest of the force see any sort of womanly weakness, so I hold a lot back, perhaps more than I even know, until it's too late—"

Clara gestured as if to say she needn't explain. "It gets to be too much, I know. That's when I would have a seizure," she said. Looking over at Evelyn, Clara reached out suddenly to squeeze her hand that was increasingly lined with age, reminding Eve that her grandmother had had many mentees and many battles in her long, unique life.

Returning that unsettling gaze back to Eve, Clara continued. "I'm sorry we seem so inured to terrible things. That must not seem very human of us. I was speaking in part from relief," Clara admitted. "Relief that it isn't the same kind of work. I'd like to think it is no longer my problem. But I do think someone is trying to throw you off."

"There's a particularly prominent family she's been warned to avoid," Gran explained. "The Prenze family. This could be an intimidation tactic."

"Likely so. I've heard the name. They deal in laudanum, yes?"

Eve nodded. "And other tonics. I don't think they know one thing about me or my department, but I think an overzealous policeman is trying to protect something he doesn't even understand."

Clara laughed bitterly, as if that pressed on old bruises.

These women who all came before her, making way for her—Eve owed them so much and felt so deeply but didn't want to be seen as some young, gushing sap to these elder icons. Still, she wanted Mrs. Bishop to know that even if she wasn't allowed to know what had transpired in her former department—a frustrating blockade she was clear came from her parents' demands rather than from Clara's wishes—she considered her still so important to the Spiritual legacy . . .

"Thank you for your assessment, Mrs. Bishop." Eve blushed. "You know . . . you could always join us at the Precinct, whenever you wanted. You're . . . so talented, we could really use someone of your caliber, I mean, if that would ever interest you . . ."

Clara smiled that half-smile again, a look that made her seem a thousand years old and weary of being dragged back through long-lost lives again. "You have migraines sometimes, don't you? Related to your Sensitivities?"

"Why, yes . . . Why do you ask?"

"Have they gotten worse as you've gotten older?"

"Not necessarily." Eve shrugged. "The pain changes, how it spreads shifts, and the density of it. It's manageable for now, provided I don't block the spirits out, that's when they break me."

"Gifts and their costs can change profoundly over time. I used to have seizures. I don't have seizures anymore," Clara said carefully, piercing Eve with that particular, eviscerating stare. "I cause earthquakes." Her lips pressed into a thin line. "Best leave me out of this."

Eve nodded, wide-eyed, having no idea what else to say.

Clara insisted they stay for lunch. Thankfully Ambassador Bishop and Gran had lots of catching up to do regarding their mutual friends in England, and they carried the whole of the conversation.

As Eve was freshening up again, trying to exit the place not looking so green, she could overhear Evelyn and Clara, back in the parlor again, discussing this latest turn.

"I'm trying to keep her parents from knowing a thing about it," Evelyn said.

"How do you all manage it?"

"Manage what?"

"Family dinners?" Clara asked bluntly. "If Lord and Lady Denbury are really so opposed to the paranormal as you say, how can any of you bear one another? I long ago gave up the hope that I would ever be able to be lasting friends with them. Lady Denbury would never forgive me for her husband's continued involvement in our work, and it was clear I was not welcome as an additional mentor to Eve, as much as I would have liked to have been . . ." Clara didn't hide the hurt at being left out; Eve could hear it radiating through her words.

Perhaps that's why this woman seemed so distant, so eerie. She didn't dare allow herself to become fond. This made Eve ache to the core. Clara Bishop had a loving marriage, but it would seem she had hardly any friends. This was likely due to the extreme secrecy of her and Ambassador Bishop's work, but Clara also had no additional family. Gran explained that Clara had been orphaned at a young age and Eve wondered if this incredible woman wasn't extremely lonely.

When Eve was first coming into her own, her grandmother had abandoned everyone save for Eve. She was her constant caretaker so that she would never know terrifying darkness. When Gran's own gifts had first manifested when she was a young lady, Gran had told Eve, the whole experience had nearly killed her. She'd promised she wouldn't let Eve suffer. Eve wondered if Clara resented Evelyn being taken from her in this way. She couldn't blame Mrs. Bishop if she were bitter; she'd be jealous of anyone stealing Gran away from her too.

Eve rejoined them again, lest she be called out for lurking in the hallway, just as Gran was saying of their family, "We manage as well as any family that has strong, different opinions; we set things aside for common interests. Bless my dear Gareth and his talk of art, it has saved us all."

"To be fair," Eve murmured, "I don't always know what not to talk about since you won't talk about it . . ."

Gran chuckled. "Well consider this my letting you know. Don't mention The Master's Society anywhere near your family. This is a copycat action. Everything in the spirit world is telling Clara and me this is different. Listen and you'll hear the same thing."

"So that this doesn't draw out any of our old enemies," Clara declared, "pale imitation that this might be, it does need to be destroyed. If you don't mind, I'll take the item."

"Be my guest."

Clara moved the item onto a hutch. "I'll take pictures of it for evidence and have it dusted for fingerprints. Yes, I know all the latest technologies," Clara added when Eve's eyes widened. "I do try to keep up to date even if I have shunned the metropolis," Clara said with a smile. "But there's a way this needs to be destroyed, so that whoever this belonged to can rest in peace." She turned to Evelyn. "I've needed to see Reverend Blessing anyway, and this is a reminder to refresh the city Wards."

Eve's eyes must have remained wide and surprised, as Clara felt again the need to explain.

"There are protections in this city against demons, and my commission, years ago, put them there. Alas, I have no such protections against misguided humans. That's up to people like you to police."

* * * *

Returning to her offices, Eve explained everything to her waiting colleagues.

"You could have left a note," Antonia murmured. "When we came in and you were out again . . ."

"The spirits told us, but we'd have preferred to hear it from you," Cora said. "Grim as it was." The group shuddered.

"I'm sorry." Eve sighed, her shoulders falling as she sunk into her chair. "We're not functioning as a cohesive whole and that's my fault. I've been dealing with spirits so long, on my own—"

As we all have, Jenny added in sign, her lips pursed in aggravation.

I know, Eve signed back. *And we mustn't shut each other out.*

"So what's to be done? About the finger?" Cora asked.

"There are protections that will be renewed about the city," Eve explained. "Wards. And I'll contact the city morgue and ask about any corpses turning up missing a finger. As for us, it was an intimidation trick I'm not going to give in to. Now," Eve clapped her hands together. "We need to talk with Susan Keller," Eve stated. "If Ingrid's mother is more coherent, perhaps progress . . ."

She tried to sound hopeful. Looking around, no ghosts were in their offices. Their usual helpful ghosts were either absent or strangely incoherent, distracted. It was as if someone were addling their spectral brains, making them dizzy and forgetful.

Eve was aware spirits could lose some of their potency through time if they were not utilized and engaged. So it went with the living; elderly people left to die with no one to talk to or interact with went far quicker into death than those who were active and interactive. The responsibility to both her colleagues and her spirit assets was overwhelming. But she could only deal with one action at a time.

Just then, a looming shadow crossed their threshold. An unmistakable, bespectacled form stood before them in a cream linen suit and boater, exuding a powerful air of import with an undercurrent of barely contained whimsy.

"Governor Roosevelt, Sir, it's . . . a pleasure to see you, I . . . wasn't expecting you," Eve stammered, glancing back to see her colleagues had all jumped to their feet. Jenny had even saluted.

"You don't have to lie about that," the bombastic man said with a laugh. "I know my arrival causes brave, stalwart hearts to tremble, as they never know what I might be up to that might turn their lives upside down."

"Well, in that case, what are you here to upend?" Eve asked with a smile. "And would you like a refreshment?"

Roosevelt kept chuckling as Eve led him to the best chair they'd been able to salvage from Department storage, a leather-covered high-backed one that Eve kept across her desk for guests.

It was clear that Roosevelt found what Eve did fascinating, and in turn, she found the man ceaselessly compelling and entertaining. Antonia wheeled over the tea tray that had an assemblage of options.

"Just water for the moment, thank you," he stated and Eve poured him a small glass from a plain decanter as he sat down.

"There was a complaint recently," Eve began, "one that I was made aware of—a powerful family in the city that has evidently quite a champion in Sergeant Mahoney, so if this is about that—"

"Oh, he's a snitch through and through," Roosevelt declared. At this, Eve allowed herself a cautious smile and the Governor continued. "And believe me, when I was cleaning up this rag-tag unit they called a police force, I needed plenty of snitches to root out the bad seeds from the good. But that one, I think he's more loyal to patrons who would like to see him police commissioner than to the greater good."

"Ah," Eve said. That made the most sense of anything. It would be quite a jump from his current post to Commissioner, but having friends in high places assured those kinds of ascents.

"So I'll not throw him onto the tracks, but know you're understood. I'm here because of your former liaison. Mr. Bonhoff has gone on to be Ambassador, and Detective Horowitz volunteered in his stead, and that's all well and good, but you can't go around waltzing with your liaison."

Eve stared at Roosevelt. "We were simply at a ball."

He leaned in. He adjusted his glasses. "Fraternizing."

"One has to talk to one's liaison, and often—"

"*Dancing*, Miss Whitby." Roosevelt waggled his moustache. "Dancing can result in an implicit bias. I'm all for a good dance, but not in my line of accountability."

"I could make a few suggestions—"

"You're not supposed to stack your own deck, Whitby!" he cried with a laugh. "I know you believe in your cause and fear the least grumble will get it shut down."

"Yes. That is it, precisely, sir." Eve was trying desperately to appear confident and perfectly in control in front of her colleagues who were all likely equally nervous as she was. A man like Roosevelt would only respect strength. "You know how passionate I am about this work, about helping this city—"

He held up a hand. "So I'm not going to set you up with anyone who's predisposed to hate you, but we do need someone more objective than someone you've not only danced with but spiritually advised."

"Am I being spied upon?" Eve asked. "I have to ask, because I'm not sure how you'd know about the dancing or that we held a séance for the detective on a case he needed help with."

"The dancing I found out by happenstance. I was asking about the party and one of my lawyers, whom I'd invited to your appreciation toast, mentioned seeing you. The Detective is the one who told me about how you helped him with his dead end, held a séance for him and everything. He's certainly in your corner. All the more reason for you to have a more objective liaison. I'm in town on other business, but I wanted to clear this up with you in person."

"Of course, sir, I'm sorry. Could you then please appoint someone yourself, not the department? These are men who are reluctant to bring on alienists or to implement dusting for fingerprints, so I'm really not their cup of tea."

Roosevelt chuckled, rising to his feet. "I'll find someone, otherwise I'll just have to come check on you myself."

"That would be just fine, sir."

He chuckled and turned to the door but then paused a moment. He turned back and sat back down again with a curious expression. "What do the spirits say about me?" he asked. "I know it's terribly selfish but I've a small streak of that sin of self-absorption that just won't entirely quit me."

Eve grinned. This man was effervescence, ambition, and roiling energy embodied. The definition of bombastic—an entertaining hearth Eve could lose track of time warming her hands in front of.

She closed her eyes a moment. Her senses saw the man before him, her ears tuned in to all the spectral chatter.

"I hear 'executive'. Something about running."

"For president? Good!" He cried, throwing a victorious fist in the air. "I've been thinking of throwing my hat in the ring! Glad to hear I have the endorsement of the ghosts!"

"Now I wouldn't go that far," said an elderly ghost's voice, but there were more hearty 'hear, hear' and 'huzzah' exclamations from the spirit world than protestations.

"Not the whole realm, mind you," Eve countered. "Don't go overestimating your endorsement," she clarified. "You've got an opposition caucus of the dead too."

Roosevelt laughed heartily. Eve turned to her colleagues.

"My friends, what would you add to the Governor?"

Peace, Jenny signed. *Be a man of peace.* Eve offered the translation.

"Ah," Roosevelt responded carefully, looking between Eve and the young girl. "We'll have to see about that. That will depend. We'll be back in touch, Whitby. Thank you."

"Thank you, sir."

He rose and everyone else did so in turn. He turned back to Eve as he stood at the threshold. "One of the stranger things I've heard from one of my contacts of late, is a strange spate of religious objects going missing, not even those of much value other than sentiment. That rubs me wrong. Put your ghosts on it."

"Yes, sir," Eve assured. "We're already involved in that."

"Of course you are! Good. Take care of yourselves." He turned at the door. "Oh, how's the book going, Whitby?"

"Slowly. I figure proving a lifetime point can wait, I am needed in the here and now."

"Needed in the here and now." He shook an emphatic finger at them, grinning. "Magnificent practical advice from my ladies of the dead!"

After he shut the door behind him, Antonia chuckled. "That should go on your business card, Eve," she said, picking up one of Eve's cards from the nearest desk and gesturing with it, putting on a theatrical voice. "The Ghost Precinct; magnificent practical advice from ladies of the dead!"

They all laughed.

Eve looked at each of them for a long moment. "Thank you, for being you. And bearing with me. Shall we see if we can make headway with the Schwerins?"

Cora nodded. Antonia went for her hat. Jenny grabbed a notepad and paper and put them in the pocket of her pinafore.

They walked east and Cora refreshed Eve on the particulars—that the mother Greta had brought eight-year-old Ingrid to her sister Susan before taking the child to Grace Memorial House, and then when Greta had taken Ingrid *out* of Grace, presumably to evade Mr. Schwerin, and returned to her sister Susan, she had done so without Ingrid and the sister had no idea what to think. Greta insisted that the child had been taken but didn't have any details about where and didn't want to implicate her sister in foul play.

"It's all fishy," Cora stated. "She's not going to be happy to see us, out of protection for her sister."

"Agreed. We'll play up the fact that no one is a suspect."

Susan's rented rooms east of St. Marks in the Bowery, a colonial Anglican and now Episcopal church that had been an anchor in the neighborhood since its establishment at the end of the 18th century, were in a narrow brick townhouse with sandstone details above a few windows to make the exterior look more appealing than the narrow, dim hallway and railroad-style rooms that were inside.

Susan came to the door, embroidery in her hand. She looked at Cora, then at Eve.

"You're back with a new interrogator?" she asked humorlessly, her German accent thick. "I've told you everything I know. I am a working woman, and every few minutes is one less of these pieces I can complete," she explained, shaking the cloth in her hand.

"I'm so sorry, I understand. My name is Eve, you've met my colleagues—forgive the crowd but we're en route to others who need our help and wanted to see you and Greta first. We are all working women and we'll be done as soon as we can. We just want to help," Eve said earnestly. "May we please come in? Otherwise we can ask questions in the hall . . ."

Susan gestured them in. Seeing Jenny prompted a question. "Young for a police matron, *ja?* Precincts adopting cheap labor these days?" Susan asked with a nervous chuckle.

"Jenny is one of our charges," Eve stated. Jenny waved and smiled. "As you know, working women don't always have many options and we take care of our own." Eve fished in one of her dress pockets—she'd had her working skirt adapted so that there were several visible as well as hidden. "Let this be a simple valuation of your time," she said, placing a dollar coin on the table by the door, and continued with a question.

"Is your sister any better?" Cora asked, with the same earnest gentleness as Eve. Susan gestured to the corner. Eve's eyes had to adjust to the dim light of the shadows before she could see a woman rocking so slowly in a rocking chair that it was almost imperceptible. The brightest light was over a center table of plain wood, where an unfished stack of panels waiting to be embroidered sat beneath the gas lantern hung from the ceiling.

"She's not very awake. I've been giving her medicine," Susan stated. "But it might be making her worse."

"I wanted to ask about Greta's employer," Eve stated.

Suddenly Greta began rocking quickly, a nervous hum, a children's lullaby escaping her lips in a raspy tone.

"I don't know anything about him, I told your colleague," Susan said, nodding towards Cora, then glancing nervously back at her sister.

"Well there's a strong reaction here," Eve said gently, "so someone isn't telling us something important."

"He lived in Gramercy Park," Susan said wearily. "She was his maid. Called him the Lion of Gramercy, that's all I know. He was . . . difficult. When she got married he didn't want her working there anymore." The name of the park rang in Eve's mind like an echo and Vera wafted behind Eve to repeat it. Eve hadn't noticed that Vera had joined them.

Greta made a desperate noise, moved to stand, and then sat back down, collapsing into the rocking chair as it jarred back against the wall. Susan rushed over to her. "Calm down, love. If there's something you want to say, just say it."

Eve glanced at Vera, who wafted back towards the wall. Sometimes people who were ill or grieving had heightened sensitivities; circumstances could open the spirit world to the vulnerable wider than one wished. It wasn't a talent for everyone.

Greta moaned and then her head lolled to the side as she lost consciousness. "She's been doing that," Susan explained, "moments of panic before a collapse. But maybe it's for the best she's out. I will tell you that I haven't liked anything that's happened since she left this apartment. We came over from Germany twelve years ago when our parents died and there wasn't enough work in our village. An aunt was here doing lacework and embroidery as I do, so I took up the business. Greta wanted something else, so she started work as a maid." Susan glanced at Greta before speaking in a quiet rush, as if she had to say everything before the ill woman stirred again.

"I think she fell in love with her employer, the Lion; she would talk about him all the time. I didn't see her during this time. She only wrote letters. If something would have happened to me, I could have died in this apartment and she'd never have known," Susan said bitterly, in a sudden burst of anger. Greta stirred and Susan sighed, going back to her whisper as she continued.

"For whatever reason she kept her "Lion" secret and said she could never have company there, so I'd best not try to find her. So I respected her wishes. She lived on site, said she had her own room. She said he treated her differently but she had to keep deadly quiet about it. Something must have happened because one day she simply didn't talk about him anymore, and started talking about one of the delivery men who would come around to the house, saying he was German and wouldn't it be good if she were married, especially to someone from our country, never mind if he was Catholic. Within a few weeks she was married to Heinrich and moved into his rooms over near Union Square. It was all hasty—I was only a part of her life through her random letters, whatever she chose to share. I do know after Ingrid was born Heinrich started getting, well . . . darker."

"Violent?" Antonia murmured.

"Not directly, I don't think, but perhaps without meaning to. Grabbing an arm too hard. To the point of bruising. I saw it on Ingrid's arm right before Greta took her to that Grace house—it was clearly fingerprints."

"The Deaconess at Grace saw marks too," Eve murmured. "It seems Greta's concerns did not go unnoticed by Memorial House. If we go and talk to Heinrich—"

"I don't know where he is either," Susan said irritably. "She would never tell me where their apartment was—she didn't want to drag me into the darker parts of her life, she said—and she never brought him here, told him I lived on the other side of Manhattan even. Perhaps she kept things secret so that this would always be a safe place for her these men could never find. I have never understood. She always had a strange way of looking at the world."

"You mentioned Heinrich was Catholic, I assume you're not?"

"Lutheran. It doesn't matter to me one way or another, we fell out of churchgoing ways, but he insisted she convert and that Ingrid be raised Catholic. She agreed, she had to before a priest would marry them. Since she left this apartment I hadn't seen her again until she came here with Ingrid, last month. It had been four years."

There was an uncomfortable silence.

"I wanted to be a better sister to her," Susan confessed, tears in her eyes. "But she wouldn't let me. She was always in her own little world."

"Did you ever live with anyone else here?" Cora asked, looking around the sparse main room. The cream-colored walls needed a new coat of paint, and the fabric hung across the threshold leading to what was presumably a bedroom or closet was sooty and threadbare around the edges.

"I was planning on leaving here and moving into my fiancé's rooms over on Fourth Avenue. He died of pneumonia before I could."

"I'm so sorry," Cora murmured. Jenny, staring at Susan, nodded her support. It occurred to Eve how difficult it must be for Jenny to be on an investigation of a missing girl her age. But she was steeled about it. Old souls inured to sorrow at too early an age.

"You know," Susan began thoughtfully, "I suppose I can trace Greta's obsession with secrecy to our childhood. When we were very young, there was a boy who she loved who was in love with me. We were children, it was all silly, but from that point on she would never bring me round anyone she cared about for fear they'd fall in love with me instead of her. It was absurd because she was always the prettier one, but so very scared of the world, so nervous. But stubborn. I couldn't tell her anything. She lived on her own terms."

Jenny had left Antonia's side and gone to the table where a bottle of tonic lay open and she was examining it.

"You told my associate what Ingrid looked like," Eve prompted, "like her mother but dark-haired. I don't suppose you have a picture?"

Susan shook her head. "She didn't look at all like her father, Greta said once. That may have caused the first strain."

"Do you think there's a possibility Ingrid wasn't Heinrich's child?" Eve whispered.

Susan glanced at Greta, then back to Eve, her eyes flashing with defense. "I don't know what to think, and I won't cast my sister in a poorer light than you're already seeing."

"Of course," Eve said gently. "We're just trying to have a greater sense of what may have happened to Ingrid and why. No further details about the Lion of Gramercy? No address on her letters I suppose?"

"None. They're here if you want to see one," Susan said and went to a metal tin set on the small kitchen counter by a bread box.

Cora glanced at Eve. Eve nodded and Cora slipped her glove from her hand and received the letter. She examined it and read it, Eve reading over her shoulder.

It was a note saying that the Lion had made intimations that perhaps they'd run away together and wouldn't that be grand. A few details about an opera singer she'd heard in the park and that was it. Baffling. No return address. Though Eve was sure Cora was getting something more personal from a psychometric read.

"Is there anything else you can think to tell us?" Cora pressed, returning the letter to Susan's outstretched hand. "I know you were constrained because she was conscious when we spoke before. Anything else that could help find Ingrid?"

Susan looked lost, tired.

"Any thoughts about Heinrich's family?" Eve asked.

"You're welcome to track down any Schwerin in New York to see; I heard of none. Greta said there was no one at their wedding. He was an orphan. I don't know if Schwerin was his birth name, or one given him."

"You have our card," Eve said. "We'll see if we can make any sense of who the Lion of Gramercy might be. Please don't hesitate to reach out, thank you for your time."

The group moved to the door. As Eve turned to follow Cora, Jenny grabbed Eve's hand. Looking down, Jenny signed, emphatically, that what was advertised on Greta's medicine bottle wasn't what was *in* the bottle—the spirits said so.

"Also, Miss Keller, you're likely right about the medicine making her worse." Eve said. "The chemist may have been skimping on the actual medication and putting in something else instead. It isn't what it says on the bottle."

Susan sighed. "Can't trust anything or anyone these days. May God turn our lot better with the turning of the century."

"Amen," Eve stated. "Please contact us with *anything* else. Neither you nor your sister will be compromised or in danger."

"You promise that?"

"I do," Eve said.

Susan seemed to be pondering something else for a moment, but she just nodded. She moved to close the door behind the coterie without another word. As they exited the building Eve took Jenny's hand. "Thank you, Jenny, what you offered was very valuable."

"Someone along the line is either intentionally or through negligent malpractice poisoning Greta," Antonia stated. "The only thing that came through for me in that house was the instinct that she knows something and someone is deliberately trying to sabotage any testimony."

"This isn't the direction back to the office, so I assume we're heading to Gramercy?" Cora asked.

Eve nodded.

"We didn't want to make things worse with the mother," Vera said, appearing suddenly at Eve's side in a burst of freezing air, Zofia appearing on the other.

"We spirits often addle grieving mothers who are ill and might be all the more able to see us. I didn't want her to think I was Ingrid," Zofia said sadly.

"Thank you both for being so wise and perceptive," Eve said to the spirits.

"From the outside of the building I could feel the sadness." Zofia said. "There was a feeling of being trapped, no way out, no way to win."

"A—how do you say—damned if you do, damned if you don't," Vera added sadly. "I think Greta was manipulated and was trying to limit the damage done but it didn't work . . ."

"I strongly feel that if we do find this Lion," Antonia stated, "he's not going to want a crowd in his parlor. Jenny and I will circle the park and get a read on what's around it."

Eve gave Antonia a grateful look. When she didn't have to delegate to separate the group it was always a kinder and gentler shift of powers and priorities.

Just off Lexington Avenue, between Twentieth and Twenty-First Street, Gramercy Park was one of the oldest in the city, small and surrounded by a tall iron gate closed to the public. One had to live facing the Park to have a key to it, and it saddened Eve that she never saw anyone in it. A caged bit of green used more as window-dressing and status symbol than as an interactive, life-giving aspect of sanity. The city's system of open parks had flourished since Central Park's installation mid-century; this was the elder model clinging to its boundaries.

The townhouses that all turned away and faced inward onto this small scrap of green always felt to Eve like they didn't want to acknowledge the rest of the city that kept tumultuously growing up around it. She couldn't blame Gramercy; she was concerned about tumbling forward into the future too . . .

Psychically, the effect of the park and the way the houses turned their faces into it trapped energy. For a Sensitive, Gramercy was like a cauldron of simmering stew; all cares, worries, and haunts could be seen and felt, emotions and fleeting sensations tasted on sooty city air. Eve didn't dare open herself to it. It was too easy to be distracted away from one case with the unfinished business of another spirit's needs.

While Antonia and Jenny crossed the lane to stroll along the park side, Cora and Eve kept to the townhouse side of the walk, taking in the varied levels of splendor from address to address, some more ostentatious than others, the more modest buildings still carrying a stately stubbornness. This stalwart aberration of an alcove was not found in any other part of Manhattan's makeup.

As they passed the beautiful brown sandstone Player's Club, Eve thought to what felt like months ago when in actuality it was mere days, toasting her Department thanks to Governor Roosevelt inside its lovely parlor. She'd been so nervous that night and anxiety had only increased with so much to prove. If she wasn't careful, the low-grade pain in the back of her skull would grow into an aura then migraine if she didn't offset the pressure.

Cora must have sensed this, for she turned to her, pausing at the steps of the club under the shade of a tree losing its leaves in an autumn breeze. Her hazel eyes were so piercing and perceptive. "What is it?"

"I fear now that we've made our department official I'll fail. It was all fine and good when I was chalking up clues and just seeing if I could help, a hobbyist, but now—"

"You can't entertain that kind of thinking," Cora replied. "You just can't. Make room. Uncle Louis always says," she added, gesturing to the air as if her spectral mentor was always just to her left, just a brush of a breeze away, his wisdom always with her even if his spectral form came and went, "that *les Mystères* need room to make miracles on behalf of the unknowable *Bondye*. Doubt takes away room for the divine."

"Thank you," Eve murmured, and they kept walking. "Doubt takes away room for the divine," she repeated. A new prayer.

The spirits that hung over the foliage behind the park bars—floating, transparent, luminous forms buffeted like laundry on a line over an imprisoned swath of green—called to Eve in a sighing, whispering mass, bidding her come talk to them and keep them company. She didn't look at them. Instead, she focused ahead on the next house and took a deep breath. Filling her lungs with air and her heart with hope she tried to make room.

Both women paused at the corner.

The house before them had rampant lion sculptures carved in pale limestone on either side of the stoop.

Cora and Eve glanced at one another and walked up the steps in unison. The building was one of the plainer townhouses along the Gramercy rectangle, white and Georgian, the lions being the only real flourish. In the front of the first floor's bay window, its white curtains closed, was a golden sign with black letters reading:

M. E. Dupont.

Undertaker

Office and Viewing Parlor now at *66 Irving Place*

"Take in whatever you can," Eve murmured to Cora. "We're moving a bit blindly."

Eve pressed the bell on a small decorative frame at the side of the plain wooden door with an etched glass oval, revealing an empty white entrance foyer with burgundy carpet within.

A young maid in a black dress with a starched apron and dark hair tucked up under a linen and lace bonnet came to the door and opened it slightly. "Yes?"

"Hello," Eve said with a smile. "I'd like to speak with Mr. Dupont?"

"He's at work," the young woman said flatly.

"Where would that be?" Eve asked.

"If you're here then wouldn't you know that?" she asked, gesturing to the sign.

"Did he used to have his practices here?"

"Used to, but he's expanded to an office and parlor now, around the corner heading downtown. You'll likely find him there, but he's very busy."

The maid made a move to close the door and Eve leaned forward, speaking quietly. "Do you remember a Greta Schwerin, nee Keller, working here?"

Her eyes widened and then she shook her head. An awkward silence ensued.

"Is there a lady of the house we could speak with?" Eve asked gently.

"Who are you here with? On behalf of? We can't be chatty with strangers, it's a solemn profession the family keeps, you know, and if you're not a client . . ."

"Of course, and we're not looking to do anything but find out what happened to poor Greta Schwerin's child, who went missing a few days ago."

The maid's eyes remained wide, her expression blank. "I don't know anything about that. There's been no children around here. Are you here asking for the . . . police? Is Greta in trouble?" the young woman asked in a tiny voice.

"No one is in trouble, we just want to find little Ingrid is all," Eve assured gently. "And yes, my colleague and I are asking on behalf of the police. Eve flashed her card, which only made the poor girl more nervous. "Is there anyone here who might know more?"

"I'll ask the lady of the house but I can't promise she'll see you. She's very busy with the accounts."

"Of course, please check."

The woman scurried off. Cora's brow furrowed as she murmured, "I can't tell if she's nervous because of hiding something or just shy. I can't read her."

"If the Duponts are indeed 'difficult' as Susan had indicated, perhaps staff are generally nervous."

After a moment, a woman came to the door. She was stern and seemed too thin—hollowed out, even—dressed in a dark brown wool with black ribbon accents, greying hair up in a braided bun.

"Come in," she said curtly. "We'll speak in the hall." The woman closed the door behind them and turned. "You are?"

"Miss Whitby and Miss Dupris," Eve said, showing her card that bore the police seal. It had been a deliberate choice not to include Ghost Precinct on her cards. It would have predisposed witnesses and suspects one way or another, and she needed neutrality. The woman glanced at the card and kept her unwavering, stern expression. "Inquiring after Greta Schwerin, nee Keller, who may have worked here? Does that name ring a bell?"

"Yes," the woman replied flatly.

"How long had she worked here before getting married?"

"I don't know, good help is hard to find and flighty girls are the worst of the lot, so good riddance after, I don't know, a few years."

"Did you know she had a child?" Cora asked.

"No, when she married, she left, and why would I know anything further?" the woman said with disdain, as if the idea that she should know anything about the lives of help was offensive to even consider, then clenched her jaw so hard Eve thought she might break a tooth.

"Did you ever see her husband? Was he a delivery man to the practice here?"

"Perhaps, the help deals with deliveries and most go to the office now. I don't know anyone I don't need to."

Cora looked around and her eyes stopped at the stairwell where a window at the first landing looked out onto a brick structure, a new building blocking what once might have been a lovely view. At the window, outside looking in, Eve saw the same thing, a grim-faced spirit of a girl in contemporary clothing, a plain dress. She was pointing to her right, where Eve assumed there was a parlor beyond an arched threshold.

"Did you used to lay out bodies here in this building?" Eve asked. The woman's eyes narrowed.

"What would that have to do with a missing child?" Mrs. Dupont countered.

"I'm more wondering about the profession of death," Eve continued. "How it's changed through the years, people not always wanting bodies laid out in their own homes anymore. Do you find that a burden, to take on what others feel they must distance? Does this place feel haunted?"

"*Haunted*?" The woman pursed her lips. "Are you with the police or the metaphysical society?"

"I'm just inquiring if those who work for you . . . feel comfortable," Eve said, not letting the brisk attitude of this woman ruffle her in the slightest.

"They know what they're getting into—there's a sign out front, and death comes for us all, Miss. Every part of life needs managing, same with death. We're practical about that here and if anyone goes on about ghost stories, well, they can pack their bags."

"Have they, though?" Cora pressed gently. "Gone on about ghost stories?"

Eve noticed the edge of the maid's black dress was poking out from around the corner of the foyer, listening.

"Not to me, and again, I don't see what that has to do with a missing child. If that's what you're on about, and not tracking the actual child, I feel sorry for the waiting mother."

Eve and Cora maintained their pleasant expressions and didn't rise to the insult. "Did you used to hold viewings in your parlor before the new offices?" Cora asked. "Might we see the room?"

"Suit yourself," the woman sighed, gesturing for them to follow her. The edge of the maid's black dress disappeared and as they entered the open white room with burgundy curtains, stately but plain, the maid was dusting the mantel of a marble fireplace. "There's nothing to see. We use it as an actual parlor these days now that my husband has the Irving Place office, so your morbid curiosity will have to look elsewhere."

Mrs. Dupont moved to open all the curtains and Eve almost jumped.

Ghosts were looking in all the windows. Floating at eye level with Eve and Cora. They didn't want to be inside, but they certainly wanted to be seen. It was a startling image. There must have been twenty or so, of varying ages and tones of grey, their clothing dating from the recent decade. Perhaps those who'd had a viewing here—they were all in their Sunday best, fit for a funeral.

"Why did you expand?" Cora said, forcing herself to look away from the horde at the windows. "Has business been good?"

The woman smiled primly. "Death is a constant, and the city is growing. We provide what people need and do so in a neutral space, which many find part of the comfort. It is a Dupont tradition, to make what is sorrowful manageable."

"A noble sentiment," Cora said.

"Do you remember anything about Greta before she left your employ?"

"I maintain it's the flighty ones you can't abide. She was always off in her own little world and then turned very religious. Kept crossing herself even going from one room to the next. Had to put an end to papal nonsense right off; told her to look for work elsewhere. She gave me an uppity response, saying she was already engaged, so it all worked out. I am sorry to hear about the child. Now if you'll excuse me, you can see yourselves out."

"Thank you for your time Mrs. Dupont."

She harrumphed and turned away, exiting into another room and calling for the maid, Berta, to follow her. When the parlor door closed behind Dupont, Berta turned to Eve. "Anything strange was all moved to the offices when Dupont took on his business partner," she whispered and hurried away.

They walked out the door, catching Antonia's eye as she and Jenny were taking another turn around the gated park towards them.

Glancing back, the maid was watching them through the glass oval of the front door. When she saw Eve notice her, she drew a curtain across the glass.

"Friendly folks," Cora said with a smirk as the group rejoined and Eve gestured ahead. "Irving Place next?" Cora asked. Eve nodded and explained to Antonia and Jenny what had gone on.

"Hiding something?" Antonia asked. Cora and Eve chorused yes, but Eve clarified.

"We can't say what exactly, or if it even relates to Ingrid at all; we may have been sensing an issue with how the help is treated. But being told "anything strange is at Irving Place" raises our stakes."

"I think the offices were the direction the ghost outside the stair was pointing—not their parlor, which seemed mostly neutral," Eve shared.

"Except for all the ghosts looking in all the windows!" Cora exclaimed. "You'd think I'd be prepared for it, but not like that. Just dead-eyed and staring. If twenty ghosts are looking into a building, not haunting it, I'm more worried about why the ghosts won't go *in*. I've never seen anything like it."

Just down Irving Place, they found a grey sandstone three-story building with a wide front window where a towering vase of white lilies stood on a bay ledge.

A brass placard to the side of the door read:

DUPONT AND MONTMARTRE, UNDERTAKERS
VIEWING PARLOR, FUNERAL PLANNING
DEATH NEED NOT BE THE END . . .

"Isn't that the truth," Antonia said, reading the sign. "Again, my instinct says to let you two interview. We'll see who comes in and out, and if any spirits outside speak about what's inside."

As they stared at the building, twenty or so ghosts wafted over in a horde and floated about the third floor—circled it, even—as if they were caught up in a procession. It was utterly eerie. They looked like the same entourage of ghosts that had been looking in the windows just a moment ago.

Jenny looked up and shook her head, signing that she didn't like the look of that and she'd be standing outside, thank you very much. She grabbed Antonia's hand, who nodded.

"Yes, we'll be waiting outside, then," Antonia stated. "Have fun, ladies . . ."

"Thanks," Eve said, setting her jaw and ascending the stoop behind Cora, who pressed the bell.

After a moment, a long-faced, clean-shaven man answered the door in a plain black suit. His hair was auburn, too much so, as if a dye had been applied to it to hide greying hair, from the look of the lines around his eyes.

"Hello, how can we be of service?" the man asked.

"May we come in?" Eve flashed her card. "Dupris and Whitby here; we're with a department that deals with missing children and I wanted to ask you a few questions."

"My child is grown," he stated as he gestured them into the entrance hall. Much like Dupont's home, this building was plain and white, with deep red carpeting, arched ceilings and a great deal of light through the front, made into a glow by gauzy white curtains on all windows. To their immediate right was what Eve assumed to be the viewing parlor, with velvet-seated wooden chairs facing an empty wooden dais with carved floral motifs.

"Is this your business?" Eve asked. "Dupont or Montmartre?"

"Dupont here, Montmartre is in France at the moment."

"Both French names, one a famous cemetery at that, fitting," Cora stated. "*Parlez vous français?*"

"*Un peu*," Dupont replied with a chuckle. "Not fluent like my partner. He helps keep me up to date with all the latest trends. Death is ever changing as are the fashions and sciences around it, and as you well know the French are the most fashionable about everything."

"Indeed," Eve agreed. "You used to work out of your home, but have you found this to be a more neutral space, and better for working in a firm? We just spoke to your wife."

"Whatever for?" he asked, lifting thin, carefully manicured eyebrows.

"About Greta Schwerin. Greta Keller for most of the time she worked with you—that would have been for what, a few years?"

"Three, yes—what about her?"

"Her child Ingrid is sickly and missing, and she herself is very ill. We're trying to find out what happened to Ingrid, and if you can think of anything that could help us, we'd be very grateful."

Dupont sat down in one of the viewing chairs.

"Missing, you say?" he asked slowly.

"Initially, we received a tip about Ingrid going missing from a charitable institution she had been left in temporarily, for safety reasons," Eve began. No need to tell the man the tip had come from a ghost. "There was reason to suspect the father had perhaps become violent. Fearing for Ingrid, her mother took her back out of that charitable institution and from there, Ingrid has disappeared. Greta has been, well, not entirely lucid, and therefore not very forthcoming."

He sighed heavily.

"Do you know something otherwise?" Cora urged quietly.

"She . . . she brought the child to me. Ingrid. She brought her here. Dead. At least we thought so. While she was here she broke from what seemed like death's grip and roused a moment. It was a last gasp, the body's last fight. It is a terrible trick of life, to rally before death, to brighten before going out. She then faded and Greta's failing, feverish mind took one more precarious step towards the brink."

Eve's heart sunk and she saw Cora waver slightly on her feet.

"I prepared her to look her best for a postmortem photograph," Dupont continued. "I offered to take care of the burial process, free of charge, but she insisted that she wanted to handle it. She wrapped her up after the photograph and took her away. I have no idea what happened after that."

"That's . . . so very sad," Cora began.

"And a bit confusing for us," Eve continued. "Greta has not allowed herself to realize Ingrid has passed and we have no idea where the body has now gone. If you have any idea where it could have ended up, as we're wondering if the father got involved, please let us know. Here is my card," Eve passed it along. "We just want closure for the family."

"Of course," he murmured, tucking the card in his breast-pocket, seemingly lost in far-away thoughts.

Eve noticed a medicine cabinet in the corner, a familiar bottle on the counter below—a Prenze product.

"Are you also a dispensary?" Eve asked, gesturing to the cabinet.

"Often when loved ones are in their final days and families come to make arrangements with me, they may be in need of extra tonic to treat pain and ease their transition. It is a tumultuous and difficult time, so I have some on hand. Nothing too strong, nothing overriding a doctor's orders, just palliative."

"You didn't happen to dispense any to Greta Schwerin, did you?"

"I did. I find that a pain tonic can often make the grieving sleep easier."

Jenny's statement that the tonic wasn't as advertised rung in Eve's mind. Was that Dupont's fault, or the Prenze Company's? And was that a matter to press right now?

"What's on the third floor?" Cora asked.

"Bodies," Dupont replied simply. "It's where I prepare them."

Hence the spectral funeral procession outside, perhaps. Eve bowed her head. "Thank you for your time, Mr. Dupont."

"No trouble at all."

They exited and, catching sight of them, Antonia and Jenny walked on ahead. Sure enough, glancing back, Dupont was watching them out the bay window, over the lilies, curtain drawn. When he saw Eve look back, he waved.

She glanced up. The ghosts had stopped circling above and instead had fanned out in an array around the top floor, watching. Nothing was said, which was perhaps the most unsettling thing about the spectacle; the spectral silence.

"You'd think he'd not want to hoist bodies up and down two floors," Eve stated. "That doesn't seem quite right."

"Something ate at me about that too," Cora replied. "Unless he has some kind of body-sized dumbwaiter, it would be pointless effort."

Around the corner, turning back to Gramercy, from where they would continue heading west, a cold blast of air hit Eve square in the face.

"*That* was the picture! *That* was the house!" Vera cried as the park came into view, pointing at the Dupont residence.

Eve looked up, trying to catch Vera's transparent eyes. She wafted down to Eve's eye level.

"The post-mortem photograph you threw into the hall for the wife to find?" Eve asked, hoping for clarification. The ghost nodded.

It was good Eve never did write up that preemptive report, as things were unfolding to be quite a bit more complicated.

Vera was floating along with them, but staring back at the Dupont residence with a worried face, as if there was something she was trying to place, and she did so until they had turned off Gramercy Place, heading west towards the Village.

"We could have used your insights in these two interrogations—where were you? I thought you were right behind us when we first entered the park," Eve stated, glad in the moment that she didn't need to be cautious talking with a ghost, since her colleagues were walking with her. Walking alone, it would appear to the majority of the population like she were speaking to thin air.

"I . . . I lost my way . . . I'm sorry," the ghost murmured. "I tried to keep up with you, I truly did . . ."

Vera was so genuinely apologetic, and baffled, as if she were experiencing a senility she never had in life that was catching up to her in death. There was no longer any doubting her ghosts were losing steam and becoming fractured fragments.

"That's all right, love," Eve reassured. "Just . . . do whatever you can to stay with us. I can't lose you too . . ."

"No, no, I . . . I don't want to go," the old woman sounded frightened and childlike. Eve reached out to the cold air beside her. Cora kept the both of them from lurching into worry and melancholy by keeping Vera engaged.

"Why was he, Dupont, keeping the photograph then, do you figure, Vera? Just sentimentality? If so, it was clear his wife didn't share the same fondness for the help."

"There was something deeply personal going on," Vera replied. "Secrets, betrayal of trust. And grief."

"Was Dupont Ingrid's father? Did they both know that? The hasty marriage after stolen virtue? Greta covering her tracks and looking out for herself, but the fact of a different father remained?" Eve asked.

"It seems the only answer for the secrecy and the discomfort."

"Did you sense Dupont was telling the truth?"

"Not the *whole* truth," Cora replied. Eve nodded in agreement. "What do we do about all this?"

"If the child died sick, as it seemed clear from Grace that she was already ill, then what a grieving mother does with the body I'm not going to make my business or that of our precinct. But why not be honest about it, even with what remaining cognizance she has?"

"If Ingrid's body went missing, the fact that she then *died* wasn't voiced to Susan, perhaps out of guilt or just trauma," Cora mused. "The death is bad enough . . ."

"Indeed. This is all just so sad," Antonia said with a sigh. "And uncomfortable."

"And unfinished," Vera murmured. "Other pieces . . ." She vanished without another word, her face determined. Generally this meant she had an idea and was off to test a theory or gather information. These days Eve couldn't be sure.

"I don't know if we should bring this to Susan or not. The only reason we started on this path was the ghost from Grace Memorial, the one who managed to use a telephone, asking me to look after Ingrid . . . It never became a police matter and I'm not sure it should now."

Jenny took Eve's hand. Eve looked down at her. Jenny signed that she should rest, that she looked tired and she wasn't of any use to anyone tired.

"I think Jenny has the best answer for the moment," Eve said, running a fond hand over the girl's hair that Antonia kept neatly braided. "Rest on it, resolve tomorrow. Those involved have our cards, and we'll keep reaching out to Ingrid in hopes her soul can find peace. That's what troubles me the most now, and that's what I'll fight for; that she above all finds the answers she needs to be a contented soul, either to haunt this earth or to move onto the Elysian Fields."

When they returned to the office, McDonnell stood, looking a bit harrowed.

"Thank goodness you're back. The Foundling Hospital has been ringing trying to get a hold of you, *milady* . . ." Again with that aggrandized foolishness.

Eve set her jaw and frowned. "What happened?"

"There was a delivery to the building." The matron shifted uncomfortably on her feet.

"Of what?"

"The dead body of a saint."

Chapter Twelve

"A saint . . ." Eve repeated slowly.

"A child, done up like one," McDonnell explained.

Eve placed a hand on the matron's desk, steadying herself at this startling news.

"Did the Sister who called recognize the body?" she asked, trying to grapple with facts.

"I can't say, but the woman, Sister Rose, sounded beside herself, whatever happened, and she said something relates to an angel so you should just go up there, please," the matron declared.

Glancing at her colleagues, Eve noted everyone's expression as suddenly worried and wary. They filed into their office to sit down a moment and catch their breaths.

Eve turned back to McDonnell, leaning over the woman's desk. She blinked up at her with her usual set jaw.

"I understand I'm hardly your favorite addition to the NYPD but would you *please* dispense with the 'milady' and all that nonsense, Mrs. McDonnell?" Eve asked quietly, trying to sound good-natured but in fact very irritated. And tired.

"If you can't take good-natured teasing then what on earth are you doing anywhere near civic duty?" McDonnell asked. "The gents take to boxing one another, the least you can do is grow a thicker skin. Until you do, I'm going to continue to call you ridiculous titles befitting your daintiness. I'm trying to help you *survive* the NYPD; you're quite welcome."

"This is your idea of support, McDonnell?" Eve said with a dry laugh.

The matron blinked at her. "Yes."

"All right then. Are you . . . trying to be funny?"

"Yes."

"You're not funny, McDonnell."

There was a beat before McDonnell loosed an echoing laugh. "You may just be all right after all, child."

"Glad someone is entertained," Eve muttered and moved towards her office door. She needed a cup of tea or coffee before she embarked on seeing whatever grim and strange resolution this had come to.

"Get to the bottom of this nonsense, will you?" McDonnell added quietly, earnestly, in a far more amenable tone than Eve had ever heard out of her. "It sounds rather dreadful . . . Terrorizing nuns and abandoned children at the Foundling Hospital? Terrible."

Eve didn't turn around, just nodded. "Indeed."

She needed to call Horowitz. She didn't recall a telephone in his office so she'd have to go through the main switchboard. He'd want to know how this was progressing, for better or worse. What had started with a stolen angel was now culminating in this. Horowitz couldn't be her liaison, but there was no reason she shouldn't update him on the case he'd been the one to drag her into.

Once the message was relayed, and she had a firm promise that it would be passed onto the detective as soon as possible, Eve turned to Cora.

Antonia was standing behind Jenny at her desk with an arm on her shoulder. She shook her head, indicating Jenny had reached her limit on this case. The young girl's eyes were wide, scared, and far away.

"We'll hold down the fort here or I'll take her back for a nap," Antonia murmured. "I don't think she should see . . ."

A dead little girl her age, dressed up like a saint in her faith . . .

"No, she really shouldn't," Eve murmured. "Thank you." She rushed out the door with Cora.

"This must have something to do with it being important that Ingrid was raised Catholic," Eve stated.

"Exactly."

They went east, took the elevated rail up and exited a few blocks from the institution.

Ringing the doorbell brought a wide-eyed novice to the door. When Eve gave her name, the young woman said nothing but gestured her inside frantically. The children must have been dismissed because there were none to be seen, though there was a general hubbub of noise above them; likely dormitory rooms. Several Sisters of Charity in their black habits and wide black bonnets stood in the entrance hall staring at them, baffled and worried.

Sister Rose, her expressive, warm face harrowed, hurried down the plain entrance hall and led Eve and Cora into the main room as she'd done for Eve and Horowitz. All chairs had been cleared out and the space was empty save for a long table at the front of the room.

Over a small casket-sized box was draped a large blue velvet curtain with gold trim at the bottom. Surely the stolen curtain from the synagogue.

"May I?" Eve asked, gesturing towards the drape. Sister Rose nodded. Eve lifted the curtain to find a body on display in a glass casket, golden paint in detailing around the edges curving into an imitation of metal filigree.

Inside lay the small body of a dark-haired girl in a white silk gown, beaded and layered with lace and tulle. A communion gown. Greasepaint makeup had been painted on her small face to mask the pallor of death, but it looked garish rather than an imitation of a sleeping child. The smell of embalming fluid was overpowering, as if too much had been used.

Eve sent out a prayer for Vera to join them, to help identify the body and see if this was the face from that post-mortem photograph. If it was Ingrid Schwerin. Her heart broke at this sight. Her next prayer was for the spirit of this poor child.

Around the child's head was a golden metal halo that radiated out from a crown of white flowers, and around her body were garlands of silk roses, white, pink, and red and at her feet sat a small stone sculpture of an angel; surely the other stolen items the detective mentioned.

The body was dressed up like an effigy of a saint on her saint's feast day. Eve often saw parades of effigies during feast days around New York, taking place in various predominantly Catholic enclaves around the city. Regional details and practices varied, but the basic principles were the same. This was created as fully as any of those effigies, the difference being this was a corpse, not a fabrication imbued with sacred meaning.

In her folded hands was a painted wooden figure of an angel. Lovely, but simple. When Eve pointed to it with a questioning look, Rose nodded.

"That's the angel that was taken."

"Which saint is she made up to be?" Eve asked quietly.

Sister Rose pointed to a small placard at the girl's feet where a word was written in red paint by a shaking hand.

Inocencia.

"*Santa Inocencia*—Saint Innocence," Sister Rose began, "some two-hundred years ago, was killed by her own father for befriending a nun and wanting to join the Catholic faith. The girl received Holy Communion and then, when the father found out, he plunged a knife through her little chest. I . . ." Tears fell from the nun's eyes. "I pray that sort of violence did not happen here to this poor child and that she is simply meant to represent Innocence itself, not a repetition of that history."

The nun shivered suddenly, visibly as the temperature of the room plummeted.

Vera appeared at Eve's side.

"Do you recognize this child?" Eve asked, both for Vera's sake and to get the answer out of Sister Rose too. She was careful not to speak to thin air. Often people of the cloth sensed spirits more directly, but she didn't want to additionally tax an already strained woman. This body was strain enough.

"No," Rose said. "I know the names and faces of every precious life that has come into my care. This is the first I've seen her."

"It's the girl from the photograph in the Dupont home," Vera confirmed. "Her spirit led me there. It must be Ingrid. She wasn't made up like this in that photograph, though . . ."

Eve circled the small casket several times, thinking, feeling the eyes of the Sisters watching her, as if they didn't dare watch the effigy.

"We believe this is the body of Ingrid Schwerin," Eve stated. "Daughter of Greta and Heinrich. We'd been looking for her."

"Heinrich Schwerin . . ." Sister Rose murmured, wide-eyed.

"You know the name?"

"Yes. Heinrich was left here. As you know, we keep a basinet out front for desperate mothers to leave a baby. He was raised here. Why, Sister Loretta was his favorite . . . oh . . ." She put her hand to her mouth, tears in her eyes. "He must have taken that angel."

"And there it is," Eve murmured, pointing to small, dead hands clasped over a wooden icon with open wings.

"So it is . . ." Rose murmured. She made the sign of the cross. "Why would you do all this, Heinrich?" she asked the air. No spirit dared answer for the living.

"What was your impression of him as a child?" Eve asked.

"Quiet. Devoted to his faith. We hoped for the best for him. He was adopted by the Schwerin family, upstate if I recall. I didn't know he had returned to the city. I wish . . . we could have helped . . ."

Cora moved around to the other side of the glass casket. Eve could see her colleague was shielding her hand from view of the nuns while pressing it to the base of the coffin to get a psychometric read.

"There were family tensions in play, and we were told Ingrid was already ill for some time," Eve explained to the Sisters. "Likely consumption. We know where the mother and aunt are, we'll give them your information.

None of this is your fault," Eve reassured, seeing in the Sisters' faces the great need for someone to help make sense of this.

"In whatever twisted way Mr. Schwerin's mind was working," Eve continued, "he likely wanted to honor you, and this place, and his faith, by this presentation of his only child. I don't think it's meant to terrorize you, terrible as this is. The minds of the ill are . . . hard to comprehend. I hope you know how much good you do here and that this does nothing to change that."

Tears fell from several of the Sisters' eyes and they nodded.

"We don't have any sense of where Mr. Schwerin is," Cora added. "If you should encounter him, please alert us and your local precinct."

"We'll alert the mother and I hope she will retrieve the body and make arrangements," Eve offered. "We can take care of anything that you don't wish to be burdened with or believe would be a safety hazard for you or the children. The blue curtain, it was taken, as were the statues and the garlands. You should retrieve your angel."

"No, I think I'll let her rest with it," Rose said softly.

"But the other items, once burial arrangements are in order, will need to be returned, the detective and I can reunite them with the sacred spaces they came from."

"Bless you."

"And you," Cora added. "Do be in touch with anything else."

That was enough, for now. It would have to be. Contacts were exchanged along with soft benedictions.

Ingrid's physical remains were a certain amount of a resolution. What and who got her to this state was as yet to be determined. Eve would fight to find out what happened, for her own sense of decency as well as closure for the family.

Exiting, Eve grasped onto the railing to keep from tumbling over, feeling entirely exhausted. She noticed Cora had gained dark circles under her eyes, so Eve felt justified in stopping for the day.

"Rest. I need to rest, I'm overwhelmed," Eve confessed to her colleague. "I can't go on anymore today. But tell me, did you see anything psychometrically when touching the coffin?"

"Yes. I envisioned a man I didn't recognize, crying as he painted on the glass. I saw him cover over the casket with that curtain. Not Dupont. He had that angel in his hands."

"Heinrich?"

"Likely. His surroundings I couldn't glean more of than a parlor in a modest apartment. More tomorrow. There isn't a life to save anymore, just a spirit to contact to be sure her voice is heard and at peace, and those who remain living must be told the truth."

"That it's related is a surprise, one odd item connected to the next."

"You shouldn't be surprised by patterns anymore," Cora declared. "What comes to you from the spirit world always seems related to a web, not a single string."

"I don't think God works like that, stitching together our every move."

"No deity does. But I think the spirit world shows us the connections. It knows we're suited to follow their pieces, even if we feel they're disparate."

Eve nodded. "I am very blessed to have you, Coraline Louise Dupris."

Cora beamed. "I'm very glad to hear you say that, Evelyn Helen Whitby."

Such extreme exhaustion took over Eve that she barely remembered the rest of the trip home, let alone greeting anyone when she got in. Sleep took over her like a sudden storm breaking over a calm shore, the crash of waves bearing on their roiling crests a barely perceptible whisper . . .

Help me . . .

Chapter Thirteen

The next morning was hard on everyone, and over warm oatmeal and jam, Eve struggled to explain the previous day's events to Antonia, who recoiled at the account, crossing herself. Even though, by her own account, she'd fallen away from that faith, reflexive habits remained.

Jenny wasn't feeling well and had been instructed to remain in bed. Antonia volunteered to stay with her.

"I can stay," Cora offered. "I don't want you to feel left out in our rounds of late."

Antonia blinked back sudden tears.

"When I left behind my family," she began quietly, "when they couldn't accept me, nor my gifts, nor *who* I am, I left behind a little sister who had once depended on me. She understood why I had to go and become the woman I am, in the way children comprehend things adults refuse to. I'd like to think the spirits are trying to offer balance here, bringing us back a semblance of things we've had to sacrifice. Jenny is a bit of my beautiful justice."

Eve smiled warmly at Antonia. "A noble sentiment and we are so lucky that providence brought you to our doorstep. Thank you for your understanding and help. But be honest with me if ever your needs or your calling aren't being met."

Antonia looked at Cora a moment before looking out the window and smiling when the sun peeked out from the clouds and lit up the dining room lace curtains in a dappled glow. "I am well met."

Cora and Eve took to the offices in silence, knowing they'd have to check in with Susan and Greta to make sure the Foundling Hospital had reached out, and if not, tell them the strange turn and see what was to be done about burial.

Eve was hesitant to go to Dupont with any of this information, especially considering the state of Ingrid's body, so heavily embalmed and prepared. It seemed hard for her not to think he'd been still involved after Greta supposedly took her away. Why wasn't anyone telling the whole truth?

Just as she'd made herself a cup of coffee, there was a knock at her door.

"Come in," Eve called.

Maria Sullivan, the eldest and most revered of Evelyn Northe-Stewart's hired help stood at the door in a blue linen dress and a flocked hat, clutching a parasol and looking extremely uncomfortable.

"Could we speak in private?" Maria asked Eve. She looked at Cora and added; "No offense, Miss Dupris, I just . . . don't want to concern you needlessly."

Eve could feel her colleague stiffen behind her even without looking at them. The dynamic was precarious and with Cora already feeling excluded, Eve merely closed the door behind Maria instead and spoke gently.

"It's all right Maria," Eve replied. "If you've a concern, then it is mine and Cora's equally, as Cora is my foundation."

She could feel this ease Cora's hackles. Maria remained uncomfortable but spoke anyway, stepping further into the room.

"I'm very sorry to trouble you, but I know you care as I do about the woman who is a mother to us all . . ."

Eve felt her heart spasm. This was about Gran.

"Has something happened to Gran?" she asked, almost choking on the words.

Eve could feel a fresh panic like nothing she'd ever encountered batter her body, as if an explosion had gone off beside her. Maria shifted anxiously on her feet.

"I . . . I hope not," Maria said, trying to remain calm, "and I very much hope I'm just a hysterical old woman, but Eve, my dear, do you remember a while ago when you told me that my instincts were very sound? And that I should listen to them more often?"

"Of course, Maria," Eve replied cautiously. "Go on," she said, forcing herself to do something physical to tamp down on her anxiety. Tea. She owed Maria tea—it was only fair the woman that had waited on her so much got her turn.

"This morning, a lady in mourning—fine clothes, thick veil, I couldn't get a good look at her—came asking for your Gran's advice, as many do, seeking her Spiritualist counsel. She bid the woman come into the parlor, where I brought them some tea and then I left them alone, as I do whenever she's a medium for anyone. I didn't get a sense of anything out of the ordinary. But then, I heard the front door close." Maria nodded in thanks as Eve handed her tea.

She continued. "I come back into the foyer, the parlor door is open, they're gone. I look out the panel of the front door to see Madame walking ahead of this woman and turning down the block, a determined expression on her face, the kind when she's trying to figure something out. Again, while her leaving without saying anything isn't common if she knows me or one of the other girls is easily within earshot, there have been many times when she just does what she likes and we've no idea about any of it. But she's been gone all day. Usually if she's with a client that's not a friend, she doesn't extend herself for hours like this."

"That is . . . unusual," Eve replied, trying to keep her voice calm. "If she's not back by . . ."

"If she isn't back within the next few hours I'd say get the folks you work with out on the streets and start looking for her."

A potent memory caught Eve, almost like a slap in her face. In her early days of understanding ghosts and the energy they could drain from you, paired with the needs of someone in mourning begging to be connected to a loved one, Gran told Eve her own boundaries.

"*I never give a grieving person, even a family member, more than two hours of my time, my gift. Beyond that, it is dangerous for me. Find your own time and you keep to it, no matter what is asked of you*," Gran had instructed.

Two hours.

"Maria, remind me exactly when Gran left the house, do you figure?" Eve asked.

"It would have been just after ten in the morning. I told the other girls this was where I was going and I told them to call you if she returned." Maria looked balefully around the room before her eye fell on the large telephone box on the wall.

Eve glanced at the clock. It was two in the afternoon. It had been longer than two hours by far.

Panic wrestled within her, piercing and tearing. A part of her was being ripped away.

Psychic bonds were hard to describe, and they varied from one Sensitive to the next. Her bond with Gran had always created warmth and comfort. At the moment she was cold and terrified. Maria was still staring at her.

"All right. Well. I'd say return to the house and see if anything has changed. I will call every associate whose phone number I have, and even her favorite cafes and restaurants if I have to. I know all her haunts. Don't worry, we'll find her. Thank you." Eve embraced the woman who was a part of their family. Maria nodded and walked away.

Eve turned back to Cora, tears welling up in her eyes. Cora came close and grabbed Eve's hands. "Everything will be all right," she assured.

"We *have* to find her . . ." Eve choked.

Before Eve made calls she darted to the séance table and sat down.

Cora joined her without a moment's hesitation and once Eve lit the candle and rang the bell, she tried desperately to calm herself as she took Cora's hand.

Recklessly she plunged into the Corridors. Just thinking of Gran was muscle memory enough to plunge her into those depths. She didn't even need Gran's guided hypnosis, she dove right in. Surely the absence of the architecture had just been an anomaly.

No.

Much like trying to look for Maggie, her psychic search went nowhere. No sign or scrap of Gran, no tether that Eve had entirely taken for granted. Perhaps Maggie had gone and taken the whole of the Corridors with her. Everything had changed. Nothing remained but shadowy depth.

Nothing.

A terrible, ungodly nothing. The worst feeling Eve had ever known. The absence of spirits tethering knowledge. A barren world. Eve had heard hell described as an absence of God. This black void, when she expected something so different, was the most terrifying thing she'd ever experienced. Pressure built in her head; there would be a headache if not a near blinding migraine.

The acute panic sharpened within her and she felt the void for what it was. An integral part of her soul was missing. She had prepared herself since childhood that those who were her elders would go before her. But they would still be there; their spirits immortal. Yet she was not here. Gran was not *here*.

Eve catapulted forward and nearly slammed her nose onto the table. The candle fell from the holder and nearly set the tablecloth on fire. Cora batted out the singed fabric and helped Eve stay upright.

"Eve, what are you—"

"Calls," she barked. "I must make calls."

Numbly she rose to her feet, went to the phone.

There were a holy trinity of people Eve had been instructed to call in case of an emergency.

Reverend Blessing wasn't in his church office but Eve left a message.

Next she fumbled at her notebook for the right number and asked the operator to connect her to Ambassador Bishop's office at the British Consulate. As an ambassador, he was often traveling, but she had been instructed to try his office first before his house and she was in luck that a familiar voice was soon on the line.

"Ambassador, it's Eve Whitby. I need to see you and your wife. It's an emergency."

Chapter Fourteen

Evelyn Northe-Stewart fought back towards consciousness.

There had been a troubled woman she'd invited into her parlor for a Spiritual counseling and medium session. She'd been dressed to the nines in mourning, thick veil and all. Said she'd been recommended, came to her door fully in tears and expressive suffering.

Or so she'd thought.

The woman who had given her name as Mrs. Calvin was unfamiliar to Evelyn, though admittedly she didn't lift the veil and she didn't get a good look past the thick layers of muslin trimmed at the edges with black lace. That should have been a warning sign, that she hadn't gotten a good look at who she was making herself vulnerable for . . . Since when did she set aside her own life-long rules?

There had been a compelling feeling about the morning, she recalled, trying to sift herself back to consciousness, when her body felt stiff and uncooperative. A shooting pain went up her back. She was sitting in a hard chair. She tried to move and found she was in constraints.

Panic flooded her and the rush of terror cleared the fog from her mind and senses, only to find she was still impaired. She couldn't open her eyes—there was a blindfold. She couldn't scream—there was a gag. Something cold and metal was attached to each of her temples and she felt supremely dizzy.

A strange sound emanated from behind her head somewhere, in this cold place she was trapped in, like the sound of a phonograph needle hissing over the silent moments of a cylinder disc or record. The sound dissipated into the darkness of a large space with a cool draft that was a distinct feeling from the wake of spirits.

This was a far more insidious chill.

What had happened . . . ? Her mind felt disjointed. She'd invited the woman in, then what . . .

Don't invite anyone in . . .

The warning. The spirit world had warned her granddaughter Eve, had warned *her*, but she'd flat out ignored it and was now paying the price. Her mind might not have been working at its best capacity but she was certainly quick to chastise herself; her self-censure was in perfect order while her body was hampered.

She vaguely remembered the conversation with Mrs. Calvin—something about a dead child. The most evocative of situations, meant to arouse empathy and aid. Because of Eve's recent cases, Evelyn, who of course was most keen on helping anyone through the loss of a young soul, perhaps gave more attention to this than she would have otherwise, in hopes it might actually relate and be helpful in Eve's present ventures. She overextended.

The haziness suggested to Evelyn that she had somehow been drugged. The heaviness to her body was unnatural, the effects of some noxious paralytic. Trying to connect missing pieces Evelyn grasped having needed fresh air. Either she had suggested it or the woman had, but she did recall leaving the house and that the autumn day had been warm. She recalled looking at the brightly turning leaves of a beautiful maple tree along the low Central Park stone wall.

Then nothing.

The woman centered in this mystery had been clearly in need. Evelyn felt confident in that; she could usually spot an insincere mourner a mile away. Perhaps someone had put the mourner up to this trap or perhaps what Evelyn had taken for sincere grief was instead a troubled soul in need of intervention of the law, not spiritual guidance. She couldn't know the intent—all she could do now was try to send some kind of distress signal.

Perhaps spirits could help illuminate what had happened and how to get out.

In the forced shadows of the blindfold, Evelyn closed her eyes in ritual and tried to reach out for spirits. Her psychic channel felt raw, bloody, as if someone had been rooting around in her soul and breaking off branches from her inner tree of life.

There were spirits nearby. Not inside but in the vicinity. She herself was near the water. Her channel did best near rivers and estuaries. She must be downtown—she knew the feel of this air very well.

The device somewhere behind her whirred slightly as she silently pleaded to any spirit that might be listening. She bid the dead heed the plea of the living, and there was a faint scratching sound, like fingernails or a pen on paper.

Please she said internally, trying to swallow. Her mouth was dry and the corners of her lips bloody from the gag. *I need your help. Any of you who can hear me . . . Send for my soldiers . . .*

There was a fluttering, a movement out of the corner of her third eye, a white-silver leaf floating through darkness towards her. The whirring of the hissing cylinder, the mysterious machine sped up.

"Hello," a spirit responded, too far away for Evelyn to see them in her mind's eye.

There was a loud zap and a hiss, and Evelyn cried out in pain.

An electrical charge. The spirit was gone.

Evelyn tried reaching out again. The machine was whirring at its same sound and pace. The movement coming towards her, ethereal light in shadow, was even more hesitant than before.

"I'm *trapped*—" Evelyn begged the spirit world to hear and she cried out, hampered by the gag, as the lashing sting of a jolting shock coursed through her body. She shook in the chair. A wisp of smoke curled up from the lace around her throat and she smelled the singed fabric.

She was alone again.

In the bare room there was no presence, no spirits—just her, the dim light beyond the blindfold, and the infernal machine. Her reaching out to spirits seemed to set off this device to maim her, set there so she could communicate with no one but herself. So that she could not call for help.

Perhaps God. Hopefully a simple prayer would not cause her pain. This was not the first time she'd been kidnapped or in danger. Mordantly she thought about how it had been a bit of a habit for a time in her life, as mentor and fellow soldier to those who had fought vile, greedy psychopaths courting demons as charges. But that was when Eve was just a baby and she was a much younger woman.

For a moment, her fear seemed shoved aside by a hum. She thought she heard a familiar voice. Calling her name. Reaching for her. But then quiet again. A mental and spiritual void.

She didn't dare try her medium skills again. God only knew what repeated exposure to electrical charges could do to an old heart, an old body, an old brain.

For the first time in many, many years, and never in quite so much terror, Evelyn Northe-Stewart wept in fear for her life.

Chapter Fifteen

There was movement behind the beveled, leaded glass that framed the hefty oak door marked THE BISHOPS.

Before Eve could even let loose the doorknocker of the dove of peace, the door opened and a warm smile from a distinguished face greeted her from just inside the threshold.

"Hello, Miss Whitby, lovely to see you though I wish it were not worry that brought you," the charming Ambassador Bishop stated, his silver hair aglow in the warm, bright gas lamp behind him. "When I heard the tone of your voice I knew I had to come right home," he said, taking her light cloak and placing it in the armoire by the door while she unpinned her straw hat and placed it on a wrought iron rack that said "Peace be with you" above its pegs, setting the light boater between one of Clara's feathered caps and one of Bishop's top hats.

"I'm glad the trains carried us both here swiftly," he added, facing her and opening his hands in a welcoming gesture. "Tell me now, what has you so concerned and how might we help?"

"I hope that I am overreacting," Eve stated, her voice shaking. "I hope that I am wrong when I say I believe Grandma Evelyn to have gone missing, perhaps abducted."

The Ambassador's arresting hazel eyes, the implements of a skilled mesmerist, darkened.

"Evelyn," he murmured. Eve knew Gran was one of Rupert Bishop's oldest friends, a devoted colleague and a fellow traveler in every sense of the word. The Bishops and Gran had laid their lives on the line for one another many times.

"Where is she, what's happened?" The sharp voice came from around the corner and Clara strode forward in a light blue day dress, standing there before the stained-glass angel and again taking on its wings, her body surrounded in the golden light, a radiant aura. Clara would always strike a bit of awe and fear in Eve, and she gaped a moment at the fierce creature who was lit without and within before remembering her words.

"That's what I'm here to find out. I . . . I've reached out," Eve said, gesturing clumsily at her own head, "and I can't find her. It's why I wanted to come here, out of the noise of the city, to see if I can *hear* her . . ." There was no artifice around the Bishops, they were earnest, forthright people. Eve felt like a child before them, because she *was* one, comparatively, and she desperately wanted to cry.

"I'm . . . we're *tied*, she and I . . ." Eve continued, gesturing to her mind, blushing because she could hear how inelegant she sounded but bumbled on anyway, unable to hold back tears. "I feel nothing and the spirits say nothing and . . . She left her house this morning with a woman in mourning and she hasn't been back. I don't dare wait to see if it's all a happy mistake. Not when I can't *feel* her, that may sound mad—"

"Hardly. We are each deeply connected to this woman, more than a mother or mentor combined; she means more to us than we even *dare* acknowledge," Clara declared.

She strode forward to stand a few feet from Eve. The woman's dark-blonde hair with slight greying shocks was swept mostly up, save for small wisps around her head that floated in an ethereal manner. Her eyes were green-gold and wide in the gaslight, luminous peridot piercing Eve to the core.

"Her being so precious to us, so irreplaceable, and so much a *part* of us means we can find our North Star. Just you and me. Come. Follow me into the Parlor." Clara gestured and darted, her movements like a bird, into the open parlor whose gauzy lace curtains were drawn shut though the golden day's sunlight made everything glow. The properties of light took on an additional ethereal quality in the Bishop home.

"Don't be far, love," Clara called to her husband.

"You know I won't be," he replied gently and took a seat at the angel's feet, resuming with the open book.

Eve knew why the Ambassador had returned home. When Clara's powers were called upon, it often had a devastating effect on her and he didn't want to be far when it did. His devotion was inextinguishable. In the parlor, Clara sat in a tall wicker chair whose spokes emanating from her back continued the theme of her sharp radiance. She gestured for Eve to sit on the low, velvet-covered stool before her.

As she did, Clara gave her careful instructions and Eve followed them. "Close your eyes. Put your palms on your knees, facing up. Focus on Evelyn. Think of anything and everything that means *her*. Feel her touch, hear her voice, and hold on to your fondest reminiscence. Relive it."

Tears poured immediately down Eve's flushed cheeks as a memory grabbed her by the throat.

* * * *

She was seven, lying in bed trying to sleep and the spirit world was swooping down around her like diving birds pecking at her skull, all of them desperate for attention and chattering away, Eve having no idea how to order her mind to keep them at arm's length, the air before her a fog of ethereal light. Eve had tossed and turned, weeping, mumbling for them to leave her alone. This escalated until little Eve was screaming.

"Shut up, shut up, shut up!"

As if she had just appeared there, landed there as if dropped from the sky, Eve was scooped up into her namesake's silk-covered arms as Gran bellowed a command.

"Peace!"

And the spirits dispersed at her demand.

Gran lay Eve back down on the bed, but Eve wouldn't let go. So Evelyn bent over her, Eve remembered she was in a beautiful saffron dress, arching over her like a protective ceiling of satin, lace and lilac perfume. Gran stayed like that, her warrior protectorate in a fine ball gown, until Eve fell asleep.

* * * *

Eve felt Gran, touched her, smelled her in this memory, and she wept now, just as she'd done as a child.

A sudden, drilling pain attacked her skull and Eve cried out, opening her eyes to find that Clara had stood, her hands out before her, fingers curved like claws.

"I'm sorry," Clara murmured, drawing in a hissing breath in empathy. "There is always a cost to these powers. Hold on to what you felt. It was *palpable*. Very good. Exactly what I needed. But always a cost . . ."

Clara closed her eyes and widened her arms, her open hands still hovering, her fingers moving as if she were playing a piano. Eve could hear a strange note rising, like music. A chord of the angels, perhaps, or just energy, raw energy in and of itself. This was why the woman didn't want electricity in this house, she herself was a dynamo. Eve had no idea what was happening other than that there was a great, raw, ancient force bubbling up all around her and Clara Bishop knew how to wield it.

"Come on, Evelyn, reach back to me . . ." Clara tilted her head to the side, as if trying to hear something.

Squinting her closed eyes as if she were trying to clench a thought, Eve kept kindling that old memory, shielded in Evelyn's loving, elegant glory, wrapping herself up in the spirit of the woman who had taught her everything, who had saved her mind and given her purpose . . .

The music rose again. A note in the air, a vibration. Ancient, tremulous and soul-shaking.

Eve started as she felt Clara's hands on either side of her head, the center of her palms white-hot, and the woman cried out, her words tumbling forth. "Hold on, Evelyn, we'll come for you . . . We've got you . . ."

Clara's hands fell away and she stumbled back, sinking heavily into the throne-like chair, a sheen of perspiration breaking across her sharp face.

"William and Broad, downtown. Open building. Warehouse, likely," Clara stated. "Go. Gather friends and reinforcements. Find her. Do call for my husband, though, please. Right now, as I'm about to—"

"Ambassador," Eve called. He was right at the door.

"I'm in a countdown, dear," Clara murmured as he entered.

"Ah, yes. We'll take it from here, Miss Whitby," he said calmly, moving to her and taking her in his arms. "William and Broad, did you say, love?"

"Yes love," Clara gasped. She closed her eyes. Her fists clenched against her husband's sides. Her speech slurred slightly. "Waste no time. Eve. Have our driver take you. Go . . ."

"Thank you," Eve stammered. "I'm sorry—"

"Go!" Clara wailed.

"Go on," Bishop said calmly. "Ring for Leonard to take you. But before you leave, call Reverend Blessing and any of your police folk you find trustworthy to join you. I've a telephone and telegraph in my study. I'll meet you there but only if Clara's in the clear. *Go*."

Chapter Sixteen

The Ambassador's study, across from the parlor, was beautifully appointed with wooden cabinets, fine instruments of measure, and lovely books, but Eve couldn't appreciate all the details. She went right for the telephone box on the wall, a telegraph machine on a ledge beside it.

She hesitated to dial the operator and ask for Blessing. The Reverend wasn't a young man any more than Gran was. But next to Bishop, Reverend Blessing was Gran's most trusted counsel, her most valiant spiritual warrior, Cora's Godfather, and a damn good exorcist. Also, the Ambassador had given her a direct order to alert him. She had to respect them and their years of service together.

While Eve had never seen Reverend Blessing conduct an exorcism, Gran's tales of him were larger than life, legendary, tales she spoke quietly when Eve's parents weren't listening. They didn't want to talk about 'the war' or to let Eve hear of its tolls. But Gran seemed to want to relive some of its glories.

As Eve had the operator connect them, there was a long sequence of rings. She remembered earlier in the year when Gran had seen to it that he had a telephone installed, and how much he'd fretted about it the whole time. He was an Episcopalian supply pastor to several black congregations around the city, and as a man of color he had taught Evelyn countless lessons about what the city and *all* its residents needed. She did her best to be his staunchest ally, supporting his missions in any way possible, and fighting alongside him against evil. This included installing his telephone—a demand, not a request. Exorcisms were emergencies, and while the practice had gone out of fashion long ago, it was still, at times, necessary, and he was called into quiet service.

Finally, there was a bumbling rattle of machinery and a rich baritone voice could be heard grappling for the bell.

"Lord help me with this thing," Eve overheard the Reverend grumble through the device. "Hello?" The Reverend said too loudly into the bell. Eve held her end out with a wince.

"Reverend Blessing," she spoke, more quietly, into the receiver, "this is Eve Whitby. Please forgive the urgency, but I need you to meet me at William and Broad when I'm back in the city. Something's happened to Evelyn."

There was a click and a hiss. It took Eve a moment to realize the Reverend had just hung up.

Police officers you can trust, Bishop had said. The only person that came to mind was Detective Horowitz.

Trying to connect via the limitations of precinct lines, no one could find or get a hold of him, so she left several wires with various desks before asking if there was a family number listed anywhere. She recalled him saying, the first time they met, that his father had insisted on getting one installed to keep up with a University colleague in a sort of engineering one-upmanship, to his mother's horror. New York University paid their professors reasonably, but it was still a lavish expense.

Once the operator connected her, after a few rings, a gruff elder voice answered with a wary:

"Hello?"

"Hello, Mr. Horowitz?"

"Yes, who is this?"

"My name is Eve Whitby, sir. Mulberry Street gave me this number. I'm calling in hopes your son, the detective, might be willing to help me with an urgent matter."

"Eve Whitby, eh?" The father sounded like there was a smile in his voice. "We've heard a bit about you."

Eve heard a gasp and a sharp murmur in the background. "She'll call on the phone but won't come around calling? Takes an emergency?" The woman harrumphed.

"Oh?" Eve pretended not to hear the additional commentary. "I hope what's been said has been pleasant! I'll say that your son is a great asset to the Police Department and has been a very wonderful colleague."

Another voice joined in nearby, that of Detective Horowitz. "Is that Miss Whitby?"

"We should *meet* her before she takes the bold notion to *call* you, Jacob," his mother admonished in the background. "This casual age, as if you can just pick up a *device* to avoid interaction and *real* communication! This thing is unnatural, David," she said with genuine concern.

A wave of emotion hit Eve; her empathy and psychic sense sharpened when encountering people who would prove important. In this moment Eve sensed Mrs. Horowitz's keen desire to have communication be personal and not at a distance; especially with her family, a strong conviction Eve could feel even across the line.

Eve blushed at the receiver, vaguely horrified. He must have told his family they were 'courting' and his mother was as skeptical and disapproving as had been expected. She hoped she wasn't complicating things further, but nothing else right now mattered but Gran and she knew that he'd want to help, especially after being so immediately fond of her. There was no meeting Gran and not becoming enamored of her.

"Let me talk with her please," the detective said in exasperation, and there was a jostling for the receiver. His voice was then loud in her ear. "Hello, Miss Whitby? What's going on?"

"Detective, I'm *so* sorry to trouble you at home, I'd never do so if it wasn't—"

"It's no trouble, what can I do for you?"

"Gran has gone missing. Earlier today in a pattern that is very unlike her. I'm *certain* something has gone wrong."

"In relation to your current case?" he asked.

"Possibly? Couldn't it be any of those she and I helped solve? Aren't there infinite bones to pick? Not to mention she's been targeted before. Many times, by an evil Society."

"Yes, I read up on that. In the early eighties wasn't it? Horrid stuff."

"This rings to me more along the lines of that complaint of late, and our daring to charge right into the Prenze home. Gran did say she was sure she was being watched, there . . ."

"You ladies do have the capacity to overturn the usual order of things," he said with a mordant chuckle. "For what it's worth, I know how strong Mrs. Northe-Stewart is—anyone who meets her, even for a moment, can tell that. She'll be all right."

"Thank you for saying so, but I must take every precaution. Are there officers you trust? I've not had the best experience being believed, let alone assisted in an operation."

"There are a few I'd stake my life on," the detective replied. "I'll reach out for them and accompany you to the location you've determined."

"Thank you, that's a great help."

"You should have someone with you who is armed, just to take every precaution."

"Oh, Cora's a good shot, I'll have her with me, rest assured. Gran hasn't been gone long enough to file an official report, but I know better. I *know* something is wrong."

"So much of our work is acting on instinct. Who am I to say otherwise? Do you have any idea where she might be?"

"Exactly the address, I can't say, but we've pinpointed William and Broad."

"Good. How did you do that?"

"Well . . ." Eve wondered how in the world she could explain what Clara and she had done. Sheepishly, she offered, "Psychically?"

"How very useful," he said brightly, to Eve's relief. It was good she'd brought him into a séance early. She'd make converts out of disbelievers any day.

"I need to rally my own troops," Eve continued. "Can you and a trusted, preferably armed confidant meet us within the next two hours?"

"Yes."

"Thank you."

"It's an . . . honor to be called upon, Miss Whitby."

Eve found herself smiling at the earnestness and warmth in his voice before the daunting task ahead sobered her and she hung up the receiver.

The Bishops' longstanding, affably detached driver knew an emergency when he saw one and Eve was back in city limits in impressive time, having taken their speediest hack. She asked that she be dropped at home. She needed to pack a bag of medical supplies just in case she found Gran in need, and gather her operatives.

* * * *

At home, Antonia and Cora had already discussed duties and support. Antonia was set up in the parlor, the materials for a séance ready, with one of Cora's most sacred items in her hands; a family bible in French handed down through the Dupris generations, with some of their own special prayers written into the margins of certain passages. When Eve raised her eyebrows at seeing it in anyone's hands but Cora's, she explained why she'd handed it to Antonia.

"Jenny still is unwell. She's congested and running a fever; we think she's fine but she needs to sleep it off, so Antonia will be here, receiving any spirit's message. She will be tied to me most strongly and to our channel if she has this heirloom in hand."

Eve nodded and thanked her colleagues. "Come, Cora, you and I need to go—"

Cora reached out a hand to halt her. "I also told your mother what was going on."

Eve rocked back on her heels. "Cora, why did you—"

"I told Cora to tell your mother," Vera said sharply, floating her ghostly form between the colleagues, her transparent eyes flashing. "You've taken the idea that they don't want to hear about your business to an *absurd* degree. She would want to know about this. She's not as delicate as you assume, and you're not as immune to needing her love and support as you think, young lady!"

Eve stood there, chastened, and blinked back sudden tears because Vera was quite right; there was a lot about her family that she'd tamped down and tried to avoid.

"She's waiting for you," Cora said, pointing to the door that joined the houses.

Eve swallowed hard, unlocked the deadbolt, and went across.

In the parlor, her mother was sitting stock still, staring at the fireplace, her jaw set. There was a black-eyed Susan lying atop the smooth, hefty oak mantel carved into a beautiful scrolling arabesque with a floral theme. Helen, her maternal grandmother who had died saving Natalie when she was a child, had made the flower, her favorite in life, manifest again. She did so periodically, whenever emotions or fears were particularly high, but it always unsettled the house. Eve felt sure the ghost wanted to help, across their generations. The bright yellow of the flower petals was a splash of color against the more muted pastel hues of powder blue and cream that the parlor was awash in.

At the sound of Eve's step across the threshold, her mother turned with a steeled look, one that exchanged the usual wariness she wore against the world to something more ferocious. It was a look that Eve recognized as a source of her own strength.

Her mother came closer and, hilt first, handed her a small knife. Eve looked between the knife and her mother with a raised eyebrow.

"I should have given you this at the start of your career," she explained, gently pressing the hilt into her daughter's hand. "But I was hoping so badly you wouldn't need it, that the work would be the sort of desk duty you'd claimed it would be." Her mother met her gaze, one set of steeled green eyes to another. "But knowing my family history, this unexpected legacy of ours, I should have known better. Stay safe. I once tucked this in my corset when I undertook utterly stupid risks to try to save your father."

"For which we're all grateful, and thanks to which I exist," Eve said. Warmth from her mother was hard-earned but worth the wait. "I will carry this in honor. And I promise any risks I take will be carefully measured against utter stupidity."

At this, her mother smiled the half-smile that Eve wore often.

"Please find her safe," Natalie murmured, and for the first time, Eve saw how truly scared she was for her step-mother. "Trouble seeks Evelyn out and it isn't fair. She's done so much to help people in this world, she deserves a medal. A commendation. Not more trouble." Natalie looked up and squinted her eyes. "It isn't fair, do you hear me?" she repeated her point to the heavens.

"We'll find her safe. We'll be having a fine dinner together before you know it."

Her mother embraced her suddenly. "Sometimes I think you're just a baby, still my little girl, but then I remember I was facing down death and a spiritual war at your age. You're far more suited for battle than I ever was. You dear old soul. I'm very glad you're strong."

"I've had the best role models," Eve stated. She squeezed her mother tighter then stepped back. "The group is meeting at the probable location. William and Broad. I must be off."

Natalie nodded and walked away. There may have been a murmur of "I love you," but Eve couldn't entirely be sure, though she murmured it back regardless. Father was at his clinic and Eve didn't plan on stopping by; her Mother would let him know of the developments as she saw fit.

Ghosts awaited Eve outside the house, coming at her and Cora in a shimmering, silvery, luminous rush of freezing air. There were so many of them that they were just a silvery grey mass. Eve could pick out no physical details, only luminous fog, all chattering their worries and theories to Eve at once. It was the kind of chaotic cloud of spirits that had nearly broken her mind as a child. She would have none of that now.

"Silence," she commanded, and the cluster hushed, wafting back from her a few feet, some fading, some separating out into forms young and old that ranged the full 19th century in fashion, class difference, and culture, allowing for the temperature to balance from frigid to manageable. "We have to focus only on Evelyn's well-being—not worry, not fear, only assurance of her safety—I will hear nothing less. I know she's important to you too!"

To be this important to both the mortal and the spirit world—Eve wondered if Gran had any real idea just how much she was cherished.

Eve darted to the nearby stables up the block, nestled between two town-houses, where her family's horse and hack rested in wait. They were soon back out onto the avenue, Eve at the helm of the small rig with Cora beside her, a bag of medical supplies, sustenance, and cloth in the back, and prayers on her lips.

Chapter Seventeen

Downtown Manhattan was the pulse of New York City. With the five boroughs having been consolidated the year prior, it beat with money and resources, speculation and desperation, glamor and grit. The government and financial centers were all located within relative walking distance on the lower mile of the island, and industry and commerce kept all kinds of hours. It was true that the restless city didn't know how to stop, its engine an ever-whirring turbine of need and greed, possibility and progress, kindness and cruelty in equal measure, forces constantly wrestling towards an uneasy equilibrium.

Eve wasn't sure what she'd find on the streets as dusk fell, other than a significant slice of the city's varied life.

"That's it, Athena," she said to the sturdy, well-tempered mare the family loved, pulling her to the side of the gentle bend in South William Street as it neared Broad. She hitched her to a post near an electrical pole first installed by the Edison plant nearly two decades prior that stood at a slight angle, wires coming off from it in an inelegant stream. Once she and Cora had disembarked from the small hack, making sure Athena was well clear of the wires, she reached into her supply bag and gave her part of an apple.

Turning around, she saw two men approach, Horowitz was in a basic black suit, his associate in a police uniform. The street was quiet enough. Most shops were in the process of closing up, though several pubs serving stock brokers after the nearby Exchange floor had closed for the day were bustling. The streets were speckled with passersby. Nothing was out of the ordinary.

"Thank you for coming," Eve said quietly. The man next to the detective was round-cheeked and broad-nosed, light brown eyes set in an olive complexion. He bore a pleasant demeanor with a neatly trimmed black moustache, and his uniform was pressed and immaculate, showcasing a pride in his work and in the details.

"This is Officer Fitton, he befriended me from my first day in the force and his devotion to justice is as clear as his mind is sharp. Officer, Eve Whitby of a special precinct devoted to cases that have little to go on." They each bowed their heads to one another. "Let's find our dear lady, shall we?" he said quietly but confidently.

Eve managed a smile, her nerves as spread out and jumbled as the industrial wires strung out along the lanes. After her initial admonishment, the ghosts hung back a few paces. None suggested a place to start, so Eve stood on the nearest two doorsteps, but felt nothing. Inside both, shop-keepers or clerks were tidying up and restocking shelves.

Eve felt the temperature around her plummet and she glanced back at the ghosts for help. Her most devoted and able to manifest had appeared— Zofia, Olga and Vera, who all shrugged. "Start anywhere, we're baffled. Can't seem to pick up a trace of her in either the physical or spirit realm."

"That's . . . troubling . . ." Cora murmured. Eve nodded and tried to mask her terror.

For a woman who had made such a distinct impression in both realms, this was unprecedented. After Maggie's disappearance, the idea that the most important souls in her life could just vanish was the most terrifying notion Eve had ever encountered. For Eve, death was only a phase of life and it meant her ideas of fear and mortality were far from average. This idea of *truly* dying, of ceasing to exist . . . It was the sort of throes of anxiety that biblical poets might have described as the outer darkness, the definition of a soul in agony.

The Bible crossing darkly through her mind made Eve wonder where Reverend Blessing was. She was sure she'd have met him on the street by now. He could easily have been here ahead of her, even. His noted absence chilled her further.

The next building, a warehouse, proved more promising the moment they began their approach. Eve began to sense a bit of Evelyn's spirit again, her power and magnetism—the sort of tether that took them in and out of the Corridors together.

She turned around to address her spirit entourage, but they were gone. Spirits winked in and out at times, were drawn to other sights or callings, or fell subject to the inconsistencies of the living's mortal senses, Eve was used to that, but this was terrible timing. Her spirits weren't usually so flighty in times of trouble. It was as if something else was interfering with their being seen and felt.

Eve's blood chilled when she approached the store window and she took in what kind of warehouse and showroom they were about to enter. Eve and Clara's mentalism hadn't been specific about the theme of the place, only offering a location.

It was a warehouse of funerary fashion.

Faceless mannequins in mourning regalia stood in wide arched shop windows. Black bombazine gowns with jet details, crepe and ribbons, black tulle, and layers of veils floated behind the showroom window hung from thin wire as if they were floating ghosts themselves. An eerie and unsettling display.

The industry of death was an elaborate one: mourning clothes, rituals, jewelry, intricate customs, and lavish monuments had been the century's great melancholic pastime and expenditure for those who could afford to make a spectacle out of grief.

Horowitz and Fitton put their ears to the door of the shop. There was no light on from within, just the static forms and racks of fabrics marching into the shadows of the showroom in shades of charcoal and onyx. Fitton shouted, "Police, open up!"

There was no answer. Eve could feel Gran more and more; every step nearer, she could feel her presence as if she were right next to her, there on the sidewalk outside. There was a dreadful, mind-numbing hum in the air.

"Do you hear that?" Eve asked Cora who stepped up beside her. She nodded. It was unlike any other industrial sound she'd ever heard and she felt the vibration of the hum on her skin, as if some force was working to get under it.

Horowitz pointed to the doorjamb which was already slightly ajar.

Fitton opened the door, causing an immediate and raucous clattering of shop bells inside. Eve winced. Both he and Horowitz had pistols drawn and swept inside, ducking beneath airborne bits of veil and ribbon hung for display like floating, wispy entrails of some phantasmagorical severed head. Everything about this place told Eve this was where she'd find Gran and everything felt full of dread, a cruel joke at her precinct's expense.

Eve touched the knife her mother had given her, palming it in its improvised holster up the cuff of her sleeve.

No ghosts were anywhere to be seen or felt, without or within the shop. Usually a few specters were drawn to Evelyn, a few more when she and Eve were together, but as had been a theme with the spaces they'd been investigating lately, this place was entirely, eerily detached. Was this what the average mortal felt? Going into a crisis with only the living to turn to, devoid of spectral insight? How lonely and vulnerable, Eve thought. Only tokens of death around but no assurance of the spirit that lived on beyond that black veil.

The shop floor was a basic department store layout, with counters and two registers, and a waist-level wooden gate to the back that was swinging slightly even though no one had gone through . . .

Wordlessly, Horowitz gestured that Fitton go forward. He pressed the gate open and with a quick, whipping motion flung back the black curtain that Eve presumed led to the storage areas and possible workrooms.

Beyond was a large room filled with racks of black dresses, and in the center . . .

Gran.

There she was, head down, her arms tied behind her back in a chair with a length of fabric around her mouth.

"Oh God, please be alive . . ." Eve whispered, rushing to embrace her. Everything she had worried she'd never be able to say to her best friend welled up in her throat and manifested in a strangled sob as she removed the gag, causing Evelyn to stir, slightly, groggily. Perhaps she'd been drugged. "Thank heavens," Eve exclaimed, repeating thanks and praise as she gingerly used her mother's knife to cut the edge of the fabric away from Gran's hands on the arms of the chair. Hands that looked so fragile . . .

"I'm here, Gran, its Eve, we found you. Everything will be all right . . ."

As she worked to get her second wrist free from the bindings, she looked into the shadows around her and saw Reverend Blessing laid out on a fabric-cutting table, just past another rack of black tulle and jet beads. Cora had two fingers to his neck to check for a pulse.

The Reverend's brown skin gleamed with perspiration. He was dressed in his finest priestly vestments, a black suit and white collar. His wrists were bound before him with scraps of black fabric. Cora was working on his bindings, speaking a gentle prayer in French.

To the Reverend's right was another man laid on a second table, a distressingly handsome man in similar vestments. Eve assumed this was the Exorcist protégé she'd heard Gran mention, Reverend Coronado.

Suddenly she felt very dizzy. There was an odd, chemical smell in the air.

Horowitz and Fitton entered the room again and Horowitz began to cough.

"The building is empty," Fitton stated, returning his pistol to his holster but making a face as if he'd just tasted something odious.

"Can you make sure both Reverends' wrists are freed?" Eve stated, and joined Horowitz in a cough. Her nostrils burned. Gran was mumbling something and Eve bent to try to understand her.

"It's . . . a . . ."

"What's that, Gran?" Eve's head spun but she blinked her eyes and tried to right herself. "We're almost there." She tried to fully free Gran's other hand but Eve slumped forward instead, her body uncooperative and her speech slurred. "We'll . . . get you out of here . . ."

"It's a trap . . ." Gran finally managed.

That's when Eve hit the floor.

Chapter Eighteen

Dimly, Evelyn Northe-Stewart was aware of the help that had come to her. All her beloveds. All were in danger, and she couldn't have warned them in time.

Bleary, she tried to open heavy eyelids. She tried to reach out for psychic and spiritual help but couldn't muster the energy, and the last time it had resulted in a horrific pain. Dim figures moved in the shadows. Perhaps she shouldn't let them know she was awake . . . Her eyelids fluttered.

What had first appeared as a black-clad mannequin, its face covered by a thick veil, a figure that had been unnoticed deep in the shadows behind a rack of black gowns, moved. From behind a wooden cupboard, a long mourning coat moved as well. The figures remained shrouded under thick veils. They turned their heads to evaluate the room, their figures macabre and unnerving.

Evelyn closed her eyes to remain innocuous as she listened to their murmurs, trying not to shudder at the fact that these captors had remained hidden amongst the clothes, watching.

"With so many of them here to show themselves, they've made themselves that much more of a target, and we've that much more data," one figure said in a deep voice. "Now that they're all unconscious, let us make sure they all stay out for as long as we need."

"They'll try to trace us. The shop," a younger, higher-pitched voice replied. It was familiar to Evelyn. *Mrs. Calvin*—the supposedly grieving mother.

"Don't you worry," the lower voice replied. "For *us*, the dead remain dead. Layers of mistrust. Layers of misdirection. They won't know *where* to look. For all their clairvoyance, they can't see what's right in front of them . . ."

"And they won't be able to . . ." the woman murmured, and there was a rustle of fabric. Evelyn shifted her head to the side imperceptibly, fluttering her eyes to see the smaller figure in a black gown sliding back a gauze curtain to reveal a device.

It was like a phonograph player but with something different in the upright box. The two black-clad figures lifted the wooden cabinet and brought it close to Evelyn. A moment later, cold metal was attached to each of her temples, the skin there already raw and sensitive. Burned. She tried to calm the fluttering of her eyes and appear to remain unconscious but she winced from the pain. It must have been taken by her captors as an unconscious reflex.

"Second readings on each to establish baseline," the deeper voice instructed quietly. "The girls are the most important of all. Then the priests. I doubt the officers have any capabilities. Leave the note and get out once it's done."

"Does the output have to account for the atmospheric conditions, such as the gas, affecting their minds?"

"Already included as a factor."

"Well done!"

Footsteps walked away from Evelyn and she took the moment to flutter her eyes, enough to dimly catch sight of the machine's interior.

A cylinder rotated slowly and above it while small needles dragging attached sticks of thin graphite edged along a paper tube, unfurling a zig-zagging line. The footsteps approached again and Evelyn lay still.

"This will never get tiresome," the deeper of the voices murmured in awe, bending over the machine. "I learned so much overseas and here we are mapping the mind, its *song*. *Now* every new line we acquire helps build the wall. Our fortress. Now that I've heard them all, seen their pattern . . . It's all so beautiful."

"But are we not registering?" queried the lighter-toned voice, and it sounded to Evelyn as if its owner were leaning over the instrument, looking in. "Are we not living minds too? How could it distinguish?"

"I am blocking our signal." The woman gasped as the deeper voice continued. "I learned so very much when I died, my dear," the deeper voice said with a chuckle. "And I've much still to learn. The whole world is new . . . And our power to influence it . . ."

"Endless . . ." came 'Mrs. Calvin's' whisper.

There was a stirring moan off to Evelyn's left, and her eyes shot open at the sound of her granddaughter's voice.

Two shadowed faces peered down at her and looked over across the room. A black-clad arm pointed. "Dose them again, we're not done here."

A black-gloved hand lifted a perfume spritzer before Evelyn's face, sprayed the air with something noxious that burned her nostrils, and she was again lost to darkness.

Chapter Nineteen

"Help me . . ."

The soft plea echoing again and again through murky depths sounded like Maggie to Eve's ears. After a few more repetitions she realized it was her own voice mumbling the request and she came up to consciousness from a black depth in a dizzying rise.

Coming to with a cry, Eve's head ached to the point where it felt like her skull could crack open. Having been slumped in a rickety chair, she was surprised to find that she hadn't been bound and in her lap sat a crudely written note:

YOU WILL CEASE YOUR UNHOLY ASSOCIATION WITH THE DEAD AND END YOUR 'PRECINCT'S' COURTSHIP OF THE DEVIL

At her feet sat an envelope. She bent down for it and a dizzy spell struck her so violently she fell to her knees onto the floor. Her throat was parched and she was starving. How long had she been unconscious? Next to her lay her supply bag and she fumbled for her canteen of water and took a drink. She wanted more but she'd need to make sure Gran had enough. Gran. She struggled to get up.

"What the hell happened?" came a nearby, rasping bark.

She slowly turned to see Horowitz slumped on the floor next to her, Fitton further on. They all looked rumpled and dazed. The Reverends were still lying on tables, but it appeared they were about to stir. Blessing was flexing his hands that Cora had indeed managed to unbind and turning his head. Eve felt like every movement and impulse to react was slowed, as if the commands from mind to body were at an impasse.

"Drugged, surely," Eve fought for words, her speech slightly slurred. "There was something in the air . . ."

"Yes . . ." murmured Gran, still partially bound in her chair to Eve's right, a rack of black dresses between them. She still had the hand free that Eve had managed and was working with fumbling hands on the last bound scrap of the other. Rising shakily to her feet, Eve tried to rush back to Gran but tripped on her own feet and tumbled to her knees.

Horowitz and Fitton, groggily shaking their heads, got up to resume sweeping the entire building. Cora, who had been slumped on the floor beside Reverend Blessing rose, shakily took out her own pistol from her breast pocket to have it at the ready for any further foe and returned her attention to the Reverends, as she had been doing before the blackout. Eve managed to right herself and collapse at Gran's feet to continue to help her.

"Thank God you're all right! Do you have any idea where the culprits are? Who? Why?" Eve asked, setting to work on the last piece of cloth holding her.

"They anticipated you," Gran said. "They were gathering information on us." She gestured to the empty area beside her. "There was a machine here, it was . . . something like reading my mind. There was a ticker and a marker scrolling back and forth . . . There were two little plates put here . . ." She gestured to her temples and winced as her finger touched raw skin. "And they may have done that to each of us. From what I overheard, we were like . . . laboratory animals. I only saw two, all in mourning. The woman's voice was the woman today who drew me into all this mess."

Evelyn cried out as Eve finally cut through the cloth and it fell away, her stiff, aching shoulders strained nearly out of their sockets returning to her sides. Eve murmured empathetic apologies and rubbed those aching shoulders quickly as she gave her the canteen and Gran took a long draught. She helped her to stand and Gran suppressed another cry of agony at stiff muscles.

"Age is hardly as kind to me as it was the first several times I was kidnapped. Really, you'd think I'd have retired from being a target."

"It's my fault, of course. I am so sorry," Eve blurted.

"No, I'm the target—always have been, it falls in around me. I'm just grateful that our captors, while uniquely driven, manage to remain moral enough not to murder."

"Yes, but they're very alarmed by my Precinct." Eve picked up the note that had fallen to the floor when she rose and showed it to Gran. "There's a letter too, I'm almost afraid to read it."

"Charming," Gran muttered through clenched teeth.

"How did you find me? For whatever reason, inside this place, I can't get the ghosts to hear me, or to stay, it's like I've been detached from the very fabric I've been wrapped up in my whole life . . . I wonder if that machine may have had something to do with it. When I tried to engage my gift at one point, I felt a surge, a sting, a shock. It was terrible."

"Clara Bishop found you. It seems I gave her the right kind of bond to get to you. She . . . located you as if she were looking for an address on a map. Uncanny."

"She uses ancient energies that travel on ley lines," Gran explained. "Her powers have grown unwieldy since she first learned them, but I'm so grateful they found me. You found me."

"That's what we do, Gran," Eve said fondly, embracing her tenderly.

Next Eve moved to Blessing's side, where he had sat up on the table he'd been laid out on. He was quietly speaking with Cora about what had happened. She had returned her gun into concealment. Eve passed around the water.

"Do you remember *anything* else?" Cora asked. The Reverend shook his head.

"I saw Evelyn, ran to her, rejoiced that she was alive, and then I fell to my knees. I wish it had simply been in prayer. The next thing I know my Goddaughter is helping me return to the living, so thank heavens for that." His rich baritone made nearly everything he said sound like an oration. He smiled before looking around the dark room. "We must have been dispatched by something in the air now dissipated. I didn't see anyone, but then again, it would be easy to hide in all this," he nodded to the racks of crepe and jet.

"Thank you for being heroic, Reverend," Eve stated. "I'm *so* sorry . . . I wish I'd have anticipated this, I should have known somehow—the spirit world hasn't been forthcoming and my assets vanished before we got in the door . . . It's like they're being kept from me."

He waved a hand at Eve as a gesture not to worry. His other hand was clasped by Cora, his large, deep brown palm between Cora's delicate light brown hands. Cora's parents had worked closely with the Reverend, particularly her father André and he credited the Reverend for saving his soul from vice and melancholy and inspiring him to be a loving man of hope. Eve knew that part of Cora's reason for moving to New York had been to be a part of the Reverend's life and to learn from his wisdom.

The beautiful man in the same plain black vestments beside the Reverend stirred. Eve went to his side and bent over him to examine his state more closely. He opened light hazel-brown eyes that took a moment to focus on Eve.

"Hello," he said softly. "Would you be so kind as to tell me what happened?" He had a faint trace of an accent—Eve recalled Gran mentioning he'd been born and raised in Mexico City. Vera would be thrilled by that fact, not to mention his looks.

"You must be Reverend Coronado. I'm Eve Whitby and unfortunately, my Grandmother and I are the reason you got dragged into this. I'm terribly sorry."

"That's all right, protecting the flock has its dangers," he said amiably, wincing as Eve helped him sit up. The moment she took his warm hand to aid him, she felt a frisson run down her spine at the touch, and he looked at her. Then he smiled, radiant. While bleary, he seemed so pleasant and undaunted, it was a remarkable quality.

"Is everyone all right?" Coronado asked, looking around. "I don't know what overcame us."

"We're all recovering. Evelyn believes there was a machine gathering scientific data on us while we were unconscious, likely from an airborne chemical," Eve explained. She offered him water and he drank, thanking her.

"Why?" he asked.

"For any number of reasons that I'm sure are further illuminated here," Eve said, moving to pick up the envelope at the foot of the chair she'd been deposited in. Typed on the front was:

An Open Letter to Those Who Court the Dead

Eve tentatively began reading aloud:

You and your kind must stop. Spiritualists. Clairvoyants. Tainted minds who can't leave well enough alone. It's unnatural talking to the dead. It is of the devil and it must be stamped out entirely. While many Spiritualists claim to be Christians, that's how the devil lures you, opening your mind to that which is beyond scripture's reach. You stray from the path so easily, as it seems so harmless. Seems generous, even, but communing with the devil is the unfortunate result.

That there has become a whole Precinct involved in such ungodly activity is what has made this letter and the actions taken to mitigate you necessary. To take advantage of the grieving in a lavish theatrical production is one thing, but to involve the New York City Police in something so unnatural? It is an abomination and we will not stop until it is terminated.

There was a long, uncomfortable silence.

"That's presumptuous!" Reverend Coronado exclaimed finally. "Deciding what God would deem unnatural. That's up to God to decide. All Spiritualists I know of, the real ones, bring comfort to the grieving, transmit messages of love, and assure us of life everlasting."

Eve smiled. "Thank you for your support. I hate to tell them that ghosts aren't going anywhere. My Precinct or no."

"This intimidation tactic might also be a cover for some other aim, crying a religious reason as justification," Cora said, helping Blessing to ease off the table and to his feet.

"Many have done terrible things, all in the name of God," Coronado said with a quiet sadness, as if the failing of any moral institution was something he took personally.

"What's their next step? I worry they'll escalate . . ." Eve murmured, staring at the paper. "I just want to be left to do my job . . ."

Horowitz and Fitton returned to them. "The building is empty," Fitton assured.

"Are you sure this time?" Cora pressed, gesturing to the racks of clothes that had hidden their assailants. The two men looked exasperated.

"I heard them say they were going to collect data, then leave," Gran said. "I don't think they knew I was awake to overhear them."

"A colleague is reporting the incident now to the nearest precinct in order to have the patrolmen make further sweeps," Fitton stated. "Are there any details you can give us about them?"

"There were two voices," Gran said. "One was that of the woman who got me into this mess with a given name of Mrs. Calvin—she was in a mourning dress and veil. The other one with her was tall in a coat with a resonant voice, a top hat also bearing a shroud, features utterly obscured," Evelyn replied ruefully.

"Not much to go on," Fitton said ruefully. "But we'll trace the owners of this shop."

"They said something about the dead staying dead, so . . ."

"A dead end," Horowitz said, and made a face at his unintended pun.

A sound at the shop door had Fitton darting out, only to return and report that his colleagues were stationed at the front and one at the rear entrance.

"Good, we need to look around more," Eve said. She motioned to Cora, gesturing around her head and flexing her hand, wanting Cora to engage all her gifts as she wished to, trying to grasp the scope of their scenario and any clues they might muster. "What were they trying to do with mental data, then, Gran?" Eve asked, walking around the room for further clues, looking behind frock coats and black bombazine gowns with high-shouldered sleeves and tapered, Gibson silhouettes.

"As that letter threatens us, they may promote multiple ways to stop us," Gran replied. "They were, in part, successful. I couldn't reach out and connect with spirits."

An article Eve had read recently in one of the psychical research magazines had mentioned a theoretical but cutting-edge field discussing brain activity and how there might be ways to map and measure it. Weaponizing it was another story.

On a rear worktable set into the shadows, Eve saw an array of glass bottles and atomizers; a veritable vanity of poison. A small metal fan with sharp blades was attached to a turbine on the table that ran an electrical cord to the wall. A shallow metal bowl of mostly evaporated liquid sat before the fan, likely one way of distributing the noxious means of their blackouts, atomizers being another. Squinting at the bottles, she recognized some of the labels as Prenze products.

This was no direct indictment of the family, of course—once a product was able to be purchased, the customer would do with it what they will. However, their products were a thread linking many of their inquiries of late, perhaps a pattern emerging. And what of their products could be mixed to create something not healing, but harmful?

A step behind her had her turning to see Horowitz staring at the table, his brow furrowed, his expression fierce. He was clearly angry at what had happened.

"Cures all your ills . . ." he read from one bottle's label. "And creates more," he added sardonically. "You know, I've mentioned my friend Doctor Lee, the imminent toxicologist whom I consult with often during cases. He is concerned with just how many opiates are in the system of the average person, prescribed any number of tonics. If the dosage is just a bit off in a compromised system, if a dispensary doesn't fill it right, any adult or especially a child, a soul, just slips quietly away. He rues that so much of medicine is palliative, so little going into *curing.*"

"And, evidently, these, when mixed . . ."

"Quite the dangerous compound. Do you think this is why you were being warned off the Prenze family?"

"I think one could be warned off any number of robber baron types in these days of gilding lilies with soaring profits," Eve replied. "Don't Carnegie coal, managed by his henchman Frick, the railroading Vanderbilts, and countless factory magnates all have skeletons in closets needing management? I feel we could be warned off any number of factors, from any number of families of note, and my spirits, generally so helpful, help me see the way through, from pattern to grasped fact. Right now all we have is this name that keeps surfacing wherever we look, in bottles that don't contain what is advertised."

"Indeed," Horowitz said, pulling a pencil and notebook from his pocket, noting everything present. "I need to retrieve the bottle found on Mr. Font that I left in Doctor Lee's care to see if he could determine what all might have been in it. I hope he can shed some light. You should meet him, his practice is just north of Chinatown."

"Gladly, thank you. His thoughts would be *most* valuable."

Fitton came further in the room, looking sheepish. "Miss Whitby, your . . . parents are outside. They . . . insist on taking you home, I'm sorry I . . . said I'd bring you out, I know that's not my place, they just . . . looked so sad . . ."

Eve put her hand to her mouth. She looked back at Gran, who had her arms around Blessing and Coronado, they were all praying together.

"That's all right, Fitton," she said. "Thank you. I should go."

She looked at Cora, who nodded, then at Horowitz.

"Please go," the detective said gently. "We'll keep sorting this out. We may not always do exactly what our parents want us to, but sometimes we need to be their obedient children, especially when they're scared."

"That's . . . very wise, Detective."

So focused on the case, so focused on the details, the evidence, sometimes she forgot about hearts, and that she remained their little girl. She owed them being a part of this recovery, for they were surely frightened, wondering when the threats would stop.

"Gran," Eve urged, "Mum and dad are outside and we shouldn't linger here."

"Yes, my dear. I need to go home to Gareth. It's so good he's been away with the traveling exhibition but I'm sure he'll be home now and worrying. I'll take the Reverends with me and we'll have dinner. You go on to your mother. It's best she not be reminded of my drawing you into all this."

"She loves you, Gran, don't ever fear that—"

"I don't, but I needn't be a constant, shadowy pall over their lives."

"They wouldn't *be* alive without you and they know that."

"Still, one needs a breath apart. Please go be with them and tell them I'm fine. Thank you for coming for me. I don't know what I'd do without you," Gran said, kissing Eve's forehead.

"The very same. I've never known panic like when I couldn't reach you."

"This damned place—spirits can't get in, and psychic calls could not get out. May have something to do with the lights. When I tried to reach out psychically for help, there was a surge."

Eve sighed, looking at just how many bulbs swung overhead from hanging lamps, buzzing quietly in their dim setting. "This damned, modern age."

"I've been saying that for decades. It is the way of all things."

They embraced again, Eve holding her close with a renewed wave of thankfulness.

Chapter Twenty

Once she was outside, up the block, she noticed her parents' carriage at the corner, a small wooden cab with their lovely white horse, her mother looking anxiously out the window. The moment she saw Eve she clambered down, her father striding to keep up behind her.

"You're . . . all right? And . . . Evelyn?" Her mother could hardly get the words out. The effects of her early life trauma and the selective mutism that had followed haunted her in times of stress. She fought it admirably and Eve's heart ached that she should be another trigger.

"Mum, I'm fine," she said, embracing her. "Everyone is fine. Let's go home. Gran is going home to Grandpa—he's finally back from his whirlwind art exhibit engagements. She's with the Reverends who came down to look after her and they'll escort her back. Honestly she's fine."

"Oh, well then, good . . ." Natalie said, staring up the street at the uniformed officer still at the warehouse door.

"Let's go home," Eve repeated. Her mother cupped her cheek and echoed the sentiment. Her father said nothing, as if no words he could have chosen suited him. He gave her a smile that showed his love in equal measure as his pain.

Would it always be like this? She wondered. Every case, every possible danger . . . Did she have any right to put them through this?

In these moments, staring at them, she wondered if worrying about them was a convenient excuse not to think about how scared *she* was. The ghosts had determined her calling, but where was *her* decision? And where in the hell were all of them? It remained unnatural that her world was so suddenly quiet. Where were her most loyal that had appeared to her outside the warehouse? What had made them vanish? She shoved aside the fear that they were all gone like Maggie, victims of whatever device was blocking their aid and communication.

Once they turned to go north up Broad Street, Eve started to see spirits again, and hear the whispers of conversation glancing off her ear. They'd been scared from the block but they were returning to the atmosphere, as if they'd been a flock of birds startled by a shot.

After long moments of silence, Eve finally asked her distant father a question, realizing that she was a fool for not regularly asking his advice as a doctor. "Father, are there ways to measure the activity of the mind?"

"Emerging studies, yes. Theoretical at this point, really. Why?"

"We think someone was trying to study Gran."

She left herself out of the picture.

Her father frowned. "Abducting her to study her? Couldn't they just have asked?"

Eve gave them only the truths that wouldn't terrify them, explaining a rough outline of "Mrs. Calvin" and the events at the warehouse, excluding the additional threats.

"Perhaps they wanted to study a mind under duress. A gifted mind, at that," her father mused.

"Do you have any idea what a device like Gran described might be?"

"No, unfortunately," her father replied, rubbing his chin thoughtfully. "I didn't think the theory was anything more than that, theory that we could map out the action, the . . . rhythms of the mind, as it were. We've a pulse, what about the mind? What is its rhythm and pattern? That's a premise. The Europeans, some London circles have talked about it."

"Will you let me know if you see anything about the field in your medical journals?"

"Yes, yes I will my dear," he said, his piercing eyes lit, seeming suddenly pleased that she was interested, and she realized what a resource in him she had squandered thus far. *Youth*, she chided herself. Taking elders for granted. Not Gran, of course, but her parents shouldn't come in so far second.

"I know I prayed for a normal life for you, I know I prayed in vain. I just . . ." her mother exclaimed suddenly, blinking back tears. Her father squeezed her hand, looking out the window at passing lamps and lanterns. Her mother couldn't seem to find any suitable words.

"I will continue to be careful," Eve said. "And I've plenty of people I trust. Just think of all the people that helped Gran," she continued, recounting every step that led them there, even daring to mention Clara Templeton Bishop, even though Eve knew her mother might never forgive the Bishops for dragging her father back into their investigations when she'd been a baby.

"They're all there to help me too," she reassured. "We've the best. New York's finest."

She was trying to reassure herself as much as anyone. Folding the threatening notes into pieces within her pocket, as if by making them smaller she hoped to minimize their psychological impact.

"Come have dinner with us," her mother declared. "Your father and I prepared a huge stew together; it helped us to have something to do while we worried."

"Bring the girls over," her father bid softly. "Let's be a family."

"Of course, Father," Eve said. "That will be lovely."

When she arrived home, Antonia greeted her with an embrace and they discussed everything that happened.

"How's Jenny?" Eve asked.

"Better; I believe her fever has lessened, and she's sleeping soundly."

Eve placed the demanding, threatening notes on the séance table.

As if the act of placing that text on the table had summoned them, the spirits of Vera, Zofia, and Olga appeared.

"There you are," Eve exclaimed. "Where were you when we tried to find Gran?" she asked. All of them looked at one another, eyes wide as they floated before her.

"We . . . tried," Olga began. "We were . . . how do I say it?"

"Repelled?" Vera stated. "That's what it felt like.

"Pushed," Zofia added. "And we couldn't fight back against the wind."

"We're sorry we failed you," Olga said, her translucent eyes wide.

"You didn't fail me. I just need you, is all," Eve said earnestly. "I really need all of you . . ."

"And we, you," Vera whispered.

"Would you like me to put on the phonograph for you spirits while the rest of us have dinner with my parents?" Eve asked.

"Yes! Music!" Zofia clapped spectral hands, the sound manifesting as an echo of a clap in Eve's ear.

As Eve moved to the phonograph cabinet, Cyril appeared, wafting in from the wall of the parlor, a dark grey spirit in shirtsleeves with a young girl in a choir robe at his side—Winnie. They hadn't reappeared since Maggie was first reported missing. Both had died of consumption and found one another singing songs, scared in the Corridors between life and death. Unsure where to go, they followed music, returning home to haunt their beloved New York, where they watched over an ever-growing number of brilliant, struggling musicians. Cyril was drawn to any kind of music Fort Denbury could manage, this was his act of summoning.

"No, we don't need the phonograph," Cyril said, his spectral cheeks dimpled as he smiled, gesturing to the upright piano against the rear wall of the parlor. "I'll play for everyone if you don't mind."

At this, Zofia clapped again and grabbed both Olga's hands. "And we'll dance!"

Vera turned to Eve and smiled. "We'll all be fine here, thank you. Go on."

* * * *

At dinner, everyone was quiet. Antonia and Cora knew not to talk about spectral matters with her parents. So, in an effort to draw out her Father and engage in an affirming subject for all, Eve asked about his medical practice and especially the children he served who seemed to brighten his life every day. This led to a comprehensive discussion on public health and what he thought could be done for the city that the many charitable organizations and hospitals weren't always able to do. There were sound points about managing a person's working hours with the ability to tend to health matters and not have either suffer. Eve promised to discuss these thoughts with Roosevelt.

The distinct drive to ease suffering was writ large in each of them, and Eve felt such a surge of righteous anger that anyone could think what she was doing with her department was unnatural or in any way akin to devilry.

A warm meal with friends and family renewed the soul. Returning to their precinct home, Eve, Cora, and Antonia joined in with the ghostly girls' dances as Cyril played mazurkas and polkas, Zofia and Olga showing each of them some Polish and Ukrainian dances taught to them by elders long passed on to peace, both cultures and communities that had deep roots in the city.

Eve turned to demand that Vera join them but was struck to find the ghost in a seated position, floating over a stool at a writing desk by the window, having managed to pick up the smallest piece of charcoal which now floated along a paper. She was drawing. A sacred heart was blooming on the page and it brought tears to Eve's eyes.

This was the very essence of the animate forces, the inner fires of the spirit that drove life itself, and she would protect it at all costs.

Chapter Twenty-One

Everyone was slow to get into the offices the following morning but there was so much to do, so much to follow up with. Jenny was feeling better and quietly asked Eve if she could come in with them, her often unused voice a scratchy whisper. The fact that she spoke at all was a testament to her feeling better. She couldn't always overcome the selective mutism, even on her best days.

"Of course, love, you brilliant girl," Eve said, squeezing the child's hand after feeling her forehead and examining her face. The four walked the few blocks and full avenue over to their offices, enjoying the bright, crisp day as autumn began to turn cooler.

While Eve made everyone coffee, Cora conferred with McDonnell about messages and post, with thankfully no fuss or teasing aggrandizement from her.

"Mulberry Street left us a wire," Cora stated once Eve had distributed cups. "For once they followed up with us on a lead," she said with a slight chuckle. "I had them put the Schwerin name out and it seems Mr. Heinrich Schwerin has been found."

"Good work, let's go ask him some questions," Eve stated, and even though she'd just sat down, she rose again.

"That . . . will be difficult."

Eve stopped and stared.

"He's suffered some kind of brain-addling trauma, according to the attending physician who admitted him. They thought he came in drunk, but he hasn't recovered long after the effects of alcohol should have worn off. He can't convey complete speech. He's currently on Wards Island. Still

. . ." Cora began hopefully, holding up her hand to indicate her particular specialty. "There's much his mind can tell us."

"While you do that, I'd like to follow up with Susan, if you don't mind," Antonia countered. "We need to discuss Ingrid and the situation in which she was left, in addition to Mr. Schwerin being found and see what she thinks. We need to find out if Greta has now claimed Ingrid's body or not, or if the Foundling was left with the details. If we need to help, we should."

"Very good. Jenny, are you up for that too?" Eve asked.

The eight-year-old nodded, took a sip of Eve's coffee, made a face, and then smiled, ready for a mission.

* * * *

The Men's Asylum on Wards Island was a sorrowful, intimidating affair that Eve wouldn't have wished upon anyone. After taking a ferry to the jagged edges, the boatman who helped Cora and Eve onto the small pier seemed just as intent on getting out of there. The island, he said, gave him the shivers. None could blame him.

The building itself was a truly enormous complex, two sprawling wings of red brick with white freestone trimmings, gothic arches, towers, and turrets. A huge, curving drive led up to its front door; its lawn was vast and there wasn't a tree in sight. The barren landscape that seemed at first to have been built with the idea of being a welcoming haven just couldn't convince. In its nearly thirty years, it had taken in and sent to rest many thousands of men. Women were taken to another isolated island, Blackwell's, for treatment—though not many were rehabilitated back into society once they'd passed into this quarantine of sanity.

It was a place she'd visited once with Gran in the earliest days of her gifts, before the precinct had been formed, trying to set to rest the soul of a woman whose body had gone missing on those grounds. Eve had helped to find her remains. At least, she'd sent someone in to retrieve the body; she hadn't wanted to see the state of it herself. That was so long ago, Eve wasn't sure what she remembered and what she'd invented. Her mind had made a sanitarium into a nightmarish place, and she wasn't sure how to separate fact from fiction. Her breath hitched. Cora placed a hand on her shoulder, her lovely face steeled.

At the dim grey reception area where one buzzing bulb flickered in a lamp without a shade, she approached a man in a drab suit who looked quizzically at the women entering this unwelcoming edifice.

"I am here to see Mister Schwerin." Eve showed her NYPD paperwork. Someday she might get a badge, she kept telling herself.

"You realize he's fairly unresponsive? That you won't get much out of him?" the man asked.

"So we were told. Did he suffer that setback while here or before he arrived?"

"Arrived as such, Miss. There was an empty bottle of what may have been poison in his coat pocket."

"Do you have any of his belongings here?"

"Yes, we keep personal items for two weeks or so if we've made contact with anyone who wishes to see the patients. There's been a letter sent to the last known address of the family."

Eve nodded. Even if the letter managed to get from the Schwerins' old address over to Susan Keller, Eve doubted Susan would be bringing her sister by anytime soon. Hopefully with Greta having stopped ingesting toxins, she would be spared the asylum fate and could make a full recovery.

"Could we see the belongings, then, of Mr. Schwerin?"

"As you like."

Down a dreary corridor was a bench and a bay of wooden boxes with chalk letters scrawled on the front of each. A box with "H. S." was pulled down and handed to Eve. It contained a worn black leather-bound bible that was nearly cloven with age and wear, an embroidered handkerchief with a monogram, a silk ascot worn around the edges, a few faux flower petals made of silk, of the same colors that were around Ingrid's body, and a large, empty bottle of Prenze tonic that had rust around the metal cap.

Eve put her nose to the cap and drew back, an acrid smell accosting her lungs. It was not a 'refreshing mint' as the bottle promised, but an acidic, sour stench. Of all the bottles she'd seen, this was the only one with rust on the cap.

Cora placed the monogrammed handkerchief between her hands and her eyes fluttered closed a moment. Glancing at the cream-colored fabric edging out from between her pale brown hands, Eve noticed the monogram wasn't Schwerin's. The letters were an entwined "M. E. D.," which Eve thought at first might be a medical reference. But then, as she noticed one umber corner of the kerchief—an old blood stain—she thought of Mortimer E. Dupont, undertaker, and her blood chilled again at the thought of his viewing parlors and all the ghosts outside looking in.

Opening her eyes again with a nod, Cora thanked the attendant, who placed the box back on the shelf again.

"Will you be sure to contact us before any of that gets thrown away?" The man nodded. "Any response from next of kin?" Eve asked.

"Tried with what I was given by the city, but no one has been by for him." The man gestured that they follow to the next part of the wing.

"There were some . . . family tensions, let's say, so I'm not entirely surprised," Eve said.

Cora hung back, taking in every detail, her mouth pressed in a thin line, her expression reflecting the grim nature of the place. Ghosts were hanging about, but not fully inside. A ghostly hand or part of a dress or frock coat through a wall or partition, a transparent face looking in from sooty windows, as if none of the haunts could bear physically fully manifesting inside.

They walked through a long corridor that was dank and grey; even the bright day or whitewashed walls couldn't make this sad place cheerier. It was quiet. Too quiet. Eve had had preconceptions of screaming and terror, but this was instead a wing of silent resignation. Perhaps the denizens were subdued into this, or perhaps it was the true weight of sorrow. Proper, caring treatment was so hard to find. There was a time when Eve had been interested in a broad-based reform of places like these, especially as the century had a troubling habit of putting headstrong, misunderstood, or inconvenient women away into various institutions. But working directly with the ghosts had won out.

None of the nearby presences murmured from the corners of Eve's attention; no flickers of forms or auras crossed directly before her to demand anything. There were a few floating specters but their forms were almost invisible. Was there a place too sad that it silenced even the chattering dead?

The warden gestured forward to a wooden door with a hefty lock and an open but barred window. Eve looked in.

In the cell, Schwerin sat blinking slowly as he stared out the tiny lancet window. He was a stocky man with wild, uneven brown hair, as if it had come out in clumps and grown back at different stages.

At the sound of the door's lock turning, he shifted, his mouth gaping, his eyes widening. He lifted his arms disjointedly. The man kept staring as they entered but made no sound. He saw that there were people in his room, but there was no further comprehension in his glassy eyes.

"He seems . . . dazed beyond any usual function," Eve stated. "Did something else happen to him besides the obvious? It's clear there's another factor."

The warden moved closer and gestured toward the side of Schwerin's head. "Yes. When we examined him more closely there appeared to be a small hole in his cranium, Miss."

And with that went the last of his ability to communicate. Dehumanized entirely. Either he had done a monstrous thing, or he was a foil for someone that had done a monstrous thing. Someone didn't want him to talk about something terrible.

The man had wide, terrified eyes, a prey animal. Eve was overwhelmed for a moment by a trifecta of misery, sensing his helplessness, her own, and Ingrid's somewhere, praying for her peace; the echo of it all, the empathy overarching, was staggering.

Cora moved closer and held her hand out. The man's eyes flicked to her as if he wanted to register her, respond, react, but he was caught in that miserable daze. The mind and body tried so hard to overcome any adversity. Keeping her hand an inch from his head, Cora closed her eyes.

The warden took a wary step towards Eve. "What is she—?"

"Shhh . . ." Eve whispered. "We're all concentrating here."

"On . . . what . . ."

"The mysteries of the mind, and spirit, sir, and that's all we can say," Eve said gently. The man withdrew a step again.

Psychometry was a gift that had first stirred in Cora earlier in the year, one she was still experimenting with. Cora still didn't quite trust herself yet—Eve could tell from the hesitancy in her posture and expression—but in this case, even just an inkling of seeing past events and scenes thanks to the talent of her touch was better than nothing.

Suddenly Schwerin leaned in, pressing his own affected cranium so that it pressed under Cora's hand. Eve wanted to ask how that was possible, how a dulled mind could know to try to connect with Cora in such a manner, but the moment was not for interruption. Cora kept her face neutral and her arm outstretched. After a long moment in which Cora was likely sifting through images, trying to navigate her way through an expanse, there was a reply.

"Magic!" Cora gasped. "My little saint." The voice she spoke in was far away and not entirely her own.

There was a long pause as Eve waited to see if her colleague would elaborate. 'Magic,' she couldn't make sense of, but 'little saint' had been clear. As Cora continued to blink, to see things in a different plane, Eve was left only with the wind against the stone walls and the occasional opening of a door, the murmur of another voice or the scuff of a patient's worn shoe. No one was alone but all were alienated, abandoned even by alienists named for that very state of detachment. There was nothing further from Cora after her exclamation, so Eve sought a bit of clarification.

"Magic," Eve repeated quietly. "Do you mean spell-casting magic or theatrical magic?"

Cora withdrew her hand from Schwerin very slowly. "Theatrical?"

"Noted," Eve replied.

"Be direct," Cora suggested to Eve. "Talk to him. Interrogate and see what you can stimulate." Schwerin's eyes flitted about nervously.

"We are here because of your daughter," Eve said slowly. "Ingrid. We are investigating her disappearance. And the strange manner in which her dead body reappeared." Silence. Flitting eyes. "What about Ingrid?" Eve asked quietly. "What do you remember?"

Eve nodded to Cora. She placed her hand back on the man's skull. He couldn't communicate, but perhaps his mind could still offer up an image that Cora could see or interpret.

Cora hissed. "I can see him taking the curtains from the Synagogue after making a delivery, drawn to the pretty blue velvet. He's bending over the glass coffin. He's in a white room, upstairs, the windows look out over a street."

The man grumbled, hoarse, not language but a visceral response.

"Du . . ." Schwerin tried to form a word.

"Dupont?" Eve queried. There was a sad, deflating sound of sorrow from Schwerin, as if his lungs were wheezing pure pain.

"It's where he dressed the body, there in the Irving Place viewing parlor. I don't see Dupont, but he might have been supervising? The man did confirm Schwerin made deliveries there. Perhaps he was training as a mortician and practicing on his own daughter became . . . too much. Perhaps it sent him over a certain edge."

"If she even was his daughter," Eve murmured, thinking of why Dupont would have her post-mortem photograph in a sentimental place in his study.

Another wave of searing pain accosted Eve. Did it matter? In this moment did it matter whose she was other than a daughter, a human being, a sick child who was lost to the world too soon? No.

"He didn't present her body out of anything but pain and a misplaced devotion," Cora murmured, as if she saw something in the shifting past parading before her that confirmed this fact.

"Were you training to be an undertaker like Dupont?" Eve asked Schwerin.

"I'm seeing flashes of other dead bodies, and preparations on them. Yes, he was," Cora replied. She took a deep, hissing breath.

"What is it?"

"I see a cabinet. It's full of . . . parts. Organs. Eyes. Some teeth. Locks of hair. So. Many. Locks of hair . . ." Cora trailed off, shuddered, and removed her hand.

"I think somewhere in Dupont's building, he has trophies I doubt the grieving families would want him to have . . ." Cora murmured. "I . . . I'd like to leave now," she said in a small voice.

Eve grabbed her hand. The attendant, who had hung back and was now looking at them with extreme caution, led them out without another word, just bobbing his head when they thanked him. The boatman on the way back didn't ask about their visit.

"Trophies. Fetishes." Eve mused. "I wonder if Dupont does anything more with them after they're salvaged. I suppose there's a market for specimens."

"The way that cabinet was organized, it felt . . . different. A twisted, uncomfortable and misguided sort of sacred."

Therein was the last unsettling piece, an aspect of the unfinished business, a reason Dupont would want his own space, not to mention whatever his new partner Montmartre had to do with any of it.

"I wish I knew how I could safely flush him out and stop the practice. I'd send our ghosts in to manifest a preventative protocol, but spirits specifically avoid the place or can't even get in. I don't know what about our cases lately has repelled them so."

"The whole matter may have to wait, unless we can get some kind of city inspector to sweep the place on a pretense and 'stumble' upon it."

Eve nodded. It wasn't a decision for today. "The best thing to do right now is to find Ingrid Schwerin's spirit and make sure she isn't suffering, and to make sure Greta has as much dignity as she can."

* * * *

Eve and Cora returned to the office in hopes of finally finding Ingrid via séance and speaking with her directly.

Her soul at this point was what they needed answers for. Closure. Understanding how she died and instructions for the living on how to best proceed.

Dupont's role in the fetishization of the corpse could wait until they'd helped Ingrid and her mother gain peace. But Dupont, and that cabinet Cora psychometrically witnessed, would indeed be cause for a future warrant, Eve just needed to figure out how to obtain one beyond spectral conjecture.

Antonia and Jenny were there awaiting them, explaining that they'd been to see Susan and Greta, who was sleeping. The sisters had agreed to let the Foundling send Ingrid's body to their plots in Queens, and a small memorial with a blessing and a visitation was planned for the weekend.

None of their usual haunts were in the office, just the living operatives.

The group called a séance to order with their usual ritual of bell, prayer, and candle.

Once Eve called for the spirits to come and advise them, there was nothing. Nothing.

Not just quiet. This was an utter void. This was beyond even those moments when the Corridors were empty.

Her eyes shot open in horror. The rest of her colleagues were staring at her and the same horror she felt was mirrored on their faces.

"What . . ." Antonia began, her voice cracking.

"Why can I sense *nothing*—" both Cora and Eve echoed together.

Being detached from Gran was an unprecedented personal terror. This, now, was a shared upending of her and her colleague's very existence.

Ever since Eve could remember there had always been a rustling. Like the scattering of dried leaves, or coarse fabric in a breeze, a soft and constant murmur. She had never really known any differently and when she first went to the ocean and heard waves on sand, she likened that rhythm of the world as akin to what she heard every waking moment, evidenced by the souls of those passing on, a tide going out. Eve couldn't relate when others described absolute quiet. Some described Hell as an absence from the divine. Eve had always translated this to mean an absence from the constant respiration of the veil itself.

This—mediumship, a companionship with the dead, was the only thing Eve was good at. Nothing else had taken. Her gifts drove her to this point and nothing else mattered. She didn't care about a single other thing, save for family, but her *purpose* . . . this was it, her animating force. And it felt surgically removed, like some phantom psychic limb lay severed while her mind was grasping wildly for the missing member.

"We can't all have lost our gifts at once," Eve murmured, willing this not to be true.

Then came the pain. A sharp stab to the side of her skull. A piercing migraine the likes of which she'd never felt.

Distantly, as if she were disconnected from her body and the sound of her own voice were a foreign noise, she heard herself groan and felt her body crumple forward, folding in on herself as darkness overtook her entirely.

Eve had no sense of time or place. No idea where, how, or when she was, there was only the terrifying darkness. And pain. A stabbing pain in her head. She tried to look down, she tried to move to touch her body to reassure herself she was still corporeal, but she could not move.

What else could she do but pray? What else could she do but *use* the pain, so sharp and so acute that it threatened to split her entirely open. Raw. Cloven.

Please . . . she murmured to the heavens, to anything benevolent and great that was listening. *Please . . . I'm not finished yet. My work is not finished* . . .

This enveloping darkness is what the Corridors had become. Perhaps she was here. The pain had taken her between the worlds of life and death.

Eve tried to take a hold of the pain as a manifest mass, grasp it in her hands and from it forge a lantern. A ward. An icon that said she wasn't done here. She wasn't coming out until she got what she came for. She thought of Clara Bishop harnessing the force of life itself, pressed upon her own heart, clenching her fist as if she were grabbing the hilt of a sword, she pulled and screamed past the pain.

"Let me be your voice!" she cried to the darkness.

Suddenly there appeared a figure floating before her, silvery and luminous. Eve blinked.

It was a familiar little girl in a white gown with a halo around her head, a wooden angel in her hand.

"I know you," Eve exclaimed. "Ingrid! Little Ingrid, in your saint's garb, you're here, we've been trying to reach you. We pray for your peace, for your eternal rest and transcendence!"

The child beamed.

"There you are, angel. You came for me!" The girl lifted up the black-haired wooden angel that had been laid in her hands. She must have thought Eve was the representation. "I once was lost but now am found." The little girl called behind her, into some inscrutable shadow. "See, Miss Strand, you were right! You called the right angel! She found us!"

It was true that spirits often lost their way in the Corridors between life and death, especially since they had become such a dark, impenetrable void of late. That's why Eve and Gran had tried to go in, before, for Maggie. If Ingrid was here, there could yet be hope for Maggie.

"I'll be all right. Tell mama I'll be all right . . . I'm going to the angels . . ." Ingrid exclaimed. "Tell Mama it's better this way, no more pain and anger over me anymore."

"Was your death painless, child? I want to bring comfort to those living who still love you."

"No one killed me but consumption. I did not suffer, I don't remember dying. Just coming here. Here where Lily found me."

"I'm so blessed you did not suffer, Ingrid," Eve said, tears moistening her face.

"Tell Mama the redbird is a sign of love. I see a whole flock of them leading me to the light . . . Will you tell her that? She'll know it's me, then. Tell her I didn't feel any pain."

"I will, Ingrid," Eve said. The power of this transitional moment of the soul was something she'd never witnessed. Not like this. Not from the Corridors. This was a soul moving on and Eve was helping. Not just listening but facilitating. "I will." Tears continued to stream from her eyes in what little control she had of her own body.

"Thank you, kind angel!" She waved at Eve and there was a growing light. A figure stepped up beside Ingrid, a lovely young woman in a blue Deaconess habit. Lily Strand, waving too, a being even closer to the angels, shepherding the little children. The white light grew utterly dazzling. Blinding. Dear *heavens* that light was so beautiful.

"Wait . . . take me with you . . ." Eve begged. She'd never wanted something so much in her life as that light . . . It was the light of every good thing, every victory, every joy . . . It was bliss. Paradise . . .

In that light, for just one moment, Eve thought she saw another figure. She thought she heard her name, called by a familiar voice. The voice sounded almost like she was being scolded.

"Maggie?" Eve cried into the light. "Maggie, are you there?"

"Damn it, Eve, get out of here," she heard a voice scoff and felt a thumping push pummel against her chest, throwing her off balance. She careened back. She fell and kept falling.

Plummeting.

I'm dying, Eve thought, horrified . . . And here I was so close to heaven . . .

* * * *

With a gasping, wrenching cry she awoke. The bright light of day hurt her eyes and she fell back as a searing, mind-numbing pain came second.

"She's awake," murmured a voice she recognized as Cora's and many footsteps hurried towards her.

Her hand grazed the fabric she was tucked under and recognized the texture immediately as the quilt her mother had made from squares embroidered with roses, a gift from when she was a child after she'd been asked what her favorite flower was. The amount of labor that had gone into this gift alone spoke to a deep well of love, and the warmth of it covering her was a comfort.

Her head still hurt as if someone had placed a vise on each temple and had been increasing the pressure.

"It's bright," Eve stated, putting a hand over her eyes as her family and colleagues rushed into her bedroom. "Would someone mind closing the drape?"

"Oh, I'm so sorry, I didn't think . . ." Antonia murmured. A heavy drape was drawn shut and Eve relaxed her brow.

"That's all right," she said with a chuckle, "but now that you've disturbed the vampire in her lair you must bend to her wishes." Opening her eyes and shifting up in bed with a groan, she realized she was in a simple shift of a nightdress, a plain bag of a garment she hadn't worn in years. One of her colleagues must have gotten her into it, reaching for the first suitable thing in a drawer.

Frowning, she looked at the clock on her mantel. It was noon. The last she'd remembered anything, she had been in the office . . .

"How long have I . . ."

"Forty hours," Cora and Antonia chorused. Cora continued. "We consulted a Doctor, of course, your Father, but he said to just let you continue resting."

The sound of voices brought Gran into the room, who was gesturing behind her to Jenny, who followed, rushing up to the bed and squeezing Eve's hand, worry evident on her freckled face. Eve reached out and bunted Jenny fondly on the nose with her fingertip.

"It will take more than a headache to rule me out entirely," Eve said, again trying to rally some cheer. "But I'm not usually—"

"Out this long," Gran finished. She plucked out an engraved pocket watch on a gold chain tucked into the pale blue waistcoat she wore over a satin blouse, snapping it open and shut, the sound accompanying the disapproving cluck of her tongue. "This is fourteen hours longer than any of the naps you've taken to weather your pains, and this marks the first full blackout in my remembrance. Girls, am I correct in this?"

"Until today, there have been no blackouts I've seen," Cora agreed. "It was frightening, Eve, you just *crumpled*. Like a deactivated automaton in some fanciful story. I mean, we all felt it. There was a hum, a surge in the room. You made the lights go out. I don't think they've been restored."

"I sent an inspector around to see about the wiring," Gran stated.

"Let's hope this is not a permanent new development," Eve stated mordantly. "Has anything come back for you? Can you see or hear any of our operatives?"

"Here, yes, the spirit world feels reachable. The office, no," Cora replied. "It wasn't just you that was blocked, it was all of us."

Everything feels more strained," Antonia explained. "Outside the office, things are mostly our normal paranormal. But the office remains a void."

Jenny signed that nothing felt clear.

The loss of clarity was disturbing. For as many vagaries as mediumship offered, there were often a few very clear and pointed directives, revealed in a manner no other communication could manage. If they couldn't prove details . . . their new precinct was already doomed.

Turning to her dresser, she noticed a bouquet of flowers, a vase teeming with carnations of every color. Seeing Eve notice them, Gran stepped forward. "Detective Horowitz brought them. He asked after your well-being yesterday. I told him you were recovering, and he seemed quite relieved."

"Oh, that's kind of him," Eve said, beaming, then blushing a bit at her own reaction.

Carnations of every color, in the language of flowers that had been such a popular method of communication, all together meant health and energy, pride and beauty. A safe sentiment. A kindness without an imposition. Would she have minded if it were a bouquet of red chrysanthemums or roses? Far too bold a statement of passion to make, she decided, even considering their ruse.

Gran was smiling down at her and Cora was eyeing her.

"Well I can't just lie here; if you'll excuse me, I'm going to get dressed. We've so much unfinished business. At least Ingrid came to me in the murk. I managed to find her. It might have taken the pain, that surge, to get through to her. As Clara Bishop said, there's always a cost. At least there's Ingrid's peace. I know now. I saw her go into the light . . ." Tears wet Eve's cheeks just recalling the incredible moment. "We owe Ingrid's family a visit," Eve declared. "She has a message for her mother."

Chapter Twenty-Two

Magic. The word plagued Eve all the way to Susan Keller's rooms. It was the one thing that stuck out from Cora's session with Schwerin and begged further explanation.

But at least Ingrid had come to her. The shock of pain and the disruption of her precinct's collective gifts had somehow cut through the spirit world to that lost little girl and she'd found her voice. Eve had managed to harness power to dive into the Corridors and make contact. Not all cases were solved, not all unsettled business settled. This child's peace was something to take small comfort in.

Susan let Eve and Cora in without a word. Moving to a small coal stove, she put on a kettle, gesturing that they sit down.

"Greta's sleeping," Susan began. "I'll wake her if you need her. Recovery has been slow. I assume you're here to tell us about the body." She sighed.

"We know. A letter was sent from the Foundling Hospital. I spoke with Greta. We went to pay our respects." She shook her head, tucking a mousy lock of brown hair behind her ear. "It was *so* strange. It was good they warned us about what to expect. The Sisters said they'd have her buried in one of their plots in Queens; they were very generous about it, dear souls . . . They've taken care of everything. I told your colleague who came by with the little one that we'll visit Ingrid's plot this weekend."

"Did either of you know that Mr. Schwerin had been left at the Foundling as a toddler?"

Susan raised her eyebrows. "If Greta knew that, she never told me; then again, she was always full of secrets and wild fancies so who knows."

"Not to excuse anything he did, but I think there was deep anguish about being abandoned and . . . I think he thought he was honoring the institution that had raised him with a . . . gift. He didn't kill Ingrid. It was consumption. She did not suffer further."

"How do you know?" Susan pressed, frowning.

"She told me," Eve replied quietly. "I can explain."

"I should wake Greta then," Susan declared "She's doing better now that I threw that poison tonic out. I'm glad you told me. No idea how you knew, I certainly had no idea it was hurting her. She was in such distress, when things are prescribed . . ."

"I know, it's terrible, to think one can't always trust what is supposedly meant to heal," Antonia offered.

"It's been a theme lately," Eve stated. "Tonics being cut with dangerous additives. Rest assured, my team will continue looking into that. We did visit with Dupont, the man Greta once worked for. He is an undertaker in Gramercy at Irving Place. There's something very off about him. We're not done with him or his parlor."

"I'd agree he's off, even knowing next to nothing about him. Just don't drag Greta back into anything to do with him," Susan begged. "He was her downfall, I believe."

"Anything further we investigate won't have to do with your family," Cora offered.

"Now that she's in better health she might be able to fill in some of the missing pieces. I'll have her tell you if you promise me there won't be any ramifications for her. Nothing about Ingrid's death was—how do you say in cases—by the book?"

"We promise. Today we're here as Spiritualists to give Greta, and you, peace on behalf of Ingrid, whose spirit came to me." Eve spoke gently, watching Susan receive this info and furrow her brow. Accustomed to those who weren't sure if they wanted to know or what to believe, Eve continued with a quiet confidence. "I assure you Ingrid is well, and has gone on to paradise, or whatever stands for peace. I can't say I know exactly where or presume to know it. But she has a message for her mother."

Susan put a hand to her mouth. Her eyes reddened. She nodded slowly. "I see . . . Good. That's . . . very good, because I was worried with everything that happened that she'd be . . . unsettled."

"No," Eve assured. "She is at peace, with a specific message only Greta will understand . . ."

"She'll want to hear it."

"I should warn you that we did go to see Mr. Schwerin, also."

"Where?" Susan folded her arms. "At his rooms?"

"No, he's presently . . . at the Men's Asylum on Wards Island. Something went wrong . . . I think he also was prescribed poison, perhaps as a chemist's accident but I find that hard to believe for both Greta and him. Especially seeing as Dupont is also working as a Prenze tonic dispensary, so he may have cut stock with something improper. The tonic ate at his mind, but a finishing blow was done by an incision on his skull, by whom and where no one knows. I only bring this up because I'm not sure if Greta will want to hear this—"

"Yes. Tell her everything. She spent so much of her life keeping secrets from me, I won't do the same to her."

"Yes . . ." came a quiet, resigned voice at the threshold, a thin hand holding back the threadbare curtain between the open kitchen area and the back room. Dressed in a plain blue smock, Greta pulled a crocheted shawl tighter over bony shoulders and stepped towards the company. Her dirty blonde hair was back in a loose knot, wisps falling around her hollowed face. "No more secrets . . . What happened?" She rubbed her head with a shaking hand. "What has been happening? You know, I'm not sure I even know how you could *find* me in the first place?"

"Grace Memorial House cared for you and Ingrid deeply," Eve said. Greta didn't need to know it had been a ghost who cared the most.

Eve and Cora took turns elaborating on what they'd learned from Dupont's offices. That Greta had gone to Dupont with the dead body was news to Susan; this was clear by the way her eyes widened and she sat back in the chair, a wave of distrust and frustration passing over her face. But soon it was Greta's turn to be surprised.

"I left the body there," Greta insisted with a growl. "I was going to retrieve it once he'd prepared it . . . the liar. I didn't take her back. When I went back for it," tears streamed from her eyes, "so that I could simply bury my girl in peace . . . He told me Heinrich had taken it. I didn't know what to think. I felt ill. Delirious. Dupont prescribed me tonic for my nerves." Greta's glassy eyes hardened. "Why he didn't tell you any of that, I don't know. He loved controlling us. Must have wanted to let Heinrich make his little presentation to the Hospital without ruining it. He did like his icons, Dupont. Obsessed with reliquaries."

"Where pieces of a saint's body are put in elaborate canisters for religious display?" Cora prompted. Greta nodded.

Cora and Eve looked at one another. Perhaps the cabinet of parts from her vision?

Next, Cora explained what she had gathered from the Asylum as a narrative account; that Heinrich had prepared the body, dressed it in the saintly manner, and gifted it to the institution he'd been left in as a child as a token of thanks. That was news to Greta too, and she sat back, reeling. Susan poured everyone tea.

"That he *let* Heinrich have the body . . ." Greta's face flushed with fury.

Eve almost asked about Dupont's advances on Greta and who the father might have been, but then again she stopped. Did it solve a case or would it just cause shame and pain? She kept quiet.

"No one killed her, in the end, right?" Greta asked in a barely audible whisper.

"No one but tuberculosis," Eve assured.

"Did Heinrich have an interest in becoming an undertaker?" Cora asked.

"Oh, yes. I thought he would one day open his own practice. He said he was being tutored. I thought by a man closer to our rooms on 14th. He didn't tell me it was Dupont . . ."

"Why *not* be honest about it?" Cora pressed.

"Because I'd said I wanted nothing to do with Dupont after I left his employ. There was a . . . pall about his business. As if there was something going on we couldn't quite place. Photography of the dead, of course, but that's commonplace. Something else. There was something almost . . . unholy."

Eve and Cora shared another look.

"Why didn't you ever tell me about this man, Greta?" Susan asked, reaching for her sister's hand. "I could have *done* something, gotten you out of there—"

"I didn't want you having to rescue me. Again. From a terrible person. I thought with Heinrich I could break free . . . But no, one prison to the next. I'm so stupid."

"Don't say that," Susan scolded. She turned to Eve. "I hope you can find something on that wretch, Dupont. I hope he goes to jail."

"If we can prove wrongdoing. We have to prove it without a shadow of a doubt," Eve said. "My precinct is run by women. We are not often believed, in life or in law, I hardly need tell you that. What we bring forward has to be ironclad and unfortunately I have to sift through a lot of . . . shall we say . . . transient, temporal, and circumstantial evidence before I can move a case forward. He struck all of us as . . . off, but that's not enough for searches, seizure, or indictments. Not yet. But we'll find a way."

"That's the thing," Greta sighed. "When I first worked for him, I thought he was like . . . a god. He dealt with the dead so reverently. He called all dead children angels. He thought death was, in its way, beautiful, and I admired that. He would sometimes sculpt small wax-works for various clients. A nativity, a magician's show. I think he was modeling his sculptures after the dead children that came through his practice. There's nothing illegal about that, using bodies as muses, but he'd always be looking at the photographs. There were so many in his offices . . . He even had to give some away, they got too much. Don't know who he gave them to."

Greta shook her head, as if trying to clear her mind of troubling contents. At the words 'magician's show' Eve sat back. She could sense Cora's mind sharpening, thinking of that exclamation from Mr. Schwerin's mind. *Magic* . . . Greta continued.

"In my first year with him he would wax rhapsodic about his oath to the living and the dead. That was all well and good, he felt about it like a Doctor does with that . . . what is it—"

"Hippocratic oath," Cora supplied.

"Yes. That. But after a while, it changed. He had a certain troublesome nature." She looked away. "He . . . fell in love easily . . . and I suppose young girls could be fooled easily." This was as much as they would get to an admission of their connection. "But even that changed. As the photographs of the dead mounted, many boxes on the top floor . . . As his interest in sculpting increased—all that happened once he got his own offices, by the way, I doubt his frigid wife would've tolerated any of it in the house—he didn't want to talk about his work, any of it, and I began to see him as he really was . . . disturbed." She put a hand over her face. "And to think that my daughter was wrapped up in that strangeness . . ."

"She wasn't. Her soul wasn't," Eve insisted softly. "What you saw at the Foundling was just a shell."

"How do you know that?" Greta asked, her eyes wide and searching.

"By our calling," Eve replied. "I deal with spirits."

"I thought you deal with the police."

"Both," Cora supplied with a smile.

Greta's eye narrowed. "Really, then, why are you here, *really*?" Greta pressed. "If there's nothing further to solve . . . I mean, I appreciate your revealing the lies for me," she looked away, her hands clenching into fists on either side of her teacup. "Is this just some sort of courtesy, pity?"

"Grief is an unfinished business," Eve began. "And in my line of work, if I can ease that particular weight, that is a part of *my* oath. If I am given information that might lessen burdens, I offer it. I have come to tell you the spirit of Ingrid is at peace."

Eve continued as Greta turned back, shifting her body towards Eve, staring at her hungrily. "We conversed. She told me to thank you and to give you her love, to tell you that while tuberculosis was her cause of death, she did not suffer. To be sure you'd know it was her, she told me to tell you the redbird is a sign of love and that she saw a flock of them on her way to the light."

Greta's hands flew to her face. Eve continued speaking gently. "We spoke before the light grew blinding between us, the heavens coming for her. I work with the dead, Mrs. Schwerin; not their bodies, their spirits. What I do is a calling of love, and I work for Peace."

Mrs. Schwerin's tears flowed freely. Eve handed her a kerchief, and she took it in shaking hands, unable to speak. Eve did not press her to. Susan just held onto her sister's shoulder, holding back her own tears.

"Can *you* find peace?" Eve asked her eventually.

"I will try. Thank you. Very much. This helps. If you'll excuse me." Greta left the table, ducking under the back curtain again, sniffling.

"Of course. We'll go," Cora murmured to Susan, rising as Eve followed suit.

"If there's anything else I can do, for my part, please send word," Susan said.

"You've been wonderful," Cora said. "If anything about Dupont, any direct evidence of malpractice—if something specific manages to surface, we'd like to be the first to know."

Susan nodded. Eve knew this wasn't the last of it.

However she measured success on Peace.

If the living and the dead could reach peace, the material, corporeal details, as odd as these had been, were secondary. That was the beauty of Spiritualism done properly. Peace. The discipline had been born out of a desire for greater understanding of the spirit as a wondrous force separate from the limitations of carbon-based flesh. Of course it had grown tainted by impostors and greedy magicians banking fortunes on the grieving, a heinous practice Eve hoped to find allies in stopping, but at its heart this was what it was about—communication for a better understanding of the life that was lived. And of the lives remaining.

"I knew we weren't done with Dupont," Cora whispered as they descended to street level and walked out into the bright day.

"We'll have to proceed with extreme caution," Eve murmured. "A man like him wouldn't hesitate to make a complaint about us if he feels in any way pressured."

They reiterated all Greta's details to one another as they walked, Eve pulling out a notebook to take it all down. Vera's Preventative protocol was yet to be filed and Eve needed to start as far back as was a concern.

When they turned the corner to their offices, Eve noticed Horowitz was on the stoop, pacing on the landing. When he saw Eve, he waved his hand and brightened.

"I'll leave you to it," Cora murmured.

"No, it's all right, I—"

"He wants you alone. I can tell."

There was something about that phrase that sent a jolt up Eve's body. Cora didn't mean it as sensual as it sounded and the fact that Eve took it so was telling in and of itself. The subsequent blush that accosted her cheeks didn't help and Cora rolled her eyes, ascended the steps with a curt, "Detective, hello," and kept going. He stood and bowed his head to Cora, turning to Eve with an apologetic look.

"I'm sorry to disturb you, but I want to know what you think about something. I . . . hope you're feeling better. I . . . stopped by your house. Left flowers . . ."

"Yes, the carnations were lovely, thank you. Gran made sure to tell me you'd brought them. I think she's becoming rather fond of you, Detective Horowitz," Eve said, leaning on the railing of the outside landing.

He simply smiled. "You can call me Jacob, you know, if you like. The pretense of courting and all."

"Ah. Of course. Yes, Jacob, do call me Eve then, that's settled."

It occurred to her, there in this warm and gentle moment that perhaps this impromptu courtship of theirs could go on indefinitely, balanced delicately for the rest of their lives as careful anticipation was so much better than what could be a disappointing dénouement.

"Ingrid Schwerin's spirit came to me when I was unconscious," Eve offered. "Once her body was found."

"Yes, your associates told me about that when you were unconscious; that she was found with the missing items from the synagogue and church, to be returned. I'm glad for that, then, at least," the detective stated.

Eve nodded. "Ingrid helped settle the case as far as my precinct can take it for the moment; the matter of her peace and those who she leaves behind."

"It's all so *odd*," he added. "I feel it's only fair to confess that I don't know how much of a believer you have made out of me. I still don't understand it, but there's something to all of it. We have to find out who is targeting your department, and how to keep it safe. I took the liberty of alerting Mr. Roosevelt to the threats made against you and he's assigned some of his favorites still on beat patrol to make regular rounds along Mercer Street. That's a boon both for your offices and the precinct offices down the street."

"Good. That's good." She looked in his eyes and spoke earnestly. "Thank you."

"As for the spirits, I'll take what progress we make as progress, however unorthodox the means. Just bear with me, as I'll keep asking for the tactile when you touch the ethereal."

At this, she smiled. The dappled light of the day danced in shadows through rustling leaves, his eyes illuminated as blue-flecked brown gemstones staring at her.

She decided not to counter with anything about tactile touch and forced herself to task.

"We're not done probing the situation around Ingrid's death, because it has illuminated troubling things. Mr. Dupont, an Undertaker who Mr. Schwerin 'studied' with, or at least whose space he used to present Ingrid in the manner of a saint, had been Greta's employer. He wasn't forthcoming about the circumstances around Ingrid's death, though it's clear she wasn't killed, consumption saw to that. But considering both Schwerins were taking toxic tonics, and Mr. Schwerin had a trauma to his skull, someone doesn't want him talking about something. We found out what we could. Oddities raise our hackles."

"Do you think he could have had anything to do with our group assault and that mental 'testing?' Any correlation to what we've been working on?"

"The poison thread continues, whether knowingly taking them to possible homicide or general malpractice. That's what I'll want to have the spirits help us trace."

"That brings me to precisely why I'm here." Horowitz pulled a tall, flat bottle from his interior breast pocket. It had a cork stopper and a decorative pattern pressed in the glass. Inside the bottle was a colorful rolled up piece of paper that showed some water damage on the edges. "If you recall my friend Doctor Lee, he confirmed for me that the ingredients listed on a Prenze nerve tonic do not, in fact, include embalming fluid, heavy traces of which he found in this bottle that was found on Doctor Font's dead body."

Eve made a face. "Embalming fluid. Sounds like something an undertaker would have done."

Horowitz nodded, withdrawing a long pair of tweezers from the same breast-pocket. "My friend also examined this label, which had ostensibly been on the outside of the bottle."

Tucking the bottle under his arm, he unrolled the paper.

The decorative label printed in tricolor with Art Nouveau floral stampings framed elaborate letters declaring 'Prenze'. The bottom of the label was torn or broken off, it simply bore the name. Horowitz turned over the label. On the back, in faint graphite, were the shakily written words:

ISN'T DEAD

Eve put front and back together. "Prenze isn't dead . . ."

A discomfiting shudder coursed down her body, the kind of shudder that old wives' tales would insist was someone walking over your grave.

"Here's the punch," Horowitz continued. "While looking into Doctor Font a bit deeper, I found out he was the attending physician who had signed off on the death certificate of one Albert Prenze."

"The dead twin . . ."

Jacob nodded at the paper. "Or not."

"Mister Lazarus, didn't you say? Wasn't that the name of whoever had checked in at the Dakota apartments asking for Font?"

"Precisely."

"I wonder if the rest of the family knows they're mourning a living brother. Gran overheard it had been three years."

"The family just became far more interesting."

Eve let out a long breath. "You don't say."

"Are you still in pain now, since your unconsciousness?"

"There's always a dull ache, but this last bout wins an unfortunate prize."

"I would never know. You hide it well—you are valiant about it."

"I don't want to have to be, but it's better than not participating in the world. The gift is unpredictable. It doesn't always show up in force, but there's always a murmur." She tried to describe the sounds for him, the constant rustling and those whispers of promise just out of range. "The quiet . . . The encompassing *reach* of this quiet I don't understand. This level of silence has never happened before."

"Maybe whatever serves as some great and benevolent being is trying to tell you to rest."

Eve eyed him. "Your work is important," Jacob clarified. "But it shouldn't come at a cost to your health."

Eve pursed her lips in a smirk. "I'm a bit surprised to hear that, coming from a man who never stops trying to solve puzzles."

"I'm attempting to take my own advice for once," he continued. "I can imagine it must be rather nauseating to be courting a hypocrite, the ruse of our arrangement notwithstanding."

Eve chuckled. "A day off. That's what you're suggesting?" she asked, as if she didn't understand the concept.

"You know, labor unions are fiercely organizing for five-day work weeks and eight-hour days. You could try to give yourself just a fraction of what they're rightly trying to balance."

"Will you grant yourself the same?"

"I should. My grandfather, much like your Gran, was my best friend. A spitfire of an academic who was constantly writing. *Constantly.* Obsessively. He went to an early grave overworking himself. If I'm not careful I'll follow directly in his footsteps. I admired his drive so very much, now I just wish I had him back."

At this, Eve wanted to reach for his hand. In friendship, of course. But she didn't want him to misinterpret. Truth be told, she didn't want her own body to misinterpret either. Touch was powerful for Eve, more powerful than she wanted to admit. That troublesome, tactile evidence. He was staring at her again.

"You have a deal," Eve declared. "A well-earned day off. Perhaps we should visit the Metropolitan Museum, they've a new exhibition on decorative glass, functional everyday objects beautifully made. Perhaps we might see tonic bottles that help us piece together the poisons—"

Horowitz laughed, a genuine, near belly laugh. "What part of 'day off' is inexplicable to you, Eve?" At this, Eve blushed.

"I'm sorry. I really don't know what to do with myself if it doesn't involve work. What do people do?" She bit her lip, embarrassed. "I've no idea, really."

"Picnic in the park?" He offered. "We can't solve everything today and truth be told, I don't know where next to start. We can agree to at least discuss that, if you *must* work."

"Ideal. Thank you. Let me duck in and let my colleagues know where I'm going."

She poked her head in the door to see all three of her team reading the local papers and circling any passages of note. "I'm running an errand, I'll be back . . ."

"Running an errand with the detective," Cora clarified.

"Yes . . . Is that a problem?"

"Not as long as you know what you're doing," Cora replied. Antonia pursed her lips, as if she wanted to giggle.

"What do you mean by knowing what I'm doing?" Eve asked defensively. "What do you think I'm doing?"

Falling in love, Jenny signed, making a disgusted face.

"I am doing no such thing!" Eve exclaimed.

"Suit yourself," Cora stated. "But make yourself useful while you're flirting and see if he can dig up anything on Dupont we could use to get into the building again. Upstairs."

"There will be no flirting, I am ashamed of all of you," Eve said, her cheeks scarlet. Bluster was hardly helping her case. "But I will of course get his thoughts on how to leverage Dupont—that was a part of my plan, you wretched gossips and slanderers."

Jenny giggled and this broke Antonia into a bark of a laugh. Eve slammed the door behind her.

* * * *

The day was one of those perfect days meant for appreciating the patches of green the city clung to, its denizens clinging to them with equal zeal. Union Square had swaths of green and benches set in patterns along paths, with street vendors selling morsels of all kinds; a boisterous kind of haven. A place to sit and set down one's cares. Horowitz gestured to the carts before them, one offering pastries, another with roasted nuts.

"The chestnuts, please, thank you," Eve replied and he came back with two small bags.

A male cardinal, a red songbird with a crest, flitted up into a nearby bush, paused, and then flew out again north, perhaps towards the greater acreage of Central Park. A redbird. According to Greta and Ingrid Schwerin, that meant love was in the air.

Eve felt suddenly very warm and it wasn't the temperature around her, which was a pleasant breeze; it was her own body, her cheeks, her blood, her nerves.

"I appreciate all you've done for me, and for the Precinct," Eve said earnestly. "You've gone above and beyond. And so far, you've played your part very well."

"It hasn't been hard," Horowitz replied. "The part."

"You do seem to be enjoying yourself at times," Eve countered with a grin.

"As do you," Horowitz replied. "At least, you seem to. Perhaps you are just a very talented actress, for all your commitment to honesty." It was a searching statement, and his eyes gave her no respite. "Though you seemed to have charmed that young new Reverend who was a part of rescuing your Gran, so I would say you could have your pick of faux suitors if he'd be willing to. He's Episcopal, right, the kind that can court and marry?"

"Oh, that? Him? What? No. He was just being kind. Reverends do that, you know, one mustn't misinterpret. We were all very emotional, having faced what we all did, together . . ."

The detective smirked at her.

Eve was terrified her blush would now become a permanent feature. She feared she would never again have a pallid face. Had he taken that much notice of her interaction with Reverend Coronado? It was true she had found him distressingly attractive, but had she broadcast the notion? "No, truly!" Eve stammered. "It's as you say, I have, despite myself . . . enjoyed myself . . . With you."

Horowitz laughed. "I suppose I should feel flattered, despite myself." Eve had to resist the impulse to bite her lip and look away like a schoolgirl. What was going on? Had she indeed fallen for her own ruse? Dear God, were her colleagues, *right*?

They stared at one another for longer than was polite. Their bodies leaned imperceptibly closer. Eve could feel everything else around her begin to drift farther away.

The entrancing eyes again. And had she ever noticed how impetuous those curls were that begged to have a hand run through them? Her heart picked up its pace. Oh, goodness. Was he about to kiss her?

Suddenly there was a tearing sound, and the temperature around them plummeted.

A young spirit with ringlets done up in an immaculate coiffure, wearing a fine, bustled dress typical of two decades prior, burst in upon the two, her transparent form hovering before Eve.

Maggie.

"Hello, my dear!" the missing spirit of Margaret Hathorn exclaimed to Eve, barreling forward in an excited rush. "Sorry I'm late! I'm very glad you didn't decide to die. I *had* to shove you there in the Corridors, you might have gone to heaven otherwise, you fool! You wouldn't *believe* where all I've been and what I've seen!" She paused, and finally looked between Eve, who felt her mouth drop open in shock, and the detective. The specter's transparent eyebrows raised and her voice took on a tone of gossip-filled delight as she gestured before her.

"Eve . . ." Horowitz began slowly. "It's . . . very cold between us. Did . . . someone just . . . arrive?"

"Yes . . ." Eve murmured.

"Oh, I'm sorry . . ." Maggie blurted. "I'm clearly interrupting something *delicious*. Far be it for me to come between a kiss . . . Eve Whitby! I'm gone a *week* and you're kissing men, what's come over you?!"

"I am . . . not . . ." Eve's face was scarlet again. "We . . . were not . . ."

"What?" Horowitz asked.

"He just called you *Eve*. Don't you lie to me. Never mind. I have so much to tell you! So much to show you!" the spirit exclaimed. "Come now, you must come if you can! Bring the gentleman with you! I was rescued from certain spectral demise and I have to show you how. Then you can get back to kissing, if you must."

"Come where?" Eve said, dazed.

"North. Two hours."

"You're speaking with this spirit, I assume?" Horowitz asked.

"Yes. I'm very sorry."

"It's all right," he replied with wonder. "I *can* hear the faintest of murmurs . . ."

"It's my darling Maggie," Eve gasped, feeling overwhelmed. "My best spirit operative. She'd gone missing, but she's come back to me! She wants us to follow her, to see an important place where she's been."

"It's a pilgrimage to an indescribable sanctuary," Maggie said, bobbing in the air, her long, delicate hands gesticulating grandly. "A place of *tremendous* power. You must come visit. I told them you would; it was part of the reason I could leave. That, and you powerfully cut through psychic walls and I was able to see you, finally. Good work, that."

"Two hours north," Eve murmured, glancing at her watch pin. They had the whole day if they had luck with the trains.

"Well. It would seem today resumes an investigation after all," Horowitz said with a smile. He turned to where he presumed Maggie to be, though she was on his other side. Maggie giggled and placed a transparent hand on his cheek. The cold press had him shift, and to Eve's eye, he was now looking directly at Maggie.

"Do you see her?" Eve asked softly.

"I think?" he said. "I do feel something. Beyond the chill. It isn't just cold. There's something . . . in the air too . . . Here before me," he said, amazed. "How fascinating!"

"Oh, Eve . . . Now I *understand*," Maggie said, staring at Horowitz in approval.

"Yes, you've got it!" Eve exclaimed, reaching out and grabbing his hand in excitement, then releasing it immediately when she felt the shuddering surge of delight at the touch.

"Lead on then, good spirit," Horowitz said, before turning to Eve with an awestruck smile.

Eve stared at this man. A partner. Someone who had become more than a convenience, more than a cover. And then she turned back to the beloved shade, one of her dearest friends. Her heart was full to bursting, even though she wasn't sure either bond could last the test of time. But that grim thought was for another day; today was gratification, as there was nothing that so suited detectives as inquiries and the chance to have questions answered.

The spirit world needed her now more than ever and the feeling was mutual.
"Onward to adventure, Maggie," Eve declared.
The spirit led on.

Coming Soon

Look for the next installment of
The Spectral City series
by Leanna Renee Hieber.

Coming in 2019 by Rebel Base Books.